MW01193768

ESCAPE TO FREEDOM

VOLUME ONE
OF THE "HUGUENOT TRILOGY"

An Historic Novel

Order this book online at www.trafford.com/05-2075
or email orders@trafford.com

Most Trafford titles are also available at major online book retailers.

© Copyright 2008 Kenn Joubert.
All rights reserved. No part of this publication may be reproduced, stored in a retrieval system, or
transmitted, in any form or by any means, electronic, mechanical, photocopying, recording, or
otherwise, without the written prior permission of the author.

Cover photography and design by Mary Peppard
www.peppardigital.com

Maps: Leigh Ann Stephenson, Victoria BC

Note for Librarians: A cataloguing record for this book is available from Library
and Archives Canada at www.collectionscanada.ca/amicus/index-e.html

Printed in Victoria, BC, Canada.

ISBN: 978-1-4120-7180-2

*We at Trafford believe that it is the responsibility of us all, as both individuals
and corporations, to make choices that are environmentally and socially sound.
You, in turn, are supporting this responsible conduct each time you purchase a
Trafford book, or make use of our publishing services. To find out how you are
helping, please visit www.trafford.com/responsiblepublishing.html*

*Our mission is to efficiently provide the world's finest, most comprehensive
book publishing service, enabling every author to experience success.
To find out how to publish your book, your way, and have it available
worldwide, visit us online at www.trafford.com/10510*

www.trafford.com

North America & international
toll-free: 1 888 232 4444 (USA & Canada)
phone: 250 383 6864 ♦ fax: 250 383 6804
email: info@trafford.com

The United Kingdom & Europe
phone: +44 (0)1865 487 395 ♦ local rate: 0845 230 9601
facsimile: +44 (0)1865 481 507 ♦ email: info.uk@trafford.com

20 19 18 17 16 15 14 13

ESCAPE TO FREEDOM

VOLUME ONE
OF THE "HUGUENOT TRILOGY"

KENN JOUBERT

A LITTLE HISTORY

France had for centuries been strictly a "Catholic" country - ruled by the King. Although - sometimes France was ruled more by the Cardinals - and Rome.

But the history of Europe shows that the Catholic religion was decaying - in a horrible way. In all the Catholic controlled countries, the selling of "indulgences" was a common occurrence. If you were a person who had lots of money but led a shocking life, you could approach a religious authority; and buy an "indulgence" - a piece of paper, beautifully written, which guaranteed you a life in heaven - when you died. There was also a tremendous enterprise in the buying of "religious relics" - a splinter from the original cross; a fragment of the cloth used to wipe the brow of Jesus on the cross; the little finger bone of a famous Saint; etc. And possession of these relics somehow made you "safer" in an unsafe world. And, of course, the notorious "Inquisition"!

It seems to have been this type of decay of religion which frustrated highly ethical people. Martin Luther was a Catholic priest who finally wrote a thesis on his anger; and in 1517 nailed it to the door of the Cathedral! The action rang all through Europe and was probably the beginning of the Reformation. Fresh thinkers like Calvin eventually settled in Switzerland and his Reformed teachings began to appeal to the masses.

France had been a battleground - for religious beliefs - for many years.

In 1209, the Pope Innocent III, launched a Crusade in Southern France - using the French Army - to "wipe out" the Cathars. Despite the fact that the movement had a very simple religious belief system, each settlement was attacked and destroyed. Most members were killed. Their hilltop castles - in ruins - are still a tourist attraction in Languedoc, Southern France.

In the 1400s, the Vaudois sect, similar in some respects to the Cathars, lived in the alpine areas of France and Italy. Pope Innocent VIII proclaimed a general crusade supported by all Catholic powers. All the villages were to be ravaged and destroyed - unless the people embraced Catholicism.

In the 1500s, the notorious St. Bartholomew's Day Massacre took place. Thousands of the "reformed religion" are murdered in Paris in a single night. So many bodies were tossed into the Seine River that the river ran red for days. The killing spree spread all over France. Thousands of Protestants fled France - many to England, where they were welcomed. Weavers, paper makers, felt makers, artisans of all types; goldsmiths, silver smiths; bankers; soldiers, etc. enriched England's industry.

1

This led to about sixty years of the Wars of Religion in France - until the crowning of Henry of Navarre - when the Edict of Nantes was proclaimed - which had provided some degree of protection for the French Protestants.

In 1685, it is suggested that Louis XIV of France had just lost a war; and a wife; and was very ill. His new wife suggested that he needed to gain favour with God - and should seriously do something about the Huguenot heretics! So, the King "revoked the Edict of Nantes".

Overnight, Huguenots began to flee France. Over the next 10 years it is estimated that about half a million fled - to Switzerland, Germany, Holland; some ending up in South Africa and America. Immense pressure was put on village families by the "Dragonades" - in which troops of Dragoons were "billeted" in individual homes where they bullied family members; and had to be well fed and served. The solution was to "abjure" the reformed faith and return to the Catholic religion.

It was only in 1787 that the French Protestants were again provided with some degree of freedom.

*　　*　　*　　*　　*

COVER PICTURES:

Front cover - The "Huguenot Cross" emblem; came into use in the 1500s - for details see: www.geocities.com/Heartland/Valley/8140/x-eng.htm; (or the "Huguenot Society of South Africa.")

Back Cover - Pictures taken in 1998 during the research tour by the author. The village of La Motte d'Aigues, on the Luberon hillside in Southern France. The whole of the hillside is now a part of the Luberon Regional Nature Park. (See www.provenceweb.fr) Select "English" language and "Luberon" For the village of La Motte d'Aigues - go to the "map"; through the village of "St. Martin de la Brasque".

-The community vineyards directly opposite the entrance the village of La Motte d'Aigues.

2

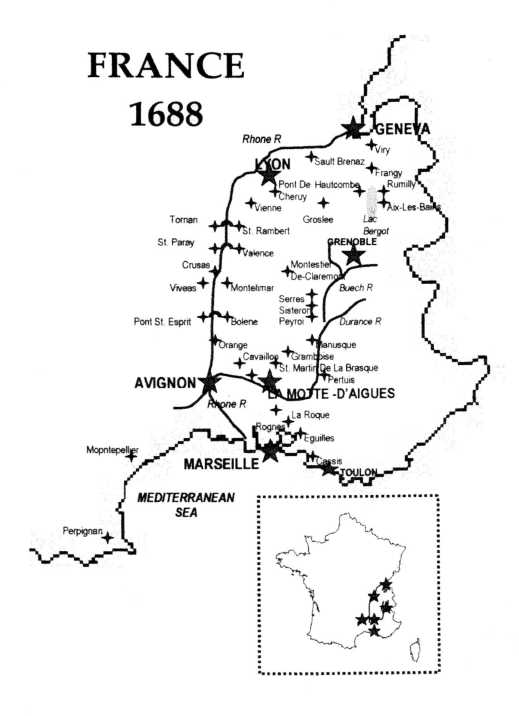

FRANCE
1688

Rhone R

GENEVA

Viry

LYON

Sault Brenaz

Frangy
Rumilly

Pont De Hautcombe
Cheruy

Vienne

Aix-Les-Bains

Tornan

Groslee

Lac
Bergot

St. Rambert

St. Paray

GRENOBLE

Valence

Crusas

Montestier
De-Claremon

Viveas

Montelimar

Buech R

Serres
Sisteron
Peyrol

Pont St. Esprit

Bolene

Durance R

Orange

Manusque

Cavaillon

Gramboise

St. Martin De La Brasque

AVIGNON

Pertuis

LA MOTTE -D'AIGUES

Rhone R

La Roque

Rognes

Mopntepellier

Eguilles

MARSEILLE

Cassis

TOULON

MEDITERRANEAN
SEA

Perpignan

3

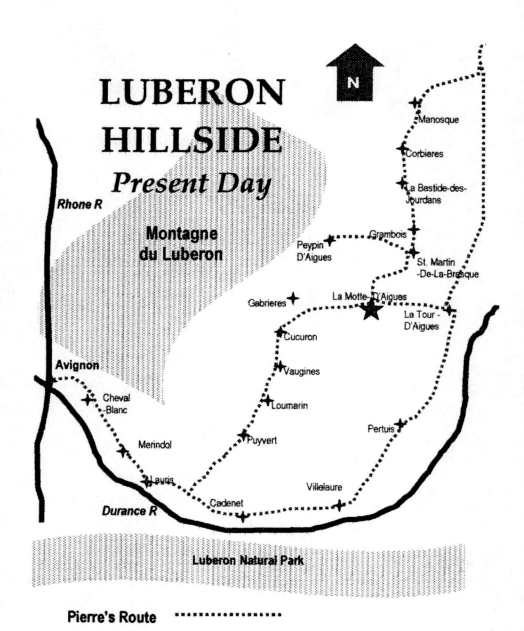

LUBERON HILLSIDE
Present Day

Rhone R

Montagne du Luberon

N

Manosque

Corbieres

La Bastide-des-Jourdans

Peypin D'Aigues

Grambois

St. Martin -De-La-Brasque

Gabrieres

La Motte- D'Aigues

La Tour - D'Aigues

Avignon

Cheval -Blanc

Cucuron

Vaugines

Loumarin

Pertuis

Merindol

Puyvert

Lauris

Villelaure

Cadenet

Durance R

Luberon Natural Park

Pierre's Route ·······················

4

CHAPTER ONE

19 June 1687.
La Motte d'Aigues Provence France

The clang of the village bell startled Pierre Jaubert as he lay in the shade of a large clump of wild rosemary. He was lazily watching the sheep graze safely and peacefully on this sunny hillside in Provence.

However, the sound did not warn him - that today - this quiet, somewhat shy man - would attempt to kill another human being.

Pierre sat up. What unusual catastrophe would have forced cantankerous old Barre, with his withered right leg, to hobble from his shady porch and urgently tug on the bell rope? Concerned, he peered through the warm haze that shimmered over the village below.

A cloud of dust rising from the winding road around the Luberon hillside leading to his village of La Motte d'Aigues warned of the arrival of a rapidly moving group of travelers.

When he spotted flashes of light reflecting from what could be polished armor or weapons; he jumped to his feet.

"Dragoons!" he grunted as a mixture of both fear and anger filled his throat. He stood on a rock, shading his eyes to try and catch greater detail. He estimated the number of horses by the column of dust. At least twenty – or more! Should I go down?

He glanced around at the grazing sheep. His father had asked him reluctantly to spend the day with the sheep when young Jacques, the shepherd boy, was sick this morning. He dare not leave them on the hillside unprotected!

But the alarm bell comes first! And, at this time of day most of the young men - the strength of the village - would all be up in the hills.

Memories returned of grim stories told over the past few months by travelers passing through the village. In a surprise move, the King had, without warning, withdrawn the protection of the Edict of Nantes from the "new believers" – like himself! And, now in the cities, "non-Catholics" had been beaten, imprisoned and even killed in the streets. But the cities had seemed so far away!

Returning home to his neighbouring village of St. Martin last week, Du Ploy, the cobbler, had told of the King's new policy of harassment by troops of Dragoons.

The"Dragonnade!"

It involved billeting large numbers of Dragoons in a household. The old men had shaken their heads in disbelief when terrible tales were told of the open theft of household goods, of physical attacks on the home owners; and even sexual harassment of the young maidens!

A picture of little Suzanne Charpentier, his neighbour, flashed into his mind. Today, she would be helping her father in his baker's shop. He winced at the thought.

"Father will be angry! But then - when the bell is rung...?" he muttered aloud. He found his breath coming in shorter bursts. The column had now entered the village. The clanging was still echoing up the hillside.

Throwing his usual caution aside, he grasped his shepherd's crook; and ran down the worn sheep trail in the direction of the village.

On the edge of the village, Pierre raced down between the vegetable gardens growing behind the villagers' homes. He heard raised voices. The louder shouting of the Dragoons made it impossible to catch any meanings.

He glanced over his shoulder. Pierre was relieved to see other running figures on the hillside paths. He recognized his good friend, Andre Roux, and frantically waved. Further behind in the dust, his red-tinted hair flying like a flag, was his cousin - both of them named Pierre after their mutual grandfather.

Caution gripped him as he jerked to a halt near the corner of the blacksmith's home. Breathing hard, he leaned against the wall. He bent slightly and looked quickly around the corner. In the center of the village, where the communal bread oven stood, he could see the backs of the other villagers. Using them as cover, he ran up behind the crowd.

Murmurs of anger rippled through the gathered villagers. The threatening voice of a man talking - with words harsh - but shrill at the same time - could just be heard.

Usually very cautious, Pierre pressed forward slightly against the others' backs and was surprised when they parted a little to let his shoulder through.

About twenty of the King's Dragoons, most on horseback, faced the villagers. Their armored breastplates gleaming under the harsh Provencal sunlight, they formed a frightening backdrop to the scene. The Sergeant had successfully quieted the gathering. Dismounted, right outside the baker's yard, stood an immaculately uniformed Captain who quietly observed the crowd.

Directly behind the Captain stood the open doors of the huge outdoor bread oven. The red glow of the embers and the bright orange flash of the flames reflected on the Dragoon's armor and brought a touch of Hell to the scene.

The Captain was a slight man, standing awkwardly as though crippled. His sword was drawn and resting with its tip on the cobblestones as he leaned on it like a walking stick. In his other hand he carried a large white silk handkerchief with fragile lace edging. From time to time he raised it delicately to touch his nose and appeared to be sniffing.

Even over the heat of the oven and at this distance, Pierre thought he could detect a hint of wild violets.

Although the faces of the Dragoons around him were grinning or sneering, obviously enjoying their moment of power, the Captain's face was oddly blank and expressionless. His eyes appeared bored. The officer turned his head and squinted into the harsh sunlight. His slight mustache moved slowly as, with a languid drawl, he spoke.

"So! You are the citizens of this ... sunny little village of ... La Motte d'Aigues?" The villagers' grumbling ceased as they leaned forward to listen. His gaze around the circle of faces was arrogant while they in turn angrily glared back at him. His chest heaved, as he appeared to draw in a large breath through his raised handkerchief

"My Dragoons - and I ... have been instructed ... by his Majesty, the King, ... to pay you a visit. I am ... a little distressed ... at our reception. You have obviously been told lies by travelers who are passing through! *Non?*" An angry murmur arose from the villagers and some of them moved slightly forward. In response, the Dragoons jerked their reins and some of the horses reared, their nostrils flaring, their front hooves thrusting. The crowd backed up quickly. Behind the Captain, some of the troopers - now on foot - waved their weapons menacingly until the silence returned.

"Now! Now! There is no need to be so ... lacking in hospitality! The King - and the Cardinal - feel that his Dragoons should be welcomed everywhere by true believers and I am certain that in this lovely village, we will find nothing but ... true believers...*Non?*" A low murmur began to run through the crowd again.

"Hah! I thought so!" The Captain turned and spat onto the dusty cobbles splattering the boots of a village elder. "You are going to welcome us - as your guests - for a while! Imagine that?" He gave a slight giggle and paused as if to gain attention. "You see - we too have to follow orders - the King's orders! We are here to root out the scum who are refusing to seek a true chance at Salvation". He paused while his words sank in.

"I will be placing my Dragoons in your households to be billeted." He paused as the rumble from the villagers rose and, with an arrogant twist to his lip, he watched them silently until the noise subsided. "I, *Capitaine* Hugo Benoit, expect my men – and I - to be wined and dined with nothing but the best! And entertained with respect! Any complaints will be ... personally dealt with ... by me!" His voice dropped to a whisper and the crowd seemed to lean forward to catch his final deadly quiet words. "And ... I can be a hard taskmaster!"

Pierre felt his chest tighten in anger. Subdued growls from the villagers now rose around him.

"I have decided to reside with the baker's family," and he jerked his thumb over his shoulder, "as I always find their food the best!" He chuckled again to himself as he tugged on his mustache.

Suddenly an old woman pushed through the ranks. Pierre gasped with fear as he recognized *Madame* Carpentier, the baker's mother and grandmother of Suzanne. Leaning on her stick, she hobbled up to stand before Captain Benoit. Pierre heard a scared gasp from the crowd and somewhere he heard Suzanne's voice cry out *"Non! Grandmere! Non!"* The old lady stopped several paces from the Captain who bent his head to face her. She peered up at him. Then she spoke with a high clear voice.

"We have heard the terrible tales from the North. We have heard of … innocent people being tortured, punished … and killed for their religious beliefs. We still cannot believe that the King would have removed his protection from our people - who want nothing but peace!" She turned and waved her hand in the direction of the crowd of villagers. "These people are not evil! They just want to be left alone!"

The Captain shifted his weight; pulled at his mustache again. Then he spoke a little sardonically: "Old woman, are you going to be the first to offer me hospitality? Some fresh bread, a little dry local wine, a good bed … or perhaps a young girl in it?" A bellow of eager laughter rose from the watching Dragoons.

"*Non!* This village is a proud village! We don't need you here!" She lifted her stick and waved it in his face. "Take your Dragoons - and go!"

The Captain looked quietly at the old dame - his expression remained passive. Then slowly he glanced back at his Sergeant standing behind him and smiled in a lazy meaningful way. Then he looked back to the old lady and nodded his head.

"It seems, *Madame*, as though your filthy peasants need a lesson in obedience? Perhaps, you do not think … I am serious?" he growled in a low tone. Then his voice raised. "*Sergent!*"

In practiced unison, the burly Sergeant and two men moved quickly from behind the Captain. Before anyone could act they grasped the old lady by the arms and legs. She screamed in a high quavering voice. They tossed her shrieking into the open oven door and slammed it closed. It happened so quickly and smoothly, that Pierre knew it had been rehearsed at another time - in another village square!

A massive moan erupted from the crowd. They surged forward toward the baker's yard. The mounted Dragoons jerked and reared their horses to crush the villagers back. They swung their swords and the crowd fell back in terror. The soldiers on foot moved forward in an organized wave and screams came from people wounded. The lines broke and villagers began to flee down the alleys.

Pierre was frozen in horror. Black smoke poured from the oven chimney. A burst of hot gasses flushed up his throat as the sickly smell of roasting hair and flesh caused him to gag.

Somehow both struggling troopers and villagers parted in front of him. An open space appeared between him and the Captain.

Both unexpected terror and anger welled up inside him and he staggered forward, then broke into a mad dash with his shepherd's crook held up like a lance.

The Captain jerked toward him and, for a flicker of a second, a light of terror appeared in the officer's eyes.

Pierre shrieked his rage as the filthy point of the crook struck the Captain's cheek and blood welled out splashing down staining his tunic front and blemishing the silk handkerchief.

Suddenly, a sharp blow from behind struck pain and lightening into his very soul and his world went black.

*   *   *   *   *

CHAPTER TWO

Her dark shining hair glinted in the rays of the late afternoon sunshine peering through the half-open shutters as her head moved rapidly from side to side in time with the scrubbing brush held in her hand. She scrubbed to the beat of a catchy little folk tune she quietly sang.

Most of the girls in the village of St. Martin d'Aigues (later known as St. Martin de la Brasque) kept their hair very long. For practical purposes, they usually braided it for comfort. But Isabeau liked the feeling of freedom it gave her to have the smooth shining wings at shoulder-length and curving forward over her ears.

As she scrubbed, Isabeau thought of her mother, Louise, and her brothers, back in their village of Peypin d'Aigues higher up the Luberon mountain slope. Due to the illness of a relative, her father, Daniel Richarde, had taken on the care of a local farm for several months in St. Martin.

This had required her to move with him to the new village but also allowed her to enhance her relationship with her betrothed, Pierre "*Le Duc*" Mallan, who lived in the same village.

She grinned a little ruefully as she thought about how much he relished his reputation as a trader - of anything! How he chortled with pride about the nickname he had been dubbed with by his envious comrades.

The sunshine picked out the little flecks of light in her hair that sparkled as she scrubbed away at the newly clean thick wooden planks in the tabletop.

"At last!" She murmured aloud as she stood upright and arched her slim back to relieve the ache. A small smile flickered across her face as she ran her eyes over the damp tabletop. Every time she had served a meal on the table in the past few months, she had winced a little and promised herself that she would find time to clean it the way her mother would have – properly!

The commotion in the near-by village of La Motte d'Aigues with the arrival of the King's Dragoons had led a lot of the villagers to rush over and see what was happening. The lack of neighbors and friends dropping in to visit had given Isabeau the opportunity to finally accomplish some of the delayed tasks that had accumulated.

She rubbed a dry cloth across the top of the table before opening the shutters wide again to allow the sun to complete the job.

She looked around for the pail and mop to wash the red tile floor in front of the kitchen fireplace. Better to sweep the floor first, she thought and picked up the broom. A single loud "thump" on the outside door caused a brief frown to flick across her forehead. She stared at the door. I don't need visitors, she thought. Maybe the dog was turning around? Then it came again - three this time! Thump...Thump...Thump! Now what?

Isabeau spun quickly and with her long skirt still swirling and the broom grasped in her hands, she ran to the door and jerked it open. Three large male figures shut out the daylight as they all plugged the entryway. Isabeau gasped in surprise and raised the broom against their chests in an effort to keep them at bay.

"Isabeau - don't be foolish! Let us in, damn it!" Despite the rough hat pulled over his forehead, she recognized the flash of red in the brown curls of hair and the cheeky grin of "*Renard*" Jaubert from the next village. Then on the far side of the trio - 25 year old Andre Roux also from La Motte. As Isabeau looked at the middle man, she realized all three were from the next village. This was Renard's cousin - also Pierre Jaubert - but his head was thrown back and his arms were being held on either side by both of his friends.

"You are *not* bringing your drunken friend in here to mess up my clean kitchen!" Isabeau stamped her foot and pushed her broom harder against their combined chests.

"Isabeau - you pesky woman - he is *not* drunk! My horribly well-behaved cousin, is both unconscious - and in trouble!" Renard chuckled aloud. "Of all people in the Luberon Mountains, Cousin Pierre – here - is the very last person I would have ever thought to get into this type of mess! "

Reluctantly Isabeau backed away and stood aside as the two men half-carried their friend across the room, his toes dragging on the kitchen tiles.

"Not on my clean table!" she cried in frustration but they ignored her and lifted him bodily and laid him roughly on the clean damp table.

"I have spent a whole hour cleaning that off," she stamped her foot again and glared at Renard. The she looked down at Pierre with a furrowed brow. "What's wrong with him anyway? Did he have an accident?"

Before the men could reply, she squealed in frustration "Look at that!" she pointed at the area under the back of his head "There is blood coming from behind his ear! And on my clean table!"

Renard collapsed onto a nearby stool. It was now evident that he had recovered his sarcastic nature. He grinned at the angry young woman and doubled-up laughing again.

"Stop laughing, Renard! Tell me what is happening!"

However, with Renard still chuckling, it was Andre Roux - Pierre's lifelong friend - who tersely recounted the arrival of the Dragoons; the tragic shocking death of old *Mme.* Carpentier; and the absolutely surprising attack of the Dragoon Captain by his friend, Pierre.

"I still cannot believe how my quiet overly cautious friend," he pointed down at the unconscious figure, "reacted like he did!" Andre shook his head in disbelief. "It is so unlike him! If it had been his cousin – here," he pointed to Renard who still sat grinning at him, "I could have understood... but Pierre?" he waved his finger at the body on the table and shook his head in obvious confusion.

When Isabeau had first met the two "Pierre Jaubert" cousins she had found the situation confusing. The cousins were both named in honour of their joint grandfather, Pierre. Both were now 25 year old Pierre Jauberts from the same little village. Except, in order to distinguish them separately, the village had labeled the irascible mischievous one with the reddish tinge to his brown hair after the cunning local red fox - "Renard". In temperament, the "other" Pierre had been more conservative and, although close, never dared get involved in his cousin's pranks.

"Well, I must agree with you!" Isabeau shook her head slowly. "The little I know of Pierre - he is not the type!" She stopped and looked at the two friends for some clarity. "But enough history - how did he get knocked out ... and why is he here ruining my clean kitchen table...!" Her voice moved quickly from concern to frustration.

"I saw a soldier hit him behind the head with the hilt of his sword. He went down like a dead sheep! But then the whole square burst into an uproar - and in the chaos we were able to drag him away to safety. We dumped him onto the back of Renard's mule and raced him to St. Martin," Andre explained: "I am sure that once the *Capitaine* regained control, he will make sure that La Motte will be searched immediately. Your village seemed safer! We need to hide him until he comes to - and then maybe, sneak him out into the countryside. At least until the Dragoons leave!"

"You expect me to hide him here - in our home!" Both shock and anger showed on Isabeau's face. "Have you forgotten that I am ... betrothed! In less than a month I am going to be married! What on earth will my Le Duc have to say!" She shook her head fiercely in utter frustration.

"Oh, come on, Isabeau...Don't get so worked up!" Renard waved his hands in the air. "We expect it will only be until ... he wakes up. Maybe, a couple of hours! We are sorry that we are dumping him on you. I am sure your father would help us!" He frowned. "These are desperate times - and require desperate measures! If Cousin Pierre had thrown a couple of rocks or yelled insults, we would not be in this mess! But physically assaulting the Captain of the King's Dragoons becomes a matter of 'Life or Death' for both our villages! There was blood all over the officer!"

Isabeau heaved a little sigh - becoming aware she was beginning to act contrary to her own firm religious beliefs. She sucked in a deep breath and she re-took control of matters.

"Well - the sooner we get him on his feet - and off my table - the better for all of us!" She dropped the broom in the corner; grasped Pierre by the shoulder and turned him slightly so that she could see the cause of the bleeding. A large lump behind the head was still weeping blood where the skin had been torn. With a wet cloth from the kitchen counter she wiped the wound cleaning up the matted blood. From a cupboard she took a small jar of herb ointment and rubbed it into the cut compressing it with a dry cloth. To the watching men, she spoke over her shoulder.

"Take his boots off and put them by the door. Then carry him upstairs to the bedroom".

With much grunting and heaving, the unconscious man was moved upstairs to the landing.

"Which room, Isabeau?" Andre's voice was breathless.

"My father's, of course!" Isabeau winced a little at how her intended would feel about another man being in her bedroom. He always was a little too proper! She gestured towards the large room overlooking the street outside.

"Wait - let me throw a cloth over the bedclothes - there is no way that I want blood and grime on the covers!" Before he was lowered to the bed, she placed the dry cloth behind his head. "I hope he wakes up soon - the sooner the better - for all of us! So, what do we do now?" she looked at Renard for some leadership.

Renard chewed on his lip thinking. "We had better be prepared ... Andre, you go to the edge of the village and watch for developments. I will stay on the street corner nearby and when I see you - or the Dragoons - coming, I will rush back in and help you hide our sleeping friend!" Both men rose and followed by Isabeau, went down the stone stairs to the kitchen.

Renard grinned at Isabeau. "Thank you for your cooperation. I cannot think of anyone who can be trusted with this ... imposition. We'll do whatever it takes to keep you safe!"

Isabeau looked at the two men. She found that her anger had subsided but was replaced with a sudden weakness in the knees. She grinned ruefully at them.

"Yesterday the Luberon hillside was peaceful and calm. I was planning for my wedding at the end of this month. Now - what a mess! For everyone! Oh well - one step at a time then. Out you go - both of you!" and she hurried them to the door and after a quick glance outside, she closed it firmly.

She hesitated a second looking back at the closed door. What next? Get rid of any signs of violence. Then check her patient. Then make some emergency plans in case we need to act in a hurry. She spun on her heel, her deep orange skirt whirling around her legs and trotted back to the kitchen. A little rubbing with a wet cloth and the dust, blood and dirt was removed. I'd better make sure Pierre upstairs does not panic when he recovers and cries out. She ran upstairs two steps at a time and into her father's room.

All was quiet, Pierre had not moved at all. I'll open the shutters and let the sunlight in so he will not awaken in the dark. She took a moment to look into the street and down the road to the center of the village. She could see Renard lounging at the street corner. All looked normal. Andre had taken the mule away. She turned back to the bed.

As she stopped at the bedside, she found herself unconsciously comparing this Pierre with her own betrothed, Le Duc - both Pierres! She stretched out her hand cautiously and touched his strong dark wavy hair. It sprang a little under her fingers. Who would have imagined that this quiet conservative fellow would have acted so rashly and impulsively?

"People always surprise you - just when you have people put into little boxes, they spring out and wreck the picture," she whispered softly and ran her fingers gently down his cheek. "You are now in a mess, Pierre Jaubert - but - what a brave mess! So unlike you!" She jumped back slightly as his head turned towards her trailing fingers and he moaned a little. "Oh - so you are coming alive again, my surprising friend?"

Isabeau crouched down beside the bed and watched his face carefully, a slight blush touching her cheeks and a slight hollow feeling of guilt inside. Betrothed girls are not supposed to be secretly touching other young men! An impish grin flashed across her face. Pierre's one rich brown eye and then the other opened slightly and then flinched a little with pain. The look was puzzled and confused. His hand rose to the back of his head and his eyes screwed up painfully.

"Oh! My head!" Then he glanced around quickly but painfully back at the girl hovering over him. "What's happened to me ... Oh yes! I remember - the *Capitaine* and the Dragoons!" Then he looked back around the room and back to her. "It's Isabeau ... Richarde ... isn't it? But what am I doing here - of all places?"

He tried to rise but she gently but firmly pressed him back on the bed. He stared at her as she explained what had happened and the precautions his best friend and cousin had taken. He closed his eyes again and groaned. "What a mess!" he whispered.

"What you need right now is to lie back and try to sleep awhile. I'll close the shutters and if something happens we will come and alert you. In the meantime, we will make some plans". Pierre opened his eyes and smiled slightly; then closed them again. As Isabeau left the room, he seemed to be dozing and she closed the door carefully and ran down the stairs.

In the kitchen she paused. Plans! We need to have some plan in case he has to leave in a hurry ... basic things ... like food and ... sleeping things! Isabeau opened a cupboard and dragged out a heavy cloth bag. She quickly wrapped a supply of bread and cheese, a flask of local wine and a knife.

She picked up some fresh tomatoes and hesitated - this is not a picnic - and then thought - why not? She rolled up an old blanket that her father used when he slept overnight in the high hills. Water! Another leather bag used on her father's travels.

Good - at least we will not be in a panic if something happens, she thought. She found she was only taking in short breaths – Hmmm she thought, Isabeau, you need to calm down! She sat for a moment at the table and felt pleased with how she had handled a dangerous moment so well.

Shouting voices echoed down the street and Isabeau ran and opened the door. Neighbors raced past her door, their faces displaying fear and distress. Renard was loping down the street and pointing backward toward the corner. "Dragoons!" he yelled out.

Oh no! So soon, she thought. Behind Renard, she saw her father also rounding the corner at a trot and heading down the street, concern showing on his face. Now I have to explain to my father, as well, she worried and stood back holding the door open for them to enter.

"I'll get him up right now! Is there a way out the back?" Renard called as he rushed up the steps and Isabeau nodded. She turned to greet her father who pushed her quickly into the doorway and slammed the door shut.

"The soldiers are coming to our village, my dear child! You need to take care! I don't want anything happening to you!" He looked around the kitchen in concern. "Who was that man who you let into the house Was that your Pierre ... Le Duc?" A touch of panic caused him to raise his voice slightly.

"No, father, that was not my Le Duc! Listen and I will tell you what has happened!" She quickly recounted the events from La Motte d'Aigues; the attack on the Dragoon Captain; and the arrival of the three men from the next village asking for help. She watched her father's face change from shock at the death of the respected old lady, to some degree of pleasure at the injury to the Captain; then to fear for his family with the arrival of the attacker in his own home. Isabeau frowned with worry.

She was relieved when he finally exploded with a grunt of stress, saying, "You did the right thing, my daughter; but we had better get him out of here and into safe hiding!" Even as he spoke, they could now hear the horses cantering outside the door.

The hoof-beats stopped below the window and they turned spontaneously towards the street. A loud knocking echoed through the house.

"Upstairs, daughter," her father grunted softly, "hide away and I'll try to send them away!" Isabeau raced up the steps and met Renard coming down. His usual grin looked strained and she passed him and watched him go and stand behind the door where her father waited impatiently. She slipped into the bedroom and closed the door.

Richarde opened the door just as further blows hammered the wood. Two tall and rough experienced-looking Dragoons stood on the doorstep.

"Who are you, old man?"

"My name is Daniel Richarde - I live here." There was a brief hesitation, then before the trooper could speak, "Are you one of the swine who murdered that fine old lady in La Motte?" The father's voice was tough and suddenly bitter. Old *Mme*. Carpentier had been appreciated by both villages for her knowledge of herbs and nursing treatments in the past.

The faces of the Dragoons both showed surprise at the outburst. Standing behind the door Renard was surprised to hear a tinge of respect and apology in the Trooper's voice as he spoke up.

"I'm sorry, *Monsieur*, the *Capitaine* can be harsh - when he is challenged!" Then the voice could distinctly be heard to harden. "Nevertheless, you Huguenots can be a pain!" His voice became more authoritative. "M. Richarde; you will probably soon be ordered to provide accommodation for four Dragoons. You will be expected to provide good wine and feed them; and provide proper lodging as long as the troop remains in the village. The *Capitaine* will punish you accordingly if service is neglected. When requested, I recommend that you cooperate," he hesitated, then added, "Unless you are willing to abjure your Reformed faith?" The trooper looked expectantly at the man.

M. Richarde's face flushed angrily.

"Never! Never! Be gone!"

The trooper sighed loudly and they turned to their horses. As they mounted with a flourish, one hesitated as though remembering something. He jerked his horse to face the doorway where Richarde stood.

"We are searching for the young ruffian who viciously attacked *Capitaine Benoit*! It appears he is known as Pierre Jaubert - the son of Jacques. Do you know where we can find him?" He glared as he leaned forward.

"Jaubert? The name is a common one in the area. I cannot help you." The voice was still angry and a touch insolent.

"The *Capitaine* expects that we shall have him by evening. Anyone hiding or aiding him will be punished! The *Capitaine* expects a quick trial tonight in the square in La Motte. Everyone is to be there! Talk to your neighbors. Do you understand?"

"You can go to Hell!" M. Richarde spoke out in anger.

The two troopers now glared at him with suspicion on their faces. One trooper - with obvious authority – stood up in his stirrups and yelled down the street to another group of Dragoons and as they cantered up the street, the troopers swung down again from their horses.

"I think, you stupid old man, that we had better first search your home!" Isabeau's father tried to slam the door but a trooper's foot was firmly between the door and the frame and it burst inward. Renard was pinned painfully behind the door as several extra troopers flooded through. A quick thrust to his chest, M. Richarde fell backward onto the floor.

"Upstairs and check the bedrooms!" The main trooper yelled at the others.

"I don't think you should do that!" Renard's voice came from behind the door as it swung slowly open. The Troopers froze.

"My daughter is upstairs - she is ill!" Richarde rose painfully to his feet.

"Then lead us upstairs, old man! And don't try anything stupid!" the head trooper announced; and looking at Renard, he spat, "You stay where you are!" Renard shrugged.

Gripping Richarde by the shoulder, the trooper followed him upstairs. They pushed open the bedroom door and glanced around. "No one here! Where is this sick girl?"

They pushed on the other door and entered. Richarde looking in quickly. The bed had been moved but a figure was lying covered with a heavy quilt. In the bed, Isabeau turned her face toward the door, a painful look on her features.

"Aha! My beauty - and what is wrong with you?" One of the troopers sneered. Richarde spoke up.

"She has a fever ... female problems?".

"Just our luck! We'll wait a few days until she recovers!" the trooper snorted and with a glance around the room, slammed the door shut. They checked the other rooms and the closets upstairs and then thumped down to the kitchen where the other couple of troopers were watching the silent Renard who was lounging against the wall with an insolent look on his face.

Richarde came down slowly and, catching Renard's eye, gently raised his eyebrows in confusion. Renard shrugged his shoulders and turned towards the door. A trooper blocked his way in reaction to a quick hand movement from the senior trooper.

"Not so fast, you yapping cur!" He swung him round with a jerk of his shoulders and pushed him against the wall. Another trooper had drawn his short sword and prodded it into Renard's side making him wince.

"What is your name!" He barked and when Renard hesitated, he whipped the back of his gloved hand across his face. Blood poured from his nose and as he tried to raise his hands to protect himself, the trooper jerked his knee forward into Renard's exposed stomach bucking him up against the wall.

"They call me *Renard*," he whispered through bruised lips.

"Sure - like a fox! And sly like a fox too, probably? What is your last name? Answer!" as he kicked him again in the stomach.

"Jaubert." he whispered painfully.

Both troopers started and stared at each other. They looked down at Renard lying against the wall. One of the troopers put his knee into the small of Renard's back and gripping the sides of his chin jerked the head back painfully. Renard screamed.

"And your real name, swine?"

"...Oh ... Pierre!" The voice came in a whispered moan.

"I think Lucien, that we had better treat this bastard with a little more care. The *Capitaine* probably wants to kill this one personally!" The senior trooper glared at Richarde standing by the foot of the stairs.

"We'll be back to see you later, old man. Make sure you are here. We will take this stinking whippet to see the *Capitaine* he injured. You may never see him again - and I think that you will soon be wishing that you had never seen him before in your lifetime!"

Two troopers came through the door and helped drag Renard out the door and slung him over the saddle and using rough cord tied his hands and feet together under the horse. One of the troopers led the horse surrounded by the other soldiers and Daniel Richarde watched them round the corner heading for the nearby village of La Motte d'Aigues. As soon as they turned the corner, Andre Roux crossed the street his face anxious and upset.

"Did they find my friend? What happened to Renard - did he let his mouth run away as usual?"

"I really don't know what happened to your friend, it's still a mystery to me. Let us go and ask Isabeau what she did with Pierre." As they ran up the stairs, Richarde explained about Renard admitting that his name was Jaubert and the trooper's reactions.

"What he did was brave - but foolish! But, it will give us some time to help Pierre escape the village. But the troopers will not be happy when they discover they have the wrong man - if they even care!"

Isabeau was standing inside the open door as they came up the stairs.

"The troopers have gone with Renard as their prisoner! What did you do with Pierre Jaubert?" Her father asked.

"I slid him down between the bed and the wall and pushed the bed tight against him. Thank God he did not struggle!" As the three of them entered the darkened room, the bed moved away from the wall and a low groan came from under the bed.

As Isabeau opened the inner shutters to light the room, Andre helped Pierre to a sitting position on the end of the bed. Pierre kept blinking his eyes, shaking his head and still looked a little dazed.

"We need to find a place to hide him - close to the villages but not likely to be searched," Andre looked toward M. Richarde with a puzzled expression. The older man shook his head.

"What about the *borrie*? He can survive there in this weather and it is probably not known to the troopers!" Isabeau burst out.

The *borrie* was a rough round shelter built entirely of local stones - rainproof and safe from animal attacks. No one knew how old they were but it was suspected they were thousands of years old and dotted through the local hills. Local villagers claimed the "Old Celtic People" had built them. The closest borrie was less than a mile up the mountain from their village well camouflaged with a copse of old trees.

"Hmm. Good idea, Isabeau," Andre looked relieved. "What about food...?"

"I've got it all packed in one of father's bags! Food, water, and covers! It should take care of him for a day or so!" Her father smiled quietly and touched her shoulder.

"That's my daughter! That's good thinking! Now let's get him down the steps and out the back."

"Renard's mule is still tied outside your back shed!" Andre grinned. "I don't think Renard will be needing it for a while! I'll lead the mule down the gully and around through the vineyards and help him get settled in the borrie. Then I'll rush back and see what we can do about getting Renard out of his mess, too."

Between the three of them, they loaded Pierre across the mule's back and carrying the sack on his back; Andre led the mule and its passenger out of sight down the gully.

M. Richarde, standing with his arm around his daughter's shoulders, whispered into her ear, "I'm very proud of your behaviors; although I don't think your Le Duc will be pleased. Maybe this whole incident had better be a family secret, eh?" Isabeau looked up at her father and smilingly nodded, and they turned back into their home.

*   *   *   *   *

The sergeant opened the door of the Carpentier home cautiously and poked his head around the corner. M. Carpentier was sitting morosely at the kitchen table. His wife was slumped in a chair in a corner of the room by the fire looking depressed and sad. The daughter faced the cottage door with a frightened look on her face.

"Bonjour, Monsieur. Where is the Capitaine?"

M. Carpentier, without looking around, jerked his finger in the upstairs direction. The sergeant entered the home, slammed the door, and ran upstairs. He carefully opened the closed bedroom door at the top.

"Pardon, Mon Capitaine," he spoke softly as he saw the figure lying on the bed in the darkened room with a white towel across his face. "How are you feeling now?"

The resting figure rolled over throwing the towel from his face and raised slightly from the bed. It was obvious that the wound was still sore and swollen.

"What do you want? I'm feeling like the wrath of God!" He grunted with obvious pain, " So - what do you want?"

"I am sorry to bother you, Capitaine. But we have some information that I think you should hear. We have developed a 'Rat' in this little village already!"

"A Rat! Nice work! A young man who wants to save his own neck from punishment – or a 'solid citizen' who wants silver for his information?"

"A scared 'Rat' who likes to look after himself at the expense of his friends! He told us where a Jaubert man has been seen."

The Captain grunted and touched his face ruefully, "You had better pick the bastard up! Maybe work Jaubert over - a little bit - so that he knows what pain is like! Then arrange the village meeting tonight to demonstrate how I feel about ... being assaulted." The Captain rolled over and covered his head again as he grunted. "I have a strong feeling that my pain will vanish ... with his punishment!" In the darkened room, the sergeant grinned to himself and closed the door quietly.

.

*   *   *   *   *

CHAPTER THREE

Evening 19th June 1687
The hillside near
La Motte d'Aigues Provence France

It was again the clanging of the village bell that brought him out of his confusing black void. Again, the bells, he mumbled to himself. Then the pain lanced through the back of his head as he turned over groaning.

His eyes opened slowly and he became conscious that he was lying on the hard packed earth on a blanket with a cover thrown over him. He could barely make out small patches of twilight coming through the ceiling of the shelter and, in the dim red light of the glowing embers in the small fireplace, he began to recognize where he was.

The borrie, he groaned. Why am I here? Then the memories began to flood back to him in little waves.

The Dragoons in his village; the terrible atrocity; the horrible burning of that sweet old lady; then - the Captain! He groaned again - I am in trouble like I have never been before! He carefully reached behind his head and gently rubbed the tender lump at the base of his skull. In his mind appeared glimpses of an uncomfortable trip on the back of a horse - or a mule.

Then a face - a sweet face - it seemed like Isabeau Richarde from St. Martin. But why her - besides, he thought: she is betrothed to Le Duc, isn't she? Everything is too confusing!

Pierre slowly pushed himself up and sat, looking around. A slight scuffling sound outside made him jerk his face painfully toward the low entrance of the borrie.

Someone was coming in! Pierre looked around for a weapon. The only thing was a stout piece of firewood next to the fireplace. He raised it above his head as a darkened head appeared in the entry. Then he dropped his hand and grinned ruefully as his friend's face reflected in the glow from the small fire.

"Andre, my friend. You scared me - a little!"

"Pierre, it's good to see you awake!" He crawled to the embers of the fire and added a few twigs to raise a small flame. "Something is happening in La Motte. You heard the bell? " Pierre nodded and grimaced as he put his hand to the back of his head.

"I feel that if I nod my head it will fall off!" he groaned.

"I had better go back in case my absence is noted," whispered Andre furtively, "But you had better stay here for safety..."

"No!" Pierre shook his head carefully, "I need to go back and see for myself. After all, I was the one who caused the problems and my parents are probably frantically worrying about me...".

"All right - but - be very careful! I imagine the Dragoons are all much on edge right now. And, I think you'll have a price on your head!" Andre rose and stretched his arms as high as he could in the low roofed building. He looked Pierre over carefully. "You had better pull your cowl up to cover your face."

He nodded. As his friend rose, he pulled the hood up over his head. The two ducked down and crawled out into the early evening light. Standing up outside Pierre recognized the soft attractive scent of crushed wild thyme and he smiled painfully.

I am glad the blow on my head did not take away my sense of smell!

"Follow me, Pierre!" Andre called as he pushed his way through the undergrowth and shrubs till they stood looking down the slope to La Motte. There were lights in most of the windows and flickering shadows indicating people moving between the buildings. Avoiding the open roadway, Andre began to jog through the vineyard toward the nearest buildings. Pierre followed but soon slowed down as he found that his balance was still awkward.

As they passed through a yard onto the small streets, Andre turned in the direction being taken by other villagers. Pierre followed feeling much better physically as his body began to recover. As they passed several of the townsfolk, despite his hood, he noted he was being recognized by the whispered conversation passing between a man and his spouse.

The villagers had begun to gather around the central square - the site of today's violence. Their attention was clearly focused on the main body of well-armed Dragoons standing before the oven. Pierre noted the doors of the oven were wide open.

The remains of old lady Carpentier had probably been removed. His nose twitched as he still recognized the sharp odor of burnt flesh. He felt a quiver of horror run down his spine. He sensed a constant rumble of anxiety and anger from the gathering.

A collection of oil lanterns lit the square reflecting off the polished breastplates and helmets of the Dragoons.

Turning his head and peering out from the hood, Pierre could view the gathering crowd of men, women and children. It seemed that everyone wanted to be aware of the dangers! Pierre ducked his head slightly when he realized that, standing in front of his biggest Dragoon, was Captain Hugo Benoit.

Dark bloodstains marred the once white dressing on his cheek. Pierre wiped the grim smile that crept across his own face. Suddenly, behind him, Pierre heard an increase in the level of growling from the villagers and, tugging his hood closer over his face, he peered round.

He was horrified to find that behind the last row of villagers, a circle of Dragoons with burning torches now stood surrounding the whole village population. He was trapped with the others!

His stomach tightened. Then the loud harsh voice of the sergeant got everyone's attention.

"Quiet! Quiet! Listen to my *Capitaine*!" A hush settled on the gathering. Pierre found it hard to breathe. He consciously took a few deep gasps.

The Captain lackadaisically strolled a few paces forward idly waving his white handkerchief up and down in the air with one hand while casually looking around at the attentive but irritated people. When he spoke, his voice was soft and low - but chillingly clear.

"Villagers of La Motte d'Aigues! This afternoon, I came with my men to take control of your village. To assist you in considering your choice of faith." He dropped his head a little and hesitated as though thinking about his words. Then he raised his face and continued, "Need I remind you that I came as a representative of his Majesty, the King! I expected ... to be treated with respect! But, instead I was challenged by a stupid old crone."

An angry murmur rose from the crowd. The Dragoons surrounding them rattled their weapons. The Captain did not appear to be in any way disconcerted. He smiled arrogantly and raised his voice.

"Let me remind you ... I didn't appreciate the challenge from the old woman. As you all saw, I have my ways of getting respect!" He paused again as his threat sank in. "Then - it appeared you had not learned your lessons well. One of your stupid young men decided to ... play the Hero!"

A murmur of vindictive pleasure ran through the crowd. For the first time the crowd's reaction appeared to affect the Captain. His cynical smile slowly vanished and the hand holding the handkerchief rose to touch his injured cheek. His voice raised again - this time appearing a little strained.

"You laugh! You laugh when his Majesty's representative is struck by a filthy shepherd!" The ripple of laughter stilled. "Then we shall let you laugh out of the other side of your ignorant faces!"

From the cobblestones, the captain raised his other hand holding the shining sword to eye height. With arm outstretched, the blade pointing at the faces of the crowd, he slowly moved his arm around the circle letting the blade focus the villagers' eyes on its point as he spoke.

"My *Sergent* tells me the young man's name was Jaubert ... Pierre!" A low groan crept through the gathering. The Captain smiled slightly as his sword continued to move around the circle of faces glinting in the light of the lanterns.

"I have decided to make an example of this ... callow young man - who dares to challenge the King himself! I have gathered you together so you can witness ... his punishment!"

He paused his sword's movement and dropped its point to the cobblestones. He leaned a little on it. "You see - about an hour ago, we captured him!" he announced and a low moan went through the throng.

Pierre froze. His breathing seemed to stop.   He was afraid to turn around and seek a passage of escape. And he felt confused. The Captain was not looking at him.   He was now smiling with satisfaction and looking well to the right. Pierre peered at the nearest Dragoon.   That soldier was also looking away. Pierre's head swung slowly and painfully backward as a commotion broke out at the opposite side of the square.

The crowd had been roughly parted as several Dragoons forced their way into the open. They were dragging a hooded man who struggled in their grasp. His hands were tied behind his back and his cloak was dirty and bloodstained. When the Dragoons reached the center, they let their captive drop on his knees on the cobbles where he swayed.

Captain Benoit stepped forward and using his outstretched sword, he tucked the tip into the front of the hood and, facing the crowd of villagers, he dramatically flipped the hood back with a flourish of his sword.   The Captain turned and sardonically smiled at the front row of villagers. A gasp ran through the villagers and several children cried out in dismay.

Pierre's gasp was both a mixture of horror and relief.   The kneeling figure was that of his cousin - Pierre "Renard" Jaubert. Above his blood stained face, his rust tinged hair glinted in the lantern light.

From the front row of watchers, a young boy's voice rang out in scorn, "That's not him! You've got the wrong one!" Then the child's voice died as a parent's hand closed protectively over his mouth.

The cry caused the Captain to spin round. He glared down at the kneeling figure with growing horror and anger on his face.   With the point of his sword he prodded Renard who fell over onto his side. The Captain leaned forward and took a closer look.   Then he spun round angrily and yelled, "*Sergent?*"

Standing behind, watching the Captain, the Sergeant sprang forward and knelt beside the figure on the cobblestones. Then he looked up directly at where Pierre stood in the crowd. He raised his right hand and pointed directly at him. Pierre felt his stomach drop again and his breathing labored.

"Claudier! Ludger!   You fools, come here and look at this man!" Confused, Pierre was jostled from behind and fell sideways as two Dragoons - standing behind him - brushed him sideways as they forced their way forward to the center of the square.

Climbing quickly to his feet, Pierre saw that the gap in the ring of soldiers had not been filled and moving slowly, he edged back into the gap until the shadow of the buildings hid his presence. He could still hear the confused explanations taking place. He carefully edged backward between the two buildings and turned and ran quietly toward the edge of the village. Behind him he could now hear bursts of laughter from the villagers and blustering threats from the Sergeant.

*   *   *   *   *

Rushing back up the hillside to the protection of the borrie, panic was still surging through Pierre. I have to get away before a much larger search takes place, he thought. Now they have discovered their mistake, all Hell will break out! He worked his way through the shrubs and trees guided by the glow from the cooling embers that led him to the entrance. As he bent to enter the doorway, he heard scuffling sounds behind him and spun round.

"It's all right, Pierre! It's me, Andre! I saw you make your escape and, when the villagers saw the Captain's folly, I slid away also." The two men crawled into the borrie and sat down to catch their breath.

"I have to leave the village, Andre! Right now! But I'm worried about my cousin, Renard!"

"Don't worry. After you left, the Captain kicked Renard once and then ordered his men to make a house-to-house search of the village. Your Uncle took him home in the confusion."

"Good!" breathed Pierre. Then Andre told him about the mistake in the next village.

"But, Pierre, we have a surprise for you! Gather your food and covers in the bags and come out to the side of the copse away from the village." Andre whispered back as he crawled out and vanished in the shrubs.

In the dim light of the fire, Pierre gathered up what he took to be food supplies with the covers and crawled out of the hiding place making his way through the trees and shrubs until in the bright moonlight, he saw Andre standing in the shadows. Suddenly a snort from an animal stopped him short.

"You've got a mule, Andre - where from?"

"It's no mule! It's a horse!"

"A horse! Where did you get a horse?"

Andre laughed. "No! It's not from one of ours! If you must escape -- and quickly - why not use one of the enemy's horses? They were all so busy right now in their house-to-house search of the village that we were able to borrow this horse for you!"

"Oh *Mon Dieu*! I have never ridden a horse!" Pierre grasped the reins and moved around the horse looking it over. "However, beggars have to take what they can get! I hope it likes me!"

"I found an extra rope for tying up the horse at night and letting him forage while you sleep." Andre added, "Isabeau said she had given you some food and coverings."

Together they tied the bundle of covers and bags of food onto the horse as it stood patiently with head turned watching the two young men.

"So Pierre, where are you going to seek refuge? Do you have any plans at all?" Andre's voice had risen a little, which Pierre knew from experience indicated that he was anxious.

"I don't know, my friend, maybe I'll ride down the road to La Tour d'Aigues or maybe even to Pertuis. The family has friends in both centers." Pierre hesitated and his eyes narrowed in thought. "I need to check with my father..."

"Oh! Pierre ... I forgot to tell you - I saw your father in the square briefly. He said he will try to meet you on the road further down the hill - if he can get away safely!"

"Thank you, Andre! That would be wonderful! I only hope my head can stand the pounding of horses' hooves." Holding the reins, he slipped his foot into the stirrup and swung himself up with difficulty. Below him the village was well lit up and shadows passed between the buildings giving evidence of the search underway.

In the moonlight, the road past the village looked deserted. He touched his friend's shoulder and nudged the unusually large animal cautiously down the pathway in the direction of the road. The dark horse trotted carefully and Pierre glanced back to wave at the black figure against the copse.

*   *   *   *   *

Evening 19th June 1687 The hillside near
La Motte d'Aigues Provence France

When the horse left the path and joined the road, the dust rose under its hooves and rapidly blew back past them. The sweet and pungent smell of crushed herbs tickled his nose. Pierre slowed the horse to a quiet walk as the lights of the village homes flickered as they rode past the grape vineyards.

Protesting voices could be heard from the village as the doors were banged upon. The moonlight was bright enough to show a good distance ahead. When the village was safely passed, he urged the horse into a light canter still wary of the possibility of sentries being located outside the village.

Suddenly, a black figure stepped into the roadway ahead and waved arms above the head.

The horse jerked to a halt nearly throwing Pierre who struggled to regain his seat.

"Pierre!" the voice called and Pierre heaved a sigh of relief - his father's voice! The horse stretched out its snout to sniff suspiciously. Then it nudged his father's arm in a friendly gesture as Pierre slid to the ground.

Jacques Jaubert was taller than his son and had strong husky shoulders. Even in the moonlight, Pierre could see that his dark hair had grayed at the sides and his shiny baldpate in the middle shone white in the dim light. He had a heavy mustache shadowing his mouth.

He threw his arms around Pierre and hugged him briefly but tightly enough to leave him a little breathless. This display of affection was unusual to Pierre and suggested that the assault on the Captain had been somewhat of a shock to his father. He had always been a man who liked his world to run in a controlled orderly fashion.

"It's good to see you still in one piece," Jacques grunted, "after the horror of the death of the dear old Carpentier lady and with your attack on the Captain, both your mother, Francoise, and I feared for your life!"

He stood with his gnarled hand still grasping Pierre's shoulder. In the moonlight, his forehead broke into a worried frown. "I suppose you realize that the matter is far from over!"

Pierre nodded. Father continued: "That shocking mistake of capturing your cousin has given you a chance to escape. All the Dragoons are searching the homes in La Motte. I must get home and explain ... I was checking on the sheep!" He paused and looked at Pierre; then shook his head sadly and continued, "Andre explained you had been hidden in the old borrie - good thinking! Do you have any idea of where to hide - right now?"

"Father, I decided to try our friends in La Tour d'Aigues; or maybe Pertuis."

"No! I think that the Captain won't settle for anything less than your head. And, the Dragoons can reach both those centers in an hour. Your mother has a godfather whose family, the Le Claires, live in Marseilles. You've been to their house on the harbor front when you were a boy. Do you remember? "

Pierre nodded - he remembered it well. As a country youth, he had been intrigued with the vastness of the ocean. They had been a warm and inviting family and were outspokenly supportive of the reformed religion. That would be a safe place to hide until matters improved.

"Good idea, Father. Once the confusion and danger dies, I will return home and we can live a normal life again." He paused, then continued, "I am sorry for all the problems I have caused you ... and the family ... and the village as well..."

"No Pierre! Don't talk like that!" The old man paused and glanced over his shoulder in the direction of the village. "I must not let you go without telling you that ... I am proud of the way you have acted today!"

Even in the moonlight, Pierre could see a glistening of tears in the corners of his father's eyes. The only time he had seen this before was when lightening on the mountainside had killed his father's favorite ram.

His father held out his hand and Pierre looked down at it in amazement. His father often shook hands with his friends but he always treated Pierre like "a son". He was supposed to follow orders; respect elders - especially father's friends; and stay in the background in conversations.

Pierre reached out his hand and grasped his father's. He felt the harsh skin and the tremendous strength in his fingers. How does this make you feel, Pierre, he thought? I feel different! Like suddenly, I am a man!

His father's mustache moved in the moonlight and Pierre could see him smiling. He grinned back. His father reached out and grasped his shoulder giving him a squeeze, then grunted:

"Better hurry on to safety. You will have to sleep along the road tonight and perhaps tomorrow." He hesitated and squinted his eyes - and then acted "like a Father again".

"With that horse, it should take about three days of riding ... through Aix ... to reach Marseilles. Beware of all mounted men - they probably would report you to Dragoons. Maybe you should ride only at night and very early in the morning ...Good luck to you, my son and the family's good wishes go with you!"

He stepped back onto the side of the road. Pierre mounted again; rubbed the back of his head; and with a wave of his hand, he cantered the horse downhill. When he looked back, his father had vanished and the lights of La Motte d'Aigues faded quickly into darkness.

The horse moved easily. Its broad back was like a comfortable chair, he thought. It takes easily to a new rider. He ran his hand over the side of the neck and rubbed his horse with pleasure. The horse turned its head slightly and snorted. We will get along fine! I hope you like grass, old horse, because that is all you are going to get for supper tonight. That rope that Andre threw in at the last moment will save my life!

A shiver ran through his body. Pierre shook his head and again rubbed his neck as the cool evening breeze ruffled his hair. I am tired and aching all over - I need to rest soon. Father's advice is good - I will canter until I feel like sleeping - perhaps after the next two towns - maybe find a safe spot at the Durance River. Then an early start in the morning!

I can't even imagine what lies in store for me, thought Pierre.

*   *   *   *   *

CHAPTER FOUR

Captain Benoit sat at the table with a bottle of local estate wine before him. He glanced at the young girl standing looking out of the shuttered window. Reaching out, he lifted the bottle and banged it sharply on the table.

"Maid! You! Bring me a glass. No! Bring two glasses!" She turned, uncertain about what to do. The Captain raised his head and looked into her face. He instinctively brought up his lace handkerchief and dabbed his lips.

"Sit down, Suzanne! We'll have a drink together!"

Suzanne glanced with a frightened expression at her father who stood in his regular place by the fire. He nodded grimly and turned his back on the table. With an obvious reluctance, she sat down on the stool facing him. The bottle opened, he poured two glasses of wine. He pushed a glass across towards her and waved his forefinger at the glass.

"Drink up, Suzanne! I think we should begin to be ... friends. I take it that you have had not much to do with young men yet." His voice was soft and earnest but his eyes made Suzanne uncomfortable.

Suzanne nodded slightly but did not drink.

"Well, drink up, young girl and perhaps we can talk a little about young men and ... the art of love." The Father grunted from his place at the fire. The Captain glanced briefly at him and concentrated on Suzanne.

A loud banging at the door interrupted this scene. As the Captain glanced up, annoyed at this interruption, the sergeant poked his head around the corner.

"Our Rat has spoken, *Capitaine*! He says that the Jaubert villain has fled from the village and, what's more, it now seems he may have one of our horses!"

"Damn it, *Sergent*! How did he do that?" The Captain was obviously angry. He stood up and joined the soldier outside the door. In the dusk they discussed what action to take.

In an effort to offset his Captain's anger, the Sergeant quickly provided more information.

"*Capitaine*, our Rat says that Jaubert may have relatives in Marseilles. They feel it is likely that he will head in that direction."

"Hmmm! All right, let's think about what we can do." The Captain stood silently looking into the dark alley.

Then, "*Sergent*, send a man on a fast horse down to the river. Have him warn the guards on the bridge; then continue on down the line in the direction of Marseilles. Make sure he doesn't miss out any of the major crossing points."

The Captain turned back towards the doorway still obviously upset and angry. Then, he turned again and waved his finger at his soldier.

"I don't like this, *Sergent*! When we catch this villain maybe his punishment should be protracted! Maybe he would like to spend the rest of his life at sea - the galley on the harbor at Marseilles might be the thing for him! And it will send a real message to the village that we do not treat assaults on the King's representative lightly."

The sergeant nodded and mounted his horse. The Captain turned and stamped his boot in frustration.

Inside, Suzanne was gone. The Captain glared at M. Charpentier.

"My daughter has gone out for some fresh air, *Capitaine*." He looked defiant.

"Well, M. Charpentier, I don't like you interfering in my social life. But I can wait awhile – after all, I have lots of time, haven't I?" His lazy grin did nothing to make the father feel he had won this battle.

"Lots of time; and a fresh young apple simply gets sweeter as it ripens, doesn't it?" He turned and stamped his way up the stairs to his bedroom. The father glanced with sympathy at his wife and shrugged his shoulders. He went out the door to find his daughter.

*   *   *   *   *

In the dark of night, Pierre avoided the main route through Pertuis on the river; and angled across the hillside on the familiar road to Cadenet. Coming close enough to the village to awaken the barking dogs; he left the road and bypassed the sleeping village traveling down the rows of grapevines. He checked the main road along the Durance riverbank before leading his horse across the road and carefully working his way into a thick batch of trees and wild shrubs. Now, over the river, he could see the lights of Silvacane village and the silhouette of the roof of the Abbey still shrouded by mist on the other bank. He unsaddled and tied the horse in a grassy area. He mentally blessed Andre for the rope! Before rolling his blankets out for the night, he ate a rough meal of bread, cheese and wine. Exhausted, he covered himself up and slept fitfully.

*   *   *   *   *

Pierre groaned and rolled over and opened his brown eyes to look up into the early morning sky. A lovely clear day? If it's such a good day for traveling, he thought, why am I not on the road already. He grunted with disgust. I have never felt more alone and more lost in my whole life than I feel right now, he thought. What is the problem?

The problem is that I know what I have to do - go to Marseilles to get help from my relatives. But how do I prevent myself from getting caught and ending up like all the other people fleeing - in chains; maybe even on the galleys? He remembered the frightening tales he had heard from villagers returning from the wool sales in Marseilles. A lifetime living and dying slowly as you pull the galley oars - never!

Pierre rubbed the growing whiskers on his face and shut his eyes. His mind seemed too full of confusion and his body's stomach felt dead. He wondered if this feeling was because the immediate drama was over?

Ever since he had acted so impulsively and struck the Captain at the village, his life had become full of urgency - mixed with action. A case of "survive or be punished"? So, do I feel dead inside because I am out of the immediate danger and away from the village and the Dragoons?

"I am safe now! At least, right now! Lying here in my dew-damp covers with a stolen horse in this copse of trees near the Durance River - I am safe! But why do I feel so numb and tired?" Pierre shrugged and rolled over to find the horse peering at him over a small shrub. Its ears were pricked up as it listened to his voice.

"Yes, my friendly old horse, what do you think is wrong with me? I should be feeling exhilarated because I am free! But inside I am feeling down and dead? Well, what do you think?" he grunted again, "And now I am even asking advice from a horse!"

Pierre sat up pulling the covers over his shoulders. Let's think this out rationally, he frowned as he concentrated. Up to now, my father - and my mother - have always been around to discuss any decision. And if it was too personal to discuss with my parents, my Uncle and Aunts were available - depending on the problem.

He had to admit it had been a comfortable situation. But, then sometimes he felt a little like one of those wooden puppets that a traveling entertainer had used at La Tour d'Aigues last summer. The strings on your hands and feet get jerked and you jump. But there is no one to pull the strings anymore! I'll have to pull my own! He grunted with some satisfaction. Maybe that is the immediate answer! I'll decide for myself!

"So, right now I am hungry - so I had better have something to eat. Clean myself up a little at the river edge. I have you, horse!" the horse stopped browsing and raised its head looking at him and snorted. "And, I have a direction. Get to Marseilles and get help from the relatives - and not get caught en route!"

"Hmmm," he grunted, "I feel better in both my head and body. Next time I feel like that I had better... get back in control ... and make some decisions - and plans!" He rose slowly and shook the cover out and hung it to dry. He scratched the horse's snout, then carefully walked to the edge of the wooded copse that had protected him during the night and peered at the nearby Durance River.

Patches of heavy mist clung to the foliage along the winding riverbank. Smoke was drifting up in tender wisps from the village chimneys over the river. On the stone bridge spanning the river was a single guard. Probably one of the local Militia, Pierre thought, the village had a large population of Catholics. The guard was wrapped up in his heavy cloak and leaning against the parapet on the Silvacane end of the bridge smoking a clay pipe. Even at this distance, Pierre could smell a tinge of the smoke.

A movement on the road from the bridge to the nearby village caught Pierre's eye. Two men were walking slowly out of the village, pikes in hand, and headed in the direction of the bridge. Glancing back, Pierre saw the guard straighten up probably looking forward to going off duty and enjoying a breakfast.

Better go now! One guard is safer than two! No time for eating! Running back to the horse he quickly saddled it, rolling up his covers and tying them to the saddle. He led the horse quickly through the masking foliage and finding the road clear except for a small cart coming down the hill, he mounted and rode out on to the dew-covered road. Nudging the horse to a canter, he approached the bridge.

Be confident, Pierre – act like you have a right to do what you are doing!

The militia guard shrugged off his coat and stood up holding his pike upright. As Pierre approached, he slowed to a trot and greeted the guard with a casual nod.

"Slow down, young fellow!" The guard rubbed his whiskered face.

"I can't! The *Capitaine* of the Dragoons in La Motte," he gestured up the Luberon hillside in the direction of his village, "has sent an urgent message to Aix," he pointed ahead as he came alongside the guard, "and he doesn't like tardiness!" As a look of confusion crossed the guard's face, Pierre simply grinned at him and nudged the horse again into a brisk canter.

"Wait!" the guard yelled and then coughed in the rising cloud of dust as the horse went by. Off to the right, Pierre saw the two approaching guards break into a frantic run to beat him to the crossroads. But, they were no match for the big cavalry horse.

He aimed the horse down the road to Rognes and glancing over his shoulder, saw the pair of guards stop in the cloud of dust and peer after him in frustration.

Pierre knew that he was safe for now. At the next stream, he would pull off the road, wash and tidy himself and have some food. Then on south toward Aix!

*   *   *   *   *

Dragoon Claude Larche, sat up straight on his horse, Parcival. Somehow, being on a special mission for the *Capitaine* made him feel more important. He smiled grimly at several young girls picking berries on the side of the road and waved to them. It would have been nice to stop and talk a while. Perhaps impress them with his questions about a rider coming this way.

He had already ridden down the Luberon hillside through la Tour d'Aigues and questioned the militia guards at the bridge at Pertuis without success. He hesitated about stopping; and then, glancing ahead, saw the bridge over the Durance near Cadenet in the distance. After this, there would be another bridge down river at Merindol; so he had better not waste any time.

As Claude cantered up the bridge the two guards rose and deliberately blocked his path but, as he drew closer, they recognized his uniform and relaxed.

"I have been given a mission by my *Capitaine* of Dragoons, stationed at La Motte d'Aigues on the Luberon, to check for a stolen horse and its rider...."

Before he could finish, the one guard snorted, "You are the second messenger today, trooper! You must not have a lot to do up on the *Grande Luberon!*"

"Who was the first?"

"Why, about an hour ago – when we came on duty – a young man in a hurry riding a big horse – rushed through on his way with a message from the *Capitaine* to Dragoon's base at Aix..."

"You fools!   That was a stolen horse!   And you let him go through?" Claude stood up in his stirrups and glared down at the two men. They then explained that they were not to blame, as they were not yet on duty. But the Dragoon was in no mood to listen to excuses. He cut them short with a threat that they may be called to account by a very upset Captain.

"Where did he go? Quick, man!" The guards both pointed down the road to Rognes. Nodding in excitement, Claude ordered one of them to run into nearby Cadenet and have a message sent to the Captain with the latest information and the fact that he would be following in pursuit. Kicking his steed, Claude left them in a cloud of dust as he spurred up the road.

*   *   *   *   *

Morning 21 June 1687
Road to Marseilles, France – near Rognes

Feeling refreshed after his cleansing in the stream, Pierre wiped his unshaven face and packed his sack of food behind his saddle. The June morning was bright and clear with warm sunshine slowly banishing the small clumps of cloud that dotted the azure sky. The horse nudged him from behind.

"All right! It's time to get moving, isn't it?" He swung himself up onto the broad back of the horse and guided him through the trees and bushes on the stream bank - following a path back to the road to Rognes. The horse needed little encouragement to break into a canter. In the distance, Pierre recognized the stone fortress built high on the hill of Fousa with its massive stone walls outlined against the sky.

There was still dust hanging in the air above the sandy road. A mule pulling a farm cart was rumbling down the road toward him. Pierre peered ahead and then reined in slightly and grinned with pleasure as he recognized the driver.

"Daniel Reyne! It's good to see a familiar face!" He stopped next to the driver, a man of his own age with shoulder length brown hair covered by a felt hat. Daniel leaned forward from his driver's seat and grasped Pierre's hand.

"Pierre – "the Good" – from La Motte!" he teased as he laughed, "as compared with your wild cousin! How is he?"

"Well, frankly, the last time I saw him he was being arrested – in error, of course!" Pierre grinned feeling relief surge through his body. He had enjoyed some happy times dancing and singing in the summer festivals at the nearby village of La Roque d'Antheron. It was pleasant to talk to someone who he knew – and trusted.

"What is new in your life, Daniel?"

"Oh, lots of work to do in the vineyard. I have delivered sacks of grain to M. Rochelle in Rognes," he explained as he removed his hat to wave away a pesky fly. "Then I ran into a big uproar as I left to drive home. A Dragoon arrived to alert the local Militia about a fleeing criminal...".

Daniel stopped talking and a frown appeared. Then his eyes opened wide and he laughed aloud.

"That *desperate man* he was describing looks a lot like you, Pierre! In fact," he leaned forward and stared into Pierre's face, "are you the man he is searching for? Pierre! What have you been up to...No, it couldn't be you! You are far too naïve and innocent to be an outlaw! Pierre?"

Pierre felt his stomach sink and his face became a little numb. It felt like a noose was tightening and he became aware that he felt short of breath.

"Well, Daniel, it could be! You may have heard that the King's Dragoons invaded La Motte. The swines murdered the old lady, Charpentier! I guess I got upset and before I knew what I was doing, I assaulted the *Capitaine*! I was knocked unconscious and since then I have been hiding and running."

Almost sensing his agitation, the horse snorted and jerked around a little. He is anxious to keep moving, thought Pierre and had to jerk the reins in order to settle it down. Daniel peered at the horse.

"Say, that looks like the Dragoon horse - the stolen one! It is! Pierre, you are a rogue who is following in your cousin, Renard's, footsteps! We heard in the village that you were being visited by the Dragoons – tough tactics from the King again?"

"Yes, Daniel, it's a question of time before we are going to be forced into a decision – and then perhaps, it will be your village's turn." Pierre turned to look down the road towards the Rognes.

Daniel turned his head and peered down the road too.

"You can't go through Rognes – the Militia was busy organizing barricades and that pompous Dragoon is thundering down the road toward Marseilles by now!"

Pierre frowned and scanned both the southern and northern roads.

"If you are determined to go that direction," said Daniel, "there is a slightly safer way around Rognes," and he pointed westward down a small pastured hollow towards some trees and brush.

"You can follow along the stream until you reach the vineyards to the west of the village. Follow a wagon track along the edge of the cliff face until you get round the village. You join the road to Eguilles and Marseilles again," he hesitated and frowned. "I don't think they will have the sense to check the back side of the hill – but, better go carefully anyway." He waved his hat as the mules pulled forward and over his shoulder, he yelled back:

"I'll pass the message on to your cousin - and parents - that you are safely through Rognes."

Pierre waved back and then urged the horse off the road and cantered down towards the trees.

The pathway along the stream edge was well used and clear. The leaves of the trees hanging gently over the necklace of ponds moved softly in the breeze. The branches were filled with a myriad of birds all singing together to the point where even Pierre winced. Brightly colored pasha butterflies flitted over clumps of red wildflowers. He stopped the horse to allow it to drink and was amused to watch a pair of wild marmots observing him from the rocky slope on the opposite side. The shade was a relief after the strong Provencal sunlight faced in the open.

This sense of peace must be effecting me too, thought Pierre as he rubbed his whiskers and felt that his face had lost the icy numb feeling he had been experiencing when told of the armed pursuit.

When he finally reached the vineyards, he carefully steered his horse close to the cliff face that now towered above him and followed the wagon tracks around the slope. The large overgrown wild olive trees hung over the tracks. The horse began to canter and Pierre had to rein him in for safety.

Something was wrong!

He felt uncomfortable and leaning forward rubbed the horse's neck to stop him. Why am I feeling so skittish – what's wrong? What's different?

There were no birds singing!

Keeping a tight rein, he rode slowly toward the edge of a grove of overgrown trees growing against the cliff face. His horse stopped   - his body tensed with a jerk.

Ah! There, in a patch of strong sunlight, lay two men – obviously Militia, with swords lying next to them in the warm grass. But both were asleep – or drunk – for Pierre could see several mushroom-shaped empty bottles lying between them.

God is on my side today, thought Pierre. First meeting with Daniel on the road and now two soldiers neglecting their duty. He rubbed his horse's neck to keep him quiet and gently urged him with his knees to walk slowly through thicker grass on the side of the path. Pierre twisted in the saddle to keep his gaze fixed on the sleeping men until he was out of sight beyond another clump of trees.

Phew! He took several deep breaths to relax his muscles and moved forward slowly and carefully – now more vigilant than previously.

Ahead on the pathway, between a gap in the trees, he could see now that he had bypassed the village. Pierre followed the path on the other side of the stream missing the open pasture and the vineyards until it met the road. At the small bridge, he carefully returned to the Marseilles road and tried to look casual and comfortable as he passed other carts, wagons and riders on the road toward Eguilles - the next village.

Despite his positive views, Pierre did not realize how quickly things could go wrong!

*   *   *   *   *

CHAPTER FIVE

20th June 1687
La Motte d'Aigues, Luberon, Provence.

As Suzanne Charpentier combed her hair, she surprisingly found herself humming the tune of a catchy folk song that accompanied her favorite wedding dance. Why am I excited, she frowned as she thought? Especially since the tragic death of her grandmother had left everyone sad and dispirited.

The arrival of the Dragoons and their presence in many homes had added to the stress and tension in all families. Perhaps it was the coming marriage of Isabeau Richarde in the nearby village of St. Martin - there was something pleasant on the horizon! She had slaved all morning to complete the housework to her mother's standards. Now finally, time for a little fun!

She and her two friends had agreed to dress up and meet in the early afternoon, walking to St. Martin to visit with Isabeau and listen to the wedding plans. Her father was out in the fields. Her mother, after inspecting the house, was next door having a tisane with the neighbor and the billeted Dragoons were having some strategy meeting in the square. Suzanne tightened the lace at her neckline and spun around to see her skirt rise in a swirl and giggled to herself. A wedding was always something to raise the spirits!

She took a sprig of wild thyme from a small bottle on the window ledge and rubbed it between her hands. Throwing the crushed sprig out the window, she sniffed her hands with pleasure and pushing back her thick brown hair, she rubbed her hands on the back of her neck.

Now I am ready to go, she thought. A slight noise from the room below made her turn her head but hearing nothing more, she twirled again with a touch of her previous joy and ran down the steps to the warm kitchen.

Glancing around to ensure that everything was satisfactory for her mother, she skipped to the front door and grasped the handle.

Suddenly a rough hand clapped over her mouth and an arm, appearing from behind, swung around her shoulder and neck reaching across her breasts and crushing her backward against a huge body.

In panic she realized that a man had been crouching in the hidden alcove where they hang their coats. As he dragged her back into the kitchen area, she fell back against him struggling.

"You smell nice, little girl!" His breath was rancid and she felt bile break into her throat. She had difficulty breathing and she reached her hands up to jerk at his arm that was strangling her at the neck. Suddenly he swung her body round and pushing her against the kitchen wall, he pinned her to the wall with his left arm thrust across her shoulder and throat keeping her breath cut off. She now saw that it was the Dragoon Sergeant - his mouth twisted in a sickening grin! He leaned his body against her right arm and hand immobilizing them; and now reached down and lifting her free left hand transferred it into his left hand. She felt the rough ridges of a stone wall behind her cut into her back. She was now pinned against the wall at the throat with both hands useless.

"Ever since I saw you, I wanted to feel what you were really like," he whispered aloud and she felt drops of spit hit her cheek. "Now is your time, little girl!" His free hand grasped her breast and massaged it through the material of her blouse. She cried out softly in pain.

"Shut up girl! If you make any noise I will have to mess your face up - so no young gallant will ever look at you again!" Then his fingers raced up to her neck and pulled the bow loose.

Suzanne felt her bodice jerked quickly open and the cloth roughly pushed aside. His harsh rough hand thrust down into the opening. She squirmed as he fumbled around until he clasped the firm breast in his hands. He squeezed hard and Suzanne moaned softly as she felt her vision fading.

"Very nice, little girl, very nice," he whisper hoarsely. "Now let's see what else you are hiding away from my eyes..."

His hand erupted from the blouse and raced down her body. When she felt it pass over her stomach, she involuntarily yelped, then slumped with her head falling forward over his arm. He grasped her roughly between the legs realizing she had lost consciousness.

"Damnation, girl – I'm not finished with you yet! But, there is no time to waste, is there?" The Sergeant swung her body up into his arms and' carrying her, crossed to the stairway. "A bed is the best place to relish a little sexual play, isn't it?" As he staggered up the stone stairs, he stopped and listened. Outside the front door, there were suddenly voices.

"Damn!" he whispered. "Get out of here right now!" He raced up the final steps, dropped the unconscious girl on the bed, hesitating a second while he ran his feeling hands over her immobile body.

Then he sped back down the stairs managing to slide out the door leading down to the stable behind the home before the front door opened.

He stood outside the stable door breathing heavily and grinned as he whispered, "Well that was real nice! Been waiting a long time!

Managed to have my way with the little bitch before the Captain got round to the same thing – even with all his fancy manners!"

*   *   *   *   *

Mme. Charpentier, dressed in mourning black, pushed open the front door and gestured her friend to enter.

"Come on in, Rachel, my friend. I have not heard Suzanne leave yet, so you can ask her about those special stitches she uses for embroidery. Suzanne?" She called and looked around the quiet room. "I was sure I heard her right here at the door." She moved to the center of the kitchen and looked up the steps and called again.

"Suzanne! Are you up there?" Hearing nothing, she frowned and slowly climbed up the stairs. Her friend heard her gasp as she saw the disheveled girl sprawled on the bed.

"Suzanne – are you alright? What is wrong with you?" she turned and called down the stairs, "Rachel – bring up a wet cloth from the water pail right way! There is something wrong with Suzanne..."

Minutes later, Suzanne moaned slightly and opened her eyes. Her hands went immediately to her left breast and then down between her legs. Suddenly, she rolled over on her side, her body slumped into a fetal position and she began crying softly. Her mother leaned over her body and hugged her asking what was the problem.

Slowly the story came out with both older women gasping in horror.

"Curse those Dragoons!" her mother whispered fiercely, "I warned my husband that they might molest our children! Damn those swines! First my poor mother burned alive..." as tears ran down her cheeks, "then the billeting; and now my lovely little daughter!" She wiped her cheeks with her hand. "What is next - little Cleo who is only 10 years old?"

Suzanne lay still now quietly listening with growing fear in her eyes.

The mother looked down at her quietly for a few seconds as though trying to make up her mind for herself. Then she shook her head in frustration.

"Suzanne – what happened is terrible! But we need to show that we are a tough family. Despite what they throw at us, we must continue to do what we need to do! And, that means that you need to go with your friends to visit the bride – as you planned! I will talk to your father and we will decide what we shall do - as your parents." She paused as Suzanne looked up in astonishment. "Now get up and tidy yourself; and go and find your friends. They will be wondering what has happened to you." There were scuffling sounds outside and a gentle rap at the front door.

"There they are now!" she placed a worn hand tenderly on her daughter's head. "Get ready now and I will tell them you are ready to go to St. Martin." Suzanne rose painfully as her mother left the room and crossed slowly over to the shelf where she kept her hairbrush.

*　　　*　　　*　　　*　　　*

As they left the village and walked down the shady road toward St. Martin, the two girlfriends were horrified by Suzanne's halting recount of the incident. Although she did not openly cry, tears glistened in her eyes. Each friend took a hand in sympathy.

"Should you tell Isabeau about this?" Marguerite's pleasant face was screwed up in genuine concern. "We don't want to ruin her afternoon! Should we say nothing?"

Suzanne looked over at her other companion with raised eyebrows.

Charlotte shrugged her shoulders at the question. "I always believe you should be open with your friends. Out of respect...? It might be better to warn others – rather than keep a secret that would make it easy for the Dragoons to fondle other girls..." she finished off softly, her eyes anxiously searching her two friends.

Suzanne looked down at the dusty road pondering the worrisome thoughts. Then she raised her head and nodded emphatically.

"Yes! I would naturally like to keep nasty things secret. What happened to me is embarrassing! But it is better to tell! And I respect Isabeau's judgment. She is worldly and wise and will want to help us plan ways to protect ourselves!"

The three girls all nodded in agreement and their pace quickened. Now that they were committed to the plan, they were eager to reach the village.

*　　　*　　　*　　　*　　　*

Isabeau skipped to the door and opened it wide. She greeted the three younger girls from the next village with obvious pleasure. Although she was older than them, she had always found their company light, refreshing and pleasant.

"You arrived at a good time! I have finished the hemming of my wedding skirt and it looks lovely!" However, Isabeau could not help noting that although the girls' comments were enthusiastic as they held up the skirt which was lying on the table with the sewing kit, she felt there was a general lack of their normal effervescent excitement.

"Is there something wrong?" Her warm brown eyes searched their faces as she stretched out the stiff white and embroided skirt material with her hands. All three girls looked at each other in despair, wondering who should speak first.

Then the whole horrible incident flooded out. Each girl taking over from the others while Isabeau listened with growing anger. When tears ran down Suzanne's cheeks, Isabeau stretched out and clasped her shoulder firmly and gave her a little shake.

"There now, there now!" she soothed her, "that's a terrible thing to happen to you. But there is a message for all of us." The younger girls all looked at Isabeau with concern. "Yes. What this means is that none of us are safe anymore!" she said firmly.

"Why?" Charlotte rose from a chair and pointed at Suzanne. "Why should the *Sergente*'s interest in Suzanne effect me?"

Isabeau turned her head and stared out the window at the distant hills, choosing her words carefully.

"What does it mean? I think it means we are all in danger! When the Dragoons arrived they brought pressure on La Motte. Suzanne lost her grandmother. Pierre Jaubert had to flee for his life. His cousin, Renard was humiliated in the village square – and beaten. All of your village has been subjected to the terrible cost of billeting the soldiers." She paused and the girls kept silent – each face expressing concern and fear. "Now they have taken another step. I think that ...no girl – or man – is safe anymore! If your father, Suzanne, tries to complain, he will probably be beaten or arrested!"

Suzanne gasped but nodded as tears came to her eyes.

"I think we should talk to our parents first. And then they will talk to everyone in the villages. Each family will have to decide for itself." She hesitated and then continued. "I hate to say this, but...it looks like either we have to decide to become Catholics..." the girls both looked horrified, "or, like other people who believed as we do, many of us may have to flee France – for, nowhere is it safe in our country any more!"

At this point, the three girls reached out to each other instinctively and clasped their hands together. Then Suzanne nodded slowly.

"It's horrible and very unfair! But I think you are right! I will talk to my family tonight." Then she looked straight at Isabeau. "But, your wedding, Isabeau? What will happen?"

"I think it is important that my wedding takes place. The way things are going, it may be the last time that we all share some joy – and what little freedom we now have." And then she outlined her plans for the wedding ceremony and the feast and dancing after.

These four young maidens never realized how quickly their cheerful plans could be destroyed.

*   *   *   *   *

CHAPTER SIX

The blazing sun was high in the sky and Pierre wiped the dribbles of sweat from his forehead with his kerchief tied round his neck. His fears in the past hour had reduced remarkably as the road traffic increased. There had been some talk in La Motte a month ago about the King's plans to build a 'canal' through the middle of Provence as an aid to movement of trade goods.

Halting his horse to let it rest for a minute on the top of a rise, he could overlook the valley of Trevaresse where the pools and streambed were being excavated and where a string of wagons moved rock and soil. He stopped a passing vendor and bought some fresh fruit and watched the merchant leave the road and steer his cart down into the vale to sell fruit, food and drink to the bands of workers.

He nudged his horse.

"Some water and a rest for you in Eguilles - and some food for me too!" As he spoke aloud to the horse, it snorted in return. In the distance he could see the village nestled at the base of the next ridge. The prominent church spire pointed up towards the old Chateau on the side of the hill above it.

             *   *   *   *   *

"Laundry day today, it seems," Pierre spoke again to the horse as he joined the heavy cart traffic through the picturesque streets of Eguilles. He paused in the shade of an old building and looked down on the ancient communal washing areas of bleached stone.

A large group of women and young girls were busy doing the week's washing and laying the bedclothes to dry on the warm grass. Several lines were tied between small trees and posts to act as clotheslines.

Pierre nudged the horse but the steed had also spotted a watering trough in the small square ahead, its smooth glittering surface broken by the constant gush of water from an ancient pipe poised above.

Eager to get to the water, the horse was now trotting forward into the open square. It was obviously a market day - for the center of the area was filled with stalls displaying a variety of colorful fruit, vegetables, meat and clothes. There was much noisy activity taking place between both merchants and local customers.

Aware that he was taking a chance - before dismounting, he slowly glanced around the busy square. The only danger seemed to be on the far end where a rowdy group of militia was seated outside a small tavern laughing as they enjoyed their wine.

Pierre was initially relieved to see that, except for a senior officer who stood leaning against the wall in the shade behind his men, the soldiers seemed to be more interested in their liquor. The officer had been casually glancing over the passing traffic but now suddenly his gaze seemed to have zeroed in on the horse.

Jerking his head around to search for an escape route, Pierre realized that the road out of the square at the far end might be difficult to reach even at a sudden gallop. Frantically, he swiveled in the saddle and spotted what looked like an entry to a narrow lane running uphill toward the Chateau.

A glance back showed the officer was calling to his men and several were reaching for their weapons. Some were loping through the market stalls and rudely pushing customers aside.

Pierre jerked the reins and nudged his horse. The horse reared slightly and then lunged forward frightening several older women with heavy baskets of fruit. A few canters and Pierre again jerked the reins to steer the horse into the darkened alley. A man smoking his pipe swore and flattened himself against the wall as the horse rushed by.

"Not that way, you fool! It's no good!" Pierre heard his words but galloped the horse up the narrow cobbled path. In the bright shafts of sunlight between the buildings Pierre realized that the lane was turning and spun the horse around out of sight of the pursuing militia. The horse reared up on its hind legs and stopped. Pierre hung on grimly and gasped in horror. The man had been right! The alley was a dead-end!

He could hear the militia jeering with glee downhill. He spun the horse around again searching desperately. Then he saw it! An old doorway had been built high up in the wall about a man's height from the cobblestones. He rode the horse to the wall and urged the horse to "stand still".

Climbing onto the saddle, he grasped the old handle and jerked it. With relief, the handles turned and with a further jerk the door opened. With a thrust of his feet which sent the horse in a gallop back down the narrow alley, he pulled himself into the doorway on his knees realizing that he was now on a cross street on the next level.

Hearing the disturbed yells from the pursuing soldiers, he chuckled with relief. He jumped to his feet and inspected the doorway. On the street side it had several metal flanges and on the floor nearby was a piece of wood which obviously was used normally to keep the door closed. Pierre dropped to his knees, grasped the plank and rammed it into the grooves as he felt the weapons being banged against the other side of the door.

He laughed out loud and stood up to regain his breath. What a narrow escape! He spun around and stopped cold. His breath locked in his throat.

Standing facing him were four huge militia guards – two with drawn swords and the other two with heavy wooden staffs.

"You look like you are in a hurry, pig!" One of the men growled at him and, at the same time, he thrust his staff into Pierre's unprotected belly. He doubled up with pain and fell to the ground gasping to regain his breath. A second blow created a blast of pain across his back. A heavy boot was firmly placed on the back of his neck and as the pressure forced his face sideways, he felt a sudden boot kick to the back of his head and blackness descended.

*　　　*　　　*　　　*　　　*

"Pierre! Pierre! Are you in there?"

The voice was low but enough to stir Pierre. A shake of his head sent pain rocketing between his eyes and lancing into the top of his head to explode at the back of his neck.

"*Mon Dieu!*" His low voice moaned through the thick layers of smelly straw. His eyes were still closed tightly in pain as he opened his mouth to respond to the voice and instead received a lump of what seemed to be like dirt but tasted worse. He spat it out in disgust.

"Who is it? " His eyes now opened and with dull senses he tried to roll over without success. He painfully raised his head as much as he could from the filthy floor and peered around. The faint voice came from a small wooden door in the shed's stone wall. His hands were tied behind his back and somehow connected to his feet that were bent backward. He moaned, as he became aware he could neither stand nor get to his knees. I could maybe roll over, he thought. Then the voice called again urgently.

"Pierre! Are you in there?"

"Yes – but tied up like a hog! Who is it?"

"Your favorite cousin, Renard."

Le Renard! The voice was still low and wary.

"Do you think there is a guard at the main door?"

Pierre bent his head at an awkward angle and watched the strip of bright sunlight showing the length of the stable's double doors. He could hear nothing and see no movement.

"I cannot be sure! But, I cannot hear anything, Renard!"

"*Bien!* Do you think you can manage to roll over to this door? There is a gap at the bottom - it might be wide enough to allow me to cut your ropes – if that is what you are tied with..."

Pierre tried to roll over onto his back but the pressure on his bound hands and fingers caused him to groan in pain. Using his bent legs, he wriggled himself so the length of his body paralleled the direction of the second door. Gritting his teeth against the pain; he rolled over on his side again. He jerked his body backward in an effort to roll over. He lay there spitting the collection of gravel and straw he had collected in his open mouth when it hit the dirty floor.

"Are you able to move –at all?"

"Sort of...but I either crush my hands and fingers under my body; then I get a mouth full of dirt! But, let me try again."

Aching all over and with bruised lips, Pierre finally managed to wriggle his back against the bottom of the door. He felt his cousin's hands feeling his wrists and bindings.

"Good – just heavy cord."

Pierre could feel the knife blade slide between his wrists and begin sawing away. At one stage he swore as the blade sliced into the skin and Renard ceased, paused and then kept sawing. The instant the cord broke, he groaned as his shoulders and legs straightened out and ripples of pain ran through his body.

"Do you need the knife for your ankles?" Renard's voice was still low and careful.

Pierre had sat up and was inspecting his bound feet. With the sharp knife, the cords fell away and he stood up gingerly. Crossing over to the large double doors, he listened carefully and could detect no signs of guards.

They probably felt that being knocked out and tied up by hands and feet were enough security. He judged by the trails on the floor of the stable that he had been dragged in through those doors. Noting the empty steel flanges on the doors, he picked up a dusty but sturdy board and dropped it into the slots. That should protect me from pursuit, he thought.

Looking back he saw that the small door was also barred from the inside and returning, he began to remove the board when he heard his cousin mutter.

"Pierre – someone is coming!" Peering through the door crack, he saw Renard pick up a hefty wooden pole and raising it above his head, stand against the building wall. He watched through the crack as a heavily built young man in militia uniform strode round the corner in the direction of the door. Too late he tried to take evasive action but Renard crunched him behind his left ear and neck. He dropped like an ox without even a groan.

Pierre opened the door and joined his cousin who knelt beside the soldier. As he bent down, Pierre noticed that his cousin had a fox tail attached to the brim on the back of his hat.

"What is the decoration for?" He flicked the tail.

"Since they call me by the fox-like name 'Renard', I felt that I might as well live up to the reputation!" he grinned up at his cousin "I'm glad I didn't kill him. He is knocked out and will be for quite a while."

"Let's drag him into the shed. Bind and gag him; and leave him in my place," suggested Pierre. And the two dragged the body into the shed and bound him thoroughly in the same manner as Pierre had been trussed.

Renard rubbed some blood from the back of Pierre's neck and smeared it over the soldier's face. Before he rose to his feet, he took his knife and cut a little of the fox-tail and tucked a segment into the open mouth of the solider.

"That will tell them who is responsible for this criminal action." Throwing some of the straw over the body, he said:

"This will disguise him a little and maybe allow us to escape without being noticed. But they will know that the 'wicked Renard' has struck again!" Before they left, Pierre noticed his personal belongings piled in a corner of the shed and took them with him. They went out through the smaller door. Then used an old bucket containing rainwater to clean up Pierre's face and hands as they exchanged information.

"I got the message in the village from Daniel Reine from d'Antheron that you had passed Rognes. Then I rode my mule down the road until I stopped at the Market at Eguilles. The whole village buzzed about your capture. They dragged you by the legs down the cobbled road – so your head should feel like a broken chicken." Renard grinned at him, "The girls in the village said that you left a trail of blood - so it was not hard to follow."

He waved his hand toward the alley ahead of them. "I have my mule tied up back there." He checked around the corner of the building. "Follow me" he said and moved into the alley. Walking behind his cousin, Pierre watched the swaying fox tail and wondered about his cousin's dangerous actions.

"Renard," he whispered aloud, "do you think it is wise to deliberately jerk the tail of the Devil by leaving a trail for the Dragoons to follow?" and he pointed to the fox-tail.

Renard grinned wryly. "You may be right, Pierre." He stopped quietly glancing up and down the deserted alley. Then he nodded his head. "I realize that up to now, I have always been a bit of a gallant fool. I loved to have fun - without a lot of thought about the outcomes of my actions." He spoke now without his usual bedeviling grin.

"I have always taken only a limited interest in our adopted religion. As you well know, I have often scoffed at the rules of our elders and made light of our young friends who were serious about what they believed in." He paused and rubbed some of the dirt from his hands.

"The ... political side of our Reform religion never really affected us in our isolated village...but after the arrival of the Dragoons and the shocking murder of old lady, Charpentier," he shook his head obviously upset by the remembrance.

Then he turned his face once more towards Pierre and grinned slightly, "...And, of course, the way they beat me up and dragged me to the square – in your name!" He leaned over and playfully punched his cousin's shoulder.

"And I heard, Cousin Pierre, that you watched the whole of my disgrace without rushing out to attack the Captain again."

As Pierre tried to protest, he nudged him again with his fist. "I tease you, Cousin! My change in behavior is my way of raising a battle flag - and fighting back! Now that the King - and his Catholics - have brought their battle to our village, we need somehow to show them that we cannot be intimidated ... is that not true?"

Before Pierre could respond, Renard turned quickly and loped down the alley disappearing behind a large overhanging tree. Pierre followed and found the Renard's mule tied to the branch.

Renard laughed quietly and pointed across the alley. Pierre turned and saw another saddled mule tied to the gate opposite - as the mule backed around so as to look at the two men with interest.

"It looks like we have transportation for you too!"

"We can't steal some poor man's mule, Renard!" Pierre protested.

"When we fight a war, Cousin, we use all weapons available! As you well know, Pierre, this is no polite fight we are engaged in!" Untwisting the reins, he mounted his mule. After a brief hesitation, Pierre crossed the alley, calmed the mule with a rub; and loosening the reins, he led it down the alley until he was behind a larger building. Tying the bread bag and roll of covers to the animal, he mounted. He was surprised that the mule accepted his rider with little fuss beyond a snort or two.

The two men rode down the alley until they could peer into the crossroads and found that besides two wagons crossing in different directions, there was no sign of militia.

Renard leaned over and extended his hand.

"Cousin, you had better continue your journey. I imagine the Militia has already boasted about their capture up and down the line from the village to Marseilles so guards will be less vigilant. I will report back to your parents in La Motte. And I will be seeking help from all our friends in the villages of our hillside. We will form a small 'Army of the Luberon' to take up the battle!" he grinned in his usual reckless style.

"You may be hearing more of "General Renard" in the future." With a backward wave he cantered his mule down behind the cart traveling back into the heart of Eguilles.

Pierre reined his mount to prevent it following his cousin and with a quick glance back up the alley from where his mule had been tethered, he nudged it instead up the hill, turning and taking the next lane traveling southward toward Marseilles.

Pierre had no way of knowing what excitement and terror this ancient city had ready for him!

*   *   *   *   *

CHAPTER SEVEN

Afternoon of the 22nd June 1687
On the road to Marseilles, France.

Pierre knew the mule was tired as the end of the day neared. He nudged the mule out of the traffic and halted it at the top of a slight rise. He stretched back and tightened and relaxed the muscles of his neck and shoulders as he watched the bright hot sunlight beat down on the ancient stone walls of Marseilles rising against the dark blue backdrop of the Mediterranean.

As he picked out the city gate he would enter, he moved his bottom around the smooth skin of the saddle to relieve some of the numbness that had grown steadily after the last couple of miles. He sensed the mule's rate of panting was slowing and he rubbed its neck in appreciation and let his own body relax a little more.

Pierre had been pleased to discover that, being in much heavier traffic, had allowed him to be less vigilant and he found that he had begun looking around with interest at the vast colorful array of travelers and spending less time peering nervously over his shoulder.

About an hour before, he had found himself behind a heavy cart filled with sacks of grain. At first, the garishly smiling face - carved and painted - on the wooden panel at the back of the cart had caught his eye. It hung down to the roadway and swung gently with the rocking of the vehicle.

Then his eyes jerked up quickly to see two attractive - and physically different - young women. They were leaning back against the sacks with obvious boredom and he assumed they might be the owner's two daughters. They had been resting back with their eyes closed and probably half asleep.

As his mule broke through the cloud of dust, he clearly saw the dark-haired girl nudge her companion who sat up with a jolt and eagerly scanned the traffic. On spotting him, the younger girl ran her fingers through her dark blonde hair to shake out some of the dust while her sister furtively ran a brush through long raven black tresses.

Pierre noted with a wry grin that they had suddenly proceeded to carry on an animated conversation with each other. Both were taking turns to glance at their watcher - to ensure they had his attention? The younger girl then openly smiled at him while the elder sister - probably more cautious - made her interest less obvious.

The driver, on hearing this increased burst of conversation, stood up awkwardly and glanced back. Finding the cause of the commotion, he grinned, rolled his eyes skyward and settled down again to his task.

It's an unusual feeling to be among so many strangers, thought Pierre. But it's also nice to be noticed by two lovely young women.

At that point he had recognized that the mule's exhaustion was severe and turned off the road. It was with a sense of regret he watched the back of the heavy cart slowly vanishing in the built-up traffic - carrying with it the two young women.

Through the dust rising from the road, he saw with some glee, the older girl try to restrain her sister from openly waving to him.

He grinned and waved back - at the same time thinking, if my mother were around right now she would be reminding me that I was not to flirt with strange women.

They don't behave in a proper manner ... like the New Believer girls of the Luberon. Too forward - too fresh? Is this the way Catholic girls act, he thought?

I don't think Mother would be pleased with you, Pierre! As he shrugged off the thoughts, he wondered whether he would ever see them again.

Pierre recognized that this pleasant experience had interrupted some serious thinking that needed to take place. His next task was to locate the godfather of his mother. He remembered the Le Claire family ran a trading business in wines and spirits on the waterfront.

He had not seen them for many years but his father always talked of them with warmth and trust. And there was no way the Dragoons would know of this close connection.

Regaining his sense of direction, Pierre enthusiastically nudged the mule into a canter to join the traffic flowing down the hill along the ancient walls of Marseilles and he mingled in the surge of carts, horses and walkers who flowed through the first gateway.

The act of entering the guarded gateway raised his fears. To hide this anxiety, he sat up taller in the saddle and tried to look around confidently. What should I do? Look like you belong, he thought! Although he did not know the individual lounging against the wall next to several guards, he smiled at him and waved his hand casually.

"Greetings. How does the world go with you today?" The man looked up in surprise and raised his hand too.

"Fine," he responded with a little surprise, "It's a long time since you were in the city, isn't it?" Pierre nodded and smiled.

Pierre had now moved well past the guards who were casually listening to the conversation. He turned slightly in the saddle and waved his hand again and then was swallowed in the traffic passing a busy inn. He hoped that the fellow would think that he had been greeted by an old companion and would be puzzling about the connection. He also hoped the guards would not have marked him by his actions.

To avoid any follow-up, Pierre turned the mule into a smaller alley that seemed to run in the direction of the harbor. The buildings were close enough to touch - obviously ancient - with wonderful heavy stone walls rearing upward at least three to four floors.

Old verandahs leaned over the alleyway and in the late afternoon grandmothers were seated in the last sunshine to watch the children at play below. After a continual life in the openness of the countryside, Pierre felt a little closed in and uncomfortable. He soon came to a wider roadway and within minutes found his way to the waterfront.

Pierre stopped the mule as he dismounted and led the animal to the edge of the roadway while he looked out at the busy harbour. The quay was lined with fishing boats, many of them selling their fresh catch to the citizens buying their evening meal. His nose wrinkled at the smell of the fresh fish. Although he enjoyed the fish from the rivers in Provence, he still preferred the taste of lamb to that of seafood.

At the end of the Vieux port, he could see the two forts that guarded each side of the port's entryway. In the distance he caught sight of the ominous *Chateau d'If* on an island out in the Mediterranean - off the coast with its rearing awesome towers stretching skyward.

The thought of being captured and thrown into some fortress sent a chill down his spine and despite the scent of the fish, he took in a deep breath of the sea air to relax himself again.

Tearing his eyes away from the waterfront activity, Pierre searched up and down the line of buildings. As a child, he had visited the home and remembered it as being somewhere further down the bay - away from the city center. He urged the mule into the traffic and simply watched the various signs. There it is! A hanging barrel above an open archway rang a bell for him.

Quick inquiries from a local woman, carrying home a fish supper, confirmed that the family Le Claire lived there.

Dismounting, he led the mule through the archway and into an open courtyard where several small carts were unloading barrels into the open doorways of warehouses. What appeared to be living quarters rose above the office and warehouse. And, to the left, an attractive doorway was fronted by a solid table and chairs placed on a cobbled stone patio. A large colored canvas that sheltered them from the strong Provencal sunshine protected this. He hitched his mule to the post allowing it to drink from the adjacent water barrel. A tall man with a heavy wiry white beard had come out of the warehouse and walked towards him.

"Can I help you, stranger?

"Yes *Monsieur*, I am seeking the family Le Claire of Marseilles," Pierre announced.

"You have found them. What is your business?" The man's voice was gruff but a smile spoke from his rich brown eyes.

"I am Pierre Jaubert – the son of Jacques of La Motte d'Aigues on the Luberon..." and before he could finish his introduction, the man yelled loudly over his shoulder, "Anne, come and meet the son of your God-daughter; hurry!"

And then Pierre was engulfed by heavy arms and crushed to the man's chest. Heavily kissed on his cheeks three times he finally recovered his breath in time to meet the same welcome from the wife who had come running from the doorway.

"I am Martin Le Claire! And ... pleased to meet you again after so many years! You have just arrived in time for dinner. And you are going to stay with us, are you not?"

"I had hoped I could do just that!" grinned Pierre as Mme. Le Claire hung on grimly to both his hands.

"Martin, let the young man wash up inside and join us for a glass of our best wine at the tables - so we can catch up on years of news! Come," she dragged him towards the doorway. "Go up the stairs; first room at the top of the stairs; wash up and come on down for wine!" And she rushed off and began to wipe the dust from the tables and chairs in the courtyard.

*   *   *   *   *

Pierre strolled through the archway onto the waterfront and stood looking at the harbour traffic in the early evening light. He glanced down the road to his left.

Then he turned to peer hard at a cart standing in a deep shadow. He shook his head and walked closer to the back of a cart and grinned to himself.

I don't believe it – what a small world!

Gleaming in the late sunlight was the painted smiling face on the dusty backboard. This is the same cart that I rode behind on the road from the North, he thought to himself. Turning, with his hands on his hips, he looked around at the nearby buildings.

A slight movement in the shadows at the top of some nearby stairs left him feeling someone was watching him.

Then a young woman moved out of the shadows onto the top step and looked down at him. It was the same dark-haired older young woman he had followed on the dusty highway.

She had a glimmer of a cautious smile on her face - not exactly welcoming. Behind her there was a flurry of shadow and the golden-haired younger girl emerged to stand behind her sister on the step.

The younger one leaned over the stone rail and peered down at Pierre. Then she giggled aloud and waved her hand frantically as she called down

"So, you found us again?"

Without hesitation, she wriggled past her sister and ran down to the bottom of the steps where she stood smiling at Pierre.

"So! How did you find us?" Then, somewhat reluctantly - and protectively - the older sister walked slowly down the stairs to join them. Without being specific, Pierre explained that the he was staying close by. The dark haired girl interrupted the enthusiastic introductions by her young sister and invited Pierre to come upstairs and "view the harbour from their verandah".

Judith Blondel, the older girl, led the way up the darkened stairs with Aleen, the younger sister following behind. While Judith walked sedately ahead, the younger Aleen continually turned to smile at him.

On the balcony, they stood in a line while Judith pointed out familiar landmarks. Pierre noted that Aleen deliberately squeezed between her elder sister and him.

After some more social conversation, Judith excused herself stating "she had to see her Aunt" in the kitchen. As she left, she frowned very obviously at her younger sister. She is probably trying to say, behave yourself -properly - Pierre thought.

"At last - the chaperone has gone!" giggled Aleen. "Here, help me up onto this bench," she whispered, "I want to show you my favorite boat." She reached out her hand, which Pierre took to steady her, and stood on the bench above him. She pointed out a pale blue boat moored nearby.

But suddenly Pierre found himself ignoring her excited chatter. Aleen was wearing a flowing white diaphanous dress and as she posed higher up on the bench, the strong rays of the facing sun were clearly outlining her pert young breasts, her shapely hips and even her slender legs.

It was like seeing a young girl in a completely wet dress. He felt a stirring between his legs and quickly removed his hat from his head and held it in front of his waist to hide the problem.

"Pierre, help me down!" Grimly clutching his hat with his one hand to cover himself, he extended the other and Aleen grasped it.

Whether her stumble was accidental or planned, Pierre could not guess. But as she jumped to the floor, she fell against him and, dropping his hat, he had to clutch her to retain his own balance.

Aleen clung onto his shoulder their faces very close to each other. Then she smiled in an encouraging way and deliberately closed her eyes, her pink young lips slightly pouted.

Confusion flooded Pierre. While still well aware that he was excited; he had never before kissed a girl. But the opportunity was too inviting! Oh well, he thought – why not?

The lips were warm and soft and he gently kissed them, then drew back.

Aleen's eyes opened and she smiled. "Pierre, I think I want more than that little peck," she breathed and putting her hands behind his head, she leaned her whole body against him and kissed him deeply holding him firmly against her. Inexperienced, he finally remembered to breathe through his nose when she broke off the extended kiss.

"Pierre, you have a knife on your belt that is hurting me...!" and pushed her hand down between them to investigate. Pierre began to wriggle a little when she pushed him a little away from her and looked down at the extended bulge in his pants. She looked up at him with wide - almost innocent - eyes.

"Pierre, that's not a knife. That's you! Oh! Did I really do that to you – just by kissing you?"

Pierre nodded dumbly. He was breathing heavily and really did not know what else to say. In his sheltered life, he had never before experienced anything like this!

Before he could bend down and pick up his crushed hat for protection, Aleen pushed him firmly against the stone balustrade and placed her young body directly on top of him. She threw her arms around his neck hugging him closely as she moved her hips against him in a provocative way.

"Oh, Pierre, I have always wanted to do this! Its so exciting..."

Enough is enough, thought Pierre! No matter how much I find this exciting and enjoyable, I need to get things back into control. I need to get out of this before something really embarrassing happens.

Putting his hands on her shoulders, he firmly pushed Aleen to arm's length. She looked up with a touch of coyness in her cheeky eyes.

"What's wrong, Pierre? Don't you like me? Did I do something wrong?"

He looked down into her hazel eyes with confusion. What do you say to a lovely young girl who is throwing herself at you? And not hurt her?

"Aleen, Aleen, I like you – a lot! But this is just too fast ... for both of us!" He whispered hoarsely. As she stood back a little, he bent to pick up his hat and carefully placed it over the extended area of his lower body. He took her hand and gently turned her towards the balustrade and placed it there.

Then he too turned somewhat blindly to face the harbor scene as he heard footsteps coming from the archway behind them. Both turned to face Judith as she emerged from the door and looked at them a touch suspiciously.

"I'm sorry, Pierre but we have things to do. I'm afraid we must leave you now." She turned to Aleen and said firmly, "Sister, your Aunt wants to see you – right now!" She accented the last word with a gentle shove on the arm.

"Oh, Judith – you are such a nag!" she turned to Pierre with a secretive smile: "It's really good to have seen you again so soon. Please come back again!" With a slight curtsey, she nodded at her sister and with a flirting backward glance and smile; she vanished into the doorway.

Judith tossed her raven hair and dropped her head slightly. From this viewpoint she looked at him with raised eyebrows.

"You look a little disturbed, Pierre! My little sister is a little wayward ... and impulsive and, of course, terribly young!" She twirled around in the gentle twilight her skirt flaring out around her. Pierre was surprised at her actions that seemed out of character.

"No, Judith – she is a sweet girl – but, as you say, very young. But I had better be going as well." He turned towards the archway leading downstairs.

"I'll walk you down and make sure you don't fall. These old stairs can be treacherous. Here," she stretched out her hand, "Help me keep my balance".

Pierre put out a hand and grasped hers and they walked slowly down the darkened passage stairs.

As they descended, Pierre noted she was gently rubbing her thumb into the palm of his hand. He glanced at her and she peeked around her swinging black hair at him with a mysterious smile. Oh no! Not another one, he thought. I don't believe this!

As they reached the landing before the closed heavy door at the bottom of the stairs, Judith gently tugged his hand to stop him. In the darkness, she turned to face him and whispered quietly.

"I am glad you found us again. And I hope my sister did not frighten you away with her wild ways. She gets a little... desperate, Pierre." She stood holding his hand and he tried to think of a polite way of breaking the bonds and leaving.

Pierre found himself muttering about not being sure of his future; about the need to get back to the country; about not knowing much about sisters because he was an only child. Suddenly, she interrupted his ruminations with an outburst.

"I have to – that's all there is to it; I have to!" And, leaning against him, she pushed him until his back was against the stone wall.

Then she let go of his hand and putting both her hands behind his neck, she kissed him firmly on the lips rubbing his lips fiercely with her own.

The attack was so sudden, that all he could do is grasp her shoulders and pull her towards him. He became aware of her firm breasts pushing hard against his chest.

He began to kiss her back as well and she moaned a little. Although he had never done this before, he gently took his right hand and ran it down the front of her chest until he felt the firm softness of her breast through her dress bodice. He rubbed his thumb around until he located the nipple and gently rubbed it. She moaned again without breaking off the kiss.

Encouraged, he raised his hands to the neck of her dress, which were laced closed with a ribbon and fumbled with the bow.

She broke off the kiss with a whisper. "Let me!" and quickly undid the bow and pulled the top of the dress open before resuming her hungry kissing.

He slid both his hands onto her firm bare shoulders and shrugged the dress off the shoulders and down her arms. Her eyes were tightly closed and she was kissing him grimly. He ran his fingers down her shoulders until each hand cupped a firm-hanging breast. He slid his thumbs so that each nudged the hardened extended nipple and massaged the ends. Her mouth was open wide now and her tongue thrust into his mouth in desperation. Pierre was completely out of his depth! He finally broke off the kiss and whispered hoarsely, "I always wanted to do this!" And, lowering his head, his mouth found each of the nipples in turn and licked and sucked each and she moaned softly with each suck.

Pierre's breathing was laboured as he found himself exhausted and leaned back to look at her. Judith's head had fallen back with her black raven hair trailing behind her with eyes closed. He gently pulled the dress back on to her shoulders and closed the top by drawing the ribbon tight.

The action opened her eyes and she took the ribbons from him and tied them quickly and neatly.

Then she raised her head and looked him in the face. She ran her fingers gently around his chin and cheeks and smiled slowly.

"I don't know what got into me ... Pierre. Sometimes I really envy my young sister. She does not seem to have any caution." She shook her head and the black curls flew around her head. She closed her eyes and breathed heavily. "I don't know why I am so... so cautious! My father says if I am too cautious I'll end up an old spinster on the shelf," she smiled in a tired way. "Please forgive me. I hope you will come back again to visit."

She leaned past him and pulled open the door. "Good night, Pierre." And, as he moved out, she closed it without another word.

Pierre stood in the twilight looking at the heavy closed door. I should have said something, he thought. Suddenly the door began to open again. Judith's slim face appeared in the crack. Her eyes were looking at him but without focusing as though she was thinking deeply. Then a slight blush reddened her white cheeks. She had evidently made up her mind about something, sensed Pierre.

"Pierre... My Uncle bolts this door at ten o'clock each evening. If you would like to... to see me again...a little later may be safest...." She closed her eyes and exhaled her breath almost in panic. Before he could reply, she had shut the door firmly and he could faintly hear her footsteps running up the steps.

Pierre stared at the closed door without seeing anything in particular. It felt as though he was separated from his body. His breathing had become labored and short. I don't believe this is happening! Right now Pierre, you are really both confused and more disturbed than Judith. What sisters! Are all Catholic girls – like that?

He turned and looked out over the waters of the bay glinting crimson in the last rays of late sunshine. He took another deep breath and exhaled it out sharply. This is ridiculous! Up to now you have not been "involved" with any young woman. He admitted ruefully that he envied his cousin, Renard's reported victories with girls from many of the local villages on the Luberon. In fact, Pierre, you are really afraid of getting involved!

He shook his head. So much for history, he thought. Here I am, catching up rapidly – too rapidly! Not one girl – but two! And strangers as well. And Catholics!

Mon Dieu, if she knew, my mother would never let me back into the home again, he grinned as he recovered from his shocking ruminations.

Finally, he retreated down the steps and, turning, walked slowly down the road in the direction of the Le Claire's warehouse. Despite the clear twilight skies, the wind off the bay was chilly and he pulled his jacket tightly around himself.

If you are as smart as you like to think you are, you will *definitely not* go out this evening! Especially after 10:00 o'clock!

If only he had listened to his own advice!

*   *   *   *   *

54

CHAPTER EIGHT

In the evening 23rd June 1687
Marseilles, France

After having spent two long days running away from his village and living off his sparse supplies, his evening meal at the Le Claire home was hearty and succulent. Martin was generous with the wine and Anne pressured him continually to enjoy more of her delicious Catalan stew and fresh bread. Sated, he finally pushed his chair back from the table with a protest.

"Enough, Godparents! I'll be bursting at the seams of my clothes if I do not quit eating! A lovely meal, *Mère Le Claire*! And enough wine too!" he gestured towards the proffered wine bottle held by his smiling godparent. "I think I would benefit from a long walk along the Quay..."

"I really don't think you should go out until I have checked to see how safe it would be," Martin interrupted. "I would have stopped you earlier if I had known that you planned to walk the Quay this afternoon, Pierre. From what you tell me, the alert has reached from your village clear to Marseilles."

Martin leaned back in his chair and thought deeply. "I will wander down to the Inn on La Canebiere frequented by the off-duty Militia and gather a little information. As a respected wine merchant I will be trusted, I think!" He rose and shrugged into his heavy coat. "You can help my wife with the pots and dishes," he punched Pierre on the arm and after embracing his wife, he left the room.

Pierre really enjoyed the time spent in the kitchen with Anne as he caught up on all the family gossip and in the process, learned a great deal about the origins of his own family. For years he had heard of the death of his renowned ancestor in the early days of the vicious attacks on the members of the Reformed religion. Now for the first time he heard details of the death of Gwilliam Jaubert in Dauphin. Finally, when the bell from a downtown church chimed 10:00pm Anne excused herself "in order to get her well-needed beauty sleep".

Pierre opened the door to the outside second floor verandah and leaned on the iron balustrade and looked at the dark harbor with the lighted lamps on many of the moored fishing ships. He found that he was deliberately not looking in the direction of the home of the two girls to the left.

I am definitely not insane enough to respond to Judith's invitation – no matter how attractive and tempting it may be! But I cannot help wondering if she would really be there? Finally, with a sigh, he gave in and glanced in the direction of the home and realized that with the curve of the bay, even in the dark he could actually see the doorway.

As he gazed at the door, it opened briefly and a small quick flash of what he assumed was candlelight, lit up the darkness.

Instinctively, Pierre felt his stomach muscles tighten up and his breathing shorten again. No, Pierre, it's insane! Nevertheless, he looked up and down the Quay and noted that there were only a few wanderers strolling the water edge. You don't need the worries that follow being involved with a woman at this time - especially a Catholic! You have enough problems as it is! However, despite the constant inner warnings, he kept looking at the doorway. When it opened again and the candlelight lit up the stairs, he finally made the fateful decision. It wouldn't do any harm to take a quick stroll on the Quay to work off that wonderful meal. But no checking at the girl's door! In a few minutes, he was down on the darkened courtyard level and smelled again the mixture of sea air, dead fish, and sawdust and spilt wine.

As Pierre strolled onto the Quay, he stood in the dark doorway and checked up and down the roadway.

He froze as a figure of a young man with a red scarf around his neck passed the entryway. He waited until he could no longer hear the hurrying footsteps and then stepped out into the moonlight. He turned slowly east and strolled close to the building walls keeping in the shadows. He found that he was taking short breaths again and made himself breathe more deeply.

Soon he was outside Judith's door. He found himself hesitating. This is idiotic, Pierre, idiotic!

It was the little sliver of candlelight showing under the bottom of the door that gave him the courage to push the door lightly. As the door swung silently open, he stepped into the opening. Pierre froze. In the dim light the single candle flame flickered in the sudden breeze. There was a grunting sound and movement from the far corner.

The sudden breeze from the open door disturbed the actions of a man who was crouched with his back toward the doorway. Pierre caught a flash of a startled olive face. Then as the man turned back, he jumped to his feet and spun round while closing his trousers at the front. Covering his face with his hand, the man lunged toward Pierre.

Raising his hand to protect himself, Pierre stepped back against the doorframe. The shoulder of the man thumped into Pierre's stomach and he collapsed against the wall as the attacker slipped past and vanished into the dark. Pierre leaned back onto his feet. Then he saw the body on the floor in the darkened corner.

The flickering candle revealed long legs covered by white stockings tied above the knees. A flurry of skirt and petticoats had been roughly bunched up at the waist. The underclothes had been ripped aside and lay between the girl's legs. Pierre could not help staring. He had never seen a woman naked before.

There was a trace of red blood staining the torn underclothes. The girl's head raised slowly and she moaned. There was blood on her cheek as though she had been struck. It was Aleen!

Finally unfreezing, Pierre heard a sound of movement behind him as he moved toward Aleen. Bending over her he pulled her skirt and petticoat down in an attempt to cover her nakedness.

Suddenly, another light brightened the scene. Pierre turned and saw Judith standing on the steps, a lantern in her hand. In the edges of the light she was holding, he saw her eyes grow wide with horror and she cried out suddenly...

"Pierre, how could you? My sister! You beastly animal...how could you?"

Pierre stared at her in horror.

She turned then and called back up the stairway.

"Uncle, Uncle! Come quickly. Aleen has been attacked by Pierre!" Then she turned back again to glare at Pierre. Suddenly she turned her gaze toward the doorway and gasped with obvious relief. "*Monsieur* Le Claire - thank God! My sister, Aleen has been attacked by this animal!"

Pierre turned in surprise to see Martin standing in the doorway. Before he could speak, Martin moved forward and grasped him by the shoulder and propelled him towards the open door.

"Go Pierre! Go back to the house – now! Don't worry, I was right behind you when you entered. So I know that you have done nothing wrong! But when the authorities come, I want you to be safe."

He pushed Pierre down the stairs and closed the door behind him. Pierre found himself faced by two immediate options; run like hell; or stay and listen. For a second he hesitated in time to hear his Godfather's reassuring words as he explained that he had followed Pierre through the doorway and could assure Judith that he was not guilty. Then he continued that the attacker had rushed by with his face uncovered, as he looked backward up the stairs.

"I saw the man who attacked your sister. It was a sailor from the sherry trading boat which is tied up at the Quay - the "Reina Negro" from down the coast at Roses in Spain."

"Are you sure? How do you know him"

"I remember him because he carried the case of wine which his captain purchased yesterday."

Because her voice dropped, he could no longer make out her speech. Turning he moved quickly through the shadows to the home archway and went upstairs. He collapsed into a chair in the kitchen and waited the return of Martin.

It was under an hour when his Godfather clumped up the stairs.

He stood in the kitchen doorway shaking his head.

"Oh what a mess you have gotten yourself into, Pierre!" he smiled slightly.

"I praise the Lord that you were there at that particular time, M. Le Claire. You are right! What a mess that was!" Then Pierre remembered again the scene downstairs and asked, "And how is Aleen? Is she alright?"

Martin nodded. "Yes, she is looked after. I think she is still in shock and the Doctor and the authorities have been called. And that presents the main problem!"

Pierre nodded, "You're right. I don't need any more attention." Then he remembered the main reason for Martin's absence from the house.

"Did you discover anything tonight at the Inn?"

"Yes. I am afraid so! There is still an alert out for you. And, after tonight, if you are questioned, you will be recognized. I don't want you to end up as a prime candidate for the galleys - here on the bay!" Martin ended grimly. "So, I propose that you leave here tonight! On my way back tonight, I arranged that you spend the night on one of my wine boats. They will sail tomorrow very early for Toulon – down the coast to the East."

"Where will I be going?"

"Your hurried plan to flee the Luberon hillside for Marseilles was a good plan. But, now they have traced you here, it is no longer safe. While they search the city for you, I feel you might be better to do what they least expect," he hesitated and grinned. "They would not expect you to go back home to the La Motte area, would they? Since you are becoming a nuisance to the authorities, it looks as if you will have to make more serious decisions."

"But – where can I go and be safe?"

Martin frowned and pursed his lips. "I think you need to escape France – perhaps through the cantons of Switzerland or perhaps Bavaria or even the Netherlands. Some place where the Reformed religion is practiced. I hear they call them 'Huguenots' - a Germanic term for a 'confederate in belief'. You will suffer the life of a refugee for a while but I am sure with your skills, and knowledge of both vines and sheep, and your willingness to work hard, you will find a new life for yourself. And - my Godson – your father – while he will miss you; at least he will be able to relax knowing that you are safe and well - if you make it!" He added grimly.

Pierre dropped his head sadly as he pondered the difficult steps he needed to take. So much change in so short a time!

"Come on, Pierre, my valiant godson. We need to get you quietly to the boat. I will give your good wishes to my spouse in the morning and explain the problems."

Pierre nodded as he rose. "And, Godfather, when the moment is right, could you say farewell - to both Judith and Aleen - for me. I would like them to know that I liked them both..." his voice trailed off sadly.

Martin nodded agreement as he pulled on his coat while Pierre gathered his belongings.

*   *   *   *   *

23rd June 1687
Luberon hillside, Provence

The shadows were lengthening in the late afternoon sun, the breeze gently brushing the petals of the wild red poppies in the ditch beside the roadway. The cart was heavily laden with special supplies for the Dragoons. The cart driver, a local man hired from La Tour nearby, was seated beside the sergeant. The officer was very vocal as he regaled the driver with his recent encounter with Suzanne. He used his hands effectively as he aptly described her - leaving little to the imagination.

He did not seem to be aware that his audience was not impressed with his story.

Two Dragoons were guarding their cart – one riding in front and the other at the rear but slightly to the side to avoid the cloud of dust thrown up behind the vehicle. Neither of the troops was alert for the danger that lay ahead.

The first rock struck the sergeant on the hand drawing blood and he cursed aloud. Immediately, other rocks clattered against the cart's sides and baggage. With his hand up over his face to protect him, the sergeant located the source of the bombardment – a copse of bush off to the immediate right.

The ambush setting was carefully chosen. The road was dug into the hill on the side where the rocks were coming from forcing the horses to ride both forward and back before they could enter the grassy meadow above.

The sergeant's shouts alerted the Dragoons. The wagon stopped. The driver and officer scuttled down and took shelter away from the bombardment. The sergeant, wiping his face, yelled as he urged the Dragoons to investigate.

The driver saw the danger first. Hearing a slight noise behind him, he turned his head and his eyes opened wide with consternation. The spot for the ambush had been carefully planned!

An apparition had slipped out from the dense bush close to the road. A man was wearing a cloth bag over his head to disguise his features. On the bag, a caricature of a fox's face had been skillfully painted with a real fox-tail hanging from the back of a red cap. A brown cloak hung from his shoulders.

The sharp knife flashed in the afternoon sun. The sergeant was not aware of the danger and hardly turned at all before the blade gashed across his throat. He fell to the road without any noise. The gush of blood quickly congealed in the heavy dust.

"Call the Dragoons back!" the assassin spoke hoarsely. "Call them, now!" He vanished back into the brush. On cue, the driver stood up and screamed at the galloping soldiers who turned in their saddles to look at the problem.

Both spun their horses and raced back to the scene. While one dismounted to inspect the sergeant, the other, waving his saber, returned to unsuccessfully search for openings in the brush.

Eventually, both Dragoons loaded the dead sergeant into the back of the cart and rode for La Motte d'Aigues.

A crowd of villagers quickly joined the cart as it drove through the cobbled street and stopped outside the home of the baker, Charpentier. A call from the doorway brought the Captain with raised eyebrows to the side of the cart.

"*Mon Dieu*, my *Sergent* - dead!" He waved his lace handkerchief to his nose as though this action would take away the bloody sight. He listened to the rattled report from the two Dragoons and shook his head as they suggested a search of the area by cavalry.

"No, these bandits know the country like the back of their hands. I'm afraid that the *Sergent* is being punished for his adventure with a certain girl from this village." He lowered his voice and spoke from the side of his mouth to the nearest Dragoon.

"I'm afraid that my *Sergent* never was one to recognize that 'you can catch more bees with honey' than with vinegar!"

Looking at the gathered villagers, the Captain raised his languid voice to address them.

"This so-called 'Fox' is beginning to become a nuisance – not a problem – just a pest! I can assure you that he will be captured soon and hung here in the village."

He turned to the soldiers, "Unload the supplies; cover the *Sergent* with a sheet and take the body to Pertuis - down the hill - for burial. I will prepare a dispatch to the headquarters to obtain another officer - one who will be feared; not just disliked like this one!"

With a flourish, he turned back into the doorway.

*   *   *   *   *

23rd June 1687
On the Mediterranean

It was still dark when Pierre awoke with the sudden noises above deck. He had been warned by the Captain to keep out of sight but could not resist at least going up the worn wooden steps to stand in the shadows and watch the ship leave the Quay. Most of the buildings bordering the Quay were in darkness also. The weather was calm but a quiet but firm breeze rattled the sails. As the lines were cast off, the sails caught the breeze and silently moved down the harbor in the direction of the Mediterranean.

Pierre had never been on the ocean before. As the gap between the side of the ship and shore widened, he went over the shadows at the rail and watched the darkened buildings and towering forts go by. He noticed the sharp tang of the salt air that was so different from the musty smell of the harbor water.

I feel a little sad inside, he thought and yet I am not really leaving my country. However, he also recognized that he felt relieved knowing that within the next day or so he would be back on his Luberon hillside.

The Captain had explained the plans made by his godfather. As the ship moved up the coast, it would unexpectedly pull in briefly at the next major port, Cassis. Here he would help unload a small cargo and in the confusion, would slip away. He would make contact with a wagon loaded with spirits waiting outside the Inn of St. Jean.

He would be provided with a mule to ride and would be one of the two outriders who would guard the shipment of valuable liquor and accompany it to a chateau outside Pertuis – which was on the banks of the Durance below his Luberon range.

Once the shipment was unloaded, he would abandon the party and ride up the hillside to his village keeping the mule as a gift from his Godfather.

Although there was little to see once the ship rounded Cap Croisette, light was beginning to show on the eastern horizon. Pierre decided that rather than trying to sleep below decks, he would enjoy this new experience instead. He threw a cover over his heavy coat, pulled his hat down against the wind and watched the rising sun slowly light up the brilliant sea and gently paint the black shoreline with a brilliant touch of gold.

*   *   *   *   *

23rd June 1867
On the road to Merindol, Provence

The brightness of the late afternoon sun caused the slowly moving waters of the Durance River to shimmer and distort the images of the trees growing on its banks.

The dust from the slowly moving cart billowed up from the creaking wheels and settled on the face and hair of the man and woman who trudged behind with their wrists shackled to the rear of the cart.

In the absence of a breeze, the dust quickly fell down to be roused again by the hooves of the two horses that followed the cart. The two mounted Dragoons rode with slightly glazed eyes bored with their dull task. To each saddle was a tether attached to a further two horses which were following behind.

The Corporal, being in command, had commandeered the most interesting job of driving the cart. He readjusted the wide brimmed hat to the sun's changing rays as he talked to the mules pulling the cart.

Behind him, leaning against the back of the driving seat, were four passengers. The faces of the three young girls were obviously disturbed and unhappy. Their dusty cheeks were furrowed with the stains of tears. Another Dragoon languished between the two oldest girls – in their late teens. Both of his arms were around each older girl's necks.

Every now and then his hand would move and take turns in cupping and fondling their young breasts. This had obviously been going on for some time for while they had previously futilely objected; they now slumped in passive acceptance.

They no longer made eye contact with their distraught parents shackled behind them. The third girl was much younger and had forced herself into the corner of the wagon box. From this vantagepoint, she could observe what was taking place and her upset glance rapidly moved from the faces of her sisters to that of her parents.

A pile of bundles was flattened in the back of the cart and covered with dust.

"Well, my big black mule...Satan, we'll call you...it won't be long now. Just short of the next village in the grove of trees on the side of the road there is an antique barn," he mumbled as he flicked the peeled sapling and touched the animal's flank. "I'll set the old woman free to make a supper for us while I shackle the father - so he won't cause any problems." He glanced over his shoulder, "And, my best friend, Jean, who sits in the cart behind me ... amusing himself with the ... attractive advantages ... of both of the young ladies ... will help one of them bring some water from the river."

Then the Dragoon in the cart turned and leered back at the driver. "I won't have to hurry back with the water, will I, Corporal?"

"No, Jean," a wide grin broke out on the corporal's face revealing dirty yellow teeth. "I, myself, may take a little special time educating the youngest of the three ladies you are escorting ...You know, I have always had a taste for really young meat..." A choking sound erupted from the youngest girl and tears streamed down re-cutting fresh furrows in the dusty cheeks.

The Corporal turned his head to meet the glare on the face of the father.

"Well, old man, you became criminals under the new laws when we caught you and your family escaping from the village of Cheval Blanc."

He shook his head slowly from side to side. "The punishment is well known to all you Reformed families...the Father to the galleys for life; Mother and older children to the Convent of St. Maria – servants for life! And the authorities will find good Catholic homes for the younger children," he paused to glance back at the curve of the road ahead. "After all, you chose your own punishment, didn't you?   You could have abjured, signed the paper, joined the old faith, become one of us..."

The two Dragoons had lifted their heads and the vacant looks were now replaced with twisted grins. The Corporal met their gaze and nodded his head.

"You two need a little fun as well.   After all, these three girls will be just...wasted in the convent. What will they learn about servicing men ... in the cloisters?" He caught the eye of the youngest, "You – yes, you, are never too young to learn something new!" He roared with laughter at his own humor and twitched the brown mule as an encouragement to reach their destination.

What happened next was so smooth and slick that none of the Dragoons reacted at all. Brush and heavy trees had hidden the five horsemen who broke from ambush. One stopped the mules by blocking their path and held their harnesses. Two rode close into the sides of the mounted soldiers thrusting muskets into their faces. Two more appeared at the sides of the cart and with their muskets threatened the corporal and the Dragoon in the cart.

It was all over in minutes. The Dragoons were swearing and cursing but that stopped when a rider smashed the musket into one soldier's face. The corporal blustered but was hauled from his seat and thrown to the hard ground.

All the riders had cloth bags masking their faces except for the eyeholes cut into the cloth.   Their leader had a vixen-like caricature drawn on his mask and a dusty fox-tail hung down from the back of his hat. All Dragoons soon had their hands tied behind their backs and a cord ran from each soldier to the next preventing their independent action.

The leader swung down from his horse behind the cart.

"Let me unshackle you, *Madame*. I fear that his Majesty's representatives know little of courtesy." He quickly had her free and used a white kerchief to cover the bloody wrists. Once he had the parents free, he helped them into the cart and asked the man to take the reins.

"Follow me," he waved ahead. Two of the riders held the other horses on tethers and led them behind him. The cart followed and another rider jogged behind the captured Dragoons and their corporal – linked together – in the dust with the final rider ensuring that they did not try to escape. It was minutes before they reached the stone barn buried in a copse of trees.

As the cart drew to a halt in the shade, the leader gestured to the father.

"Take your family down to the rivers-edge down that path," he pointed "and get your family cleaned up and refreshed. You've had a tough ordeal! But you are free now!"

"Bless you, whoever you are, bless you!" The man stumbled down from the cart and shepherded his dusty family out of sight down the path.

By the time the family returned, the band of Dragoons were all shackled to heavy beams in the deserted barn and one of the riders had started a fire to heat a meal of stew and bread.

"You must excuse our masks, *Monsieur et Madame*, but the less you know about us, the better – in case you are captured again, God forbid!" The leader explained.

"Are you the one they call *'Le Renard'*?" The leader nodded.

"Thank God you came when you did! None of my family would ever have been the same...after...Thank you! Thank all of you!" Tears ran down the father's face and the girls hugged their mother's arms.

The leader then explained that when they received a message stating that the family had been captured while escaping from their village, the band had trailed the cart for half the day until they could develop a plan to free the family. Following their escape at night from their village of Cheval Blanc, the family had planned to seek refuge with friends in Marseilles.

"There is no time to lose, *Monsieur*. Once you have eaten, you need to travel in a different direction. Do you have friends in the north? Yes? Good! Where abouts? You are now a short way from Merindol. You need to travel back up the road; past your village of Chevel Blanc; then overnight at Cavaillon; and rapidly to your friends at Orange. That city is big enough to hide you until you can journey to Lyon and from there across the border to the cantons of Switzerland."

The father nodded in agreement.

"Two of my men, dressed in the clothes of the Dragoons, will accompany you as though you are in trouble with the Law," he chuckled as the girls gasped in astonishment." We have done this before and are getting good at the 'game'. We will keep the soldiers locked up but fed and watered for about three days to allow you to escape and hide."

A short time later, after all the band had been hugged by mother and all the girls, the family, guarded by two uniformed "Dragoons", set off back up the road following the Durance River.

Needless to say, within a couple of days this latest exploit of the elusive "Le Renard" was being told through all the villages on the Luberon and within a week both laughter and snarls were being heard in inns all over Provence.

*   *   *   *   *

CHAPTER NINE

25th June 1687
La Motte d'Aigues, Luberon, Provence

Jacques Jaubert turned in his bed and groaned as the old pain ignited in his hip again. His eyes opened slightly and he found himself wondering whether it had been the pain that had wakened him.

His nose twitched as it sensed a strong smell of a beast - either horse or mule? Before he could rise, a strong hand pushed him back on the shoulder while another hand, smelling strongly of sweat, covered his mouth tightly.

"Father, keep quiet - please!" Jacques relaxed, as he immediately recognized his son's voice and the grasping hands were both lifted simultaneously. He turned over slightly trying not to wake his wife. However, proving again that she was always alert where children were concerned, her soft voice whispered from the edge of the covers.

"So – the men in my life are conspiring again to have private conversations without me, are they?"

"Hush, dear mother," Pierre's hoarse voice crept over the heavy quilt. "It's good to be back at home again – but I must talk with you both – right now – because I have to leave the village again before dawn."

"Ssh! You may have forgotten we are billeting two Dragoons in the next room. But, they were drinking heavily tonight," she hesitated. "We can go downstairs; and then into the stable below. It will be safe, *non*?"

"Good idea, mother – let's go quietly!" grunted her husband. The two rose; pulled on warm robes; and the three of them quietly left the room. His mother closed the door to the next bedroom quietly and followed the men down into the kitchen and then into the stable area.

"I'll bar the door to the kitchen from this side. If we are interrupted, you can leave and we will have time to let you escape before we re-open the door," mother whispered, then hugged her son fiercely.

"I am so glad to see you again. I thought you would be gone forever! But... why are we blessed with this surprising – if uncomfortable - visit, Pierre?"

As his parents seated themselves on the bottom step, Pierre shuffled his feet in the heavy straw on the rocky floor and then crouched down on his haunches.

In low tones, keeping details brief, he quickly recounted his trip to Marseilles including his brutal capture in Eguilles, which drew sharp gasps from his mother. He brushed over her concern as he told of his cousin's orchestrating his escape – which pleased her.

He carefully provided little detail about the affair with the girls from Marseilles but was heavy in his appreciation of his father's godparent's help in escaping the authorities and returning to the Luberon range – and home.

"Godfather's strong recommendation is that it is too dangerous for me to remain in France now that I am regarded as a criminal - with a price on my head. If I am caught, it will mean the slave galleys in the Bay of Marseilles – for life."

Again his mother's gasp of horror was overridden as he continued "Frankly, I hated the idea of leaving my country, my dear parents, but as I rode the ship to Cassis, I had time to think it all out. And, although it will be a real challenge, the future of living in peace ... anywhere...seems better than living without freedom under the yoke of the Catholics."

"Pierre, there has been a lot of discussion in the villages since you left," his father interrupted. "Sad as parting is, we – both – feel we would rest easier if we knew you were safe somewhere." He gestured in the moonlight to his right leg. "My hip and leg are giving me a lot of pain and I would not be able to handle any long rough travel. And, I can well afford to hire people to carry out my daily work." Pierre winced but nodded.

"Pierre, there is a lot of fear in the local villages and some families, and many of the young people are wondering about escaping over the border to the Swiss..." mother whispered as she reached out to touch him on the shoulder.

"I too, since I completed my task of escorting the wine cart to Pertuis, have taken the time to secretly visit all the villages on the eastern slope – Peypin, Bastide des-Jourdans, Pierrevert and many of the hamlets and farms where I sheltered in the last couple of days. There are many who are preparing to flee – probably by following the river, Durance to the Alps..." he fell quiet and turned his head to listen to a creak from an upstairs floor.

"You had better go quickly," his father whispered. "You will be in the borrie?"

Pierre grinned in the shaft of moonlight and nodded.

The family embraced fiercely and then Pierre slipped out the stable door knowing his parents would check around the villages to seek out would-be escapees.

As he blended into the bush, he heard voices in the home as his father explained to a Dragoon that "they too had heard a noise downstairs and come to investigate..."

Reaching the borrie safely after checking the area carefully, he wrapped himself in his covers and found sleep came easily after the decision about his future had been finally made.

*   *   *   *   *

The sun was setting with its traditional late June warmth offering a slight breeze to cool the heat of a Provencal day, as Pierre slipped upward through the brush towards La Motte. He paused to listen carefully for signs of danger but all seemed suspiciously peaceful. As he approached the lower gardens of the houses, he had expected to hear the raucous voices of Dragoons enjoying a glass of wine before supper. But all was subdued.

Pierre had spent a good portion of the afternoon discussing the planned escape of villagers with his good friend, Andre Roux.

Names of potential refugees had been mentioned with their proposed destinations. Many were planning on joining relatives in Switzerland but some were traveling further afield to areas of Bavaria. Others were talking of reaching Princedoms in different parts of Germany and the lowlands of the Dutch provinces. Some were even going as far as Scandinavia. There was a great deal of conflict as to who would lead the escape party; it was not yet agreed upon.

Crossing through several garden areas, Pierre eventually arrived at his parents' land. All seemed quiet here too. Feeling uncomfortable, he was extra cautious crouching low in the shade of the massive rosemary bush, its pungent scent leaving its traces on his face and hands as he listened carefully before flitting into the shade of the stable doors.

He was startled as he reached for the handle only to have the door swing towards him. His father's low voice welcomed him inside.

"It's safe, my son. The *Capitaine* has taken most of his troop out on a sweep of the lower valley in an effort to seize the infamous 'Renard'! Your cousin is, however, safe on the heights above Cabrieries watching their maneuvers below like a Bonelli eagle watching a rabbit," he chuckled as he pulled Pierre into the cool of the stable, "others will be joining us shortly."

"I wondered why everything was so quiet and peaceful."

"We are enjoying it as well. It's good to move around your own home and through the streets with your neighbors without having to watch what you say; and who is listening..."

Pierre saw glasses and an open bottle of wine on the lower step and helped himself to a glass.

"Pierre, your mother and I have decided to do the safe thing," his father shook his head and grimaced, "I am a little too old and crippled to fight the crusade. So, we have decided to abjure. We will sign the agreement to recant our Reformed belief. We will twist our tongues and cross our fingers – and play the game...knowing that you will be safe and free somewhere else." He shook his head again as though to rid himself of the disgust in making the decision. "Maybe someday soon the King and his advisers will regain their senses and move to protect us believers. Maybe then you can return to claim your inheritance...who knows?"

The door upstairs opened and closed. Pierre looked sharply at his father but his father smiled and waved his hand up and down to indicate calm and safety.

"Our neighbor, poor Charpentier. He has a task for you!"

"A task?"

The door opened above and his mother appeared followed by the village baker. Pierre was shocked! The once strong and hearty neighbor had aged dramatically since the brutal murder of his mother in the oven. His cheeks drooped and his eyes were sad and dull. He gripped the man's hand in welcome and with great sincerity.

"Pierre, it's good to see you again!" the man's voice quavered a little, "I have not seen you since the sad death ... of my mother. And I have not forgotten! It was your brave action which has led to you having to lead... the life of a criminal...!"

"*Monsieur* Charpentier, I must be honest and tell you that I acted without thought. And I certainly don't see my self as ... brave! Since then I have been running like a frightened rabbit..."

"Enough, you two," broke in his father; "our friend has a task for you..." Charpentier nodded slowly.

"Yes, Pierre. Although we have heard a great deal of your adventures between here and Marseilles, things have been happening here as well. None of our families are safe anymore!" The man's voice broke a little and he bent his head and shook it to recover his composure.

"My wife and I have made a difficult decision! You have always known my daughter, Suzanne. I know she respects you; and although she has had eyes for your rascally cousin, I have always hoped that she would choose you for a husband when the time came,"

Pierre looked in shock at his father who simply raised his eyebrows and shrugged. He looked back at the baker. "Suzanne...?" he questioned.

"Yes, Pierre, I would like you to take her to safety ... over the border to Switzerland. Despite the fact that she is the prettiest girl in the village, I think she will also make you a good wife when you reach a safe place." With this he held out his hand and gripped Pierre's fiercely. "I trust no other, Pierre! Will you honour a sad old man's wishes?"

The shock was so great that it took a second before Pierre realized that he was not breathing. He took a deep breath to help him regain some control. He looked deep into his future father-in-law's sad and sincere eyes.

In this shocking second, he realized his life was to be decided for him! It was traditional amongst the Reformed religion that these decisions take place for young men after the age of 25 years but usually are proceeded by long and involved negotiations ending with a written marriage contract with firm restrictions as to dowry and many gifts. Sometimes, the negotiations took months – even years!

Suzanne is beautiful, he thought, and popular. She could have her choice of any man on the Luberon range, he thought. It is a prize ... worth dying for, but...he made up his mind swiftly.

"I hesitate, *Monsieur*, not because I do not value your offer – but, because I am not sure I am good enough for the hand of your daughter." He jerked his eyes in the direction of his father as though looking for guidance. But his father's eyes said nothing - waited for his response. Pierre looked back into the face of his future father-in-law and nodded.

"So I say now, *Monsieur* - I am honoured!" his voice was hoarse and weak.

The baker smiled with obvious relief, turned and called up the stairs.

"Suzanne…"

After a long minute, the door at the top of the stairs opened and Suzanne herself stood in the doorway. She peered into the semi-darkness of the stable until she recognized his form. Then she walked down the stairs slowly and with great dignity. On the last step, she held out her hand to her father. Meeting Pierre's nervous - but very obvious look of pride - her smile was a little sad and subdued.

"Father?" she said simply.

"My daughter, I have arranged for your betrothal to our good neighbor's son and your childhood playmate, Pierre." He hesitated obviously trying to choose the right words, "I know … both of you… would have wished for… more time …and more choices, but I am afraid that Fate – and the quest of the King – have made that impossible." He led her down the last step and, turning to Pierre, he placed her hand into his. "I give you both my blessing and pray that when you are safe somewhere, that you will be properly married and enjoy a new life together…"

The couple stood holding hands and looking at each other. Her hand felt cool and detached in his and he knew that his was wet and sweating. He thought he saw the sadness leave her eyes and be replaced with a glint of mischief at his obvious discomfort.

"I will go with you, Pierre…to safety - for I trust you!" Suzanne said slowly and quietly.

"Suzanne, I honour your father's request." Pierre's words stumbled and he could not find appropriate words to express his fortune. "I feel … very fortunate … that you will - one day - become my wife…" His mother now stepped forward with enthusiasm and broke their grasp. She swung Suzanne around to hug her in congratulation. Pierre stood back with his father's arm around his shoulder while good wishes were offered.

It was much later that night - after he had crept back alone to the borrie - that Pierre realized that Suzanne had never said that she would "marry" him. She had simply said that she would "go" with him…Hmmm, he wondered - what does that really mean?

*　　　*　　　*　　　*　　　*

From the window of her bedroom, with the shutters pushed well open, Isabeau, by leaning out and straining her neck, could see the old tree in the square in the center of St. Martin. I'm puzzled, she thought? Instead of feeling excited inside, I feel slightly depressed today. I'm surprised - this day is supposed to be the most important - and exciting - day of my life! She leaned back once more into the shade and coolness of her room and concentrated on her feelings.

Why am I feeling like this, she thought. What is wrong with you, Isabeau? In a short time, she knew she would hear the "tock, tock" of the little hammer being used by Jean Cappel, an elder of their Reformed Church, as he tacked the third reading of the marriage banns on the old tree.

Ever since the temple building had been destroyed by order of the King, the tree had been used instead.

What a wonderful ceremony it would have been to be married in a real temple, she thought with a touch of sadness. Even a ceremony in the "Desert" would have been exciting.

With the King's destruction of the church buildings, the church members had, in protest, organized their church services at secret places in the countryside – the location known only to the local trusted church members. These sacred locations had been in beautiful rural spots. In big caverns; or beside waterfalls; and in small hidden groves in the forest – referred to by all those in the "reformed religion" by the code words: "the Desert".

Quietly they had left their homes at the special times; families split up into little groups to meet at agreed spots where they joined with other families as they trekked through the brush and bush to the secret locations. Times and places had been passed on only by word of mouth. The authorities had tried desperately to discover these "Desert" spots and arrange for mass arrests – sometimes mass killings. But the Reformers continually changed their locations and roving ministers secretly held religious services, baptisms and weddings despite the King's ban.

Isabeau heard the sound and peered out the window again.

"Tock, tock, tock." There he was, in the strong morning sunlight, hammering away. She leaned back hurriedly to avoid being seen by neighbors who would check her window with glee on hearing the sound. She was not supposed to look too eager. Brides were supposed to be a little reluctant!

Maybe that is what I am right now, she pondered...a touch reluctant - I am not scared; but I am not eager as well? Getting married is important. Starting a new life and a couple's lifestyle should be exciting! She turned and looked at her wedding skirt and blouse hanging up on the hook in the corner. A little smile creased the side of her mouth as she remembered watching her aunt embroider the hem as she talked about the "old days".

Just behind the wedding clothes, she could see the green and white skirt of the gown she had worn at the day of her betrothal.

How tense everyone had been as the wedding arrangements were negotiated. A faint smile emerged at one corner of her cheek. Her father and her future in-laws, the Mallans, had met in the kitchen with the meeting presided over by the Notary who drew up the wedding contract.

All the traditions had been carried out beforehand. The couple had met at a village festival - carefully watched by their parents, of course, she thought ruefully. The fathers had met to get a mutual agreement. Then the mothers had joined them to ensure that the wedding plans were not mismanaged. And the future groom had called on Isabeau's father and, perspiring greatly, had asked for her hand in marriage. She had had to wait upstairs in her bedroom while the discussion took place. She remembered giggling into her frilly apron as she had heard her father try to inject a little humor into the suspense.

But Pierre "Le Duc" Mallan had not been amused. He really needs to see the funny side of life... a little anyway, she thought! Finally, she had been brought down and had her hand put into his sweaty palm. He had been obviously pleased to get her as a bride. How he had beamed! Then he had kissed her in front of her father. And his mustache had rubbed her mouth almost raw. That was something she had not even given thought to!

Everyone in the families had finally settled down to planning the wedding and the couple had taken time to talk a lot to each other about their wishes, desires and plans. As was expected traditionally, Isabeau had made sure that her husband's wishes had been given priority – at least, until they were married - Isabeau smiled to herself.

But, it was during this period that Isabeau had realized for the first time that her Le Duc Mallan might not be the easiest person with whom to live. And matters had worsened with the legal marriage negotiations.

The bridegroom, accompanied by his well-dressed parents, had arrived on time – after the Notary had been settled in the middle of the biggest room in the Richarde home – the kitchen. Isabeau had scrubbed and shone everything in sight the day before. The pots hanging from their racks gleamed. The tiles on the floor shone. Not a speck of Provencal dust could be seen anywhere.

A chair and small table had been borrowed from a neighbor and placed in between the two groups of chairs – one group for each family. Isabeau smiled as she remembered her excitement in getting dressed in her new clothes – with the green and white skirt and the fresh white blouse. Special vases with matching lovely white flowers and bright fresh greenery had decorated the room.

Since all the basic details had been discussed well in advance by both families, it should have only been a routine legal affair. However, despite clear understandings, the Mallan family arrived, unexpectedly accompanied by his uncle and aunt, as well as the parents. Isabeau was embarrassed and had to quickly arrange for a couple of extra chairs from neighbors.

And things had got worse! Beyond the confusion about the number of guests, the Uncle, who seemed to be highly regarded by Le Duc's parents, completely broke with tradition by questioning the details of the dowry and raising issue with the plans.

Although there had been no question of the suitability of the marriage during the early negotiations, it was obvious that the Uncle – who apparently was regarded as the "patriarch" of the Mallan family – had some strong views about the acceptability of the proposed bride and her family background.

Even now, Isabeau found her cheeks flushing with hurt and embarrassment. She felt sure that her betrothed, Le Duc, would have stepped in to object to the sudden changes in plans. But he had simply sat, apparently unconcerned, and gazed with some awe at his officious and interfering relative. His parents showed some sign of discomfort and studied their hands and looked up at the ceiling as the questions by the Uncle continued. Isabeau felt an added mix of emotions – anger had joined humiliation.

Suddenly her father rose to his feet after listening quietly but with growing astonishment,

"I must apologize," he said, looking directly at the Notary who had put his pen down on the table and was staring at the Uncle, "for this unexpected change in the arrangements, because I know what a busy man you are. I can assure you, *Monsieur*, that I am as shocked as I am sure you are also." His voice became a little shaken and hoarse. "As is the tradition in the Luberon villages, all arrangements have always been settled well before we meet to sign the contract. I have always trusted and honoured the Mallan family..."

At this point, the groom's father rose quickly to his feet and cleared his throat but before he could say anything, Isabeau's father continued, "but it seems that, maybe, my trust has been misplaced."

He turned to look at Isabeau and with a gentle smile; he stretched out his hand and raised her to her feet. "But, above everything in my world, I honour my daughter, Isabeau. And, under the circumstances, as the father of this lovely young woman, I feel I should withdraw my blessing until I am sure that both parties to this contract are satisfied with the agreed arrangements." And with that, he led her to the stairs. With a gentle wave, he directed her to leave the room and go to her bedroom.

Pleased at her father's intervention but also worried about the sudden change in plans, she, nevertheless, had walked sedately up the stairs. Without looking directly at the families below, she had seen that Le Duc had now also risen to his feet, his face flushed, and in a loud voice was actually remonstrating with his Uncle. By the time she closed the door, a tumult of voices was raised below but she noted that her father had withdrawn and was now looking out the window at the activity in the street.

It had ended up as a "stormy Mistral in a soup bowl". Her father later had recounted to her that he had remained cool and calm and steady in his resolve. "You were not to be haggled over like some sheep or goats! As a daughter, I regard you as priceless! Even without a dowry, you are the most valuable thing in my life! So, I simply waited until they arranged their own affairs and then listened patiently." He paused to grin at her. "In an effort to somehow recover control of the situation, your future father-in-law actually increased his gift to you by fifty sheep! I think he felt he needed to recover his honour; and, of course, I accepted gracefully..." he pulled her to him and hugged her with enthusiasm. "I think you and your husband are going to have to watch the antics of that Uncle with some care. He seems to be very ... managing!"

So the contract was drawn up and signed by all concerned. And, the wedding date was set for Wednesday, the 2nd of July in this year of 1687.

"And, it's coming too quickly for me..." she said aloud pensively as she realized that it was only seven days away. She peeked secretly down the street and noted that many of the local women were discussing the banns in the shade of the old tree.

Several gentle raps on the door below, jerked Isabeau away from the window and she hurriedly pushed her dark shining hair behind her ears and straightened her skirt as she raced down the steps.

When the door opened, her two friends, Suzanne and Charlotte were framed by the strong sunlight outside.

"Oh, I am so glad to see you two!" she cried joyfully. "You're what I needed today! Please come in..." As she waved them through the doorway and closed the door, she was concerned at their obviously distressed faces. "Is there something wrong?"

Suzanne broke into tears and Isabeau moved to hold her tightly.

"She has to leave! Suzanne has to flee!" Charlotte was obviously also upset.

"No! What has happened?"

With broken speech, Suzanne told the story of her father's arrangement made the previous evening with the Jaubert family.

"What I am really sorry about, is that I will not be able to help you at your wedding – as we had planned," burst out Suzanne.

"Oh, I am sorry too, Suzanne. You know how much I wanted you to help me in my bridal duties. But, if you are at risk, then ... so be it!"

"But it is happening so quickly! The plans are being kept secret and a group from many of the villages on the Luberon will be leaving the day before the wedding. The people, who arranged it, felt that this type of exodus would not be expected. The Dragoons will also be enjoying the celebrations and will not realize what is happening," Suzanne paused, "But, it seems so unfair to you, Isabeau!"

"Don't worry, Suzanne. My wedding will go on anyway. I am pleased that in some way, it will play a part in your – and the others' – escape. And I would be honoured to have you, Charlotte help me...will you?"

To say that Charlotte was surprised and obviously overjoyed would have been an understatement. She had always regarded herself as somewhat of a "foreigner" on the Luberon hillside. Unlike other parents, her father had been born in Italy and she had inherited his warm and olive complexion. Unlike other girls, she never seemed to have the physical capacity to blush. The sudden new role as helpmate to the bride was surely evidence of being accepted into the Provencal society.

Suddenly, turning to Suzanne, Isabeau grasped her by both her arms and swung her round.

"So, Suzanne, Pierre Jaubert is going to be your betrothed? I never thought he would ever get round to taking a wife!"

Out of breath, Suzanne gasped, "I am not really sure that poor Pierre had to make much of a decision. I don't even think that his father guessed what my father planned to do! In fact, even I was a little stunned when father arrived at this decision."

She finally caught her breath, frowned a little and then said, "Just between us friends," she glanced at each companion in turn, "I have always..." she shrugged his shoulders, " sort of *known*... that I might marry one of the Jauberts. But... since Pierre is so ... well, reserved and cautious, I guess my first choice would have been his cousin, Renard! But...since he has always been sort of wild in his ways, my father decided I would be safer with Pierre."

Suzanne looked earnestly at both her friends, "Of course, I really trust *my* Pierre and know that he will be a ... really strong - and reliable - husband. And, lately, of course, his manner has changed quite dramatically!" She frowned again. "In fact, in the villages he has become something of a 'quiet hero', hasn't he?"

Isabeau smiled at her friend. "You are right there, Suzanne, it's really quite amazing how courageous he has suddenly been! And how well he has handled the horrible things that have happened to him."

She smiled impishly at Susanne, "I should tell you a secret! Last year, when I was considering who I would like to marry, I looked hard - very hard - at your Pierre!"

Both of the girls' eyes opened wide in astonishment, as she continued, "Yes! I really liked that strong secure feeling you get when you are with Pierre. But I felt I needed a little more ... direction in my man. So I made my choice...and the rest is history. But..." she grabbed hold of Suzanne's hand "I am really pleased that he has chosen you! I cannot think of a better partner for him!"

"Wait girls! Since you are dividing up the village's main supply of eligible males, what about me?" Charlotte broke into the hand grasping pair and shook their arms.

"Charlotte," they both cried, "there is lots of room for you. And lots of time as well!" And the three girls hugged each in mutual glee and friendship.

*　　*　　*　　*　　*

CHAPTER   TEN

28th June 1867
The road to St. Martin, Luberon, Provence

Crouching in the brush at the side of the dusty road, Pierre waited while the cart, loaded with sacks of grain destined for nearby St. Martin, had passed.   In the dust rising from the wheels, he hoped to cross safely to the security of the vast vineyard.

As he tightened his muscles to make the first leap, the image of a young girl appeared through the haze and he dropped quickly to the ground.

With relief, he realized that he knew her well.   Charlotte had her face covered against the cloud of dust and was quickly covering the fresh herbs she had collected in the basket on her arm to also protect them from dust.

As she stopped to remove her wide brimmed bonnet and wave it over the herbs to blow the dust away, he called out quietly to her.

"Charlotte!" She started and looked up and down the road.

"Charlotte, I'm here...in the grass.   It's me, Pierre Jaubert." Clever girl, he thought, as she stopped and turned away deliberately and faced the vineyard as she casually waved her hat before her face as though taking a break on her journey.

Without looking around, she talked in a low voice. "Pierre, are you behind me?"

"Yes, Charlotte," he called back. "I am going back to take final leave of my parents."

"This is a safe time, Pierre! Although the Dragoons are all back from their search of valley," she shook the dust from her bonnet and fidgeted with her herbs, "it was an unsuccessful search for the 'Renard' outlaw!" She chuckled: "They are all sleeping right now; or recovering from heavy drinking.

"It's a sad time, Charlotte," he paused, "I may never see them – or you – again! That is such a terrible thought. I expect you are going over to St. Martin, are you?"

"Yes, Pierre, I have collected a fresh load of herbs.   Both to decorate the homes and to use also with all the cooking that is being done for the wedding two days from now." She paused and glanced over in his direction with a sad smile. "I am sorry you will miss Isabeau's wedding."

"Yes! Well, I had better get going. As you probably know, the escape party is gathering soon. We are hoping that by leaving before the wedding, there will be enough commotion in the villages about the wedding preparations, that our absence will not be noticed."

She nodded without looking at him.

"I would like to have bid Isabeau farewell and wished her well in her life," he flushed a little as he said, " for she was...always a little special to me..."

"I always suspected that, Pierre...but you have a new betrothed - in my friend, Suzanne - don't you? I'll bet that was a sudden surprise, wasn't it?" She turned with a little flourish and strutted towards St. Martin.

"Charlotte," he called after her impulsively, "I'll try and be in the quiet grove at the bottom of the Richarde yard in the early evening on 30th June – 2 days from now! Just in case..."

Over her shoulder she casually called out, "I'll pass your message on to Isabeau! But, with all the fuss and bother, she may not be able to meet with you..."

When she had passed out of sight around the bend, he checked the road again and crossed quickly to vanish down the rows of protective vines.

*   *   *   *   *

30th June 1867
La Motte d'Aigues, Luberon, **Provence**

Pierre furtively wiped the tears from his eyes. The farewell had been painful for both he and his parents. They all realized – but never voiced – their unspoken fear that they would likely never meet again.

His mother had carefully packed basic food supplies in his canvas backpack. His father had presented him with a new sharp knife that he had attached to his belt with pleasure. His mother had hugged him grimly and he had to push her firmly to break the clasp.

"I hope, when you have ... your children with Suzanne...wherever you may be...that you will tell them about their grandmother... Oh my son, how I will miss you!"

He leaned over and kissed her forehead with love and respect.

"I will miss you both – greatly! And, maybe, one day, it will be safe to return."

He reached out and touched their hands and then turned and quietly slipped down the path to the bottom of the garden. In the gathering dusk, keeping to the protective bushes, he worked his way carefully up the little path that led to the village of St. Martin.

I should not be doing this, he thought ruefully, but somehow, it means something to me! He crossed the little stream which marked the end of the Richarde property and chose his steps carefully as he pushed through the heavy brush and entered the glade.

He chose the dark shadow of a large tree to drop his backpack and crouch beneath. I'll wait for an hour, he thought. Then I need to join the gathering party at the borrie.

Suddenly, without any warning sounds, Isabeau appeared in the shadows at the farther edge of the glade.

"Pierre?" she called tentatively. "Pierre, are you here?"

"Here, Isabeau." He stood up and stepped out of the shadow.

The two young people looked at each other.

"I got your message from Charlotte. I should not be here - you know that! But I wanted to say ... *adieu*." As she spoke, she touched her face with her hand. He guessed that she had flushed.

"It's been a sad day for me. I have ... probably...seen my father and mother for the last time," he paused. "but I wanted to wish you well at your wedding...and in the future..." He paused awkwardly. "But I'd better go..."

Pierre broke eye contact with Isabeau and bent to pick up his backpack and turned to shrug it onto his shoulders. He felt uncomfortable and awkward. I don't know what I want to say, he thought. But - I had better go! He turned and simply called "farewell" over his shoulder as he walked away down the path. He only got about ten feet before she called out.

"Pierre! He stopped and looked back at her.

"Yes?" Even in the dusk, he could make out a frown masking her sweet and earnest face.

"We will probably never meet again, Pierre."

"No – not likely."

"I feel there is something I need to say..."

"Something?" he said. Isabeau looked down at her hands clasped in front of her. Then she looked up; both determination and a hint of something like fear showing on her face. Pierre felt tense and confused.

"I feel you should know..."she bit her lips in anxiety "...that when I thought about a future husband...that ...I had strong feelings about you!"

"Me?"

"Yes! I found you thoughtful and kind; and steady on your feet; really firmly on the ground." She hesitated and looked down again. Pierre found it hard to breathe. Many thoughts were racing through his mind. Then, through his confusion, his words broke out...

"It seems ...there is a 'but' in there... somewhere?"

She jerked her head upward and even at this distance; her eyes were sincere and steady.

"Yes...I must be honest! My father felt that you were the best man in the two villages. But, I guess, I wanted to find a man with a little more ...well...confidence and spirit." She hesitated again and he anxiously waited. "You didn't seem to have much direction to your life? You did not seem to be going anywhere? Is that terrible of me?"

But before he could speak, she continued: "And then, after I was betrothed...you did a foolhardy – but very brave thing! Then you fled the village to the coast. You got captured, then escaped, and finally came back to help escort the group to Switzerland." He waited for her to finish because he did not know what to say.

"There is part of me, Pierre, that wishes that I had been ...less hurried. That, if I had waited, I might have... made a different decision." She suddenly smiled and he saw the sheen of tears in her eyes. "There! I have said it! I felt I should say it because ... well ... we will never meet again, Pierre." She looked at him earnestly, "Pierre – did you ever...well, ever know I felt like that...?"

His throat felt choked up and he coughed nervously.

"No!" He saw a flash of disappointment on her cheeks. "No, I never knew you felt that way." She looked relieved. "But, I often watched you dance at the festivals. You had so much spirit - and such ... *la joie de vivre*, Isabeau, I saw you as a beautiful; and talented, wonderful person..." he broke off and took a breath, but she interrupted his thoughts.

"I too think ...there is a 'but' there as well, Pierre," she was smiling at him - in an almost flirtatious manner.

"Yes," he said carefully, "It always seemed ...that you were ...too confident...too self assured...too much in control - for me! You were somehow meant for someone better and more successful than me."

"And now...?"

"And now, Isabeau, I," he hesitated, "I...realize that I was much mistaken." He paused and returned her smile and his body felt relaxed and he was breathing freely again. "I am glad we spoke our feelings, Isabeau! But, we are going different paths now – you and I! However, I will never forget this moment!" He paused and looked slowly around the valley spread about below them. "And I will never forget you!"

They simply stood and smiled at each other with an obvious touch of both sadness and respect. Then Pierre turned and trotted down the path through the brush. Isabeau spun around her skirt twirling and ran back up the path toward the house.

Neither of them looked backward.

*   *   *   *   *

30th June 1687
La Motte d'Aigues, Luberon, Provence

The Captain was tired and frustrated and in no mood for any interruption in the period of quiet reading he enjoyed after his supper. He looked up and glared scornfully from his choice spot at the kitchen table at his new Sergeant who was standing in the open doorway.

"One of the things you should learn quickly, my dear *Sergent* Cappel, is that there are times during the day that are...somewhat sacred to me. And, this is one of them!" He breathed out in obvious frustration and prepared to deliver a lecture of some importance, "Surely, after the completely tiresome exercise in chasing around ... and not finding ... the elusive Fox...and his band of criminals..."

The Sergeant interrupted quietly but firmly.

"*Mon Capitaine*! You know I would never interrupt you without cause! I know how you enjoy your relaxation," he nodded his head in the direction of *Mme*. Charpentier who was hovering after opening the door,

"But my information is immediate and," he turned, "private. I will meet you in the street!" Without further comment he turned and left the doorway.

The Captain sat back his mouth open in shock. Damnation to him, he thought. While the new Sergeant was a slim quiet little man, the Captain had heard rumors of a traumatic childhood with thrashing from both a German father and a Parisian mother. He was said to be a man who, despite his diminutive appearance, was brutal in actions. He was one you disregarded at your peril. Oh well, he mused wryly, I will humor him this once...

Shrugging on his dress coat, he nodded to his hostess and walked out onto the cobbled lane.

"Well, *Sergent* Cappel, what is this mysterious revelation that needed my rest interrupted?" He waved his lace kerchief towards the seeping scar below his eye. "Well...?"

The Sergeant turned to face him and spoke quietly.

"*Mon Capitaine*, I have recently received special intelligence from your favorite 'Rat'!" He paused and looked around carefully noticing that the Captain's frustrated face now showed interest with his raised eyebrows. "It seems that on this very day – the day before the villages celebrate the Richarde wedding in St. Martin - there is going to be a secret exodus of a group of the Reformed faith! They are planning on fleeing France for the so-called safety of Geneva!"

"*Mon Dieu*! We shall snap this in the bud! People fleeing from my territory? Never! I will not tolerate such an action!" He spun on his heel and faced the Sergeant. "Do you have the names of the families? Have you not gathered the Dragoons?"

The Sergeant stood quietly looking patiently at his officer.

"Well, *Sergent*? I believe in action – fast action!"

"And I, *Capitaine*, believe in making sure that, if and when we act, we make the greatest impact possible." He hesitated and carefully spelt out his words. "If we intervene now," he spoke so quietly that the Captain had to lean forward to catch his words, "we will have to prove each case. And soon there will be another escape. And, very likely, we will lose our informer as well – a valuable source. *Non?*" He hesitated allowing the Captain time to absorb the picture.

"So, you have another plan?"

"Of course, *mon Capitaine*. That is what you would expect from a good *Sergent*...*Non?*" He continued while the Captain listened with growing interest. "Right now, we know... where they are gathering; the time they will depart; the direction they will be going. What's more, the village folk will believe they have pulled the proverbial wool over your eyes! Hmm! They will be sad at the departure but happy that their loved ones have escaped. Each day they will grow more proud – and relieved. And at the last minute, when the escape is on the edge of success – at the border near Geneva – we will capture them all! Dash their hopes! And march them back to this village where all can share in the disaster - and the disgrace!"

"Well that's good, but why delay so long?"

"Because, *mon Capitaine*, I understand that despite the harassment of the Dragoons being billeted in this village, there have been few successes in having the Believers abjure? Is that not so?"

A flash of embarrassment crossed the senior officer's features.

"And how will this plan improve the number of abjurations?"

The Sergeant paused, looking at the Captain with a firm stare, as a grim smile appeared on his face.

"With this one blow we will smash all the hope that this escape has given birth to! And when the refugees are all punished; the men shipped to the galleys in Marseilles; the women sent as slaves to the Abbey; the children torn from their families and adopted out," he paused as his voice had taken on a threat of steel, "I promise you, *mon Capitaine*, that we will wipe out the Reformed faith from these two villages so fast, you will probably receive a commendation from the King himself!"

The Captain instinctively took a step back and grunted, "Hmm, you're a surprising fellow, Cappel! And, the plan has merit. In fact, it will give me great joy to relish in the fun of the wedding, knowing that I have the upper hand while the villagers snigger as they think we are ...fools? Eh Cappel? What a glorious joke on them!" he frowned. "But how will we know when they are ripe to be captured?"

"Our informer, your 'Rat', will be a member of the escape party!" The Sergeant smiled as he enjoyed the look of surprise on the Captain's aristocratic features. "We have arranged for him to leave a 'trail' to guide our party of Dragoons who will be shadowing them!" The Sergeant broke from character as he actually chuckled aloud. "It's almost a joke, *Capitaine*. It amuses me to play the cat with these unsuspecting mice."

"You have depths I was not aware of, *Sergent*. Good work! We will follow your plan." He turned back towards the Charpentier's door, then looked back. "You have made my evening, Cappel, I shall enjoy the free wine tonight with extra gusto!"

As the Captain closed the door, the Sergeant's face bore an unseen sneer. He may be the aristocrat, but he has a lot to learn about intrigue, the Sergeant thought as he turned and strolled down the cobbled lane.

*   *   *   *   *

1st July 1687
On the Luberon hillside, Provence

This first day in July of 1867 had proved to be a warm one, thought Pierre as he rested on his bedroll inside the ancient borrie as the sun dropped on the horizon. The light from several candles flickered when slight puffs of breeze slipped through the gaps between the rocks that made up the uneven sides of the old dwelling. He lifted his hand and placed it on one of the rocks next to him. Even the old men in the village did not know whom the ancient people were who had built these conical shelters of stacked rock.

Pierre had suggested this temporary hiding place - this borrie - buried in a tangled grove of bush on the slopes of a hill - as a meeting place for the escapees.

It was safe because many of the villagers were scared of these mysterious hovels. He was sure the Dragoons did not know of their existence. Each little group would slip away from their homes. Family members would travel separately and join up at selected sites outside of their village. Backpacks with food and clothing had been smuggled out the villages the day before. He knew it would be hard for people to leave special momentos behind. What to take and what to leave?

As rocks rattled down the path, Pierre rolled over on his side to take advantage of the deep shadows but was relieved when his friend, Andre, called out softly to him. He stood up to grasp his hand in the darkness and then saw the smaller form clinging to Andre's hand.

"So your parents decided to send young Theodore with you?" He whispered.

"Yes. You know Pierre, don't you, Theodore?" he nudged his younger twelve year old brother into the dim light of the candles. Pierre saw the boy nod in agreement, the whites of his eyes showing up in the poor light.

Further cracking of a twig down the path alerted the small group to another arrival and they too stood in the shadows until two people emerged. The larger figure had a packsack on his back. Suzanne's father spent little time in ceremony. He hugged her briefly and kissed her twice before turning to grasp Pierre's hand firmly and without a word, dropped the pack and vanished back into the darkness.

"My father is sad. But, soon, he will be relieved when I am safely away from the village." She reached out and found Pierre's hand in the shadows. Her clasp was slight and he suspected that she was frightened. He pulled her slightly towards him and she came easily resting against his shoulder.

"I trust you, Pierre," she whispered softly. He gently bent down and kissed her smooth forehead as her head tilted back to look up at him.

"We'll be alright, Suzanne," he reassured her quietly.

Further shadowed figures came up several paths now and the two men separated to greet and reassure each group. Soon a large number were gathered around the entrance to the borrie. Pierre looked around and recognized people from both the villages.

Andre Roux and his younger brother, Theodore; Suzanne Charpentier, his betrothed; the Deleman family with father, Henri and mother, Claudine Cheron, and their three young daughters. Pierre later got to know them well – Catherine aged 16 years, Francoise aged 12 and little Jehanne aged 10 years.

Suddenly a rider on a horse startled them all! The tension was enough that both Pierre and Andre drew their knives. However, Henri Deleman recognized the rider from his village of St. Martin and called out greetings to them.

"It's Alexander Cramer from my village," he called out to Pierre, "he has offered to lead the party. He has also generously provided a horse for emergencies and a mule to carry food and extra baggage," he explained in a hoarse voice. "You know, his cousin, David Blosset, from La Motte – he has the mule with him. Alexander says he has traveled this route many times to Geneva."

Pierre was shocked as he looked at the man who held the horse with one hand and greeted the rest of the party with the other. Pierre had personally done enough planning during his visits to the villages and had expected to lead the group.

But Alexander gestured towards the entrance of the borrie.

"Let's go into the borrie and I will explain the system we feel will work."

Pierre noted with a touch of resentment that everyone followed his directions without question. Following Alexander's cousin, David, who had tied the mule to a nearby bush, Pierre crept into the borrie. Another couple of candles had been lit highlighting the anxious faces of the party.

"The villagers of St. Martin have asked me to lead your party safely to Geneva." Alexander gestured to his companion, "David Blosset, whom you from La Motte know well, will act as the scout up ahead for the first day using my horse. Once you all understand and know the dangers and the survival routines, you will all take turns in scouting duties."

Everyone listened intently. As this new leader explained, they would travel in the early morning and in the late afternoon and evenings when the roads would be safer. The route each day would be outlined and the scout would ride well ahead of the party using hand gestures to tell them to come forward; to hurry; to hide; to go back. Where possible, they would join the field and vineyard workers along the route for their lunch each day.

"Many people like us are fleeing the country. Those remaining are helping feed and hide the refugees along the route. When we join a vineyard work group, they will feed us and at the same time send a villager on to the next village to prepare them."

Pierre admitted reluctantly to himself that Alexander seemed to have prepared a well-organized plan - which he had explained with some degree of past experience. He caught Andre's eye and received a shrug of approval. He turned and looked at Suzanne and the shy smile she gave him made a warm jolt inside.

"I assume you have all eaten tonight...Yes?" He looked around the group and nodded. I think we should sleep in the borrie. It will be a little crowded but will protect us all from a heavy dew. Andre and ...Pierre, can you take turns outside on guard?" He received nods from the two men. "And we will wake you at just before daybreak; eat quickly; and set out for Grambois and La Bastide en route to Manosque. Good, then let's get organized for the night. We will need all the sleep we can get!"

Pierre agreed to take the first duty outside while Andre slept inside the entrance. Suzanne reached out and squeezed his hand before turning to make up her sleeping roll. Standing outside in the moonlight at the top of one of the paths, Pierre could hear the children's murmuring for about an hour before silence settled in for the night.

Little did he realize that this was to be one of the only nights when everyone felt secure and safe to sleep without fear.

*   *   *   *   *

CHAPTER ELEVEN

Vicar Zave coughed aloud several times and the gathering quieted down; people stopped their whispered conversations and turned to face the couple.

"Our help is in the name of the Lord, who made heaven and earth..." the Vicar's voice echoed throughout the large room and he went on in the traditional Reform wedding manner to describe God's making of man and woman.

Holding her small bouquet of pale mauve military orchids tightly in her damp palms, Isabeau turned her head slightly to glance at her groom standing beside her. His profile showed that his mouth was slightly open; beads of perspiration were shining on his brow and openly running down his cheeks and chin. Isabeau, seeing that Le Duc had a familiar glazed look around his eyes, felt her forehead furrow in a slight frown of frustration.

Why had he found it necessary to drink so heavily before the ceremony? Especially, someone who prided himself always as being very much in control of his life? She caught herself with a guilty start as she recognized the lines being spoken by the Vicar about St. Paul recommending that a marriage be an honourable estate...

"...likewise, let the wife see that she reverence her husband; and submit herself unto her own husband - as it is fit in the Lord...." Am I wrong, then, to look with critical eyes at my future husband? That is not the honourable thing for a new bride to do; or to think; Isabeau shook her head slightly and concentrated on the ceremony.

"... it is not to be entered into unadvisedly or lightly, but reverently, discreetly, and soberly, in the fear of God and with holy purpose." The Vicar broke his speech to take a breath. "...to live therein in all purity, according to His will." The Vicar paused dramatically in his reading of the ceremony from the black book he held and looked at the faces of his two subjects.

"Pierre and Isabeau. Are you willing to enter into the holy state of matrimony...? And, do you desire to make known here," he paused and looked around the room, "before God and this congregation, this, your purpose?"

"Yes!" Isabeau's voice whispered clearly in the quiet of the moment. Then she realized that they should have responded together!

But Le Duc had said nothing! The Vicar coughed loudly; looked at the groom and, leaning a little in his direction, whispered:

"Pierre!" The groom started, glanced around a little anxiously and spoke like someone waking up from a dream state.

"Err, Yes! Yes! Sorry...." The Vicar nodded, smiled at Isabeau, and continued with the prayer urging the Lord to bless the couple and influence their "affections and conduct throughout their lives..."

The Vicar, in an obvious effort to ensure that Le Duc remained aware of his obligations, made direct eye contact as he asked him to "promise to love, honour and protect his wife" as is the duty of a good husband, to which he dutifully responded.

It's like being in a dream of some kind, Isabeau thought. Like watching some other young maiden take her vows on a stage. Somehow, she did not feel like she was actually taking part in this ceremony.

A slight shiver of disappointment ran through her. She clenched her teeth slightly to re-gain control. This is not the honourable way to behave, Isabeau, she told herself, as the Vicar turned to her for her vows.

"Do you, Isabeau, also acknowledge here, before God and this congregation, that you have agreed to take, and that you now take, Pierre for your husband! Do you promise to love, honour and obey him; to comfort and cherish him, in health and in sickness, in joy and in sorrow, in prosperity and in adversity; to lead a holy life with him, being faithful unto him in all things as is the duty of a good wife, according to the word of God?" As Isabeau, who had been listening to every word, took a long breath, the silence in the room grew and even Le Duc turned slightly and peered at her.

"Yes!" she said clearly and with obvious determination. It seemed that everyone in the room - especially her father - seemed to relax   - and smile.

From then on, even Le Duc, seemed to have woken to the fact that they were embarking on a major journey in life. He smiled slightly as he slid the ring onto her left hand. Then the Vicar took both of their right hands in his and announced simply, "You are now Man and Wife!" After he had asked for God's blessing on the couple, he had added the Benediction. However, as he turned the two of them to face the gathering, they – untraditionally - broke into impulsive applause.

Her new mother-in-law, Marguerite came forward and fondly embraced her. She had made it clear for some time that she was going to cherish this new daughter-in-law.

Her new "father" gave her the traditional three-cheek kiss, his eyes filled with tears. Since she had been betrothed to his son he had learned to admire and respect her judgment. After her mother, Charlotte, her handmaiden, had hugged her in excitement, her own father finally made his way forward.

"I'm proud of you, my dear dear Isabeau!" he whispered in her ear. "But, not for this moment! I have always – and will always be proud of you!" Tears flooded her eyes and she hugged him in sheer joy.

"Father, you have been exactly the way I feel every father should be!" she whispered back. "However, I have set you up as a model for my new husband and I fear - I truly fear - that he will never reach that level of perfection...."

Her father glanced around the room quickly and then bent his head to whisper, "Be gentle, my daughter. And be patient. All young men need to grow - from experience they will learn - and you can help him with your patience..." They hugged again.

Her brother, Francis standing talking to the young men at the end of the room raised his voice:

"Time for the festivities, everyone! Good food and wine is outside in the street! Let us toast the couple; dance and have fun!" And with a roar of approval, the gathered crowd surged out the doorway and joined the other neighbors in the street.

The ceremony had been held in a neighbor's home because it possessed a large enough living room to hold the wedding party. Since the Temple in nearby La Motte d'Aigues had been destroyed in the name of the King many years ago, most wedding ceremonies had been held in local homes.

On the arm of her unsteady groom, Isabeau walked carefully into the middle of the street. She was relieved that no military presence had invaded her wedding ceremony. But they could still be expected to arrive at the street festivities and cause embarrassment and distress.

I must not worry about things that might not happen, she reminded herself. I will act confident and hope that I will be strong enough to deal with any problem that may arise. As she moved into a patch of shadow from an overhanging tree, she again felt the tug on her arm from her new husband – reminding her that he - not she - must take care of problems now!

*   *   *   *   *

Clarice Aubertin carefully touched her furrowed brow with the cloth she had used to whisk the flies that were hovering around the rich garlic sauce and glanced a little frantically up and down the groaning tables along one side of the square. She was proud that her daughter, Charlotte, had been chosen – even if a little late – to be the handmaiden to that lovely bride, Isabeau Richarde.

She allowed herself to feel a little bit pleased at the way that she and *Mme*. Charpentier from La Motte had been able to organize all the ladies in the two villages to provide so sumptuous a wedding feast.

She rubbed her aching back and straightened her spine with a sigh of relief. I know Charlotte will be pleased with our success, she thought. She was so worried at the delays in getting responses from some of the other mothers. Worried that there would not be enough to feed the two villages? And yet, look at that feast...

She walked slowly down the long heavily laden tables. It was just minutes before the bridal party would emerge into the street. And everything is just right! She waved her hand threateningly at several gaily-dressed youth that were trying to steal the legs of a wonderful roasted goose still steaming gently.

"Wait, you young piglets! Be gone!" She smiled at them as they dashed away to take their place in the growing line of males waiting to be introduced to the newly married couple who would take their place at the special table in the corner of the square.

Not three – but four yearling lambs – had been grilling over red coals while the drops of hot grease burst as they struck the embers. Three enormous pots of rabbit stew gently bubbled and sent up a rich scent flavored with local rosemary herbs. Covered bowls of hot vegetables richly flavored with herbs. Even some freshly cooked wild partridges.

At each corner of the square were barrels of specially selected local wine – both red and white – with spigots ready for filling the tankards and cups. She nodded as she checked to see that each table around the square also had its own tall toasting glass. Clarice smiled as she remembered the age-old "rule" which required any male guest who "wanted to leave the feast early" having to drink an enormous wine toast and how the merry crowd laughed as they watched the men choke as they struggled to "down" the contents.

Clarice smiled as she recognized village ladies arriving bearing baskets of freshly baked bread and baskets of many different local cheeses. She crossed the center of the square noting how carefully it had been swept clean and strewn with sprigs of freshly cut local herbs and flower petals. The scents of rosemary, thyme and parsley would rise up to twitch her nose as she crushed them with her dancing feet later.

As she stepped between the smaller tables on the edge of the square, she looked with pleasure at the bridal table which her daughter, Charlotte, had personally decorated. The table stood in the coolest corner of the square under shelter of an old olive tree. Behind the table a large mirror had been hung on the outside wall of an ancient home framed by an enormous heart made of peeled saplings and decorated with green boughs and early lilac blossoms and other colorful wild flowers. She tucked a pair of bright red poppies back in place.

She hurried over to the serving table and helped the four struggling men place the freshly roasted pig on the center spot of honour. Traditionally, a bright ripe orange had been placed in its mouth for luck. In all her long life, she could not remember any wedding feast without an orange for the poor pig. The rich fragrant smell of the roast pork was so tantalizing that she could not resist touching the slick flesh and licking her finger. Hmmm, she thought. Tonight, I think I am going to really enjoy this feast.

Clarice looked around the huge crowd that was gathering from her village of St. Martin and recognized some of their neighbors from La Motte and many other villages on the Luberon. Despite the plague of the Dragoons and all the worries of the attack on their religion, she wished that on this day they would forget their woes. She also hoped the military would stay away; and everyone would have fun.

Raised voices from around the corner made her forget her memories of weddings past and Clarice hurried to the corner of the square and peered into the next street.

They were coming. A small crowd of well-wishers had been standing outside a home waiting for the wedding party to open the door.

Standing with them she could see the famous musician, Paul Gaston - from Peypin d'Aigues on the top the ridge - raising his famous Provencal flute to his mouth as he thrust his snare drum to a safe position out of the way over his shoulder.

The trills of the wedding promenade filled the street as he began to walk down the middle of the dusty road toward the square. She had a glimpse of the bridal party forming behind the musician before she rushed back to ensure that the two young squires were standing in their traditional spots. Their honourable task was to take each family and introduce them to the newly married couple at the special table.

Her own young eight-year-old daughter, Rochelle was to escort the men; and young Marcel Duvall was to introduce the women. Both the children were wriggling with excitement as they too heard the bridal music echoing off the walls of the homes. She touched each to calm them down and hurried to the edge of the special table to make sure everything was satisfactory before handing over her responsibility to her daughter, Charlotte.

Suddenly, everything was perfect. The wind had cooperated with the sun and the weather was wonderful. Everyone was clapping the couple and their parents as they approached the table. Charlotte hurried up and hugged her mother in thanks for all the care she had taken. Breathless and with eyes wide open, the bride, Isabeau, smiled sweetly at Charlotte and nodded her head in thanks.

As the bridal party settled down the young children, Rochelle and Marcel began to bring the guests up and introduce them to the "new" *Monsieur* and *Madame* Mallan. Charlotte stood behind the bride with Le Duc Mallan's cousin, Paul, to add to the introductions where necessary.

Satisfied and also relieved, Clarice Aubertin quietly withdrew and stood behind her husband at a side table looking with silent joy at the gathering crowd of excited neighbors. Then with a start, she turned and trotted to the edge of the square and peered down the dusty road towards where the village of La Motte lay. She sighed with relief as she saw only groups of villagers striding purposefully down the road walking carefully to keep their good clothes clean.

No sign of the Dragoons – yet, she thought as she turned with relief towards the festivities. Now, to enjoy the wedding!

*　　　*　　　*　　　*　　　*

2nd July 1687
On the Luberon hillside, Provence.

The day on which Isabeau's wedding was to be held started with a bang. The black sky burst apart with a massive lightening flash and a thunderous roar which jolted all the refugees awake at about 3:00 o'clock in the morning. Little Jehanne broke into brief tears. Her oldest sister hugged her quiet. However, no rain fell and the group was relieved when the storm passed quickly. The clouds scudded away leaving a clear starlit sky.

Everyone was busy finding a place in their backpacks to stuff last minute items. In the darkness, each member shared bread and cheese with a dried apple for breakfast, as the mule was loaded. Pierre was pleased their preparations were carried out with a lack of fuss and worry – and so quickly.

David mounted the black horse and squirmed in the saddle as he made himself comfortable for the long morning's ride. Looking at the moonlit upraised faces, he grinned at their obvious apprehension and then, glancing over at the leader, Alexander, for his nod, he turned and trotted his horse down the path in the direction of the road to Manosque.

Within an hour, despite the stormy start, the day had proved to be bright and sunny. Now, this is going to be a great day for Isabeau to get married, thought Pierre and he smiled with a mixture of joy tinted with a touch of regret.

Both the villages of La Motte and St. Martin had suffered in restrained behaviors with the arrival of the Dragoons and really needed some relaxation and excitement. They would have a lot of fun with the wedding feast and the folk dancing and, as he trekked along the dusty road, he winced as he hoped that her partner, Le Duc Mallan would prove a better husband than he had been a single man.

Pierre remembered over the years being at a few festivals when Mallan's raucous humor and heavy drinking had been a nuisance. Maybe in the past couple of years he has settled down a little, Pierre thought pensively.

He was jolted out of his reverie by Alexander's urgent call to the group to get clear of the road and hide.

The party was strung out along the dusty roadway well sheltered by the overhanging trees with their self-appointed leader handling the laden mule. Peering ahead to the next rise, he could see David on the horse gesturing with his hand "to hide" as he hurried the horse off into the bush.

Andre had moved quickly ahead to alert Suzanne who was walking and talking to his young brother, Theodore, who grinned and flushed as he enjoyed the attention of an older pretty girl.

The couple slipped into the bush as Pierre ran past them in time to slap the mule on its rump, as it was being difficult about leaving the road. The animal, surprised by the slap, leapt forward and vanished dragging Alexander along with it. Pierre followed them in and stood next to the mule rubbing its soft nose to settle it down while the leader held the halter tightly under control. The fresh scent from the crushed thyme beneath their feet wafted upward. Once settled, Alexander led the mule further into the bush while Pierre crept back toward the road to check the scene.

Crouching low, he divided the green foliage between himself and the roadway in time to see a well-loaded mule cart escorted by several Dragoons.

Supplies, he thought. So far, the makeshift system of alarms seems to work, he thought with some chagrin. He crept back to the road and lying down in the short grass crawled up to its dusty edge. He watched the rear of the cart pass around a corner and raising his head, he saw that David had returned to the roadway on his horse and was waving them on safely.

He stood up and called softly. Slowly the party returned to the road looking disheveled and scared. Alexander arrived last with the mule and urged them to hurry to the next rise and await another "all clear" signal. However, he did remember to compliment them on their quick response and they set out in small groups showing renewed confidence.

Theodore grinned up at Suzanne. "We beat the Dragoons, didn't we? It's like a game, isn't it?" She smiled back and nodded.

"We should be close to Grambois soon," Alexander called out, "and, when we get alongside, we will send someone up to the village to find where the refugee group are hiding and join up with them. Keep things tight!"

As they turned the corner, David ahead waved back indicating safety. Pierre and Andre brought up the rear, walking easily together and discussing the wedding they would be missing. But Pierre found it hard to concentrate on the discussion. Despite the carefully prepared alarm system, he felt something was missing. It was when he found himself glancing back over his shoulder for the third time that it struck him. There was not protection from the rear!

"I'll be back!" he called to Andre as he jogged up past the walkers to where Alexander was leading the mule.

"Alexander, I think we've missed something!" Alexander frowned but kept walking as he scanned the line from David on the horse ahead and back to Andre in the rear.

Then he frowned, and said in a low voice, "Pierre – I know you expected to lead this escape party but I want you to know that I know what I am doing! So, all I can ask is that you ...trust me ...and we will talk about your concerns ...tonight!"

He turned away and jerked the lead to the mule that had slowed down. Pierre stopped and stood astounded with his mouth slightly open. Then he frowned and followed the leader. But he continued in a low firm voice: "Listen, Alexander, it looks like we are protected from the front; but we have nothing to protect us from Dragoons coming up behind us!"

He saw the man's head jerk slightly as he continued walking away. Then he stopped, turned and raised his head in a commanding way.

"Pierre, I think it would be a good idea if you...or Andre...maybe, hang back at each turn in the road. Your partner should be behind the last member of the group and watching for your signals. Hand signals, yelling - if appropriate; or sharp whistling to warn your partner." He spoke in a loud authoritative voice – as though Pierre had never raised the issue. "Better get on to it right away!" Then he turned away again and led the mule down the road.

Pierre stood in the road, a wry smile breaking out slowly wiping the frown from his forehead. I don't believe it, he thought, all I made was a suggestion! He turned to meet Andre who finally caught up to him.

"What's the new strategy, Pierre? What does Alexander want us to do now?"

Pierre explained the additional system and Andre nodded.

"I'll take the first turn, Andre. You watch for my signals and warn the others!"

They began immediately at the next turn in the road with Pierre waiting in a position to be able to look backward a good distance and Andre keep checking as he followed the others. It seems like our leader is not as sure of himself as he pretends, Pierre thought as he watched the dust settle on the road. This early in the morning the road was deserted but they all knew that this would soon change.

Like many ancient villages in need of protection, Grambois had grown high on a little hill, its stone buildings shining in the breakfast sun. Between the batches of trees and bush on the slopes were small patches of gardens. A stony road winding its way up the steep hillside clung grimly to the ancient yellowed cliffs. Small wisps of smoke rose from some of the chimneys as breakfast was being prepared. David found the group a safe hiding place in a tight copse of trees from which they could watch the road and the village.

Suzanne had dropped onto the grass and removed her shoes and was busy massaging her feet. She smiled up at Pierre as he crouched down opposite her. The Deleman family grouped together drinking from a water bottle.

"Phew! I am not used to early morning exercise...but I feel good – except my feet!" Suzanne turned her head gracefully and smiled down at Theodore who was lying flat on his back looking up at the morning sky. "My brave companion, Theodore, has been doing a fine job of both protecting me and entertaining me as well."

Theodore flushed – but grinned at Pierre – and rolled over on to his stomach to hide his confusion.

"Good for you, Theodore," he grinned at the boy whose blush had reached round to his ears tips. He glanced back at Suzanne. "What's happening now?"

Suzanne gestured at the mule tied to the branch nearby.

"Alexander has sent David into Grambois on his trusty steed to contact the local Elder's family and make arrangements for their group to meet us somewhere up ahead," she waved in the direction of the village "and Alexander has gone to the bottom of the roadway to wait for him."

Pierre frowned a little and then stopped by the Deleman family to check with each of them. Blushing, Catherine admitted that she had enjoyed the walk so far but was still a little scared at being captured. Her sister, Francoise, glanced scornfully at her older sister and brushed aside her fears, "My sister worries about everything...it is like being on a herb-picking trip!" The youngest, Jehanne, smiled shyly and nodded her head seriously, "I'm all right." The mother, Claudine, nodded her head while she rubbed her back and winced.

"Thank you for asking about me!" She rolled her eyes at her husband who was leaning against the trunk of a tree enjoying his pipe. "But, it makes me realize I am older than I thought I was!" Henri Deleman removed his pipe and nodded at his wife, "You haven't aged a year since I married you! Still like my blushing bride!" They both smiled at each other fondly while the girls exchanged glances and grinned. A nice family, thought Pierre.

He pushed his way through the shrubs until he could safely view the village and the road. The horse with David had vanished into the village.

Further down the road, Alexander had reached the junction and had stopped under a large tree and appeared to be studying the ground at his feet. He bent and seemed to be picking up things from the ground.

Probably, last year's nuts, thought Pierre. He looked back up at Grambois. A pretty little village, he remembered. Several years ago, he had gone to attend a sheep sale and his mouth watered as he remembered eating freshly baked bread in the early morning.

He glanced backward as Andre pushed through the brush and crouched with him.

"Anything happening?"

"Nothing much. David is in the village. Alexander is waiting down there," he pointed and noticed that their leader was still picking objects up from the dusty road corner.

"What's he doing?" Andre queried.

"Don't know. Maybe getting nuts for his lunch?"

"He is pretty sure of himself, isn't he?" queried Andre with a frown. "He hides us in the bushes and then stands out there! Oh well..." and he turned away and vanished into the shrubbery. Pierre's frown remained, as he stood there puzzled. Then he saw David on his horse trotting out of the village and down the road to join Alexander at the junction. After a short conversation, David pointed to the north up the road to Manosque and then cantered his horse down the road towards the hiding place. Shrugging his shoulders, Pierre turned and re-joined the others.

Swiftly the group hurried down the road that bypassed Grambois and a short while later pulled off the road to meet the next small group of refugees in the woods.

The escapees from Grambois comprised the Gervaise family with two nine-year-old twin blonde girls, Nicole and Nadine, with their father, Isaac, a mason. He related that his wife had died two years ago. Accompanying them were a brother and sister, Joseph and Rochelle Daillon, in their early twenties.

A couple of uneventful hours later, the group safely arrived at the village of La Bastide-des-Jourdans. It had been arranged that at noon the group of refugees would join the workers hoeing the vineyards where they were provided with lunch. In this way the group could be fed and at the same time, would not be noticed by people traveling by.

While the children played in the trees, the adults worked alongside the villagers of La Bastide. Five more had joined the party. Two single young men, Pierre's age, Daniel Carle and Thomas Brunet, both laborers; and the Claude family, Theodore, a wine dealer, and his wife Laverne Coulan carrying their two year old son, Albert.

"The party is now big enough. Any more would make us conspicuous," announced Alexander. "With luck, we should be in Geneva in twelve to fifteen days! We will sleep in Manosque tonight." He took some time to explain to the newcomers, the rules for safety on the road and appointed experienced travelers to take the initial posts of responsibility. "We will change you from time to time so that you all understand how we can keep ourselves safe."

He had David check the road before mounting his horse and Alexander stood on the side of the road positioning the groups as they hurried into their convoy.

"You, Pierre and Andre, is it?" Andre nodded his head to Alexander; "You take up the rearguard patrol as you did before. We will change you later on." He turned and leading his pack mule trudged off up the dusty road.

Pierre clapped his friend on the back raising a small cloud of pale yellow dust. Then he walked backward down the road until he could see around the corner. He turned and waved to Andre before peering alertly into the distance. I wonder how safe we really are, Pierre mused?

*   *   *   *   *

2nd July 1687
The Wedding at St. Martin

I have really entered a different world, Isabeau thought, as she turned to smile at her replacement bridesmaid, Charlotte, who was standing behind her at the wedding table. Charlotte looks lovelier than I have ever seen her before. The touch of Italian blood in her veins really gives her a beautiful sunny natural tan. Isabeau found it hard to concentrate being the center of such lavish attention.

Myriads of thoughts were rushing through her mind and she needed to pay careful attention to what she said and did.

I am now a married woman – for better or worse! Better I hope...? No! Better I will make it! I must learn to handle my life differently! I hope my husband manages to shake himself out of this stupor that he is in. Maybe encourage him to eat some food. No more wine for awhile: but how to do that without angering him?

"Let me introduce the Courteen family from La Motte – and their daughter, and my friend, Lizette." Pretty little Rochelle was introducing a newly arrived set of guests to her and Le Duc. Concentrate! Touch your husband's arm to get his attention – but gently.

"Le Duc, the Courteens!"

Le Duc seemed to rouse himself and thrust out his hand. "Of course, Jacob and his beautiful wife. Welcome to the festivities!" He grinned at the little girl. "Are you going to drive all the little boys mad in that new dress, Lizette?" She blushed and clung to her mother but seemed overjoyed to be given special attention. The parents beamed and wished them good health and luck before turning away to join friends at the nearby table. Lizette turned and grinned back at Le Duc who pointed his finger at her and winked.

Good, thought Isabeau with some relief. Just try to keep him on a straight road for the rest of the afternoon. Something to eat for both of us. She turned and Charlotte responded immediately. She described the menu for the feast and after both the couple placed their orders, she rushed away to fill their plates. A heavy plate for the husband and a small bit of everything for the bride.

*   *   *   *   *

With some good Luberon food in him and a little wine to help the meal, Le Duc's control was rapidly improving, thought Isabeau, as she carefully wiped a little gravy from her lips. Several times during the meal, the crowd had roared for the bridal kiss. With much of his usual gusto, her husband had obliged, embarrassing her with the length of the kiss. She was relieved when she noticed that while his presence still smelt of brandy, his lips now tasted of roast lamb.

She realized now that once she admitted that things had changed in her life – that she was married to Le Duc – she had begun to feel she was again handling herself better.

Long rambling speeches had been made by her new father by-marriage; her own father had been short but so sincere that tears had sprung to her eyes.

A surprise event, without her knowledge, was a group of the young unmarried males in the two villages had written a song about her which they had sung with great enthusiasm – but limited musical ability. With some truth, it had listed all the beaus she had turned down when offered romance - and how distraught they all were! To show their remorse, the entire group – plus many others in the audience – proceeded to howl and wipe their eyes in their misery. The gathering loved it and cheered the performance.

Le Duc rose and turned to her. As she stood up, he picked up her hand and raised it high.

"Of course," his voice rang through the courtyard, "in the end...you, Isabeau, sweetheart of Luberon, married the *Best!*" to the roars from the crowd. Isabeau smiled openly up at her groom and nodded her head. "The Best!" she repeated.

Under the hot afternoon sun, the gathering really enjoyed their wedding feast. All were relieved that the Dragoons had not made an appearance - yet! It reminded them all of the joy and peace they had all enjoyed on the Luberon mountain range for so many years.

Some of the men eating with their families had had to leave to take care of farming duties with their flocks of sheep and watering of gardens. There was much excitement from the crowd as the men tried to slip away unnoticed. Neighboring tables, however, demanded a special toast of wine be drunk, to the bridal party. Before the farmer departed, they quickly pounced upon him. It was obvious to many that they had "expected" to be caught because they put up only token resistance. They were dragged back, the huge glass on each table was filled to the brim and they had to empty it to the last drop! The successful men banged the empty glass down on the table to the roars of the crowd. The less successful spilt most of the wine down their shirt-front and apologized to the bridal couple with wine still spilling from their open mouths.

As the sun slowly sank toward the horizon, the musician from Peypin d'Aigues, Paul Gaston, rose and strolling to the end of the open square, raised his Provencal three-holed flute to his ready mouth. Isabeau never failed to be amazed at his ambidexterity. She watched as he held the instrument in his outer two fingers of his left hand and piped the tune with the middle three fingers. His right hand hung free to keep time beating the *tabor*, a snare drum, hanging from a strap in the crook of his flute arm. The quickly lilting tune floated around the warm square and people sitting at the tables began to beat their hands in time with the catchy rhythm.

"Oh, good!" whispered Isabeau, "It's *La Farandole!*" The traditional folk dance was always used to start weddings and festivals for probably one hundred years since it was first danced at Arles. The round chain-like dance allowed everyone – especially the men in the villages - to show off their styles.

"They are waiting for us, my bride!" Le Duc stood up and held out his hand. Isabeau smiled up at him as she rose and let herself be led out to the center of the square.

Her long green wedding dress, delicately embroidered with large white daisies around the hem swayed gracefully from her trim hips. The dress fitted tightly at the waist and emphasized her firm breasts. A fine lace shawl was looped over her shoulders and joined at the waist with a broach. Charlotte had rolled her hair up into a knot on the top of her head and capped it with a delicate white lace ribbon that flew down the back.

Everyone kept time with clapping as Le Duc proudly paraded his bride around in a circle before grandly waving the other couples to join up in a chain behind him. Le Duc had danced this number many times and loved the control it gave him as the leader.

He gave his left hand to Isabeau and placed his right hand on his hip. She in turn held his hand with her right and gave her left to the next dancer – making each dancer in the chain face the opposite way. Soon everyone was facing different ways and chained together as Le Duc led them through a series of traditional designs. The "Snail" design wound the chain into a smaller and smaller circle and then led them out again. In the "Bridge of Avignon" design, the bridegroom, held Isabeau's hands, to form a bridge for people to pass through; they then created further arches behind them. And, finally, the "Maze" in which he turned and ducked under Isabeau's arms and then turned and led the chain under the next upraised arm until the whole body of dancers braided themselves in an intricate design.

Finally, he threw up his arms and hugged Isabeau and everyone crowded around and applauded.

"Oh, Le Duc, you did the dance so well!" She complimented him as he led her back to the wedding table.

"Dancing is always wonderful – and today, with you, it's very special!" he gasped as sweat ran down his face. "I need a little rest and we can watch the others in the next dance."

She nodded as she settled herself and the musician, Paul, changed the tune. As they recognized the lilting air, young girls and men ducked under their tables and held their objects in the air to the cries of pleasure from the older women – the men held baskets of flowers and the girls held up saplings gaily plaited with colorful local flowers.

"Oh good, Le Duc – they are going to dance "*Li Jardiniero*" – I haven't seen that for a long time!" Isabeau clutched his arm in excitement, "I think it was when my father and I attended a festival in Apt – the "garden" dance..."

The crowd of excited young people formed into couples; and the couples into two lines. The women bent the hoops of flowers to form an arch over their heads. They began singing "*Sinai to it gento jardinie – ro Que n'a ven...*" as they moved to the tune. They did a polka step as they danced to the side of their partners and reversed, then moved as couples in a circle; then the girls formed a circle with the first male in the middle and the men on the outside. Then, with another girl, they formed arches with their flowered wands and the men ducked through. Then each girl gave one end of the wand to the single man in the center and they all circled forming a flowered merry-go-round. After circling several times, they gracefully returned to their lines and finished by singing the song again. The whole gathering roared its approval when the beautiful dance ended.

"Did you see that, Isabeau," whispered Charlotte from behind, "not a single mistake – that must be some sort of a record, *non?*"

"Yes, beautifully done! We should dance the garden-dance more often!"

*   *   *   *   *

3rd July 1687
Outside Manosque on the Durance River

Pierre stood in the deep shadow of the huge door of an ancient stone barn peering out in the late afternoon sunshine. Behind him he could hear the muffled voices of the group as they prepared to get to sleep for another early start on the road to Geneva. Gervaise, the mason from Grambois was trying to settle an argument between his nine-year-old twin girls, each raising the stakes as they quarreled. He felt a grin appear as he listened with one ear while he searched the countryside outside for danger.

The group had been directed to the farm by a church elder in Manosque. They were isolated enough on the farm located up a small ridge but close enough to be convenient in reaching the road north towards their next destination, Sisteron.

To the left, the worn path led from the barn to the ancient stone farm home with a whisper of smoke floating from the chimney. From this elevation, he could see the deserted dusty road down the hillside until it vanished in the trees. Safe, in that direction!

To the right another worn path led through a grove of olive trees towards the stream that meandered and splashed down the hillside. Before bed, Pierre wished to drink some cool water, wash himself and relieve himself. Seems safe, he murmured and slipped quietly out of the protective shadow and crossed quickly to the safety of the olive orchard.

I hate this constant need for vigilance, he thought. I'll be eternally glad when we finally reach safety in the cantons of the Swiss and can stop having to live on half-breaths.

A couple of birds broke cover with an explosion of wings and startled him into freezing his movement. He remained in his stance until all was quiet except the whispering rustle of the olive leaves as the late sun dappled the path ahead with broken shadows.

He moved quietly down the dusty little path until he saw the wink of glittering water cascading gently over the rocks and heard the refreshing murmur of the stream. Pierre glanced around again before kneeling at the edge of a little pool. Bending his head, he cupped his hands and rinsed them well before dropping his mouth to suck in the clean taste of mountain water.

He was still swallowing when rough and firm hands grasped both his shoulders and his body was forced backward to lie in the crushed wild herb-covered bank. In a panic, he was only able to spit the water out before his mouth was covered tightly by a hand.

Two burly men in Dragoon uniforms were pinning him helplessly on his back. They used their bodies to keep his hips tightly controlled as his feet kicked uselessly. Looking over their shoulders he saw another figure emerge from the bush on the other side of the stream and stand in the darkness of shadow peering at him.

"Well, my Cousin, it looks as though we have you at our mercy!" The figure jumped over the stream and landed at his feet. The hand was removed from his mouth as he stared with relief; but still mystified; at the fact that his cousin, Renard, was wearing a Dragoon uniform! The two troopers released his shoulders moved away to the side.

"Renard, what are you doing in that!" Pierre gestured towards the uniform.

"Oh that! Can you think of another disguise that would be better for fooling the enemy?" Renard grinned down at him.

"Hmm...you scared the Hades right out of me!" He sat up and brushed the broken weeds from his chest. "Still, it's good to see you again. It seems like weeks since I saw you last – what's been happening in your world since then...?"

Renard settled himself down carefully on the bank and grinned at his cousin:

"Well, Pierre, I've seen you daily – but from a safe distance."

"What? What do you mean?"

"Well, that's the reason we are meeting like this. There is something really mystifying going on and we thought we should meet to discuss this problem." He paused as Pierre stared across at him, waiting patiently.

"We decided – with the village elders' wisdom – to act as your 'Guardian Angels' until you were safely across the border. We were going to trail behind you; but allow you to act independently so as not to reduce your strength as a team...to let you run your own show; and you are all doing very well!" He paused and then nodded in support, "There will be other parties after yours and the elders felt that you needed to develop a practice that others will use later."

"Well, it's good to know that we have 'angels' at our back! But, what's the mystery?"

"Well, Pierre, if you think you are safe, you are not! Although you are not aware of it, there is a troop of Dragoons, dogging your trail ever since you left the village!"

"What! That's madness!" Pierre sat up, his face in a frown. "We have been so careful. And, why have they not moved in and captured us? We are refugees, escaping; and under the King's orders, we are 'Royal game', are we not?"

"That's why we are checking with you! That's the mystery! You see, Pierre, they seem to be watching you, careful not to be close enough so that you are alerted; but always shadowing you!" He paused and grinned at his shocked cousin, "It's really quite amusing...they are following and observing you; and we are watching them. It's a funny game," he paused and pondered the situation. "In fact, it seems to me that as long as you don't know they are there, you are probably safe. I can't help wondering what their game is though – it's mysterious, isn't it?"

Renard rose to his feet and extended his hand, which Pierre grasped firmly.

"Pierre, you keep this a secret – maybe discuss it with your friend, Andre – but not the others! And, we will find a way of meeting with you when we are able. Not too often. And, between us, we should be able to come up with an answer to the mystery, Eh?"

He broke away, jumped the stream easily and with a casual wave of his hand, silently slipped back into the bushes. Pierre stood and stared at the moving brush without hearing any parting footsteps. Just like a sly fox, he grinned and then turned and carefully moved back up the path, the flashes of broken late afternoon sunlight speckling the little frown on his forehead. What's going on?

*   *   *   *   *

4th July 1687
At Peyruis on the Durance River bank

A smattering of light cloud had provided some relief from the strong July sunshine as the small group of refugees entered the dramatic stone gateway of the ancient town of Peyruis on the banks of the mighty Durance. The regal 14th and 15th century massive stone houses reared their ancient facades and added to the shade of the old plane trees providing the party of refugees with a gentle coolness.

Laverne Coulan, Theodore Claude's wife, stopped gratefully at an ancient fountain and used her hand to scoop cool crystal-clear water into her warm and parched mouth.

Choosing a passing elder woman carrying a basket of freshly picked herbs, Andre explained that Laverne was feeling ill and they wished to locate a woman who was familiar with herb treatments.

"Oh, yes," the woman smiled with understanding at the sick refugee and waved down the cobbled roadway. "Widow Fleury – at the green door over there," she gestured towards the right side of the street, "is highly regarded for the ailments of women."

She nodded at his thanks and smiling, went off into a side street.

The small group had separated from the main party early in the day. This had arisen because Theodore, Laverne's husband had grumbled as he toted his baby son, Albert, on his back as they left their overnight camp at Manosque early that morning.

"She's feeling ill," he had gestured at Laverne who was bending over as she walked behind him, "Does not feel strong enough to care for our son. What can we do?"

Alexander had clicked his tongue in frustration. "Is this going to be an ongoing problem, Theo? It's not a good idea to try to find a Doctor – it will draw attention to our travels, surely?"

"She has been a little sickly since the baby was born," he murmured, "she usually rests for a day and recovers – but we cannot rest now."

Overhearing the conversation, Andre broke in and suggested seeking out a mid-wife at the next village and Alexander reluctantly agreed.

"When we get near Peyruis, the party can join the field workers for a lunch break and I will escort *Mme.* Claude and you two," he waved, indicating Andre and Pierre, "and I will wait outside the gate – by the signposts – to keep watch for trouble. You two, can see if you can find …some treatment for her." He gestured to the father, Theo; "You will need to look after your son. Is that alright?" Theodore nodded with obvious relief and turned to pass the information on to his wife.

*   *   *   *   *

When they stopped in the fields outside Peyruis, young Theo had also rushed to join the party as they began their trek into the town. The lad had been upset at being separated from his older brother and reluctantly, Alexander agreed to let him join the party – but only if he waited outside the town. "The less people on the streets of a strange town, the less they are noticed…" and Theo nodded his head.

*   *   *   *   *

The Widow Fleury had been cautious and a little suspicious as she observed the three strangers through the door that was slightly ajar. At hearing their request, she looked carefully at the woman and then opened the door and gestured them inside.

"You have not yet recovered from childbirth, my dear," she nodded, a caring note suddenly entering her voice.

"I think that is what is wrong, *Madame*," Laverne whispered as she crossed her hands over her stomach.

"Come – all of you sit in here," she led them down a dark passage into a sunlit sweet-smelling kitchen. She turned and regarded them all carefully, "You are strangers to Peyruis?" The two men looked at each other and back at Laverne who now sat leaning on the scarred wooden table.

"Are you running away...it's alright...I am of the Reformed faith as well. Well?" Pierre nodded and the widow broke into a wide smile.

"If you are running away, then...you need ...special help! And quickly, without a lot of questions from a curious old widow..." She turned and took a flask from the shelf.

"Here, you men can have a cup of my famous mead. Everyone in the village loves it! I will take this lady to the bedroom and ask her some questions. Just to make sure that I am not missing any special signs." She whisked Laverne out with her and up the stairs into the darkness.

Both men were enjoying the excellent mead when the widow returned in a few minutes.

"Yes. I can help her. She has taken a special potion and needs to rest for a while." She gestured up the stairs. "The pain will be eased greatly ... soon ... and I have given her a supply to take on the journey with her."

As Pierre rose to his feet and drew out his moneybag, she waved her hands in the air. "No – no money! It's nothing! I am too old a lady to escape. But for people of my Reformed faith, I can at least do something to help!" she paused and then sat down, "I will however, share a cup of mead with two handsome young men while you tell me what has been happening in your village."

Pierre and Andre were overwhelmed with the noticeable difference in Laverne when she returned to the kitchen. She was walking upright and smiling as she gestured to the earthenware flask she carried in her hand. "It's like magic...and thank you so much, Widow Fleury!" She hugged the old lady who brushed aside the gratitude.

*   *   *   *   *

Theo was obviously overjoyed as he saw the three travelers come through the gate of Peyruis and despite the gestures of Alexander, he rushed to meet them.

One look at Laverne was enough to reassure Alexander that the journey could be continued. He walked ahead down the dusty road in the direction of where the group was hiding. Theodore grasped his brother's hand and swung along between the two friends.

When they turned off the road and into the bushes, everyone in the party rose and gathered around them to ask about Laverne's condition. Relieved, they began to gather their packsacks and belongings and Alexander took control and set out positions for their convoy.

Pierre was surprised to find Theodore clutching his elbow and looked down at the serious face of the boy.

"Pierre," he looked around anxiously, "Our leader, Alexander, has been...building castles again."

"Castles?"

"Yes...I don't know what it means...but he was doing the same thing outside the village of Grambois. You know, building a little castle – by the signposts." He glanced around anxiously and said, "I thought you ought to know. Is that alright?"

"Hmm, yes, it's alright, I think." He hesitated and picked up his packsack. "Thank you, Theodore, for telling me. I don't know what it means also, but...perhaps it would be better if you don't mention it to anyone else. I will tell your brother, is that alright?" Theodore nodded and grinned.

"I'll have to hurry now, Pierre; I want to catch up to Suzanne." And he dashed away through the brush.

Pierre shrugged on his pack and walked out cautiously onto the road to join Andre in their rearguard watch. That's a curious pastime, he thought, and a mysterious behavior for a leader like Alexander.

*   *   *   *   *

CHAPTER TWELVE

Everyone seems to be really having a lot of fun, thought Isabeau as she smilingly watched the happy crowd. Suddenly, an unusual raucous beat began to fill the air and everyone looked at the musician. Paul had been joined by "Old Pierre" Porvier from Merinidol – down-river. As he played his instrument he waved it high in the air.

"A hurdy-gurdy," exclaimed Le Duc, with sudden interest. "I have never seen one in this area. I wonder where he dug that up from...?"

Suddenly an ominous hush filled the square and the music died out.

"*Mon Dieu*! Where did they come from?" Le Duc groaned. Isabeau's eyes flashed around the square. Twelve – no, sixteen Dragoons, armed with swords had suddenly appeared from seemingly nowhere. They had evidently come unnoticed through alleys and were spaced in a careful protective arc covering the whole circle of the wedding area.

The ominous silence was broken as both old and young men sprang up in response and began to move unarmed towards the soldiers.

"Stop! Wait!" Le Duc's Uncle had risen to his feet, "I will pay them to go away and leave the wedding in peace." The village men hesitated and looked at the wedding table for leadership. "Good work, Uncle, good idea!" Nodding in agreement, Le Duc slowly returned to his seat. The Uncle strode toward the senior soldier and talked with him but was brushed aside impatiently. The soldier looked towards the end of the square for guidance. All eyes turned in that direction.

There stood the Captain in a flamboyant dress uniform, the large feathered plume in his hat waving in the breeze.

"Payment? Ridiculous!" The Captain touched his delicate white handkerchief to his nose and removed his hat with a flourish as he bowed to the bride's table. "We have come to honour the bride! I regret to say that our invitation has not yet been received...a mistake, perhaps."

A low rumble moved through the ranks of the gathering and men began to move forward.

"Enough! Enough!" Isabeau's father had climbed onto a table, "We forget ourselves. Remember friends, this is Provence! We are famous for our hospitality!" he waved his hand around the circle. "If they will put their swords away, let every table make room for a guest. Feed them and give them lots to drink."

Noting the hesitation at some tables, he continued, "Since they haven't the wisdom to follow our excellent religion, perhaps we can demonstrate to them how real Christian people behave..."and his smile covered every table.

Quickly there was space made and, at the Captain's lazy nod, the Dragoons joined the gathering and slid their weapons under the tables.

The tune for a new dance rose above the slowly rising hum of conversation. Isabeau's father, M. Richarde, had himself gone and invited the Captain to the parents' table. Before the Captain sat, however, he turned and wandered over to the bride's table.

Isabeau had been reaching for her fallen serviette and as she raised her head, she met the languid gaze of the Captain.

Startled, she became flustered, "Captain? Hmm... welcome ... to my wedding?"

Enjoying her confusion, he waved his handkerchief lazily in the air. "I wish to honour the lovely bride...and the timing is right...I think I hear the lilt of my favorite dance," he turned and touched his ear as if listening. "I was right! It is the zesty and exciting *La Volto*, is it not?" And he bowed gracefully to her and as he rose, he extended his hand in invitation.

Isabeau felt herself flushing. Of all the dances, this was the one she should have danced only with her new husband. It was one of the most lively and energetic but also notorious for its intimate embrace. She well remembered that some disgusting older men, under the guise of failing physical strength, often fumbled their holds on their young female partners and grasped their breasts. And, of course, they always apologized profusely!

She glanced at her husband, hoping that he would recognize her entrapment and, with good humor, apologize to the Captain and claim the privilege as the Groom's – as was his entitlement on this, his wedding day. Disappointment struck home as Le Duc grinned from ear to ear and waved his hand – in consent!

Turning slowly, she rose to her feet and touched his hand slightly in acceptance before stepping back and coming alone around the end of the bridal table.

"I will be honoured, Captain," as she now gave him her hand and he led her slowly through the upturned – somewhat bemused – faces. Men's faces were grim; women's were shocked or embarrassed; the children's faces were innocently pleased and smiling.

A circle of couples was gathering in the dance area and the Captain led Isabeau to her position. He placed her with a grand gesture and faced her. Then he turned and took the traditional stance with his hands on her waist as she faced him and she slowly placed her hands on his shoulders. In this close proximity, he smiled lazily at her then dropped his gaze to her breasts, which he seemed to examine carefully. Isabeau felt her face flush at this distinct lack of politeness.

The dance started and the partners performed the balance movements forward and backward accompanied by turns. Isabeau felt angry feelings in her chest.

So, you think you have me at a disadvantage, you Catholic pig, she thought, I will dance like I have never danced this before!

]

She readied herself for the grand leap. A woman slips her right hand round the man's neck from behind to keep her safe; while with her free hand, she controls the height that her skirt rises as she flies through the air. The partner, putting his left arm around her waist, grasps her hip and swings her high in the air while his right hand is supposed to hold her firmly against the stiff busk below her breasts.

Determined now, Isabeau really enjoyed the high upward flight – her skirts rising displaying her many petticoats and legs. She was prepared for the drop to the ground and - as expected - the "accidental" slip of his hand on her waist allowed him to fondle her breast. She froze! The roar of enjoyment from the onlooking crowd encouraged the dancers to swing their partners even higher the next time.

As the final notes played, Isabeau breathed to herself; at last it is over! He has had his fun but somehow I will make him suffer for it, she promised. Inside she was cool and determined. I have never danced the "turn" dance - so well - or so gracefully, she thought fiercely.

Covered by the roar of approval from the crowd watching, the dancers left the floor. But the Captain held her back slightly as he whispered: "In my area of France, I have ...the right of ...the old Aristocracy...I think, left over from the Medieval days... if I remember rightly...where I could bed the new bride... before – or despite – her husband's needs!" He smiled down at her with a lecherous twitch to his lips, "Oh, how I would enjoy you!"

After his disgusting behavior in the dance, Isabeau was prepared for his remarks and smiled back with confidence, as she replied: "Don't underestimate the strength of the girls of Provence, Captain Benoit. As a young bride, I would probably push pins into your eyes as you slept afterwards – and enjoy it too!" He had obviously expected confusion and embarrassment but she was pleased to see his mouth fall open in evident shock as his face turned white.

"Thank you for the dance. There won't be another today!" she smiled sweetly and, without allowing him to return her to her seat in the traditional manner, she turned to walk back to the bride's table touching hands of children and receiving compliments from the adults.

When she turned to sit down, the Captain was still standing in the middle of the dance area staring at her. Finally, he wiped his face with his handkerchief and wandered on his way to the edge of the square looking somewhat shaken.

"I never knew you could dance 'La Volto' like that!" whispered Le Duc. "I have never seen it danced so well before – anywhere!" Then he paused thoughtfully, "But ...what did you say to the honourable Capitaine...he seems like someone took the wind from his sails – or is it old age creeping on...?"

"Oh?" Isabeau smiled slightly, "It's probably old age – or maybe...he has been taking us Provencal girls for granted?" And she turned round to talk to Charlotte.

* * * * *

Ahead, the late afternoon sun lit up the fortified 16th century fortress, La Citadelle, crowning the City of Sisteron which had protected the city for a hundred years.

A stranger surprised Pierre, coming out of the bushes on the side of the road. However, Pierre, on looking up the road at his own separated group, quickly realized the man had mistaken them for groups attending the festival now occurring in this village.

After stopping to chat for a few minutes to prevent any suspicion from arising, Pierre nodded thanks to the man who continued his journey south to Manosque. Quickening his steps, he caught up with Alexander and passed on the information.

"Hmm, that's good. We already have a contact in Sisteron who has a large warehouse where we can sleep overnight and be fed. The festival will cover our entrance very well." Alexander waved his hand in the direction of Andre who was waiting on the last rise in the road behind.

"Thank you, Pierre, you can wait for your partner," and he continued leading his mule up the dusty road along the banks of the Durance towards Sisteron.

*   *   *   *   *

Inside the huge warehouse crates of goods had been pushed back and stacked against the walls to make room for the travelers. They had enjoyed a fine Dauphin stew with crusty bread and local fruit and were getting settled for sleep using piles of sacks stacked in the corner for mattresses. Even the thick walls of the warehouse could not keep out the lively music of the Festival as the locals danced and sang in the streets.

For once, Pierre enjoyed some quiet time with Suzanne because Theodore was engaged quietly in the corner playing a solitaire game with a pile of pebbles. He had been taught by the older youth who had used the game to while away lonely hours as a shepherd.

Pierre sat down beside her in a private nook between two crates and reached for her hand. Suzanne glanced anxiously at the other folk as they prepared their children for bed and seeing that they were not being noticed, leaned against him and smiled shyly.

"I'm afraid we don't get much time together ... for a couple who are betrothed?" she whispered.

"Not as much as I would like," he whispered back. "My competitor," he nodded in the direction of Theodore, "for your attention, gets a great deal more, doesn't he?"

"Oh Pierre, he is really so sweet!" She dug a finger into Pierre's ribs, a little cautiously, "I always wanted to have... a little brother...and, now I have." She started a little as he bent to awkwardly kiss her neck. "Pierre! That scares me!" She turned slightly away from him. Then seeing his disappointed reaction, she reached her other hand out to touch him on the shoulder and smiled anxiously. "Remember Pierre, I never had much training about...what people do when they are betrothed!"

Pierre felt the flush reach up his neck and warm his cheeks. Awkwardly, he whispered back, "That's alright, Suzanne, but ...maybe we should find time to ...practice a little...?"

Before she could reply, the outer sounds of revelry rose. Pierre looked up to see two young men of their party gently opening the door of the warehouse. With a quick guilty glance backward they slipped out and closed the door behind them.

A glance told him that Alexander was sound asleep in the far corner. His mouth quirked wryly as he remembered that their leader had been firm about not leaving the safety of the warehouse until early dawn. He knew how much the sounds of fun outside had challenged all members of the group – especially the younger children.

"Better take a look and see what the boys are up to outside," he whispered to Suzanne as he rose to his knees and rested his head against her shining dark hair in a note of affection, "I won't be a minute!" He stood up and crossed to the door quietly closing it behind him as he stood in the darkness of the doorway. As he walked down the little alley to the main street, the cheers of the dancing couples and the spectators watching them made him completely miss the sound of a door opening and closing behind him.

*   *   *   *   *

In the flickering light of the decorative lanterns hanging from the walls of houses, the *La Volto* was being enthusiastically danced on the cobbled streets. The excited cries rose as the girls flew into the air and tried desperately to keep their skirts from flying out of control. The men's faces were dripping with sweat as they spun and turned - their colorful red and blue waistbands flying in the air.

Standing quietly in the shadows, Pierre spotted the two men from his party. They were standing openly on the street corner cheering aloud and nudging each other as a girl's skirt whipped up higher than normal. He grinned to himself as he thought of how all of his party would have really enjoyed the wedding of Isabeau Richarde. Instead, us young men are spending our days trekking the roads to the freedom of the Swiss cantons.

Suddenly a hand grasped his and he spun round in fear. The flaring lanterns lit up Theodore's bright eyes and grin! Oh no, he thought – not now! As he bent to tell the child to return to the warehouse, Theodore's eyes grew large as he pointed urgently toward the street corner. Pierre turned back suddenly.

Three well-armed militiamen were standing surrounding the two youth. They had them backed to the wall and the foremost soldier was pressing his short sword into the ribs of Daniel Carle from La Bastide while his partner, Thomas Brunet stood beside him, hands upraised and placed on the wall. The soldier was nudging the youth as he questioned him.

Oh oh, he gasped, what do we do now? A glance told him that no one from the local people had noticed the situation. They probably wouldn't interfere anyhow, he thought; they are having too much fun. I need to do something now!

Turning he looked down at Theodore. Could the boy handle it? He bent and whispered urgently in Theodore's ears. He stood back and stared at the child. Theodore was frowning and looking at the militia. Then he grinned up at Pierre.

"It's scary...but it's better than doing nothing! Pierre? Do you think I can do it?"

"Yes," he bent and whispered reassuringly, "It's really scary, but it might work," and he bent and pointed past the militia down the street.

Theodore left his side and ran behind the dancers passing the militia and vanished around the corner. Pierre followed him down the street staying in the heavy shadowed areas and soon stood on the street corner opposite the militia.

Suddenly, Theodore came racing up the other street and tugged at the coat of the militiaman standing behind.

Pierre could hear his shrill voice echo across the street. "Soldier, Soldier!" as he tugged. The men turned and glanced down at his upturned face.

"Hurry, there is trouble down there!" He pointed desperately back down the street to where the tumult from the Festival was rising. "The Captain says there is trouble with the crowds." His voice raised higher. "You have to all come now!"

The militiamen looked at each other and then at the youth standing against the wall.

"You stay here – and don't move! We will be back right away!" And with a final smack on the backside of Daniel with the flat of his sword, the three militia guards raced down the street.

Before Pierre could move, Theodore grasped the hands of the two youths and dragged them across the street to him. The relief at seeing him showed on their faces. He hustled them down the street and with a glance backward to see that they had not been seen, he pushed them into the darkened alley and hurried them to the warehouse door.

"Enough excitement for one night," he whispered to them in response to their grateful thanks, "let's slip in quietly and hope that Alexander has not wakened!"

Inside, he bent and hugged Theodore.

"You were a real hero tonight, Theodore! Thank you!"

The boy flushed as he grinned back and quietly slipped away in the gloom of the warehouse to find his bed. Before Pierre closed his eyes, he checked the quietly sleeping form of Suzanne and smiled.

*　　　*　　　*　　　*　　　*

The Captain felt angry and bitter. The little bitch had not had the courtesy to be embarrassed or confused. He began to suspect that his behavior in the dance had been noted by many of the experienced matrons and probably their husbands as well.

It was not like him to have let things get out of control! His plan had been to take charge and cut into the joy and merriment of the occasion and somehow he had lost the day! Even now, his show of strength with the surprise visit by his horde of Dragoons had been subverted. Look at my stupid animals, unarmed and quickly getting drunk and tamed. He had better do something ... now!

The Captain walked over to the musician and after paying the traditional compliment on the quality of the music, asked for a special request. Nodding in approval, he turned to the crowd and clapped his hands for attention.

"Friends of the Luberon! I thank you for extending your warm hospitality to me...and my men...but," he paused for effect, "I am afraid we must go!" When several of the Dragoons slapped their hands on the wet tables in disgust, he glared at them until they cowered quietly. "In respect of your ...lovely bride and lucky groom...I invite my Dragoons to take their swords and present for you ... the famous Sword Dance of Provence!" At the roar of approval from the crowd, he continued, "Aha! You did not know that my men were so well trained." He waved his hand around the square and obediently, the Dragoons retrieved their weapons and reluctantly gathered in the middle of the dance area and took their places.

The Captain continued, "However, when this dance is performed, there is always a comically dressed "Fool' who is the center of the dance," he threw up his hands in consternation, "but we don't have one! So... we shall pay honour to the groom himself – not a fool – but a hero today!" He waved his hand grandly and smiling, Le Duc rose unsteadily to his feet and to the roar of the crowd joined the Dragoons in the dance area.

The music started and with some errors but a lot of zest. The Dragoons – sixteen men with swords – danced, their intricate movements leading them to finally form a platform of "locked" steel swords onto which the "fool" traditionally stepped in confusion. On this sword platform, he was raised shoulder-high and paraded around the floor. High above the congregation, with a wide grin, Le Duc's intoxicated state became obvious to the cheering crowd as he waved to the gathering until the dance ended.

The Captain was pleased that he had regained his control at the expense of the new husband. The little bitch would soon pay for her "female pride"! All his men were now armed again and he marched them off to the cheers of the gathering. The mills of our Catholic God may grind slowly but they will grind things exceedingly small when they are finished, he thought as he caught the eye of the bride. And ...she is even smiling at me? Bitch!

*   *   *   *   *

In the excitement of the sword dance, Isabeau had risen in concern at the swaying antics of her husband as the sword platform was paraded around the square.

"Oh, Isabeau, I pray he does not fall!" whispered Charlotte as she desperately clutched her friend's hands in her own. "I fear, my new bride," she grinned weakly showing her obvious embarrassment, "that your new husband...may not be able to," she raised her shoulders and opened her eyes wide with a mischievous quirk. "May not be able to...to...consummate? – Is that the word? ...The nuptials?"

"Ssh, Charlotte. You are too young and innocent to talk of such things! Or, have you been keeping secrets from me? Eh?" Charlotte's warm brown face was even showing a flush as she shook her head with some confusion before turning back to the successful – if questionable – end of the sword dance.

Isabeau was smiling at her husband who stood waving farewell - somewhat like a proud General - to the marching Dragoons when she caught the eye of the Captain who was watching her with obvious menace in his gaze. She felt a touch of fear race through her body. He is now a personal danger to me, she thought. Was I vain and foolish to strike back ... so viciously? But now, I must not show my fear. Despite her feelings, she smiled sweetly in his direction before turning to greet her husband as he came to the bridal table. When she dared to look back at where he had stood at the corner of the square, he was gone

*   *   *   *   *

A traveling troubadour led the whole celebrating party in some old time songs of joy - which were sung at weddings. More dances filled the evening hours.

Although she was aware of the wedding traditions, she was unprepared for her unexpected "capture" when it suddenly occurred.

A favorite Aunt had crouched in front of her table. She told tales bringing back old childhood memories with much laughter. A crowd of young girls gathered to listen to the stories and joined the laughter. Her mother-in-law and Charlotte, her bridesmaid, hovered around like moths to a candle.

Isabeau nearly spilt a glass of red wine she was holding when her chair was pulled back and her arms grasped from behind.

"Time! It's time, Isabeau!" The whole gathering of females, led by Charlotte began to chant and pull her firmly from her seat. *Mon Dieu*, whispered Isabeau to herself, how did they catch me by surprise. She had taken part in this traditional capture herself many times. Now, she was on her feet, being rushed away from her seated groom whose mouth was hanging open in astonishment. She tried to struggle loose but was firmly gripped by her new mother and bridesmaid on both sides. Glancing in some terror over her shoulder she saw that she was being pushed from the back by her close female friends from both villages - all laughing joyously and chanting the cry, "It's time, it's time, Isabeau!"

]

She saw the buildings racing by as she was rushed down the street to the home of her new husband. Her last look back to the square had seen her husband trying to race to her rescue and being pushed back into his groom's chair and a large glass of wine being thrust into his hand. His hair was flying around his face, his head tilted back and wine was being poured into his open mouth. Oh dear, she thought, that's the last thing he needs now...

As she was pushed through the doorway, she remembered she was traditionally supposed to demand that she be returned to the wedding party and to struggle to be released. It was all part of the performance, she thought.

"Let me go! You are supposed to be my friends!" she called out as she struggled, to be met by even firmer grips and cries of, "No! No! To the bed chamber of the bride!" by all the party of women. She was carried up the stairway. She saw her mother-in-law grinning as she was thrust through the doorway into the second bedroom of the Mallan home.

Around the large bed, the wall was covered with garlands of colorful flowers. The sweet scent of rosemary and thyme rose as the feet of the women crushed the sprigs on the floor. Even as she kept up the traditional struggle, she was quickly divested of her clothing. Ornamental broaches were unclipped and her wedding skirt was whipped off followed quickly by her petticoats leaving her naked lower body barely covered by her camisole and cotton pantalets. The bows holding her stockings were undone and the hose removed in a whisk. The clips and ribbons were slid off and her rich brown hair swung on her shoulders. The traditional scarf over her shoulders and her wedding blouse vanished in a flurry of white and she finally managed to free her hands and covered the breast area with them in an effort to regain some dignity.

"Aha! We have plucked the bride as a cook plucks a chicken!" called out her mother-in-law as she clapped her hands. The other members of the party, led by Charlotte, joined in the clapping and chanting. Isabeau felt her face flush in embarrassment at finding herself sitting on the middle of the bed in an exposed condition. She quickly rolled onto her side and closed her legs while all those gathered around her clapped and cheered.

"Oh! I never knew that it would be so embarrassing!" she whispered aloud only to be met with giggling responses. She was pulled to her feet and felt her last shred of dignity vanish when the camisole and pantalets were whisked up and down from her naked body. The shock turned quickly to relief as a dainty white embroidered nightdress was slipped over her shoulders to the cheers of the excited girls. She was pushed back onto the bed which had been now opened up and she was rolled over to the one side and the covers pulled up to her neck.

"Now she's ready!" cried out another Aunt as everyone clapped. "Let the bride await her gallant man!" called out Charlotte in a shrill voice and hurried everyone from the room. Turning to face the wide eyes of the new bride peering over the top cover, she grinned shyly. "I will wait to keep you company until the groom's party arrives, Isabeau," as she perched on the bridegroom's side of the bed, "I am sure I am as excited as you are – are you, Isabeau? Are you excited?"

Isabeau lay back and looked at her friend. I don't know how I feel right now, she thought, realizing her breathing was short and labored. Is this the way I thought I would feel? She looked up into the brown anxious eyes of her friend.

"I don't honestly know, Charlotte," she finally whispered, "although I am older than you, I really haven't had any experience in being a bride, have I?" She thought back to conversations with her married friends and could not remember much of value. Some had been quite distinct in their dislike of "the things that husbands do" and shuddered even when they could not describe what took place. Others, who, from their grinning and flushing behavior, seemed to like what took place in the bridal bed, but became too coy to tell her much of value.

"I guess, dear Charlotte, I will have to wait and hope that my new husband is knowledgeable in the ways of ...bed-work?" and she ducked her head under the covers and giggled hysterically.

Charlotte jerked the covers down to expose her convulsive friend. "And you had better remember everything to tell me later! Do you hear me, Isabeau? And, do you promise to ... educate me later?"

The two girls lay side by side on the bed and chuckled together.

*　　*　　*　　*　　*

5th July 1687
Leaving Sisteron for Eyguians, France

Before leaving the warehouse in the morning, Alexander, in his role of leader, had drawn a rough map on the warehouse floor to illustrate a decision he said he had made during the night. He pointed out that, up to now; they had been following the banks of the Durance River. At Sisteron, the river divided and instead of continuing their normal daily practice, he had decided to take the Beuch River joining on the left that would take them rapidly north into the Haut Alpes range towards Grenoble.

"We will follow the Beuch all the way until it becomes an alpine stream. I plan on staying overnight in Eyguians, Serres, the village of Lus-la-Croix-Haute, the Monestier-de-Clermont and then we will reach Grenoble," he hesitated while he thought, "at that point we will be in Savoy. Although the land of Savoy does not belong to France – it belongs to the Duchy of Savoy - I am afraid that our King Louis is bringing great pressure on him not to help us refugees. However, the people of Savoy are sympathetic towards the people of Provence – even many of the Catholics!" This statement brought gasps of disbelief from the older refugees.

"Really? I find that hard to believe," the mason, Isaac Gervaise breathed, "people of the Catholic faith...helping us out?"

Pierre nodded in support of the leader. "Yes! I have met many Catholics – who know us very well – who feel that the King and the Cardinals have been too harsh on us ... Huguenots."

"Anyway, we will travel from Grenoble through Chambray, Aix-les-Bains, Annecy and then cross into the safety of the Swiss cantons," he hesitated again as he calculated in his head, "and, it should be about ten days of travel through the mountain passes. I have chosen this route because there are less people living in the Alpes-Haute with a lot less travelers."

He stood up and pointed to David Blosset. "David and I have saddled and loaded the horse and mule outside the door. Divide up again into families and groups of two and three; walk apart from each other through the streets back to the city gate. I will be waiting with the mule outside at the sign posts and you will see David and his horse down the road to Eyguians." He shouldered his backpack and slipped through the door.

Pierre turned to his pack and found Theodore's eyes on him saying - without words, "There! Did you hear that?" He grinned wryly and patted the boy on the shoulder.

"Go along with Suzanne! Good luck! I will be watching, Theodore..." and shepherded them out of the door into the darkened early morning streets of Sisteron.

*   *   *   *   *

In their rearguard position, Pierre and Andre stood watching the small groups of their party set out on the road. From where they were standing, they could overlook the timeworn tile roofs of different shapes on the villas reaching down the steep banks of the Durance and catching a glimpse of disturbed water as the early morning sun reached the river.

Stretching up the dusty road, he could make out several clumps of their party dispersed between local carts and mounted travelers. He caught a flash of Suzanne's face as she turned to look backward and was pleased when he received a return wave from her.

"It's time." Andre picked up his pack and shouldered it. Turning, he looked down at the base of the ancient battered signpost and pointed to the pyramid of pebbles. "There they are again," he pointed, "I wonder what it means?"

Pierre grinned. "I don't know, but, since we're changing routes, I think I might destroy it and ... see what happens." And, with a quick brush of his foot, he knocked the pile down. As he turned to leave, he flicked the pebbles with his foot to spread them around in a more natural fashion. Shrugging, he raised his eyebrows in a question and pushed Andre's shoulder to get him in motion.

*   *   *   *   *

It was soon clear to all the refugees that they were entering the mountains. The banks on either side began to lengthen and steepen even though the dusty road seemed level. The steep mountain peaks still covered with snow that they had seen from a great distance had now advanced and were beginning to rear up on each side of them. Theodore stated that the vivid blue sky was even more immense and Suzanne claimed that the air seemed to be fresher and more reviving.

The small villages that they passed, even though they had typical Provencal accents, had steeper roofs to deal effectively with snowfalls. Henri Deelman, the farmer from St. Martin pointed out to his daughters that when he had traveled this route some years before that they could expect to see chamois – even ibex - deer and goats- "if they kept a sharp watch – and were lucky…"

"We are going into Dauphin territory soon. There have been many rulers here – the old Romans – this used to be Burgundy - then my father used to say that it belonged to the Carolingian Kings – I think that was what they were called; then the King of Arles, I think. And, lastly, the Dauphin of Vienne – but it will probably be traded to France. It's a long time since I heard the whole story," he apologized as he scratched his head and wiped a bead of sweat from his brow. "We are getting higher already," as he pointed out pinewoods were now sharing the landscape with small groves of olives and lavender fields.

The night spent in a small stone barn alongside the road north of Eyguians had been so much quieter than the festival noise of Sisteron, that some of the adults had trouble going to sleep. The building was so small that the single members of the party had to climb into the hayloft and leave the main floor to the families.

Pierre thoroughly enjoyed the distinctly different flavor of the farm-made goat cheese and the crusty freshness of farm-baked bread.

As he watched, the Pere Blanc vulture swooped down from the sky and scattered a family of marmots on a nearby slope. It reminded Pierre of the shy dugo owl he had spotted hunting when he slipped out of the barn early this morning.

Because the vineyards were now smaller and less numerous, they now carried food with them and gathered off the road in a hidden spot on the stream when signaled by David to take a mid-day break.

The sight of the ruined watchtower on the mountain ahead warned them of the approach to the village of Serres. The famous castle had been destroyed by Cardinal Richelieu fifty years before in what was now termed the "Wars of Religion" by the Catholic authorities.

Pierre waited patiently for Andre to pass him to take control of the next rise in the roadway. Looking backward over Andre's approaching shoulders, he spotted a horseman emerging from the foliage on a high bank. His shock quickly subsided as the rider waved his plumed hat in the air and Pierre recognized the fox's tail flying in the wind. Responding to the shock on his friend's face, Andre jerked his head around to check the horizon but before Andre could catch sight of the horseman, he had disappeared.

"Did you see something, Pierre?"

"No. I thought I saw someone but it was … only a frightened deer – it's gone!"

Still showing a little apprehension, Andre kept checking backward over his shoulder as Pierre remained behind to protect their rear. So, my devious cousin, Renard, is still watching our backs, Pierre grinned to himself. I guess I can expect another personal visit – maybe tonight?

*   *   *   *   *

2nd July 1687
The Wedding, St. Martin

Le Duc Mallan rose in confusion when he saw his new bride being dragged – protesting – away from the bridal table. Why were they taking her away? His head felt thick and slow and he was upset at not having her by his side. Although he tried to act confidently in public, he had learned quickly that Isabeau was not just a pretty face and a fine young figure – she knew what to do and how to do things in social situations, where he had always been somewhat clumsy and bumptious.

Rough hands grasped his shoulder and pushed him down onto the chair.

"Steady, my friend!" whispered an old drinking companion with long experience in wedding attendance in many villages in Provence, "Remember, we have to keep you here while your lovely bride is being ...prepared!" He thrust a large toasting glass of wine into his upturned face and poured the liquid into the open mouth resulting in a spray of wine on the table and the surrounding males. "You are supposed to struggle – but – you are not going anywhere until we let you! So there, my fine rooster!"

All around him his companions slapped him on the shoulder and pummeled him while Le Duc gasped for breath, his eyes glazed and his dripping mouth dribbling wine onto the table. Around them, the hearty beat of the drum and the plaintive call of the whistle were mixed with the exuberant cries of both old and young folk dancers as they celebrated the marriage of two popular youth despite frightening times.

In contrast, at some tables, some of the older people were sitting pensively, watching the joy and laughter, but thinking of individuals and families "missing" from the village on this day.

*   *   *   *   *

It was the shrieks of laughter and drunken teasing coming from the village street outside the house that broke into the warm serenity of the bedroom conversation of Isabeau and Charlotte.

Startled, Charlotte's mouth fell open and, with eyes wide, she blurted out, "That's him coming! What do I do now?" Isabeau reached out and pressed her hand.

"You open the door, Charlotte, and let them all in. And, then you must leave before they strip him of his clothes...I think".

"Of course! Of course! I'll go right away." She turned towards the door and then hesitated, looking back. "You'll be alright, won't you? Isabeau?"

Isabeau smiled a little weakly feeling her stomach turning over and feeling suddenly a little nauseous. "I'll be fine," she reassured her "and, I'll probably see you tomorrow."

"So soon!" Charlotte grinned, "That's good. Don't forget any little thing!"

They both faced the bedroom door as the sound of the downstairs door bursting open reached them and then everything seemed to flash by suddenly for Isabeau.

The thumping of the feet up the stairs; the encouraging yells of support; the door opening suddenly with Charlotte pushed behind the door; and an assortment of young men and women flooding around the bed. As was the tradition, no parents were allowed in this group – just other married young couples.

Le Duc was only just standing - held up by two stalwart friends. He was grinning in a slightly lewd way but she saw that his eyes were glazed over. Again events rushed by.

His outer clothes were whisked off with much zealous fumbling. With a horrified look on her face, Charlotte struggled from behind the door and vanished down the stairs to many ribald comments from the married men. There were shrieks from the women as they left the room before his pants were removed. His bedclothes were pushed aside and they sat him down to remove his stockings. Finally, they whipped off his undershirt and dropped the long white night clothes over his head.

"Do your duty, you wild rooster!" A final nudge on his shoulder spun him onto his side and someone threw the bedclothes over him as they left the room taking the candle with them. The room was plunged into the inky darkness with only the dim moonlight from an open window throwing a white patch on the couple.

Isabeau lay absolutely quiet and still on her back waiting. Suddenly, she did not know what to say or do. A grunt came from Le Duc. Then another. Then a warm fumbling hand crept up and touched her arm and she started. Her breath, short and shallow, frightened her a little.

"Isabeau...Isabeau," he breathed in a slurred voice, "where are you?" The voice rose somewhat plaintively at the end. She felt the covers move as he crossed over to her side of the bed. Her shoulder was grasped by another fumbling hand. The original hand now felt its way slowly across the firm but soft breasts. It cupped each in turn and rubbed each nipple.

Her breath quickened and she felt herself having to remember to breathe. The hand now raced down her body, across her quivering flat belly and dived down between her legs. Instinctively, her legs closed fast. Then she opened them quickly because she had trapped the hand between her thighs. His hand grasped the material of her nightdress and tugged it upward to her waist level. It stuck a little under her bottom but his other hand rolled her slightly to release it.

She found herself holding her breath, as she looked downward in the dark watching the traveling hand. Suddenly the moonlight was shut out; he was above her, grunting as his knee kept her legs open. He leaned on one elbow as he drove the other hand downward to help guide

]

his direction. Then he grunted again and collapsed – his full weight pinning her to the bed. Isabeau could not breathe but managed to call out frantically, "Le Duc, Le Duc..." but realized by his snoring that he was not able to help her.

Mon Dieu, she thought desperately, I need you now! She wriggled her left hand under his shoulder and pushing hard, managed to get a little breath. At the next breath, she pushed harder and rolled at the same time. Gratefully she felt his body slide – still grunting – off her body. He moaned and turned on his side and immediately his heavy snores filled the bedroom. Her breath was coming in short pants but soon settled down as relief flooded through her. I guess there is some kind of blessing for heavy drinking of bridegrooms at weddings, she thought with a little chuckle.

Reaching down, she tugged her nightgown downwards and rolled over the opposite way to her husband. Am I disappointed or pleased, she thought lightly. Either way, it's been an exciting day. She closed her eyes slowly and allowed a sense of quiet to slowly creep up from her toes. She rubbed her stomach to help it soothe itself. Slowly, she felt peace seep into her head but before the blackness took over, she had a wild thought.

What on earth shall I tell Charlotte in the morning? She chuckled quietly and slept.

*   *   *   *   *

CHAPTER   THIRTEEN

The party waited patiently in this hiding spot in a small treed valley off the road.   The parents, though tired, took time to play adventure games with their children on the grassy slopes highlighted by alpine wild flowers. The young women gathered at a small waterfall where they washed their faces and feet of the day's dust.

Alexander, accompanied by David on the horse, had made their way cautiously into the town of Serres where the day-long Saturday market was concluding with mule carts loading up to return to their farms. Once contact was made with a church elder, David returned by horse to gather the party together and in their now clean – but tired - little groups, they made their way through the town and along the cliffs on the river bank.

As Pierre passed through the town he noted that many new homes had been obviously built from the remnants of the razed citadel. They passed heavy carts bringing more mason-cut rocks down the street. Although the fortress was a great loss to their leaders, somehow Pierre felt better that something good was coming from the destruction of the castle.

After being led down a wandering riverbank path, they were turned and led through a path well hidden by overhanging tree branches. David now had to lead his horse followed by Alexander's mule.

After crossing a rushing small stream, the path turned abruptly and ran along the edge of the steep cliff face. When they reached their hidden lodging, gasps ran through the party.

They were standing before the dark entrance to what looked like a small cave.   The guide did not hesitate but after lighting a firebrand hidden beside the entrance, he led the way into the darkness. As more torches were lit, the tremendous size of the cave became apparent. It was also obvious that this cavern had been used to host other parties of refugees.   Wooden cots had been constructed laced with thongs and covered with straw filled mattresses.   There were closed areas for changing of clothes; tables and benches for eating; and a central fire pit for warmth and gatherings.

"We often used to meet here in the "Desert" for our worship services," explained the guide from Serres as he pointed to a wooden cross on a distant wall. His voice echoed around the galleries above their heads. "Someone will bring food to you soon. A stream of fresh water is

]

running into a natural stone basin over there in the corner. The fire and smoke cannot be detected from the outside; so you are safe here."

The party quickly settled into their new home. Even the older people, with open enthusiasm, explored as eagerly as the wildly running children did. The parents, now relieved of their responsibilities, sank onto the benches and chatted.

Pierre walked back with the guide to the entrance asking questions about the history of the cavern. He noted that both David and Alexander were busy grooming their steeds and unpacking them. Back on the banks of the stream he shook hands with the guide who vanished down the path to the river.

Pierre stood silently and listened carefully to the sounds of the river and forest but heard nothing. I wonder whether my cousin is still following, he thought. Well, it worked last time and bent on his knees to wash his face and swallow some of the fresh cool water.

Again, he was taken by surprise as hands grasped his shoulders and he was dragged to lie on his back as on the thyme-covered bank. This time he did not struggle and simply raised his head and smiled at his disguised captors. Now, they wore sacks over their heads with a fox face sketched on in black colours. He turned his head as a shadowy figure slipped from the bushes and stood on the other side of the steam. A gesture of the hand waved the men away and they left silently going down the path toward the cave to guard against interruption.

"Greetings, Cousin! I hope you are well?"

Pierre sat up and rubbed the scent of the wild thyme over his face and hands.

"Are you always so rough with relatives?" He grinned at the hooded figure with the fox-tail hanging from his hat.

"Ah, Pierre, we may be good at what we do; but we take no chances at all! Any mistake could be our last! It's a little like walking on the edge of a sharp blade. A mistake in any direction and you could fall into oblivion. And, carelessness with each step, could slice you in two... Should we act any other way?"

Before Pierre could answer, a soft birdcall crept through the trees. Renard beckoned with his hand and springing to his feet, Pierre leapt the stream and followed him silently as possible into the deep bush.

"Pierre, are you out here?" Alexander's voice called out. Renard shook his head and Pierre remained silent. "Pierre!"

Getting no response, the footsteps retreated back towards the cave mouth. Renard pointed again and Pierre followed him along the cliff edge. When he had covered a safe distance Renard gestured to Pierre to climb a rocky path and finally they sat on a ledge and gazed out over the strongly flowing Buech River with the mountains framing their view.

"Have you discovered anything to explain our mysterious shadowing band of Dragoons?" Renard had pulled the canvas fox-like bag from his face and wiped the perspiration from his brow as his teasing grin raced across his face.

"Well, Cousin, I am not sure! Are they still behind us?"

"That's a new problem. Up to the city of Sisteron they were behaving in their mysterious shadowing operation – checking on your movements several times a day using a scout. Then they raced up the road towards the town of Gap? We knew that you hadn't gone that way and were unsure whether to follow them to discover what they were up to; or to follow you and find them following us!"

"Hmm, so maybe we do know something after all. And we gave confusion to our enemies as well!" Pierre leant back against the rock face and chuckled. Then he related to his cousin about the pyramids of pebbles under the town signposts.

"It sounds ridiculous – but – if the piles of stones are a signal to the Dragoons as to the directions being taken, why would our leader, of all people, be leaving messages for the Dragoons?" Pierre stared at Renard. "That's mad thinking!"

Renard raised his knee to the ledge and rested his chin on the knee. "Maybe your honourable leader has sold his soul to a high bidder? Maybe this journey is the beginning of a whole series of refugee parties that will vanish into oblivion somewhere up at the Swiss border? Who knows what dirty schemes have been hatched by our devious Captain languishing in La Motte?"

"So, what do we do?"

"Hmm, I think what you have done before. Whatever you do, don't let him know that you have discovered his message scheme. Since he is always under observation en route, there are probably no messages coming the other way. Just be careful to keep things normal. Nod your head, take orders and don't rock the cart! And, remember that we are following you! If the troop of Dragoons re-finds you and begins its shadowing again, we will leave a signal for you along the way," he paused and frowned, "A red – like a fox – ribbon tied to ...a signpost! Why not use the same spot! Excellent, Pierre, we may have lost the war, but we shall win a few little battles along the way." He rose and grasped his cousin's hand in farewell.

"Come, I will lead you back. It is safe. My men are watching the cave and will warn me if there is danger."

He stopped Pierre under a large tree and spoke in a quiet but serious voice. "Pierre, you should also know that the news of my little victories has spread all over Southern France. We have become a 'real thorn' in the side of the authorities. They pray for our capture and execution. And, executed we will be, I can assure you! But, if you need to get a message to the "Fox", you can trust any villager en route. Tell them to pass the message on. We have a lot of willing spies out there – shop keepers, peddlers, market folk, any member of our faith... Don't forget! Good luck!"

As his cousin turned, he picked up a bulging cloth bag from the stream bank and handed it to Pierre.

"My men picked fresh ripe berries to use as your excuse. Enjoy them!" And he turned and silently vanished into the bush. Pierre stood by the little stream and looked around him. Nothing could be seen or heard. The "Renard" had simply vanished again.

Pierre removed several heavy ripe berries and crushed them between his fingers until they were stained to his satisfaction and then entered the cave. And the "excuse" worked better than expected. Even Alexander was enthusiastic about the fresh fruit.

*   *   *   *   *

6th July 1687
La Motte d'Aigues, Luberon, Provence

The late evening sunshine created tall grotesque shadows on the home walls as Captain Benoit and his sergeant strolled through the village of La Motte d'Aigues past the water fountain. The junior officer was more inclined to glance suspiciously at villagers passing by while the Captain made a show of nodding his head and smiling widely in response to courteous greetings.

When they felt they were safe and no one was coming by, they carried on a terse conversation.

"Well, *Sergent*, as I foretold, we seem to be finally getting results to our billeting pressures?"

"*Oui, mon Capitaine*! After much soul searching, your host, the Charpentiers, have agreed to abjure."

"Ah, *Sergent*, once he felt that his daughter was safely on the road to the Swiss, he rolled over nicely," he chuckled with some relish, "and do we have a surprise for him? We shall certainly see how solid his abjuring is! And even cranky old Jaubert limped over to admit his willingness to sign the document. Curse that family!" He touched the seeping and sensitive red scar under his eye in memory of the attack by the son of the family.

"And, many others join the list, *mon Capitaine*. Once the dam broke with the Charpentier and Jaubert families, many others gave in quickly. You have arranged for a Notary to visit soon...accompanied by the priest? It should be a large impressive mass!" The sergeant grinned at his superior with open relish evident on his face.

"Yes, it's arranged. So maybe time has come to open up a campaign on our neighbors at St. Martin down the road? Do you expect any problem there, *Sergent*?"

"*Non, mon Capitaine*," he grinned as he spoke, "I think the wave will continue across the hillside. Everyone knows how La Motte has suffered. You agree?"

"Certainly! We shall see if our... attractive bride feels quite so ... free with her insults when I invite myself to stay with them." He wiped his lace-edged handkerchief across his mouth as he simpered, "I look forward to putting that little ...bitch...in her place. You know, *Sergent*, that's the second time in my life that I have lowered myself to call a woman a bitch. It makes me wonder if I am ...losing control of my emotions? Hmm?"

The sergeant knew better than to reply – he knew better than to get mixed up in the emotions of a superior officer.

*   *   *   *   *

120

Isabeau turned over cautiously in her warm bed. A chink of hot summer sunlight lit up the hints of dark red flecks in the thick brown hair hanging over her face. She opened only a single hazel eye and moved her head to evade the brightness of the morning sunbeams. It was too early to wake up yet - another two hours before she had to get the breakfast ready for her husband. Her Husband! It still seems new to me, she thought.

As she lay still, she was now aware of the extra warmth that percolated though the bedclothes from the other body in the bed. Turning her head a little more she could see the quilt-covered form - with the covers concealing even the top of his head.

A little frown crept onto her forehead. Will it be a whole week ... tomorrow? She closed her eyes again; frowned; and thought, with a stab of reluctance, about her marriage. She recognized more than a twinge of disappointment.

When she had first met "Le Duc" Mallan, he made her laugh! Everyone around was always so serious - and he had been so different! He had made a joke of everything! She had quickly recognized that her favorite Aunt had had some dubious thoughts about someone who found the world so funny.

But Father had been eager - in these troubled times - to see his daughter safely wedded. Le Duc's aggressive manner and his confident way of speaking had been very attractive - at first! But she was beginning to see his strength of confidence had rapidly shown him more as ... aggressive and ... perhaps even a little ... bumptious!

Isabeau winced at her thoughts. But that's who I am married to! Even his joking manner and his quips now seem heavy and hurtful - at times. She thought back to her discussion about her reservations with her father several nights ago. He had brushed them aside - "You will get used to it after a while, my sweet girl! You have chosen, Isabeau! You have made your bed - now you must learn to sleep in it. Soon you will have children - lots of grandchildren for me to spoil and enjoy - and you will not have time to worry about his small mannerisms..." He had given her a hearty smack on her bottom. He had not realized that what he had said had hurt her more than his heavy hand!

Isabeau gently rolled onto her back again and closed her eyes. If father could have heard the upsetting discussion between me and my husband last night, he might have listened to me with a little more interest, she thought.

She had tried teasing him about getting pregnant and he had been blunt and firm. "No screaming babies for me! Not for a long, long time! I am still a young man - only 23 years old - and I want to have a lot more fun out of life yet."

How shocked and horrified I felt, she thought with some anguish! She was beginning to enjoy the feelings generated by sexual activity; but she had also begun to feel "used"! Le Duc would become excited and

]

then withdraw! That left her feeling unfulfilled – and removed the chance of becoming "with child"!

During our courting, she remembered, I had talked many times of my desire to have children. Lots of children! I wanted the wonder and joy I had experienced looking after other people's children. And the excitement I had felt at watching children - even little babies - when they begin to make small steps and develop into real people. Her lips curled slightly as she remembered how proud she had felt when little Angelica had laughed for the first time - while she was holding her! It had been a moment of absolute joy! She knew at that moment that she wanted to marry and have lots of children. And, now - it all adds to my disappointment!

Thank goodness that the Captain's threat to move into their home had made them appreciate the freedom of their marriage home - without extra lodgers. But the threat still hung daily in the air. Most homes in La Motte had been billeted bringing discomfort and misery to families. I had hoped that Le Duc and I would have used this free time to create the warm, loving relationship that my parents enjoyed, she thought. But why is it that I still feel we are like strangers living in the same house?

She sighed - gently, so as not to wake her husband. I might as well rise and start the day early. I can think better when I am busy! She carefully slid out of the covers and flinched as her bare feet touched the cold wooden floor. Summer is going too quickly - already it is losing its heat!

She slipped on her warm robe and tiptoed to the bedroom door. Le Duc stirred in the bed, rolled over and the covers fell away from his face revealing his round open face and his dark black lank hair curling under his chin. His mouth fell open and he began to snore loudly. Isabeau clutched her hand to her mouth to smother the impulsive giggle. Some people have no dignity when they sleep! When she was sure he was sleeping soundly, she gently backed out of the room and onto the landing quietly closing the door behind her.

As she trod carefully down the wooden stairs to avoid the usual creaking, she could feel the remaining warmth from the kitchen stove. Isabeau prided herself on her ability to bank the red-hot embers at night so they could still provide a quick fire in the morning. The iron stove was built into the archway at the far end of the long room. The plates and mugs standing on the shelves of the kitchen cupboard were already reflecting the early morning sunbeams coming through the shutters. The wooden kitchen table and chairs that Le Duc had brought from his father's home had a look of burnished gold in the early light. The dark orange tile floor ended in the middle of the long room where it met the wooden floors of the living room.

Stopping halfway down the stairs and turning her head, Isabeau looked with pleasure at the simple but comfortable wooden sitting room furniture gathered around the open fireplace that commanded the opposite wall. She had made the cushions from material given to the couple for their wedding.

Despite my uncomfortable thoughts, I am really trying to be a good wife to my husband! Oh don't be silly, Isabeau Richarde - now

Mallan! You know how independent you are; and how strong you are - treat it like another chore to be handled and everything will be all right!

She ran down the rest of the stairs and across the rooms to open the inside shutters to let some of the stuffy air out and some of the cool morning air into the kitchen. Leaning out she opened the outer shutters wide and looked down onto the little stream at the bottom of the gully.

Leaning out she could see portions of her neighbours' homes. "St. Martin was a good village to live in!" she whispered to herself with grim determination. She spread her arms wide, took a deep breath of the fresh Provencal morning air and turned to the stove to build up the fire for breakfast.

*　　*　　*　　*　　*

7th July 1687
Close to the Monestier de Claremont, France

Over the last few days, the mountain villages they had passed through had received them warmly. The villagers had openly greeted them and offered food and fresh water and wine. The absence of militia and troops in these isolated valleys reaching up into the Alps made the refugees feel safe for the first time since leaving their villages in Provence.

They walked each day up narrow cart tracks; down darkened steep valleys reaching sharply to the awesome ranges towering above them with most of the peaks still topped with ancient white snowcaps.

Everyone from children to their parents struggled with breathing at the ever-steepening slope but still enjoyed sucking in the clean clear fresh air that quickly invigorated them.

After some delay, while Alexander made a directional decision, Pierre turned to face Andre and murmured behind his hand.

"Am I mistaken, my friend, or is our leader acting...a little lost?"

Andre frowned in consternation and nodded, "Yes, Pierre, I thought the same!" he shook his head again. "He has always been quite emphatic about how confident he is about using this route! Now he hesitates at the cross trails and ponders them well before he makes his decision." Pierre had also noted that while previously Alexander had been rigid about the careful spacing of the small groups in their trekking line, he had seemed to become sloppy in his controls.

Several villages back, Alexander had lingered at the turn-off to the small hamlet. He was resuming his task of leading the mule up the slope as Pierre and Andre arrived.

Pierre had since shared his secret knowledge with Andre. Without being obvious, Andre scattered the pyramid of pebbles with a furtive kick of his foot when Pierre nudged him and he glanced up to see a grimy piece of red ribbon waving gently in the mountain breeze.

"As I told you, Andre, that means the Dragoons are back on our tail again! Not good news - but it also means that the 'Fox' is watching them!" The friends punched each other's shoulders in satisfaction and waited patiently until the mule was over the next rise before plodding upward.

]

Both Pierre and Andre, knowing they were now being shadowed by the militia, checked behind them at each occasion when they could observe without being seen watching.

"They are back, Pierre!" called Andre as he caught up with him on the rise. "It's really funny but, when you know you are being spied on, it is ridiculously easy to see them watching. There is a Dragoon on horseback! He is watching from the shelter of the firs on that rocky crag above the stream."

"Good watching, my friend. I will check before I leave this rise. You go on as usual – don't show any awareness."

Pierre waited a few minutes in clear sight at the turning of the trail.

Then he moved out of sight of any watchers; stopped and ducked into the thick underbrush. He crawled backward and parted the foliage to stare up the narrow valley. Andre was right, he thought, once you know what you are looking for; they are easy to spot.

In the clump of thick conifers on the side of the trail, two soldiers could be seen watching the trail. He carefully crawled backward and loped down the trail to the next rise.

*   *   *   *   *

The length of daylight in the mountains was noticeably short. At this time of the year, back on the Luberon hillside, you could hunt for much longer hours before turning safely homeward. Darkness began to fill the valleys early casting great shadows under the steep cliffs. Andre and Pierre, acting as rearguards, saw the excited waving ahead from Suzanne and Theodore and knew that their destination was in sight.

"And none too soon," grunted Andre. "I must be getting old! The villages down the road 'promised' us a surprise at La Monestier de Claremont. I wonder what it could be?"

"Hmm, well, we'll find out soon enough" agreed Pierre who had decided that not just his muscles but even his bones were aching.

The party was gathered on the side of the trail in sight of the village but hidden by a grove of trees. Alexander was conversing with a warmly smiling fat friar in a long brown gown. Catholics, thought Pierre? As he drew nearer, he heard the priest explaining to the cautious refugees.

"...I don't want you to be afraid. Not all Catholics believe that folk of different beliefs should be persecuted. My leader, the Abbot, in our small Monastery, has welcomed many groups of Huguenots who flee for their lives. We think it is a great pity that the Edict of Nantes, which promised your sect protection in the past, has been canceled! We do not wish to see you flee France, but ...we offer what help we can." He hesitated, seeming to select his words carefully, "However, despite the Abbot's word, there are still some of my brothers who ...frown on his decision. So, we meet you at the road and help you avoid being seen publicly."

He looked over the group smiling warmly. "If you will follow me, I will take you down this side trail and lead you to our Hospitality barn which is warm and comfortable."

Pierre noted that while the rest of the party seemed relieved and willing to follow the monk, Alexander was somewhat reluctant.

"Is there something wrong, Alexander?" he said softly as he reached the mule which was tugging anxiously and determined to travel with the group.

"Well, I am not sure," he frowned. "I do not like surprises." He looked at Pierre "What do you think? Is he to be trusted?"

"I think he can be trusted," grunted Pierre and he turned and followed the rest of the party up the trail. At the bend, he looked back and saw Alexander still struggling with the anxious mule as he stared back down the cart track. I wonder if he is deliberately waiting to be sure that the Dragoons see the change of direction, mused Pierre.

*   *   *   *   *

8th July 1687
Village of St. Martin, Luberon, Provence.

Cecile Aubertin grunted as she sloshed the water over the newly washed stone doorstep. Stretching backwards to counter the old familiar pains in her back, she thought of what had been plaguing her memory all morning. She shook her fifty-year-old cheeks in frustration.

When packing the work lunch, she had forgotten to provide extra apples for the younger children. Early this morning, her husband, Augustus, had not only taken the older members of her family but also the children who were going to help carry the pruned grape vines into piles for burning in their fireplaces. Her pleasant face creased into a smile as she remembered that, because Martin, the littlest, had not been feeling well, he had gone to play down the street.

"Mama, Mama, they are coming! The soldiers are coming!"

Cecile turned quickly as Martin's shrill voice echoed off the ancient stone walls. His running figure came round the corner of the lane. She saw his wide eyes and open mouth and obvious fear on his face. She moved quickly toward him with hand outstretched to slow him and to calm him down. For the first time, she heard the sharp thump of the hooves of many horses coming down the dusty entrance to St. Martin.

With a gentle push, she sent him towards the open door of their home, while she trotted quickly towards the entry to the roadway and peered around the corner. A warm little hand grasped hers as she realized that, despite her orders, her son had returned to her side and clutching her apron, was peering from under her arm.

In the middle of the street, rode Captain Benoit, the plume from his wide hat waving against the blue sky. She noted the red angry scar on his face. Through the rising dust cloud she could see a long line of

]

Dragoons in double file. She counted quickly – two, four, six, eight, ten...and at least another ten. A lot of Dragoons!

The Captain noticed her and touched the hand, holding a white handkerchief, to the brim of his hat in a courteous salute. She swallowed in fear – but bobbed her head in response. The greeting overrode her inner fear and clasping her son's sweaty little hand, she simply stood in the billowing dust and watched the large troop ride by and circle round the corner to apparently gather in the square. A community bell was now ringing – late – and heads were popping out of windows and doors down the street.

Thoughts flew through Cecile's head. There are very few men at home! They are all out in the fields and vineyards. Only some of the older crippled men are in town. What do we do? As some of the other residents began to move down the street towards the square, she made up her mind.

Grasping her son's hand, she ventured out and followed the dust towards the square. Appearing through the dust, as she turned the corner, was a figure of another woman. The woman dropped her apron with which she had been covering her face against the dust and Cecile recognized her as the new bride in the village, Isabeau Mallan. They clutched each other's hands and came out together from the settling dust cloud.

Small groups of mounted Dragoons were clustered in the four corners of the square. The Captain had dismounted and climbed onto a stone bench and was fanning himself with his plumed hat as the villagers gathered with curiosity before him. Another group of Dragoons, led by the Sergeant, was gathered in support behind their officer.

The more assertive villagers asked questions of each other in loud voices. The Captain smiled vaguely at the gathering but ignored the questions while he seemingly waited for a greater number of people to arrive. As the residents fell silent, he finally replaced his hat, wiped his cheeks with the white handkerchief and spoke.

"Residents of St. Martin, thank you for greeting me! I am ... sorry that your menfolk are not present...but work will be work...won't it?" He wiped his face again and continued, "I and my men," he waved his hand around the square, "would like to thank you ...for your kindness."

He nodded his head at the front row. "Your kindness in allowing us to ...share the joy ...of that wonderful wedding feast ...of our beautiful new bride," he smiled as he nodded in Isabeau's direction, "and sincerely hope that we will be ...treated as pleasantly as we were at the feast." He smiled broadly at the sea of faces – many of them displaying a mixture of confusion and curiosity; but others with distinct hints of dismay and distress.

"Ah, you don't understand. Of course, let me explain." His voice now softened and some of the closer residents either leaned forward to catch his voice or turned their heads to use their better ears.

"For the last...two weeks...is that correct, *Sergent*?" He hesitated, turned and looked down at his subordinate officer who was perched on the edge of the fountain.

The sergeant nodded his unsmiling face and turned his gaze to check his mounted men in the corners of the square. "Ah, my *Sergent* agrees! Yes! For the last two weeks we have been kindly ...billeted in your neighboring village of La Motte d'Aigues. What a fine village and... what fine people! And, in a short time...many of them have ...become much wiser! They have been ...persuaded... to abjure and have voluntarily again joined the Holy Catholic faith...and I salute them!"

A menacing murmur had increased in both volume and gesture in the disturbed crowd. The Captain did not appear to notice as he removed his hat and fanned it in front of his face.

At the gesture, the mounted men from the corners reared their horses and with a clatter of weapons they surged forward to surround the gathering. The murmur died out suddenly. As the Captain continued, his voice was firmer and less gentle.

"Residents of St. Martin, at the request ...of your King...I and my Dragoons will be visiting with you...and we expect to be well treated – as we were in La Motte! Now...I know that this is a surprise to you all. So, while my men ride around looking at your village, I will return to this square early this evening," he grinned at the upturned faces, "so that you can inform your husbands - and make up your mind ...just how many of our soldiers...you would love to billet." At this, he jumped to the ground and mounted the horse that a Dragoon had led forward.

From his increased height, he looked down on the faces. "Let me remind you! Those who volunteer will be treated much much better than those who are ...reluctant!"

He gazed directly at Isabeau who stood holding her upheld apron to her lips. "I shall naturally...stay at the home of your ...new bride...won't I?" And, with a wave of his hand to his men, he cantered out of the square and vanished round the corner.

As a group, the villagers turned and glared at Isabeau, as though she was personally to blame for this sudden unwanted burden in their lives. She looked at the upset faces, dropped her apron and held up her hands in helplessness.

"Don't all look at me! It's not my fault!" She looked with sincerity at their disturbed faces. "This is a shock to all of us! We all knew, didn't we, that we would be next after la Motte ... didn't we?"

She kept looking at them until reluctantly, they began to nod their heads and smile with a touch of guilt. "Look, let's meet this afternoon ...at your home, Cecile?" She got a frightened but willing nod. "I will bring some of my special herbs for tisane and we can...at least...talk about this before our husbands come home. Agreed?"

There were many nods and the crowd dispersed quickly while some of the smiling Dragoons sat on their horses and watched.

* * * * *

CHAPTER FOURTEEN

"This is truly a heavenly end to our day. I don't think I have ever tasted so good a mutton *ragout!*" Suzanne licked the wooden spoon delicately as she smiled at Pierre. He reached out his hand across the wooden table and rubbed the back of hers. Smiling, she put down her spoon and covered his hand.

As he watched from the seat next to Suzanne, young Theodore rolled his eyes upward and grimaced. He disliked Suzanne showing any affection to anyone! A hush around the barn interrupted the interplay as Father Paul, the Friar, entered followed by several of his band - all carrying steaming trays.

"Friends, we hope you all enjoyed your meal!" Spontaneous applause broke out from the wooden tables echoing around the huge building. He smiled and held up his hand balancing a metal tray high in the air.

"In our little monastery, we love to eat good food - especially because it is made with our own fresh produce! But for a sweet treat, we would like to introduce travelers to a specialty of the area! This has been made from an ancient recipe - and is called *Pogne de Romans*! It is a fine *brioche* made with eggs; and flavored with orange flowers and excellent liquor. We know you will enjoy it!" Excitement twitched around the gathering as the monks went to the various tables to share the desert.

Groans of pleasure could soon be heard around the room and the Father smiled with obvious enjoyment. He held up his hand to gain attention and announced: "Friends, we will now serve a local herb tisane which will help you sleep better this night than you have ever before and take away the aches from your body in the morning."

More clapping broke out and he beamed. "And, I have heard from some of you that villagers - down the road - promised you a 'surprise' when you reached our little monastery?"

Theodore stood up on the bench, his face alive with excitement. "What is the surprise? What is it?" Then he received a downward jerk on his jacket and sat down in embarrassment with his hand over his mouth.

"Ah, yes my dear little friend. Most people who live in La Monstiere de Claremont take our surprise for granted. We have enjoyed the secret for years! But to visitors, it is always a surprise - and, an enjoyment!"

At that moment, he bent his knees and pointed both his index fingers downward. "Beneath us, deep within the bowels of God's earth, there is very hot water. And it gushes out in a hot torrent in a grotto in a valley close by. We have made safe pools for the convenience of our folk. So, once we have the ladies and men separated, we can enjoy a wonderful free hot bath in Nature's own beauty!"

"And, "he continued, "for the mothers - you can bring your dirty clothes; and wash them lower downstream; and they will be clean and dry when you wake tomorrow." Both excited and curious murmurs filled the room - for many had never seen a wonder such as this!

Looking around the party, Pierre nudged Andre.

"Look at Alexander! He looks puzzled and a little shocked?" Andre furtively glanced over and nodded. "This is obviously another surprise to him, I think!"

Pierre nodded his head. "I am more certain than ever, that our leader has never been this route before – despite what he says!"

Soon, Father Paul led the way out of the barn and down the twilight path to the hot pools. At the major split in the paths, he pointed out the path to the "women's pool" and *Madame* Deleman led her giggling daughters down the path followed by the other females.

Once the genders were separated, several young men slipped past the friar and raced down the path wildly. Coming through the thick bush they all arrived at the banks of the huge steaming pool at the mouth of the dark grotto. Andre was already bending at the pool edge and gingerly stuck his hand in the water and grinned up at the others.

"It's wonderfully warm. I'm first in!" Clothes were abandoned in piles along the bank. Soon just about everyone - after a mild bout of modesty - splashed into the pool and lay back in sheer enjoyment sucking in the hot steam - which Father Paul said - was healthy.

Theodore shot up from under the warm water with an upward rush splashing Pierre and Andre and spluttering with pleasure. He waved over in the direction of the rocky bank.

"Is Alexander not coming in as well?" The friends turned to stare at their leader standing in the shadows behind the smiling friar. "Alexander," Andre called out in a teasing manner, "are you too modest to join us?"

Alexander shook his head. "I need to go back and look after the mule!" He turned away but called back over his shoulder. "Enjoy your fun!" And he slid in the darkness of the path.

"Oh well, everyone to his own choice!" Andre gasped as he sank carefully under the water. Not noticed, Theodore slid his body up onto the stone bank and slipped into the darkness.

Finding the hot water overpowering and, slightly dizzy, Pierre climbed out onto the bank and moved away from the pool to sit on a large rock. He waved at Andre to join him. Andre slid out – followed by Isaac Gervaise, the mason from Grambois and Henri Deleman from St. Martin, came out for fresh air as well.

Suddenly Pierre felt a tug on his shoulder and turned to find a disturbed Theodore standing behind.

"Pierre, You have to come and see!" The youth was obviously angry.

"What's wrong, Theodore?"

]

"Come and see, Pierre!" And he tugged Pierre's arm making him rise. "Theodore, I have to get dressed first. I cannot wander around unclothed!"

"Never mind that – just come! Now!" And he rushed off down the path.

All four men rose and jogged down the path in the moonlight uncomfortable in their nakedness. In the back they could hear the fat friar huffing along behind them.

Suddenly, they rounded a corner and saw Theodore ahead standing in the deep shadows at the side of the path. He was pointing through the brush.

Slightly ahead of the other men, Pierre stopped beside the youth who still pointed off the path. As he followed the direction of the boy's finger, he instinctively gasped. The gap in the underbrush clearly showed the women's pool. Seated sideways on a large rock recovering from the effect of the hot water was Suzanne! Her lovely pale legs were stretched before her and her arms were raised up in the air as she busily dried her wet hair with a towel. Her beautiful breasts bobbed with the arms drying action.

Pierre found it difficult to breathe. He had never seen anything so stimulating and lovely before! But he was also shocked at the boy's behavior. He turned and frantically whispered in a hoarse voice.

"Theodore! We should not be here! This is not an appropriate thing for you – or I – to do!" He grasped the boy's naked arm and pushed the other men back down the path and away from the scene but Theodore struggled loose.

"No, Pierre, you don't understand! Look!"

Frustrated, Pierre turned back and followed the boy's finger. Then he saw – with horror – what Theodore was angry about!

Lying in the deep shadow of the bushes several feet beyond the path was a vague figure. As Pierre stepped forward a twig cracked beneath his bare feet and in the moonlight, the head turned to look back in fear. It was Alexander! Pierre stood in shock. An angry growl came from the other men behind him. Before Pierre could act, Alexander rolled over swiftly and rising to his feet ran back down the path towards the road. From the pool, there were shrieks from the women who had seen movements in the darkness.

Andre grasped Pierre's arm and pulled him into the shadows with the other men.

"You cannot chase him – like that!" he pointed to his nakedness.

"That's right, young man," Father Peter pushed through, "you should all come back to the men's pool – the boy was right to come for help!" He patted Theodore on the shoulder and led the men back down the path. Pierre still felt confused – inside he was excited at the view he had had of his future wife but he was also upset and angry at the treachery of their appointed leader. The swine, he thought, what do we do now?

*   *   *   *   *

8th July 1687
Early evening in St. Martin, Provence

The home of Cecile Aubertin was too small to accommodate the large crowd of neighboring women and children who gathered quickly following the announcement by the Dragoons. Isabeau, who arrived early, helped her move the benches from the kitchen and living room out onto the courtyard where, under the shade of several ancient trees, the women gathered and chatted nervously while the children played in the sloping ground at the rear of her home.

The early afternoon sun glowed on their upturned faces lighting up their obvious anxiety. Cecile peered over the stone wall to ensure that no Dragoons were eavesdropping on the conversation and turned and nodded to Isabeau.

"Friends," Isabeau began, "and, I think this is the time when we really need all of our friends!" The women's faces all nodded in unison and some broke into a slight smile of relief. "We all have good friends in La Motte and know what they have been doing; and going through; and the terrible pressures the Dragoons have placed upon them!" She hesitated and chose her words carefully.

"I, for one, hate the thought of having to billet the troops because I hate being told what to do!" Many of the woman's faces broke into smiles of recognition. Isabeau had already been known for her tremendous desire for independence.

"However, as we know well, what happened to sweet old *Mme.* Charpentier is what happens when you confront the Dragoons - and this particular Captain - with open resistance!" Again the womens' faces showed a mixture of sadness and anxiety as they nodded.

An older woman, whom she recognized as Angela De Laine, the wife of a crippled sheepherder, raised her hand a little timidly and said, "Isabeau?"

Isabeau smiled at her encouragingly because she really wanted this to be a discussion and not a lecture, and nodded.

"We are all of the same faith," Angela looked around the group in confirmation, "and although we are used to being under ... constant pressure because of it, we all know what happens when the Dragoons arrive!"

She stood up and ticked off her fingers as she looked around the gathering. "One, the Dragoons arrive! And two, they fill up our homes to the point of bursting! And, three, they eat us out of food and wine! Then, four, all members of the home are treated with constant insult and disrespect - especially the woman and girls! Five, the pressure increases until we fear for our lives; and then, we just give in! And we have to!"

Her husky voice had risen until it was a shrill cry. She stopped and anxiously looked over at the nearby walls as tears showed on her worn tired cheeks. Several of the other women rose and touched her in understanding.

"Regrettably - you are right, Angela. I think we could all wish to be left in peace! But, we all know what the end will be! I have also heard from the other villages, that, when you give in too quickly and sign the abjuration, the authorities don't believe you are sincere ... so, they leave the Dragoons billeted with you for longer periods of time! So, ... I am suggesting that we put up with the billeting as long as we can - provided we feel safe - and then, abjure ... with dignity."

"How do we know how long that could last?" called out another voice.

"What about discussing ... our frustration levels each morning when we get water at the well. That way, the 'grapevine' will keep us all informed?"

All around the group heads were nodding. Women began to sip their herb tea again and Isabeau felt they all looked less stressed. I only hope we can survive this punishment without losing anyone, she thought. She helped Cecile fill the cups and chatted to several of the children who rushed through the group. It is so good that at least the children are still happy. And, now knowing the Captain the way I do, I think I'm going to be the receiver of the toughest pressure of all!

*   *   *   *   *

9th July 1687
Morning in St. Martin, Provence

"Isabeau, Isabeau, Isabeau... there are times you vex me with your worries!" Le Duc Mallan had obviously reached his final level of frustration. "My wife, you worry too much. So we might have Dragoons billeted here – maybe even the notorious Captain? So what?" He rubbed his hands over his hair and smoothed it downward to settle it. As he turned at the table to face his worried wife, he reached out and pulled her roughly onto his lap.

She hugged him quickly and then slid gracefully out of his arms and onto the bench beside him.

"But Le Duc, I don't trust a single bone in his body. You know what a black-hearted devil he is – remember dear old grandmother Charpentier in La Motte?" Isabeau felt anger rising up in her breast. Her breathing had become a little labored. "I told you about the wedding dance. How he had fondled me in La Volto!" Her husband leaned back and simply grinned at her.

"Come, Isabeau. With a fine figure like yours," he leaned forward and poked her breast with his index finger, "you can expect a few feels from many men..."

Frustrated, Isabeau sprang up from the bench and her skirt swirled as she spun towards the kitchen stove. "Le Duc, I have never allowed any man to feel me! Not even you!" She glared at him from the safety of the kitchen. "You know that!"

Le Duc's mouth twisted as he grimaced. "You're right there, Isabeau, I could never understand why you would not let me touch you, even when we were promised to each other! Well, I will have a talk with the Captain when they come for billeting! So enough worrying!"

He arose pushing the remnants of his breakfast to the middle of the table. "As I said, I am going to see our neighbors in Grambois this morning to see if I can negotiate some good deals. See if you can keep yourself out of trouble until I return this evening..." and, walking to the clothes pegs next to the door, he grasped the brim of his wide hat and with a scornful flourish he made a sweeping bow and slammed the door as he left.

"*Mon Dieu!* How frustrating a husband can get!" She spoke aloud to the closed door and felt a touch of sadness between her eyes. He brushes aside my worries as though they were dust on the table. He makes a joke of everything! And, then he leaves with nothing settled. It's almost, although married, as though I am very much alone in this relationship!

Outside, she heard the stable door close followed by a clatter of hoofs as her husband rode away. Well, Isabeau, if you are alone in this world, you had better sit down and make a plan for yourself. She quickly cleared the table and wiped it clean. The sunlight on the golden wood of the tabletop brightened her world. Through the open window she felt comforted by the drifting scent of the lavender that was blooming outside. She filled her cup with her favorite herb tisane and settled down to think.

Listen Isabeau; you have always been independent about how you would like to be treated – by anyone – even a Captain of the Dragoons! Even in dangerous situations, you have always managed to remain in control – so what's different? Keep control of your temper; remain calm; and, you decide what are appropriate behaviors. She took a deep breath and sighed. Just remember who you are and everything should come out right in the end.

There, she thought, I feel I have feeling back in my body again. She rose, cup in hand, and went and opened the door and peered into the street to see whether any of her neighbors were taking a break.

*   *   *   *   *

7th July 1687
Monestier de Clermont, France.

A buzz of disturbed conversations greeted Pierre and Andre as they entered the large barn. Faces turned toward them asking an unspoken question. A solemn stillness settled over the band of refugees. Suzanne rose to her feet from the bench and raised her eyebrows quizzically.

"Alexander?" she raised the question on everyone's mind.

"He seems to be gone! With the mule and our emergency supplies!" Pierre growled aloud with frustration. Small cries of anger and consternation rose from the group. Pierre raised his hand and the voices slowly died out.

"I think ... we are well rid of him! What we need to do now is to decide on another leader and leave early tomorrow towards Grenoble. It should be ... no more than two days journey from here." He looked around the group for a response.

]

"What about you, Pierre?" Suzanne smiled up at him from where she sat with young Theodore.

Henri Deelman, the farmer from St. Martin, broke off from a whispered conversation with his wife and daughters and rose up with his hand in the air. Pierre nodded at him with some surprise.

"I, as the oldest man in the party, would be willing to lead you to the cantons of Switzerland! The men in my village had asked me to lead the party – before Alexander volunteered," he countered, "I feel it is unfair to put such a heavy burden on a young man of ... only 25 years," he peered at Pierre and raised his eyebrows.

Pierre shrugged. "My father has traveled through Grenoble across the mountains to Geneva some years ago. He often described the journey to me and I remember his stories well! And, we are now far enough away from our villages to be ...much safer now!"

Andre nudged Pierre and, seeing his friend hesitate, stepped forward.

"There is something we should be sharing with the whole party - at this point!" He glanced again at Pierre and, on receiving his nod of agreement, proceeded to recount the suspicions they had shared about Alexander and the shadowing of the troop of Dragoons. Pierre noted with some relief that he did not mention any contact with cousin Renard's band.

Cries of dismay arose again as he spoke and Henri Deelman rose to his feet again his voice now tight with anger.

"Why did you not tell all of us about this threat? We share the same danger, so why not the same knowledge?" It was clear from his gaze that he was accusing Pierre.

"Henri, it was not ... certain! At first it puzzled me alone! Things I could not understand! Then Theodore and Andre, both, shared their pieces of the mystery. At that time we did not know who – or how many – were involved in the conspiracy," he spread his hands and shrugged, "Or - if there was any conspiracy – or a plot?"

Henri was obviously still not mollified but obviously decided to act instead. "Listen, I am not happy with this information! But," he gestured at Pierre and Andre, "I shall lead the party – with the help of you two – and we start early in the morning. We will use the same system as before. David," he pointed at young Blosset seated next to his daughter, Catherine, "will lead with the horse - as usual - and we will follow in small groups with Pierre and Andre acting as rearguard." He looked around the party as though challenging any objection and, finding none, continued, "Let's all get to sleep now – we will need our rest – and strength!" And everyone did.

*   *   *   *   *

8th July 1687
On the road to Grenoble, France

The trail from Monestier-de-Clement was narrow and steep under the massive peaks crowding the small rough road. A heavy mist filled the valley in front sometimes making it difficult even to see the guide, David, ahead on his horse. The party suddenly bunched together and Pierre trotted up to see Henri beside David crouching at the side of his horse studying the animal's front hooves.

"Trouble?"

Henri, his face a picture of frustration, turned and nodded.

"The horse slipped. It has hurt itself. It will have to be led slowly!" He hesitated and looked up the trail. "Pierre, you go ahead and leave Andre and Theodore in the rear." Pierre nodded and moved into the lead bending over and shrugging his pack onto his shoulders as the path steepened. As he moved past Suzanne, she smiled shyly and touched his shoulder. He grinned at her and strode on.

*   *   *   *   *

Later in the afternoon, Pierre looked over his shoulder at the rest of the party struggling up the trail. Climbing the steep path had been obviously tiring for them. Their faces were bent down looking at their feet. Even at a distance, he could hear them panting. Mostly, he could see the tops of their heads with the braids identifying the women. Some wore scarves over the head covered with thick layers of dust and wet with the mountain mist. They had originally welcomed the arrival of the midday sun now slanting down into the narrow confines of the valley but now were becoming overheated in their heavy cloaks.

Glancing upward, Pierre saw that the path ahead was passing under the welcome cover of a large tree before it vanished over the ridge at the top of a small rise.

Maybe it's time to rest and make sure the way is safe, he thought. As he entered the cool covered area, he turned and called back softly, "Stop and rest! We need to scout ahead anyway!"

He threw his pack on the ground, sat down and leaned against it. The line of people bunched up around him. Some of the women were reluctant to sit down. It probably meant that they were worried about having to get up again shortly, he thought. However, some of the men began to shrug their heavy packs prior to removing them.

But the new leader, Henri, arrived and hesitated. He gripped his shoulder straps defiantly - seeming determined to challenge any decisions made to his leadership.

"Let's keep moving! We are so close to the top, I don't think we should stop now! You rest, Pierre! We are going over the ridge and will rest on the other side!" He laughed, turned his back and nudged several of the other men. "Come on, let's move on!"

Some of the others hesitated but Henri pushed his way through and they began to stumble after him. Even Suzanne, catching Pierre's eye with a weary glance, raised a tired frustrated eyebrow and also turned and trudged up the hill.

Pierre slumped and sighed in frustration. They all needed a little rest. But the leadership problem seemed to worry Henri! Then a stab of

]

sudden fear broke through his weariness. He rolled over and called up the path.

"Take caution!" he cried. "Check over the hilltop first!"

But they were already over. Suzanne slowed and looked back at him briefly and then vanished from sight too. Pierre pulled on his pack straps, rolled onto his knees and rose to jog wearily up the rest of the hill.

Cries rang out ahead. He quickly threw himself into the long grass beside the path, but too late! A uniformed figure stepped out from behind a tree trunk. Pierre felt a boot placed behind his neck pressing his face firmly into the dust-covered damp alpine grass. Oh no, he thought, in despair. No! No!

Pierre lay still deliberately keeping his breathing shallow. Then further screams echoed in the glade ahead. He gathered his muscles intending to roll his body sidewards.

"Oh no! You rascal," the rough voice above put more weight on the boot behind Pierre's neck, "I'll have to put you out of your misery!"

Pierre groaned as he was hit on the back of the head by what was probably the flat side of a heavy sword. He blacked out briefly as millions of stars floated through his pain-filled mind. His body jerked again as the tumult of a struggle close by billowed through the trees. He vaguely felt the second blow; darkness followed the pain. And then, nothing!

*   *   *   *   *

9th July 1687
St. Martin, Luberon, Provence

Having made her firm resolutions about how she would handle the arrival of the Captain had allowed Isabeau to really enjoy the warm summer day. On the table, she carefully sorted the fresh herbs she had collected that morning and tied a fragrant bunch of rosemary into a neat bundle for hanging.

The door opened without a knock and Captain Benoit stamped onto the kitchen tiles. Following him and towering over him were three of the biggest and ugliest Dragoons Isabeau had ever seen. Without invitation, the soldiers swept the herbs off the table and slouched on the benches behind the table. The Captain seated himself elegantly at the head of the table and gestured the astounded girl to sit opposite the Dragoons.

"Really, *Capitaine Benoit*, is this the way in which an officer of the King behaves?" Taken unawares, Isabeau had desperately tried to remind herself of the decisions she made earlier.

"You have had enough warning, *Madame, n'est-ce pas?*" Without waiting for an answer, he waved his hand at the Dragoons. "I have brought some of my fine fellows along to meet you." A glance at the soldiers was met by insolent, leering and suggestive grins.

She turned her head to avoid their looks and found herself facing the Captain's sardonic smile. "As warned, *Madame*, we are going to billet

with you – all of us...maybe more...until we ...reach an understanding."
Isabeau took a deep breath and resolved to somehow take control of the situation.

"*Capitaine*...I am a reasonable person. I think we can handle...three in total..."

"You misunderstand, *Madame Mallan*! We will decide how many you will entertain." The Captain broke into her statement abruptly and Isabeau realized that the number of billets was not the most important item on his agenda.

"*Madame*, may I call you Isabeau?" He continued with confidence, "Ever since I first saw you at your wedding, I have found myself ...obsessed ...with you. Unlike most of the village maidens in Provence, you are different! You have an air of independence; a freedom of spirit; which is a challenge to me..."

In desperation, Isabeau broke into the discourse. "*Capitaine*, while I appreciate your compliments, I must remind you that I am a newly married woman. And, your statements are ...inappropriate!"

"Frankly, my sweet little flower, I don't care a sou for your opinions. What I need to make clear to you ...from the beginning...is that when I billet with you, we need to develop...a *special...relationship*."

"*Capitaine*, enough is enough," and she made an attempt to rise from the table.

Swiftly, the Captain's left hand shot out and grasped her behind the neck and Isabeau was jerked with her face close to the Captain's. The pain in the back of her neck brought tears to her eyes and although she struggled, the Captain was not finished.

"Isabeau, the choice is yours! Either you can show me ... special personal favors, or," his right hand slid across the smooth table and grasped her left breast as it rested on the table edge, "or, I can give my Dragoons my permission...to...how do I describe it...use you at will!" She winced as he squeezed her breast.

He let her go and her body moved back so quickly that she had to grab the table edge to stop herself from falling backward. She found her breath difficult to control as she stared at the officer. The Dragoons were grinning and nudging each other in sheer pleasure.

She rose to her feet and stepped back from the table. "Listen *Capitaine*, and listen carefully! I have no desire to have a *special relationship* with any man other than my husband. And, I am sure that when I tell him of your threats, he will deal with you personally. Now go!" and she waved at the door.

The Captain rose slowly and lackadaisically to his feet. "You misunderstand, *Madame*, your husband has nothing to do with ...our relationship. Like any husband, he might ...object...to my offer. But I am sure," he waved at his Dragoons as they rose to join him, "that my fellows here, can change his mind?"

As the Dragoons left, the Captain hesitated in the doorway.

"Isabeau, I understand that you are seen ...somewhat ... as a leader in the woman of St. Martin. Despite your meager protests, do not be surprised at your husband's lack of zeal to defend your honour. We do not want to spend our lives on this *godforsaken* hillside. The joys of

]

Paris call back to us. I am sure you can persuade the families that it is better to be ...safe than sorry." He turned, hesitated, and looked back.

"*Madame*, I can assure you ... I always get what I want! Always! And, despite your angry spirit, I would enjoy convincing you of my... deep desires!" He smiled and vanished leaving the door ajar.

*   *   *   *   *

CHAPTER FIFTEEN

The first thing he felt was intense pain on the side of his head. This soon became coupled with a strong smell of a stable. *Mon Dieu*, he thought, am I back in the stable at Rognes again? It brought back memories of being captured and imprisoned by the Dragoons as he escaped to Marseilles. But I am moving; and, I feel sick – like being on board that ship on the Mediterranean. Confused, he groaned aloud. Suddenly his world stopped moving and he was conscious of loud voices.

"Time you came round, you black rascal! Almost everyone else in your party of criminals has to walk! So, now you can as well!"

Pierre painfully opened his eyes to find himself upside down looking at the stony trail. He slowly realized that he was slung stomach down over a saddle of a mule. He groaned again in pain and closed his eyes. He did not feel the Sergeant cut the thongs binding his wrists to his ankles.

But when his exhausted body slid headfirst onto the stony trail, he blacked out again momentarily. It seemed ages later that voices began to penetrate his painful world and slowly he opened his eyes.

In agony, he first recognized Suzanne's large brown eyes peering anxiously into his. Despite the ache in his head, he smiled slightly. Then he became conscious of another face – that of the Sergeant standing further away and peering down at him with a wolfish grin on his face. Suddenly, he could smell the sweet lilac scent Suzanne wore and realized that his head was in her lap and she was leaning over peering down at him.

"I think, *Monsieur*, that judging from the attention you are getting from this lovely lady, that you must be the ... swine that gave my *Capitaine* the infamous festering scar on his face – the one that does not want to heal?" Suzanne jerked her head up and glared at the soldier. "Hmm," he continued, "so it seems, then! When we get you back – in chains – to La Motte, I think my *Capitaine* will be ... pleased with me? *Non*?" He leaned back and laughed aloud and the rest of the Dragoons joined in.

"So, Mademoiselle, if you will help this cur to his feet, we will fetter him in place and get the party moving again." A Dragoon ran to Suzanne's side to help her lift Pierre from the ground and steady him. "Link them together so that she can care for him – for awhile, until... we find ... better tasks for her!" Holding his head with his one hand and clinging to Suzanne, Pierre began to stumble down the trail.

]

*   *   *   *   *

The sheer exercise of walking did more for Pierre's physical condition than anything else. And, as he stumbled along, Suzanne's soft voice whispering in his ear, filled in the gaps of the last half-day.

"You were ... so right, Pierre!" she acknowledged as she recounted how the group had been led over the rise by Henri Deleman into a well-laid trap by the Dragoons.

He was shocked to hear that their horse rider, David Blosset, had become the first tragedy of their escape. He had come to the rescue of little Theodore who had been swinging a heavy stick at a couple of Dragoons. "One of them had drawn his sword and really intended to rid the world of this little pest! But, before he could stab the child, David broke loose and challenged the soldier – and was cut down!" Tears washed trails through the dust covering her sweet face. Pierre grunted in dismay.

She recounted how two of the party had managed to escape during the melee. Daniel Carle and Thomas Brunet – both of the village of La Bastide des Jordan's - had vanished.

All the adults in the party had been fettered with chains to their wrists. Suzanne's tender wrist was already bloody and she had stuffed pieces of cloth into the iron clamp in an effort to protect her skin.

The Sergeant had made Henri Deleman drive their supply wagon with both he and his wife chained to the cart. Their daughters were allowed to walk alongside the vehicle. "For this special treatment, they have been told that it will be their duty to prepare meals for both the Dragoons ... and us ... prisoners," she explained in a low voice, "and, the children are not fettered but have to stay alongside their guardians."

She gestured down the line to where Theodore was strutting next to his brother, Andre. He looked back over his shoulder to smile at Suzanne. Pierre raised his head enough to grin grimly at the youth who grinned back.

*   *   *   *   *

10th July 1687
On the road back to the Luberon, Provence

The next day, as the shadows deepened towards night, the group was finally given a break for their evening meal alongside a tumbling mountain stream. Many of the prisoners were cut and bruised from the "encouragement" they received along the way.

The Dragoons did not hesitate to use the flat of their swords to strike the slowest - hitting them on the back of their legs or shoulders. Some, in an effort to avoid the blows, had turned slightly and been gashed instead.

Time was allowed for each group to stand in the shallows of the stream to both drink and wash their hands, face and feet before being led into the shelter of some trees. Here the Dragoons pegged down the ends and middles of each chain – keeping them spaced apart from contact and in three rows.

"Listen, all of you!" The Sergeant stood below them on the trail. "I want no complaints from any of you! To me, you are the scum of France – and you will be treated as such! I have no intention of wasting my time coddling you back to the Luberon. You will be fed three brief meals each day. Eat well and sleep well - for you will need all of your strength to reach our destination. If you cannot keep up – or you give us any trouble - I will simply get rid of you!"

"How?" A hoarse voice came out of the shadows. Pierre could not see who had spoken.

"Easy! I will cut your throats – like the pigs you are!" A gasp went around the group.

"Where are you taking us?" This time it was Isaac Gervaise, the widowed mason from Grambois – sitting holding his twin girls, Nicole and Nadine.

"It's no secret! Back to your villages! So all can witness what happens when people try to escape!" The Sergeant smiled grimly as he gazed around the group of prisoners. "You all know the punishment! The women and girls will be placed in a special convent – for life -as slaves to the Sisters. If the children are unable to work, they will be adopted out into good Catholic homes."

A gasp rippled through the group as he continued, "And, the men and youths will be shipped to Marseilles where they will spend the rest of their lives rowing the famous galleys." A roar of anger burst from the group.

The sergeant did not seem to be affected by the anguish.

"Shut up! All of you! The King has made it plain that France is going to deal with the heretic problem - once and for all! You knew you should both abjure and become practicing Catholics – like all of us – or you will be punished! You knew that!"

"Can we abjure then – right now?" Henri Deleman, their appointed leader from St. Martin – growled – with some hope in his voice.

"Of course not! You," and the Sergeant waved his hand around the group, "had your chance! But, instead, you ran away! The punishment for trying to escape France to Switzerland or over the sea to England is clear! You will either be killed out-of-hand, or put away where you will be a constant warning to all others of your belief."

He hesitated and gazed around the group. " I want it to be very clear! You will all be punished! You will all either go to the convents – for life; or row the galleys – for life – but at least you will be alive!" He lowered his voice ominously, "Or - you will die on the journey back!"

During the silence that followed Pierre felt a queer mixture of both anger and defeat. The vibrant hope that had been so alive as they came closer to the end of their journey was now replaced by feelings of doom and despair. As he gazed around the group he could sense desperation and fear.

"You will now be fed – by the ... Deleman family ... before they are chained up as well for the night. My men will be on guard constantly and

]

severely punish any troublemakers! Sleep well for we start early tomorrow morning!"

As he stalked off, the Dragoons gathered around, with weapons ready, to watch them eat. The Deleman parents helped their three girls serve the party. Each person was given a bowl of their mutton stew, a chunk of bread and a couple of handfuls of dried fruit. Leather water bottles were passed along the chain lines.

Once the food was eaten, the Deleman parents and their oldest daughter, Catherine were also fettered and chained together. However, the two youngest, pretty ten-year old Jehanne and budding 12 year old Francoise were instructed to take the cooking pots down beyond the bend of the stream to clean them.

Their mother, Claudine watched anxiously as they vanished. She tried to rise but a close swipe of a Dragoon's sword forced her back.

Pierre reached out and grasped Suzanne's hand and she squeezed his in response. Tears were trickling down her cheeks as she smiled faintly.

"Don't give up hope, my dear one," he whispered softly, "we have to hope that the infamous Renard ... is watching over us!"

"Oh, Pierre, do you still hope? Surely they would have done something before this?" He gripped her hand again in a desperate attempt to build up hope in both his betrothed ... and himself! They had had so little time!

Faint cries could be heard from downstream. Many of the group tried to stand up and were driven back down by the guards.

A Dragoon emerged from the path the children had taken and called out to the guards.

"The girls have been causing trouble. They object to doing their duties! They'll be back soon! And, they'll behave better next time!" He vanished back down the path.

The climate among the prisoners had become desperate and sullen. No one talked and all watched the path. As the darkness grew, the Dragoons and the girls finally emerged carrying the serving bowls and drying cloths.

Jehanne ran ahead. Her face was twisted with anguish as she ran back up the slope and clutched her mother.

"I don't like washing the dishes! But, it's alright – I'll do them anyway!" Then she rolled over and lay curled up on the grass. Her sister, Francoise, came walking slowly, her face pale and expressionless. Pierre thought that she seemed to be wooden in her manner and walk. She dropped on the grass next to her sister; stared at her mother who spoke to her; shook her head and silently rolled herself up in a blanket. Her mother leaned over and shook her but she lay still and unresponsive. Her mother shook her head and lay down again to sleep.

*   *   *   *   *

A sharp arrow of disappointment mixed with anger struck through Isabeau as her husband came through the doorway. She had been silently praying that he would be completely sober when he returned from the nearby village of Grambois.

Stop thinking about yourself, Isabeau – a good wife always respects her husband – always! But I need you to be strong for me now, she thought fiercely.

"I'm home from the hills, my kitten. Is the supper ready?" He glanced at the pots in the fireplace.

"Le Duc – I have some bad news!" She chose her words carefully to try and guarantee the end result. Before he could reply, she told him of the visit from the Captain and his Dragoons and the threats.

Le Duc sat down heavily with his head dropped onto his hands. He shook his head and raising it, she saw that his eyes seemed empty and vacant. Too heavy for him to deal with, she thought in desperation.

Finally, he grunted. "That's terrible news! You don't have much of a choice, do you?" She nodded and waited. "I suppose I had better go and face him – he and his Dragoons are in the village square." He got up and shrugged his coat off; tossing it on the table. He turned to her as he approached the doorway.

"I don't suppose you could put up with the *Capitaine* ...for a while?" Her sudden sigh, filled with despair, convinced him this was not the road to travel. "Hmm. No, you are not made that way!" Shaking his head in frustration, he left.

How could he? How could any newly-wed husband even consider that? Angry tears ran down her cheeks and she scrubbed them away with her hands. To keep herself from thinking, in desperation she got up and checked the pots. Enough food for them and the billets? Better check the bedrooms and get them ready. She turned and went upstairs.

*   *   *   *   *

It was a good fifteen minutes when she heard the door bang downstairs and Isabeau rushed and peered down the stairs. Her husband stood in the middle of the kitchen and looked up at her fiercely.

"Well, it's done!" he threw his arms up in the air in frustration, "Because of your relationship with the *Capitaine*, we have no options now!" Isabeau gasped in dismay as he continued, "For the sake of a stupid religious belief...it's not worth it! I talked and talked but the *Capitaine* was firm. We sign the papers to abjure tomorrow at the notary!"

"What! Le Duc, this is our life ... our culture ... our soul we are talking about! How could you make such a grand decision – all by yourself? At least we should discuss it together! And what about the neighbors?"

"Damn the neighbors, Isabeau. I don't have to remind you that I am your husband! Despite the way your father raised you, I am responsible for the decisions in this family." As she raced down the stairs, he turned to face her.

"Yes, I did this by myself! I told the *Capitaine* that we - both you and I – would abjure in the morning – and we will! And don't look at me that way! I did this to save your honour – do you understand what that means to a husband?"

Isabeau slumped on the bench and looked up at her husband's reddening face. Her honour! Well, at least that is something!

The whole situation rushed through her mind. The meeting of the women in the neighborhood and their decisions; the visit by the *Capitaine* and the choice between his crude touching – or worse; or the rude attentions of the Dragoons – all day. At least, my husband has been returned to me in one piece – not beaten up as the *Capitaine* promised! And – he protected my honour!

"I am sorry, Le Duc, that I questioned your actions! That was inappropriate of a good wife! I guess, there is nothing to do but abjure – under the circumstances. And it was an option we considered when I talked with the other women in the village."

"I accept your apology! Let's not talk about this again. And, No! The soldiers will not be staying with us tonight or any other night. With this decision, there is a good chance that the whole village will abjure and we shall be safe from now on."

Isabeau rose and touched Le Duc's shoulder as she passed.

"Let's eat!" He simply grunted ignoring her touch.

*   *   *   *   *

10th July 1687
St. Martin, Luberon, Provence

As soon as her husband had left early the next day to visit the village of Peppin d'Aigues on the heights of the Luberon, Isabeau threw a shawl over her shoulders and hurried up the street towards the home of her friend, Cecile Aubertin. As she crossed the square to enter the back gate in the wall, she waved to passing villagers. But instead of a cheerful return greeting, they nodded and turned their faces away. Hurt, she looked back over her shoulder in wonder.

As soon as she touched Cecile's back door, it opened before she could knock.

"Come in, Isabeau." Cecile's voice was low and restrained. "Sit!" she waved to the bench at the kitchen table and shooed the children out into the backyard.

"Well?" Cecile sat opposite her at the table, her face appearing downcast but blank.

"Let me first tell you, Cecile, what happened yesterday evening." She then recounted the whole incident including the threats from the Captain. Instead of her usual animated manner, Cecile listened quietly but without her usual warm concern.

"So that's that! For all of us!"

"Cecile! It was my honour at stake! Despite all my resolve, there was nothing I could do – except abjure!"

She saw tears come to the eyes of her friend. She reached out and touched her hand squeezing it in understanding.

"Oh Isabeau, I am so sad and sorry for you!" Cecile withdrew her hand and looked out the window with hints of reluctance on her face.

"For me, Cecile? Why are you sad for me? We all face the same problem!"

Cecile turned back and tears streamed down her face.

"I don't know how to tell you! You are my friend!"

"Tell me! What do you have to tell me? Are you keeping something from me?"

Cecile raised her head and wiped her tearstained face.

"It is so difficult for me...but I'll try! Isabeau, you know that nothing that happens in the village is much of a secret." Isabeau smiled and nodded. "Well, we all knew that you were the 'key" target in our village. We knew that the *Capitaine* and his burly Dragoons had visited you. We did not know the outcome but we all held our breath. That fact that the *Capitaine* and his rats left your home relieved all of us! Then your husband, Le Duc, came home. And soon after he came marching down the road to the square..."

"Yes, but what is it that you are reluctant to tell me? He came down; confronted the *Capitaine*; realized that they were firm; and decided to abjure – to save my honour!"

"Is that what he told you, Isabeau?"

"Of course, my friend – what else is there...?"

Cecile dropped her head and her voice became softer. "I am ashamed of myself for doing some things. But I sneaked out the back door quietly and crept down the yard until I could listen to the *Capitaine* – I eavesdropped, Isabeau!"

"And..."

"I heard the whole thing – Le Duc confronted the *Capitaine* with his threats. The *Capitaine* laughed at him..."

"Well, Cecile, with his huge Dragoons at his back, there was little my husband could do! You don't blame him, do you?"

Cecile looked down again and shook her head.

"That's not the bad part! But you are my friend! Please just listen; don't talk until I finish – or I may not be able to tell you..."

Isabeau nodded and waited impatiently.

"You know the way your husband blusters when arguing? Well, he blustered and they laughed at him. Then your husband...he offered to turn his back and let the *Capitaine* have his way! At least for a little while, anyway. "

"What? Cecile!"

"Wait! You promised. Don't talk!"

Isabeau nodded her face both angry and dismayed.

"It's worse. The *Capitaine* is a very determined man! After Le Duc gave away your honour ... the *Capitaine* was evidently not satisfied! He turned and asked the Dragoons what they thought of the deal." Cecile faltered and tears began to run again. Isabeau waited silently.

]

"...The Dragoons said they were more interested in all having a sexual party – not with you – but with your husband!"

"They were going to rape him?"

"Yes, Isabeau – and then he made the deal to abjure. It was not your honour he was protecting, it was his!"

Isabeau sat stunned, her eyes wide open seeing nothing. Cecile clutched her hand and hammered their joint hands on the wooden tabletop. Neither seemed to feel any pain.

"I didn't know how to tell you. You have been such a good friend. Please forgive me, Isabeau, I didn't know how to tell you..."

Isabeau stood slowly and Cecile rose as well and they held each other tightly and silently.

"Thank you, Cecile – for telling me! I don't know how to deal with it – right now! Please don't tell anyone else! I will have to think about what to do with this horrible secret. I'll bury it for awhile until I know what to do. I need to go for a walk – by myself – to get my head straight." She turned to go and at the door, turned back. "Thank you, Cecile". She whispered and left.

*　　　*　　　*　　　*　　　*

12th July 1687
The road south to the Luberon

Two days later, before they slept, the Sergeant, with his full complement of Dragoons, re-organized the membership on each chain line. Pierre was upset about being separated from Suzanne but understood the need when the officer explained that the division was being made to allow the Dragoons to ease the toilet problems. All the men were now on separate chains to the women.

The guards also limited any speech after sleeping time - probably because they feared prisoners conspiring about escape. The chains were now fettered on their ankles allowing them to use their heavy coats as sleeping covers.

Pierre rolled over awkwardly as the early morning mist crept beneath his coat to chill him. But soon, the awakening of the Deleman family to prepare breakfast, ended a poor nights sleep for most of the prisoners. They were taken away for toileting and washing and pegged down again for breakfast.

Young Jehanne broke into tears and sobbed in protest when ordered to join her still subdued sister, Francoise who stood looking down at the grass at the edge of the path - avoiding the frantic gaze of her mother.

Finally, a burly guard dragged Jehanne away holding her head firmly in the crook of his arm and whispering harshly into her ear. Pierre was amazed to see her instantly stop struggling and without further whimpers, run to join her sister whom she hugged fiercely. But, even then, Francoise stood woodenly and ignored her clinging sister. The guard glared back briefly at the mother and muttered, "You have to be firm with children like her!" And he stalked away down the path following the girls.

The Dragoons checked the ground pegs before they loaded the mules in preparation for the day's travel. It was soon evident that the return of the Dragoons - assigned to the cooking detail - was delaying departure. The Sergeant finally, sent a runner down the path.

Eventually, the gang of men emerged from the path. They jostled and teased each other in a crude manner while laughing and nudging. Suddenly a pitiful wail broke out from the direction of the path. All heads spun and focused on the terrifying sound.

The Sergeant himself rushed down the hill followed by some of his men. The cooking crew eyed each other - startled fear on their faces. Suddenly, Jehanne, her face wrenched in utter anguish, raced up the path frantically ducking each of the Dragoons trying to stop her. Her screaming continued non-stop even after she had hurled herself into her mother's embracing arms. Crushed against her mother's heavy coat, the wails died into a hopeless whimper.

"What's wrong, my darling? What's wrong?" Claudine shook the child until finally the screaming stopped and Jehanne pointed frantically down the path and screamed, "Francoise, Francoise, Oh, Mother, ... Francoise!"

"Jehanne, what about your sister. Jehanne...?"

All faces turned again to the path as a Dragoon emerged staggering with the body of the young girl limply hanging. Blood still ran from long deep gashes down each wrist and further blood stained her chest. As her head bobbed up and down a deep jagged cut could be seen at her throat.

A terrible moan rose from the frozen prisoners.

Claudine dropped Jehanne and tried to run forward but fell when she reached the end of her chain. As she lay on the ground, her hands stretched out and upward in the direction of her daughter's body, and a low moan issued from her open mouth.

The Sergeant stepped forward and took the limp body from the Dragoon. He brought the body to the mother and laid it in her outstretched arms.

"The silly little bitch! Why would she kill herself?" He growled roughly as he raised his heavy black eyebrows.

"Kill herself?" Claudine's face was shocked, "My Francoise ... kill herself? I don't know!" She rolled slightly and looked back up at the face of her husband, who was standing holding his head in his hands, his face twisted in anguish.

"She was sad lately!" muttered Henri in a low voice, "But things were not that hopeless! I don't know..."

"It's not her fault!" Jehanne's voice croaked as she lay behind on the grass, tears running down her face. "It was the soldiers! Mother, it was the dirty things they did to both of us!" She rolled over onto her face and buried her face in the grass. But still all the shocked onlookers could hear her voice.

"When we were doing the pots at the stream, they would pull our dresses up ... and do things! She wouldn't let me tell! I wanted to tell!

But, they said, if we told, they would strip you, Mother ... and Catherine as well – naked! They promised they would do it to both of you – if we told!" Her hands clutched and tore out lumps of grass with her talon-like fingers. "I told her! We should have confessed! Oh, why didn't we tell!" Then her sobbing voice faded into mumbles.

The Sergeant had risen and turned and glared in the direction of the cooking crew as they stood huddled in a group. Before he could address them a scream of rage and anguish shattered the frozen silence. All turned to the sound.

The father, Henri, kept in place by the chains, had grasped a large broken branch from the grass and struck out violently at the nearest target - a Dragoon standing a few feet away. He had crushed the soldier's exposed throat and the guard was choking out blood as he rolled on the ground. As Henri turned and raced towards another startled Dragoon, the peg holding the chain jerked from the ground allowing him to strike the soldier on the side of his face. The Dragoon fell screaming to the grass.

"Get him!" screamed the Sergeant and several Dragoons jerked out their swords and cut Henri down. But it was too late!

As the Dragoons stood looking down with bloody swords, other prisoners - women and men, had - working together - jerked the pegs from the ground and without weapons were attacking the soldiers.

Pierre saw Suzanne, a rock grasped in her right hand, smash the burly Dragoon who had forced Jehanne to go to her duties that morning, in the face. Blood spurted from his nose. With a roar, he slapped her across the face. While she hesitated as she held her face in her hands, he pushed her backward and reaching for his knife, he leaned over and slashed her bodice ties. Then, kneeling, he grasped the top of her blouse and ripped it downward exposing her naked breasts.

Pierre exploded. He jerked the peg ferociously from the ground and swung the loaded chain around in a circle in the air before swinging it in the direction of the burly Dragoon. As the chain curled around his thick throat, Pierre jerked the end and the man gave a choking scream as the rough chain ground into his throat. He fell back gasping. As Pierre jerked again, a tremendous blow on the back of his head, staggered him and as he tried to recover, darkness descended as another fierce blow struck. Then there was nothing!

*　　　*　　　*　　　*　　　*

11th July 1687
St. Martin, Luberon hillside.

The early morning sunlight broke through the closed shutters and touched the shining crown of Isabeau's rich brown hair as she sat at the wooden table with her head bowed in abject misery. Her hands held up her head as she stared – without thinking – at her cold cup of untouched tisane. Even my favorite herb brew has no taste for me now. She closed her eyes tightly in disgust.

I wonder if all the other people – especially the women – in my village feel the same way. All this month, starting with her joyous wedding feast, had simply plunged uncontrollably downhill – down into a valley of disappointment, sadness and depression. All my plans have been shattered; all my dreams dashed. I have no – that's right, absolutely no direction in my life! She shook her head – the smooth dark tresses showing disapproving disgust!

But, with her hair still swinging on her shoulders, she sat upright and lifted her eyes to gaze at the fireplace as she reviewed the last few days.

The Captain had made his very open threats to her body – her integrity!   Her plans to handle his behaviors had failed dismally to protect her. She had had to resort to appeals to her husband – the one person who now had the responsibility of protecting her – and all that had happened was sheer bluster followed by betrayal! What respect she had earned in her short life with the village had been totally destroyed by his decision to abjure!

She remembered with horror the degrading inner feelings she had experienced as she visited her friend's homes the morning after her husband had made the decision. The unbelieving shock on the faces of the women when she tried to explain her husband's decision hurt her deeply.

Their eyes had glazed over as she talked. They could not understand how she, as a leader of the village opposition, could have plunged to that level of surrender. They had shaken their heads in frustration and disappointment and appealed for assurances that what they were hearing was not real. But it was! And she remembered the utter degradation she felt - after visiting so many homes – trying to walk home upright with head held high – while inside she felt she was crawling like a crushed snake on the roadway.

Villagers had even gathered the next day on the street to openly view the arrival of the Captain and his Dragoons with the Notary and a priest. They had waited on the street in disbelief as the agreement was competed in the crowded kitchen. And when she joined her husband in showing the party back outside, Isabeau had witnessed open tears running down the shocked women's faces.

What happened next was still indelibly etched in her memory. As Le Duc, her husband, had publicly shaken hands with the Notary to traditionally seal the agreement – with honour – the Captain had stepped up close to her, grasped her unwilling hand tightly and firmly in his. As she had stared at him, he had leaned forward and whispered.

"Do not, my little mountain flower, think that this...piece of paper... changes any of my plans to ...satisfy my...is it lust...or love?"

In shock, she stared up at his leering smile; her hand still firmly clutched in his. She tugged but he held it firmly. Nodding his head he whispered again. "Nothing you do will thwart my ambition.   I look forward," he shook his head solemnly, "to picking...the time and the place..." Then he released her hand and made a gracious bow sweeping his hat from his head but keeping his eyes firmly fixed on hers as he bent forward.

]

Isabeau stood frozen, her mouth open in shock. The little bit of guilty freedom she had experienced vanished in the slight morning breeze that brushed her face. Her husband had turned from the Notary and was frowning in a puzzled manner. She still stood frozen in shock as the Captain and his Dragoons mounted their horses and with a wave of his hand escorted the carriage bearing the rest of the party away.

As her husband shook her arm a little roughly, she jerked her head round to witness all of the women, as a body, turning their backs on her as they retreated down the street and into the homes to lament the situation.

"Isabeau! Did you have to make things worse than they are by flirting with the *Capitaine*? You are my wife!" She stared up at his frustrated and angry face.

"Flirting?" She felt a burst of fury rise up her throat but controlled it.

"Inside! Le Duc!" She broke from his grasp and turned her skirts flaring. She looked back and with controlled fury pointed at the door. "Inside! Now!" Dismay broke over his features and glancing around with some embarrassment, he followed her back into the house and slammed the door behind him.

Once inside, his embarrassment and anger began. However, it was immediately and completely overshadowed by her intense rage. It boiled over - as he had never seen it before.

Despite her upbringing to "respect the man of the household in all matters", her need to cleanse her stomach of all the unuttered insults to her integrity vomited out. Le Duc stood with his mouth hanging open in dismay as she, in a low but firm intense tone, repeated the Captain's recent threat. Her disgust at his decision to abjure her faith; the manner in which he had destroyed whatever support she had in the village; and the helplessness she was feeling at the direction her whole life was taking; left her utterly distressed.

Finally, she stood silent looking at the floor, her body exhausted and spent. Her husband stood looking down at her; obviously feeling helpless.

"So, Isabeau... what do you want me to do?" he grunted hoarsely.

She raised her head and looked at his helpless face. As her eyes roved over his round face and his confused brown eyes, she felt a desperateness begin to well up inside her.

"Le Duc – right now, I want us to escape this ... mess! But...something inside me says...that running away from something horrible is ... not the right thing to do!" She shook her head slowly, her thoughts churning inside as he wisely stood silently looking at her. "But, I think...we need to ...get away!"

"Get away! You mean ... flee the country – like many of our faith are doing?" He shook his head in frustration. "We would have nothing, Isabeau, nothing!"

A glimmer of hope rose in her mind and she felt her face soften as she smiled, a little, for the first time in several days.

"Nothing – at least I would have ...my faith, Le Duc! Yes – we might not have...anything valuable - that we could sell! But we would be

...doing something ... rather than just ...standing still!" She saw his face tighten a little with stubbornness and thought desperately how she could loosen the tension.

"Le Duc, we don't have to flee! Because of the contract to abjure, we are now able to at least travel! They arrest people who are escaping the country. But we could...take a trip! Until the Captain loses his mad obsession for your wife or leaves the Luberon hillside."

She desperately searched around for reasons. "Your Uncle had been keen on us visiting your relatives in ...Lyon, was it not? So, why not?" She saw immediately that her arrow had gone home, as his self-confidence seemed to lighten his features.

"Yes! Why not? Uncle did seem eager to introduce my new wife to the family. I am sure he would even pay for the trip from his own pocket!" he smiled with some glee as he saw a way to escape the horrors of the recent events and do so without costing any of his own money. He looked back at her with some pitiful eagerness, "Would that make you feel better about what I have done?"

She leaned forward and grasping his shoulders kissed him on the cheek. "Oh, Le Duc, that would allow me to leave – without running away from anything."

"Good, my wife. I will visit my Uncle immediately and see whether this can be arranged." He hugged her briefly and with some obvious relief, he swung out of the kitchen to saddle his horse.

Isabeau sank onto the bench and, leaning on the table, breathed heavily until she felt comfortable inside again. Having made some definite plans made her feel better. She knew that Le Duc would have little trouble convincing his Uncle – as head of the family – to make the visit to Lyon.

This would give her a break from having to deal with the attentions of the Captain and also allow her to develop a little of her new role as the newest member of her husband's family. But, what would she do about regaining the respect of all her neighbors? I will have to wait for the right opportunity; she winced with a little dismay, at the challenge. But, right now, Isabeau, open the shutters and let a little of that wonderful warm sunlight into the kitchen – and your soul!

*   *   *   *   *

]

CHAPTER SIXTEEN

13th July 1687
On the road back to the Luberon

The buzzing in Pierre's head overrode the pain above his eyes. The side of his face was rasped in the constant motion of his body and he recognized quickly that he was again being slung over the saddle of a pack animal as it ambled down the steep path. He twisted his head slightly to relieve the abrasion of his face and turned it enough to see the Dragoon leading the mule.

His curse at the soldier brought his agony immediately under control as the mule stopped and the sergeant appeared at his side to slice through the leather thongs. With a painful jarring, Pierre hit the ground and rolled away from the stamping hooves of the steed.

The Sergeant motioned to the dazed man with his out-thrust sword and Pierre rose to his feet, shook his head painfully, wiped the dust gently from his bruised face and staggered up the trail until he reached Andre. He nodded and stood silently until the Dragoons had again fettered him to the chain. Then walking as gently as he could, he half closed his eyes at the strength of the sunshine and followed Andre down the dusty trail.

"Pierre, psst! Pierre!" It was only after several attempts in hoarse whispers that Pierre realized that Andre was calling quietly to him. He glanced back to make eye contact and then grunted as he turned forward and listened carefully.

"Pierre, they've made contact!"

"Who's ... they?"

"Renard!"

Pain wracked Pierre as he jerked his head around; his eyes wide open in spite of the strong sun. Then he looked forward again quickly.

"Yes! At that last signpost – at the turnoff to the village of Lus - there was a little red ribbon waving in the breeze!" Andre's voice was low but filled with excitement and a touch of hope. Pierre felt his body warm with a jolt of fresh energy. Maybe tonight, he thought. Somehow they will find a way of contacting me!

"We must leave an acknowledgment ... somehow!" he grunted.

"I did! I remembered what you did before. When they stopped to get a drink of water, I sat down to rest. No one noticed ... but I built a small pile of pebbles!"

With a painful grin, Pierre turned and smiled at his friend. "Andre – you never fail to amaze me! I am proud of you, my friend!" He turned forward and marched for several paces with a much lighter step. Then, he remembered and grunted aloud in dismay. "Andre," he whispered hoarsely, "How is Suzanne?" Andre said nothing. Pierre asked again, a little louder. Andre said nothing. Now he turned his head and was shocked by his friend's pained expression.

"Suzanne? What's happened to her, Andre?"

Andre's voice was low and filled with anguish. "We don't know, Pierre! The riot was a disaster! For us ... and for them! We all got beaten! There was screaming and bodies all over the place. From the ground, I saw Suzanne... being dragged away ... from the mess!"

Andre's eyes glazed over as he whispered. "Henri and his daughter were dead – we had to dig a grave for them! And another for the Dragoon that Henri struck in the throat. He died before we had the first grave dug! We buried him too. But, we never saw anything of Suzanne!"

He was quiet for a second. "We never saw her again! Theodore," he motioned backward where his young brother was lagging with head hung in misery, "misses her greatly! And, I have no answer for him either!"

Pierre turned back, his head and stomach had become a churning mixture of emotions. *Mon Dieu, non!* Not Suzanne! Not my beautiful ... and sweet little Suzanne!

He closed his eyes and shook his aching head. Oh, if there is a God, let him care for her! Of all the gentle creatures in the world...he did not know what to think! Pierre remembered how cheerfully and bravely she had accepted the dangerous journey – all the way from her village to the mountain passes. Never a complaint or whine! Always a sweet smile and a cheerful word! And, all this had now turned into the most horrible of disasters!

As he stumbled and almost fell on the trail, he opened his eyes and looked up at the peaks overshadowing the trail. Above him birds were swooping as they fed themselves in the late afternoon. Wisps of white cloud gently moved across a deep blue sky. All this natural beauty, he thought with pain, together with all this horror in our beautiful world! He felt he wanted to vomit and clean his stomach of all this madness! Tears ran down his cheeks and he hurriedly brushed them away.

Suddenly the line of prisoners stopped walking. People, who were trudging forward automatically, crashed into others who had stopped. Confused cries ran through the group and the Dragoons slapped them quiet with their swords and sticks.

The cause of the incident soon was whispered up the line. It was reported that several Dragoons who had evidently been riding ahead had stumbled on two further heretics who were evidently trying to escape up the same trail to Switzerland! They had been captured and subdued.

The two new prisoners limped up the trail, their heads bowed and covered by their hands - escorted by Dragoons and the Sergeant. Next to Pierre, the party stopped and the officer motioned for the prisoners to be chained ahead of him. Once the task was completed, the line again moved forward, Pierre staring at their backs puzzled. Finally, one of the men turned and rubbing his head painfully grinned at him.

]

Daniel Carle! And Thomas Brunet! Of the village of la Bastide-des-Jourdans!

"But, you escaped ... just before Grenoble?" he whispered hoarsely.

Daniel smiled, and nodded. He looked forward down the line to ensure that he was not being watched, then answered.

"Yes, Pierre! But, the day after our escape, we were captured by ...friends of ours!"

"Renard?"

"Yes! At first, we were horrified – that we had been captured ... so soon! We agreed to help them! They were shorthanded! However, after we put ourselves at risk - we will be helped to cross the border." He looked ahead again, then continued talking over his shoulder.

"It was Renard's way of getting a message to you! We went ahead ... and allowed ourselves to be captured!"

"Can they help us?"

"They don't have enough bodies to make an open attack – not against soldiers! But they will make an attempt ... tonight or tomorrow night! They will be watching you and do the best they can!" He turned and grinned again; then turned his head forward.

Pierre looked back at Andre – who had been evidently following the conversation – and Andre grinned back at him.

"That's good news, Pierre! Especially, after all our disasters!" He shook his head with some astonishment; "We needed this!"

Pierre even smiled a little as he continued his plodding ahead. Then the smile died and was replaced with a grim jaw. Suzanne, he thought with pain, we need to escape and find Suzanne!

*   *   *   *   *

13th July 1687
St. Martin, Luberon, Provence.

In the light of the candle, Isabeau sat on the bed and peered at her wedding dress. Shall I take it; or leave it, she pondered? A trip to visit her husband's relatives in Lyon required that she have suitable clothing for feasts and celebrations but was this to be a regular trip spent meeting new Aunts and Uncles; or would this turn into a secretive dash for the Swiss border?

"Hmm! I suppose one good dress wouldn't be a problem." she murmured softly and holding the garment close to her chin, she sank back on the covers and closed her eyes. Remnants of memories flashed before her eyes. Being the center of the whole village – no, two villages! She had never danced better – even her husband was surprised at her abilities. The special sword dance with Le Duc – with too much to drink – swaying proudly as the platform of swords held by the Dragoons swept around the square. Then uncomfortable memories shattered the pleasant memories! Being insulted and assaulted by the Captain during the dance. Plus her growing fears of the expected and unknown sexual demands.

154

Her eyes jerked open as she heard footsteps on the stairs. She sat up and folded the precious dress carefully and placed it in the bottom of the wooden trunk as her husband opened the door.

"Can you be ready soon, Isabeau?" Her shadow cast by the flickering candle showed her head nod on the white walls. He sat down heavily on the bed, his face clearly showing traces of anxiety as he looked up at her.

"I think I have planned well ... but? Uncle Antoine agreed to have the carriage arrive at our door at the same time that the village carts are leaving for the market in Pertuis." He chuckled a little – but without his usual bragging self-confidence.

"Those lazy drunk Dragoons are usually sleeping and the noise of an extra carriage should not cause any alarm." Isabeau kept packing her clothes as he talked. "By the time they realize we have left, we should be ... in the streets of Cavaillon!" Isabeau knew from the tone of his voice that he was "whistling in the graveyard". Despite his calm manner, he was worried about the responsibility of having to make such dangerous decisions.

Outside an early cart's wheels creaked by. Le Duc stood up and helped Isabeau close the hasp of the wooden trunk. He lifted one side and finding it lighter than expected, grasped it by the rope handles and strutted through the doorway and down the stairs with Isabeau trailing behind carrying the flickering candle.

Their luggage was now piled at the doorway. Isabeau gazed around the kitchen and living room and ran her hand on the smooth clean tabletop. This had been her first home in marriage and she had really enjoyed housekeeping - for herself.

"Don't worry! We will be coming back ... once things settle down ... when the Dragoons – and that ... obnoxious swine leave the hillside!" Le Duc's voice in the semi-darkness sounded eerie and somewhat artificial. It was like he was playing a role in a traveling drama, she thought. The early sunlight was lighting up the cracks in the shutters and lancing arrows of light across the kitchen floor tiles.

Moving wheels and a clatter of hooves stopped outside their door.

"It's time!" whispered Le Duc hoarsely. "Open the door...and hold it open!" he grunted as he bent to lift the wooden cases. She grasped two cloth bags to follow him into the street.

After quietly greeting her husband's Uncle as he descended from the coach, she handed up packages and bags to Le Duc who was helping the driver pack and tie the luggage. She closed the outside door quietly knowing that any home in a village in Provence would be safely left in the care of its neighbors. She was helped into the interior of the coach and hugged by her new Aunt – Isabelle! Soon the two men joined their wives and the crack of the whip sent the carriage bumping over the cobblestones.

Isabeau had traveled by cart to the local markets many times before but had never experienced coach travel. While her husband peered anxiously out the cracks between the window edge and the hanging leather blinds, Isabeau ran her hands over the leather covered padded seats. She leaned back and smiled at her new Aunt.

]

The road out of the village should have been a straight drive so the sudden turning of the coach threw the passengers against each other.

"*Mon Dieu!*" Le Duc's voice was high pitched and held a note of terror. Without thinking, he jerked the blinds aside and stuck his head out.

"Dragoons!" he gasped and his face visibly paled even in the darkness of the coach. Isabeau found it difficult to breathe and gasped several times. The Uncle's eyes were wide and distressed while the Aunt simply covered her eyes with her hands in dismay.

Then the Uncle shook himself and took charge. He jerked the blinds up and tied them in place. Then he opened the door of the coach and turning, descended to the dusty cobblestones. A glance outside revealed many Dragoons on horseback and that the carriage was now in the middle of the village square with a dismounted Dragoon holding the bridle of the lead horse. The Captain, plumed hat in hand, was astride his horse and peering towards the interior of the coach.

"*Capitaine! Bonjour!* Is there a problem?" The Uncle's voice rang out over the dusty square.

"If you are ... leaving the village...yes!" The Captain's lazy voice drifted into the coach.

"But why, *Capitaine?* Both our families – both my nephew, Le Duc Mallan, and I have abjured as you wished. It is all legal - is it not?"

The Captain lackadaisically replaced his hat as he winced at the strong early morning sunlight. "Well ... legally ... Hmm, yes! I suppose so." He leaned back in the saddle and stretched his arms in the air and yawned.

"Well, I don't understand then, *Capitaine.* We plan to pay a visit to my relatives ... up country ... and..."

"Ah ... *Monsieur* Mallan ...your plans! That, then ... is the problem! You see ...I too have plans ... for your family ...and they don't include dashing off to visit relatives."

It was obvious to Isabeau that secrets are hard to keep in a small village. Their secret escape was obviously not a secret to the Dragoons and the Captain. And it was also apparently not a secret to the neighbors – for already the areas behind the Dragoons were filling with the villagers and their families.

She could see her late friend, Cecile Aubertin, holding onto the arm of her husband; and many other women whom she had considered her close friends – before she had failed them!

Uncle Antoine waved his hands in the air and stamped his foot in the dust.

"I don't understand, *Capitaine!* How do your plans effect our travel?" His voice sounded truly mystified.

The Captain said nothing. He waved his hand lazily at a fly that was buzzing in his face – and simply waited. The murmurs from the crowd of onlookers died to complete silence. Everyone waited.

There is no other way, thought Isabeau! I will have to do something! She closed her eyes a second and breathed deeply to get into control. Then, as she stood up and bent to step down from the carriage, her husband grasped her arm.

"What are you going to do?" he grunted. "If my Uncle cannot do anything, you certainly cannot!" Isabeau turned slightly and whispered. "I think you know what his plans are – and I am the only one who can deal with him!" She looked deep into his eyes and then firmly said "Trust me, Le Duc!" Then turning again, she shook off his hand and backed down the steps of the carriage.

"Ah, *Bonjour, Madame* Isabeau." The Captain removed his feathered hat with a flourish and bent forward and nodded his head as though to honour her arrival. Except for the odd clatter of a horse's hoof, there was dead silence in the square and his voice echoed clearly around the buildings.

Isabeau stood as tall as she could – unsmiling and poised – and nodded her head slightly in response.

"You know my plans, *Madame*! And, you know that ... I always keep my promises, don't you?" He grinned lazily at her and then turned to include all of the watching villagers with his smile. Isabeau took a deep breath - as the Captain performed for his audience - and was ready when he turned towards her again.

"Let me talk to my neighbors, my dear *Capitaine*!" Despite her resolve, she found her voice a little hoarse and anxious. The Captain lifted his head and started with some surprise.

She gazed at her neighbours. "My friends... I am afraid the *Capitaine* and I have a secret! I think it is time I shared it with ... all of you." She forced a bitter little smile to crease her face as she caught Cecile's eye and got a hint of support. "The *Capitaine*," she raised her left hand and waved it in his direction, "has made it very clear to me that he intends to ... diligently ... explore my body!"

The Captain's eyes widened in shock as a ripple of incredulity swept through the watching crowd. Behind her, she heard her husband hiss, "Oh, no, Isabeau!" but continued feeling her voice strengthen as her voice rose.

"You do not know that ... on my wedding day," a gasp ran through the villagers, "during the dancing of the *La Volta*, he was quite ... deliberate ... in handing my ...personal parts," and she gestured to her breasts.

The speechless women raised their hands to their mouths in dismay. The Captain glanced around at his Dragoons whose mouths were generally hanging open.

She continued: "Since then, he has come to my home several times to openly state his purpose – to ... violate me!"

She dropped her head momentarily, took another long breath and continued. "My husband is now aware of this ... pursuit! And has confronted the brave *Capitaine*. But it is obvious from his actions today... that he has not given up his insulting plans."

"*Madame* Isabeau," the Captain finally replaced his hat with a flourish and tried again to regain control, "I am afraid that you have ... misunderstood ... my respectful efforts at ...flirting a little..." Isabeau overrode his anxious explanations:

]

"*Mon Capitaine*, by your demands, you have insulted me ... and my husband. And since you obviously ...are going to continue your demands until I finally ... surrender," she threw her hands up dramatically to demonstrate her frustration, "I will do that - now! I will surrender! Openly! Right now!"

She turned and removed her shawl and spread it open on the cobblestones while her husband's hissed warnings issued from the coach. Then to the gasps from the watching villagers, she knelt down and lay flat on her back on the shawl. She looked up at the Captain, silhouetted on horseback against the blue morning sky. She raised her hands in a welcoming gesture.

"Well, *Capitaine*, let's get it over with! Why don't we stop this flirting ... and get down to your dirty business! Instead of all your secret threats ... let's show all of your subjects how you ...carry out the King's work in Provence!"

The villagers had moved a little closer to the action and Isabeau could see the incredulous smiles appearing on the faces of the watching neighbors. Cecile was biting her lips to prevent her breaking into laughter. The Captain's face was white with shock and anxiety.

"Well, come on, *Capitaine*! This is your chance to show your men how ... manly you are!" She turned her head towards the frozen officer. "Do I not excite you now?"

A further gasp echoed around the square as she reached down and tugged her skirts up above her knees to the point where all could see the tops of her stockings tied with ribbons. "Come *Capitaine* – either you carry out your secret threats now; or ... leave me in peace!"

She spread her legs wide open as the watchers gasped in horror. "There, *Capitaine*, I open my legs for you! What more can I do?" This was too much for the villagers and a roar of laughter raced around the square. Women were covering their mouths and men holding their stomachs and bent over laughing.

Isabeau saw the Captain jerk his head round to put a rapid end to the roars of the watching Dragoons. Then he slowly turned towards Isabeau lying prostrate on the cobbles looking at him with an earnest look in her face.

"*Madame*, you ...shock me ... and insult me! You must have misunderstood my intentions! My plans today were simply to ... carry out the King's orders ... to prevent any of you Disbelievers from possibly ...fleeing the country!" She watched him glare around at the amused villagers – who stopped smiling with some difficulty; and then looked back at Uncle Antoine.

"I apologize, *Monsieur*, for delaying your trip to visit your relatives. You may continue ... on your journey!" He reluctantly glanced back at Isabeau, now smiling mischievously up at him.

"I will not forget this behavior, *Madame*! I never forget ... or forgive ... insults, such as these!" Then jerking his horse, he galloped out of the square followed by his troop of Dragoons – all of whom grinned openly and with obvious sexual interest at the prostrate young woman.

Uncle Antoine turned and bent down to extend a hand to his niece. The corners of his mouth were creased in a hidden smile.

"That was outrageous, my dear child – but courageous! There are ... hidden depths to you that ... my family have not yet seen."

She slowly stood up and grinned at her Uncle. "I guess ... I'd had enough and felt that I needed to do something dramatic ...to stop his threats." She looked around the square. "I think that we had better go quickly before the *Capitaine* decides to ...regain control?"

"I agree, my dear child, let us go quickly before a bruised and bloodied Officer changes his mind." He helped her up into the coach where she settled next to the Aunt. "Let's go, Driver!"

As the coach turned tightly in the square and re-entered the road, the villagers as a body spontaneously broke into clapping applause that continued until the dust finally settled and the coach vanished from sight.

Cecile hugged her husband openly in the dust filled air.

"That was wonderful, wonderful, Isabeau! We are all so proud of you!" She called out down the road and the other villagers echoed her sentiments.

*   *   *   *   *

14th July 1687
On the road south from Grenoble

The next day the capture of the two additional prisoners, to replace those lost in the riot, seemed to exhilarate the Dragoons who all joined in chanting out marching songs as they tramped down the dusty trails. Needless to say, none of the "heretics" joined in despite urging from the soldiers.

Pierre tried to control his mixed emotions so as to allow the secret knowledge of a possible escape to override his anxiety over Suzanne's disappearance. There were many times on the trail when he found himself grinding his teeth or tightening his jawbone. To relieve the pressure, he would puff a blast of air from his lungs; breathe deeply; and force himself to reduce the tension in his whole body. After several attempts he discovered that, while his body was more relaxed, he would also be a little light-headed and stagger a little before regaining control.

"Pierre, Pierre, are you alright?" Andre's hoarse whisper would creep over his shoulder; or, sometimes Theodore would appear at his side, his worried face peering up into Pierre's. Pierre would lean over and punch the boy's shoulder lightly and grimly grin at him in reassurance.

With the uplifted spirits of the Dragoons, the party was kept marching down the trail much longer than normal. Long shadows were forming on the hillsides and the air in the deeper chasms was beginning to feel cold and damp before the guards began to seek a suitable camping spot.

A hurried whispering consultation took place between the two new prisoners and Pierre and Andre; and when the party finally was led off onto a grassy tree-shrouded bank above a tumbling mountain stream, the men in Pierre's group used their clean-up time quickly. Since they were finished first, they then moved voluntarily as close to the brush on the upper slopes as possible – ensuring that no group got above them. They lay down immediately and rested quietly so as not to raise any suspicions from the Dragoons.

Later, when the depleted Deleman family of mother and daughters – hesitated about settling down for the their rest prior to cooking the supper, Pierre encouraged them to settle below his party on the slope – which they did despite some curious frowns on Claudine's face.

Pierre and his group ate quickly and settled down to rest without any unnecessary conversation. Theodore was upset when his older brother urged him to control his normally boisterous behaviours and "fake" his sleep. Pierre saw, through barely open eyes, that the guards were strolling between the prostrate prisoners and being obviously deceived, had left only a single Dragoon on guard near the edge of the brush. The young soldier rolled himself up in his blanket and was soon snoring. The rest of the Dragoons gathered down across the stream around a bonfire and were soon singing – and drinking – together.

Hmm, thought Pierre, now we wait – and see. He forced his ears to try and ignore the crackling of the fire and the singing and concentrate on the sounds from the forest above on his darkened hillside. He started when he heard rustling but, although he held his breath and listened, it became obvious that this was the noise of some field mouse looking for food in the leaves.

Slowly heavy breathing from his companions indicated that they had drifted off. Well, thought Pierre, if something is going to happen, I guess it will. So, I might as well sleep also. Slowly, he felt himself drifting off in oblivion.

Suddenly, a feeling of being trapped brought him to his senses quickly. His head was pinned to the ground ... by the ear! Terror made him open his eyes. Warm breath touched his cheek and he realized that someone was lying close to him and holding his ear in a tight grip of fingers.

"Keep still, Pierre!" A soft whisper allowed him to relax his tense body. The fingers released his ear. He turned slowly to face the whisper. A dark shape had apparently crept silently through the undergrowth and now lay next to him.

Pierre glanced around and was amazed to see that everyone – including the Dragoon – were still deep in sleep. As he lay on his back, the shape turned in the direction of his feet and with some quiet tinkering, he felt the chain separate from his fettered ankle.

A hand pushed him hard onto the cold ground in an effort to keep him still. From his prone position, he sensed - rather than saw – another dark figure slide out of the bush and slither over to the sleeping Dragoon.

What happened next was both quiet and effective. The creeper raised itself slightly above the Dragoon's head and then lowered itself on top of the blanketed soldier. With a hand over his mouth to silence him and a heavy arm across his throat, there was a muffled grunt followed by a struggling trapped lower body which quickly reduced to complete silence.

A quick tap on his shoulder encouraged Pierre to quietly unwrap his body from the blanket. Silently gathering his limited belongings, he crept forward past the first blackened figure and slid through into the hollowed-out escape route in the brush. Glancing back over his shoulder as he entered the "pipe", Pierre could see down into the hollow where the major portion of the Dragoons was sleeping around the still burning campfire. He realized with deep pleasure, that the flickering light of the fire prevented any Dragoons still awake from seeing anything beyond their immediate area.

From the faint whispers and grunts behind, Pierre realized that his comrades were being awakened silently as well and he crawled carefully on up the escape route as another figure crept behind him. Suddenly, his outstretched hands were grasped eagerly and he was pulled to his feet in the deep dark gloom of the forest.

He was turned south – back down the trail - and passing from hand-to-hand, he was directed past other dark figures standing on the edge of the trail. He glanced back and counted other figures being hurried down the trail behind him.

Suddenly, he was stopped and his hand was placed onto a sturdy rope and he stood silently until finally the party was linked together and a push got him moving downhill in the dark behind one of his rescuers who held onto the end of the rope. No words were spoken and except for the soft padding of feet, he heard no other sound than the night wind rustling the leaves of the trees.

Finally, after about an hour of tramping, the leader turned off the trail uphill and over a small ridge. Down below in a hollow, Pierre could see a small lantern towards which they were headed. Pierre let out a heavy sigh of relief and felt for the first time that he was able to actually breathe freely again.

As they approached the lantern, Pierre became aware that there were figures standing in the trees ahead. And, he could hear the muffled stamping of hooves and the quiet soft whickering of mules - or horses. Finally, the leader stopped and took his hand from the rope and began to wind the rope up as the prisoners gathered in a group.

"Andre! And Theodore!" He hugged each in turn. Then he recognized the dark grinning forms of Daniel and Thomas – the new prisoners who had carried the rescue message. Then the sobbing figure of the widow, Claudine, hugged him gratefully. Then he was grasped eagerly by both her daughters in turn, Catherine and young Jehanne.

A hand grasped him by the shoulder and he was turned to face another figure wearing a hood. Even in the faint light of the lamp he could recognize the inscribed cartoon-like features of the fox on the hood.

"Welcome, cousin!" the hoarse whisper warmed him inside and he grasped the outstretched hand. "I wish we could have rescued more ... but we had to make sure that what we rescued, we saved as well!"

"*Mon Dieu*, my cousin! Anything is better than nothing!" Pierre whispered back.

"Now, friends," the hooded figure addressed the small group of prisoners, "We have deliberately set a false trail up the path," and he

]

gestured to the north, "and my men have covered our climb up the hill so the Dragoons will not recognize our escape path."

He gestured to the animals standing nearby. "We have enough animals here to move you quickly and safely to a secret spot where you can rest the night. We will then make plans for you to reach Switzerland quickly and safely." A flurry of excited voices echoed around the hollow. The rescuing team quickly got the prisoners mounted and a stream of riders guided by Renard moved up into the dark hills.

*   *   *   *   *

15th July 1687
Hidden in the mountains of France

Pierre had not slept well despite the fact that they were bedded down on comfortable straw filled bags with enough blankets to be almost too warm. He peered up into the dome of a huge cave knowing that they were all safe. But his sleep had been punctuated by many startled awakenings. And, several times in the night, Andre's concerned face had bent over him and Pierre had felt his hand on his forehead calming him down. Now, with the fire only composed of glowing embers, a flash of early sunlight emerged from the cave entrance. Still weary, Pierre sat up, and with difficulty, pondered his condition.

Why didn't I sleep better? He looked around the vast cavern again. We are safe and warm and well fed. Almost half of the prisoners have been rescued. I am back in control of ... my own destiny! We have been promised quick and safe entry into the Swiss cantons. At last!

He sighed and drew a draught of fresh air into his lungs. What was interfering with his sleep? Have I been hit too often on the head in the last few days? He rubbed his scalp thoroughly feeling the many sore spots still tender from the many blows he had received. I shouldn't wonder if I have had damage of some kind done, he thought. He remembered the sheepherder from Spain who had been beaten up by robbers some years ago and who had ended up being slow of thought and speech ever after.

No, he reassured himself, my thoughts seem to be all right. So, have I unfinished work of some kind ... of course, Suzanne! That's what it could be! My good Cousin has promised me freedom – forever! But I have to finish what I started! I made a promise to a father...he took another deep breath and finished his thought ... and I owe him an accounting! Pierre threw off his coverings and quietly found his way to the entrance where he greeted the sentries who were crouching behind a woven entry cover of branches and ferns. The guard nodded his understanding and when the guard's whistled birdcall was responded to, he pushed the cover aside so that Pierre could exit and stroll toward the edge of the ridge, remembering to crouch down prior to possibly being seen. Now, he wriggled forward and peered down from their aerie to the panorama of mountain ridges and treed valleys below. He drew a heavy breath of crisp fresh air into his chest and forced his body to relax. He found the bigger breaths he took, the easier the weight became. When his head was clear and his mind made up, he crawled back from the brink and re-entered their hiding place.

*   *   *   *   *

As he emerged from the cave entrance, he saw that the whole party was sitting on the floor including - most of the rescue team – their faces still hooded for protection against recognition. His cousin was standing against the wall – also hooded with his "fox" face on the bag. Renard turned and waved to Pierre.

"Pierre, I have been explaining how the rescue was carried out – and regretting that we had not acted earlier to … save the lives of some of the people. We did try to act – but the opportunity did not come at the right time. And, so two brave … souls died!" A soft broken sob came from the Deleman family area. Renard turned and faced the group again as Pierre seated himself beside Andre.

"Pierre, your group is anxious to leave for Switzerland as soon as possible. Daniel and Thomas, here," he gestured to the two young men sitting in the front, "were promised that for their dangerous task of surrendering to the Dragoons, they would be helped to cross the border safely! And, they shall! But," he waved his hand to take in the rest of the group, "what are your wishes…?"

Catherine's hand rose quickly. "My mother, my sister and I … would like to also cross to safety as quickly as possible!" She looked back at her mother, Claudine whose face was freshly tearstained and nodded her head with some force. Slowly, in return, Claudine nodded back and then raised her eyes to Renard; "Our family has been … punished enough for wanting … freedom! We cannot change the past… but we can go forward! Thank you all for …trying so hard!" and this time, she turned and nodded in Pierre's direction. Both the girls smiled at him also and Pierre felt his face flush in response. Renard's hood bobbed and he turned towards Pierre.

"Well, Pierre, we have not heard from you. Is it Switzerland – and soon?"

Pierre looked down at the rocky cavern floor and took several deep breaths. The whole gathering waited in silence for his response. Pierre felt tears flush into his eyes. Not now, he thought, not now!   I need to be thankful but - I need to be firm! He raised his head and looked around the faces that had shared his journey.

"The thought of being … so close to freedom and safety, … scares me a little!" He grinned wryly as the group's laughter echoed around the cavern. "But, although I … fear the worst … I have to search for Suzanne!" Unwept tears flushed his eyes again and he shook his head. He looked up at his cousin and continued, "I promised her father I would protect her and…"

"You did all you could, Pierre!" Andre grasped his shoulder and shook him.

"Yes, Andre, my friend, I really think we all did! But, I have to make sure ... for his sake – and mine!" He looked around the group. "I feel that the rest of the party should not delay any longer. Help them get across the border." A murmur of satisfaction rose from the gathering. "All I need is a mule for myself – to try to discover the truth! Then, maybe my mind will be clear again – and I can continue my journey."

Renard's head nodded. "Very well, Pierre, I understand the need. Its unfinished business, isn't it?" Pierre nodded fervently. "Right, everyone else in the escape party, pack your belongings – take the covers with you. Within the hour, the troop will leave to escort you through Grenoble, through Chambéry, Annecy and across the border to Geneva." An excited cheer rose from the group of five.

Andre turned to Pierre and grasped his arm. "You understand, Pierre, that we – both my young brother and I – intend to join you on your hunt for Suzanne!" Pierre started to shake his head but Andre continued, "No, Pierre, we both loved her! And Theodore has not been the same since she disappeared! He needs to be part of the search!"

Pierre looked at the two quietly – Andre determined and Theodore with tears running down his cheeks, begging.

"I would be proud to have you both with me!" And both the Roux brothers leaned forward and grasped his hands tightly. "Let's make plans with my cousin!" and they rose and pushed through the crowd to meet with Renard.

*   *   *   *   *

... several days earlier - 13th July 1687
On the road to Lyon, France

"*Sergent*, come to me! Now!" It was obvious to both the Sergeant, and to the Dragoons surrounding him, that the Captain's overt calm and tranquil appearance, was definitely not his current condition. The officer spurred up alongside.

"*Sergent*, if you are thinking that your *Capitaine* has been publicly mocked by that little bitch – back there in the village – you are very short-sighted!" The Captain, for the first time, turned in the saddle to gaze at his underling. Sergeant Cappel had long enough experience in the Dragoons to recognize a dangerous quagmire when he crossed one. He looked straight-ahead and answered carefully.

"Mocked, *mon Capitaine*?" The Captain kept staring at the sergeant but a slight smile caught the corners of his mouth.

"Oh, come on, *Sergent*! Don't act like the village idiot!" He gave a short abrupt laugh and lowered his voice grimly, "Though ... of course, I forget that you've had enough ... political experience ... not to answer my question! Hmm!" He grunted, then turned his head forward. "Probably the best response, *Sergent*! Very wise! Anyhow, it may have looked like I was being mocked. I expect that the villagers – and that bitch felt so too." He glanced over his shoulder and turned back. "But, *Sergent*, she was not just making an ass ... of me! She was really mocking ... every

Dragoon! And, even the King and Cardinal too!" The Sergeant squinted his eyes against the bright morning sun and nodded his head slowly.

"Hah! You get my point, *Sergent!*" It was apparent to the officer that his Captain was recovering quickly from his poorly concealed embarrassment. The Captain continued in a steady voice, "That little bitch must pay dearly for the insults she presented today! *Non?*" The Captain accepted the nodded agreement and continued in a slow and thoughtful tone.

"I want you to personally arrange to take a small detachment of men – make sure that at least two of them can read and write - so that you can keep records? They should be on the road shortly. Hmm ... maybe seven men. I want you to get in sight of the carriage. Then, drop two men behind to act as a rearguard. Then, approach rapidly – close enough so that the driver can alert the passengers. But not so close that they stop! I want you to frighten them ... so they try to flee! Gallop after them but not quickly enough to catch them! I think we can be sure ... that they will head for a public area of some kind – a village maybe? Where there are witnesses...?"

"Then, we arrest them?" The Sergeant knew he had misunderstood the Captain's strategy when his officer tossed his head in frustration.

"Don't be an idiot! Listen – don't think! No! Once they stop in the village, you will gallop right through the village! And, then keep out of sight and watch. My plan: is to destroy their present sense of victory! Destroy it: and leave them all both frightened ... and confused! Nothing like a confused enemy, *Sergent!*"

"Ah, *mon Capitaine*, just harass them! But, make no aggressive moves!" Seeing the Captain's eager nod, he continued with slightly more confidence, "Frightened and confused – yes! And the purpose...?"

"I cannot legally take any action: unless they are seen to be fleeing France! But I need to be aware of their every move – their every contact – so when I do arrest them, there is no argument about their guilt! And, I can also punish all their friends as well. When we strike, let it be massive!"

The Sergeant nodded in understanding.

"And, *Sergent*, I will follow ... leisurely ... in my carriage with a contingent of men. And, we will plan our moves carefully." As he smiled, the swollen scar on his cheek twitching slightly, "Maybe, an arrest at the border – and bring that bitch and her stupid husband back in chains!"

"Right, *mon Capitaine!*" And, turning, the Sergeant called out a carefully selected troop of men and spurred away down the dusty road past La Motte d'Aigues in the direction of Lyon.

*   *   *   *   *

16th July 1687
Searching the trail north to Grenoble, France

After a flurry of tearful farewells, the escape party left - escorted

]

by heavily armed riders. After giving orders to the rest of his gang, Renard joined Pierre and his friends at the ridge where they watched the line of riders winding their way down the wooded path to the main trail in the valley below. For the first time in a long while, he was not wearing his fox-like mask that hung now down his back.

"Pierre, I have arranged for three riding mules – one each for you and Andre; and another to carry your supplies and Theodore." Theodore nodded his head eagerly. "Two armed riders will lead your party up the trail towards the valley where Suzanne disappeared. As you requested, they will take leave of you there. For your information, you should know that my lookouts tell me that after a confused and anxious morning, the Dragoons continued to march their remaining prisoners down the trail south towards Serres. We have a small troop shadowing them – as usual!"

"How soon can we start, cousin?"

"Right now, if you like. But, you must travel carefully! I suspect that once the Dragoons feel they are again in control of their mission, they may send a troop up the trail north again – in the hopes of re-capturing their lost prisoners."

Pierre nodded. "Yes, of course, cousin, we won't take any unnecessary risks. Our freedom is too valuable!"

He stood up and grasped his cousin's hand. "Thank you again for all your help. And, look after yourself, Pierre!" Renard pulled Pierre roughly towards him and hugged him. Then Pierre turned and gestured to his two friends to rise and they went about doing their final loading and soon were following their guides down the steep trails into the valley below.

*   *   *   *   *

17th July 1687
Searching the trail north to Grenoble, France

The mules snorted and turned eagerly in an effort to follow the two armed guides as, with a wave of their hands, they turned and galloped down the trail to re-join their patrol. Both Pierre and Andre had to hold the reins firmly to keep their mounts from following the departing riders. Soon, only dust remained gently settling in the late morning air.

All three riders now looked with some bitterness at the stream-side tree-shadowed camp area where they had last seen Suzanne.

I dread this task, thought Pierre as he turned his mule to survey the grassy slope where the crushed grass still outlined the sleeping areas which had been the scene of the angry riot. Two piles of packed sods covered by round river rocks reminded him that the father and daughter, Deleman, lay in one shallow grave while a dead Dragoon lay in the other.

Reluctantly, Pierre nudged his animal and, with a tossing of its head, the mule moved up the slope. Andre's mule followed with a tether bringing the final animal with Theodore perched on top. Pierre guided his mule past the crushed grass areas and the grave sites, his eyes searching the foliage for some sign of disturbance.

166

"Over there! Pierre!" Turning his head and nodding grimly, his eyes followed Andre's pointing finger. The ends of the shrubs were broken and the long strands of grass bent leaving a rough trail into the thicker bush. As he guided his mule's head in that direction, he turned in the saddle and using his right hand, he unconsciously grasped the hilt of the sword that his cousin had fastened at his waist. He pulled and pushed it to ensure that it was loose enough in the scabbard. His eye caught Andre's nod as he also checked his sword. I wish I were more familiar with weapons like these, thought Pierre as he gripped the hilt tightly. I think I would have been happier with a good sharp hunting knife!

The mule hesitated at the entrance to the brush but with a further nudge from Pierre, it leaned into the faint trail pushing the bushes aside.

"Pierre," called Andre hoarsely, "I will stop and tether the pack mule!" Pierre acknowledged the message with a nod. "I will leave Theodore hidden – watching the roadway. He can warn us of any danger – with his birdcall."

Pierre nodded and turned to grin back reassuringly at the boy who waved back at him. Then he turned forward again to concentrate on the mule's passage through the bush. The overhanging trees caused deep patches of gloomy darkness. Ahead, Pierre could also see some open glades of heavy grass in small patches like linked islands separated by growths of heavy bush.

His mule emerged into a grassy patch and stopped. Pierre stood up in his stirrups and searched around. He could hear Andre's mule now coming thorough the bush behind him. A faint trail of broken grass led out of sight slightly to his left. He dismounted quickly and tied the mule firmly to a heavy branch. Then, drawing his sword, he walked slowly up the faint trail. With a sickening feeling, he heard the heavy buzzing of flies. As he turned the corner the grass sloped downward into a little green hollow.

Then he saw her! Or, what was left of her! Even at this distance, he could see that she had been stripped almost naked. His eyes closed in horror. How could they? The filthy swine! Even with closed eyes, he could still see an image that had been mutilated as well. He found his breathing tight and his stomach churning in revolt.

"Mon Dieu! Mon Dieu!" he heard Andre's shattered whisper at his shoulder as his friend grasped his arm tightly. "Oh! That's terrible! Too terrible!" Pierre forced his eyes open and swallowed hard. The horror was still there! The body had rolled onto its face but even so, he could see that her breasts had been hacked. And, a sword or knife had gashed the side of her sweet face. What showed of her slim stomach had also been carved with the whole body stained by drying blood – and humming with buzzing flies.

"How could anyone – anyone – have done that to a girl?" The horror was evident in Andre's voice. Pierre could not speak; he nodded his head and closed his eyes again. He raised his hand up to pinch his nostrils as the stench of dead flesh struck him suddenly.

He did not know which sound he heard first. The strangled

birdcall - or the hooves clattering up the trail south. Both heads spun round and faced the sounds. Then the two men raced up the grassy slopes and parted the high brush to look across the stream to the broken glimpses of the trail.

"Dragoons! Five of them!" Pierre took several deep breaths and watched carefully. But the patrol of five men went galloping by and up the hill to a small rise. Suddenly, they pulled their horses to a dusty stop.

Pierre grunted as, even at this distance, he recognized the senior Dragoon in charge. The burly corporal who had wrestled Suzanne to the grass the night of the riot! His stomach heaved and hot spittle filled his mouth. Silently gagging, he spat it out.

The squad circled while decisions were made. Then the big Dragoon waved two of the men onward up the trail. As they left in a cloud of dust, he turned, and gestured the other two soldiers backward while he quieted his horse and settled it facing north to watch his disappearing troops.

The two Dragoons seemed to know exactly where they were going as they turned off the trail and followed a path down to the stream and crossed it, heading in the direction of Pierre and Andre.

The two friends ducked over the rim of the little hollow and wriggled their way backwards into the heavy bush with their swords held in front of them – neither breathing properly. They peered through the heavy overhanging leaves.

The low brush could be heard crackling as the horses followed each other - coming closer with each step to the little hollow - from the other side.

Pierre could hardly contain a breathless gasp as the first horseman broke through the covering of bush and cantered into the grassy meadow, spinning and stopping on the rim of the hollow. Shadowing his eyes against the glare of the sun, he leaned over and peered down.

"Still here ... but what a bloody mess!" he called back over his shoulder to his companion – who was still struggling through the heavy growth. With a visible grimace on his face, he swung out of the saddle and thudded to the grass – dropping his reins while the trained horse stood still.

As he strutted down toward the body, he drew his sword and swatted at the cloud of flies that raced toward him. Behind him, the crouching watchers saw the other Dragoon stop his horse next to his partner's mount and, covering his eyes, peer down at the back of his comrade.

The first Dragoon walked a wide circle around the corpse and with his back to the two hidden men, leaned over and took a long look.

"Well, the little bitch is good for no one now, Anton!" he called hoarsely to his companion, "But she gave us a good fight, didn't she?" Then raising his sword, he playfully smacked the bottom of the corpse with the flat of his sword.

As he heard the uttered words, Pierre felt a surge of anger rush up from his stomach. Suddenly the consuming rage reached a crescendo.

With a grunt of utter loathing, he wrenched himself upright.   He burst out of the brush.

At the other Dragoon's yell of warning, the soldier had turned too slowly - in time to see Pierre's ferocious face grow larger as he raced down the slope. His overhead sword moved downward in a looming arc. The Dragoon spun in a futile attempt to bring his sword into play but as he jerked his head around, he left his neck open to the vicious downward slash.

As he fell, blood gushing down his breastplate, his sword left his hand and sailed in a lazy arc through the air past Pierre to stick upright in the heavy tufts of grass. Pierre stopped with a jerk and smashed the sword again into the upturned twisted face – gashing the nose in two.

As Pierre froze over the now dying body of the Dragoon, he was suddenly aware of the danger of his position.

The other Dragoon had drawn his sword with a sharp rasp and, kicking his horse, was thundering down the other slope of the hollow in a well-practiced style. He was aiming the horse to the left of Pierre and, leaning out of the saddle with the sword held high up in the right hand, obviously intending to strike a downward blow as he passed.

Pierre was petrified. He stood frozen as the horse approached. Then, in a crazy unexpected gesture, he threw himself sideways - towards the outstretched front hooves. As he rolled across the path of the thundering hooves, he managed to come to his feet and as he tottered, out of balance, he struck upward with his sword.

He reeled over, felt his shoulder jar abruptly and fell. But he knew with a biting pleasure that he had cut into the Dragoon. He lay on his back panting in the dusty grass and trying desperately to struggle to his feet.

A delayed scream followed by a heavy thud made him roll over and stagger up. Through the cloud of dust and flies, he saw the horse prancing rider-less; turning as it tried to free itself of the moaning Dragoon whose one booted foot was still trapped in the stirrup.

"Pierre! The road!" Andre's muffled yell made him turn and look at the road for the first time. The battle in the hollow had alerted the Corporal. Now, sword held high, he was racing his horse down the same path.

Pierre looked down at the bloody sword in his tired hand. Most of the blade had snapped off – probably in the body of the downed Dragoon. Then he remembered the other sword still pinned into the grass. He staggered over and jerked it out. He struggled back to where the two bodies lay together in the bottom of the hollow – those of his Suzanne and the body of the dead Dragoon and stood with his back against the heavy brush forcing the approaching Dragoon to come to him.

It seemed like time had slowed down. He could not keep his body still. As he struggled, his body shook and swayed around. I need to keep control! I have to!

In a dreamlike state, he heard the Corporal break through the bush and thunder onto the meadow; spin and then race around the outside of the hollow, shrieking at the top of his lungs. Then jerking his horse - until it reared to a stop - he glared down at his swaying victim.

]

"You – will die – right now," he screamed as he twirled the point of his sword in the air, "you filthy heretic!" Pierre stood frozen – and deadly tired.

Raising his sword high in the air, the Dragoon began to kick his horse into motion.

Then suddenly, his mouth went agape, his eyes rolled closed in agony and with a surprised look crossing his face, he fell forward onto the neck of his horse.

As the horse thundered down the slope in a charge, the body of the Corporal slid over to one side and slipped with a thud onto the grass. Startled, the horse broke from its downward rush, reared, and spun around, finally standing confused in a cloud of dust. Andre's frightened face appeared out of the dust and against the blue sky.

"I got him, Pierre! I got him!" he yelled. "He never knew I was there! He stopped right in front of me!"

Pierre collapsed back onto the grass oblivious of any danger – or the dust, blood, flies or bodies.

Inside, he was aware of no feelings at all other than he was tired – and overwhelmed! Andre, his sword dripping with blood, collapsed on the grass next to him. His hand clasped Pierre's shoulder and shook him. Then he brought his face close up to his friend's.

"Oh, Pierre, Pierre! I have never, never killed anyone before!"

Pierre found himself laughing. And, he could not stop!

"I know, Andre! I know!" he controlled his wild laughter down to a hoarse chuckle, "I have never even hurt anyone before!" He stopped, "No! I did! I did damage the *Capitaine*'s face back at La Motte! But, Andre, it was never ... like this!" and he waved his hand at the bodies of the three Dragoons.

Then he stood slowly – still swaying a little - and looked over at the still moaning third Dragoon. He staggered over and with a jerk, loosed the boot from the stirrup. Then, with his boot, he rolled the man onto his back. The soldier's eyes were closed; his mouth open and dripping blood; a soft gurgled moan erupted from the mouth.

"Enough!" said Pierre. And leaning over, he ran his sword sharply across the open throat. As it severed, the blood gushed out and the moaning stopped. "Enough!" he whispered again and turned away, tired but a little more at peace with himself.

Suddenly, they heard the birdcall alert again. The two men were galvanized into action - grasping the reins of the Dragoons' horses and holding them tight to keep them calm and quiet. Galloping hooves were heard approaching from the north. They peered out of the heavy foliage in time to see the two missing Dragoons pull their horses to a dusty halt at the rise in the road.

They stood confused peering in both directions. Pierre was relieved to note that none looked in the direction of the hidden hollow. They had evidently not been involved in the assault on Suzanne. Both men stood unconsciously holding their breath.

Finally, after some discussion, the two Dragoons leisurely continued their journey south. Pierre waited until he could no longer hear any hoofbeats before he moved again.

"Now," he said to Andre, his voice calm again, "Now is the time to bury my betrothed."

Together they wrapped up the cold body in a blanket taken from the Dragoon's saddle-roll. While Theodore, with tears on his face, watched the roadway in both directions, the two men dug a shallow hollow in a bank close to the road. After placing the rolled body in the hollow, they used their swords to collapse the bank over the body covering it completely. Then they gathered stones and built a noticeable cairn over the grave. As a last gesture, Pierre took the broken sword and plunged it into the crest to make a permanent cross.

"If her father would like to visit her grave, we can describe exactly where it can be found," he explained to his two friends. The three friends stood silently for awhile looking down at the rough grave.

Then Pierre, with hoarse broken voice, murmured some phrases of a Psalm he had liked. The words interrupted the constant bird-songs from the trees above.

"Though I walk through the valley of the shadow of death..."

The bodies of the Dragoons were left in the hollow and the horses were unsaddled and turned loose to return home.

"Enough!" said Pierre. "I need to go back to La Motte now – I have to ... report back to a father!" Andre and Theodore both grimly nodded.

*   *   *   *   *

]

CHAPTER SEVENTEEN

Isabeau rubbed her eyes in frustration. Suddenly, she felt dreadfully tired. In the carriage, her Aunt, Uncle and husband were still discussing the frightening events of the morning; and Isabeau could not keep her eyes open. She straightened herself up, determined to stay awake. Suddenly, a yell from above stopped all conversation.

"*Monsieur! Monsieur Mallan!* The Dragoons! They are coming...!"

Uncle Antoine, facing the rear of the carriage, leaned out of the window opening and peered through the dust trailing behind them.

"*Sacre Bleu!* They come ... at least five – or six!" He turned his head and called up to the driver. "We cannot race them! How far to the next village?"

"Eh! Cucuron ... is ... over the next rise!" The driver and footman had been conferring.

"Speed up! Don't mind us! Hurry! Stop in the village Square – so there will be other people around – as witnesses!" Uncle Antoine ducked back in and wiped his dusty frightened face.

The carriage surged forward rocking violently and everyone in the coach grasped for the hanging straps.

Oh that villain, thought Isabeau, does he never give up? Now, I am going to really suffer for my insolence! She caught her husband's ferocious frown and shrugged her shoulders. 'I told you so': he is going to say!

Soon Isabeau saw houses and stone walls flashing by as they rocked into the village. Suddenly, the carriage swerved as it turned into a large open expanse. At the end of the square was a beautiful little shining pond. As the vehicle stopped in a cloud of dust, Uncle Antoine jerked open the door and sprang out closely followed by her husband. Both turned to face the Dragoons' arrival. Isabeau also leaned through the window opening.

To her amazement, they saw a small column of Dragoons race by the entrance to the square and vanish in the cloud of dust.

Shaken, the Uncle broke into a trot and ran to peer down the roadway. He returned shaking his head in utter amazement.

"They went by! Just rode right on! I guess ... they were in a hurry – and not chasing us at all!" He grinned ruefully up at Isabeau. "We must remember that we are now free! We must remember to ... act like we have no guilty feelings!"

Her husband, Le Duc, turned also to face her.

"Since we are stopped anyway, maybe we should have a break – for a drink. That will also allow the pesky Dragoons to get well ahead?" They helped the women from the carriage and entered the small inn – all a great deal relieved.

*   *   *   *   *

Despite his shrill warning whistle and the frantic waving of his hand, Pierre realized with a sinking feeling of desperation, that Andre on the leading mule was going to run directly into a troop of mounted Dragoons coming down a side road from a small village – south of Serres. He was relieved when Theodore on the pack mule heeded his alert signal and diverted the animal into the heavy bushes on the side of the road and hid.

What can I do, he breathed aloud? He groaned as he saw Andre vanish over the top of the rise and Pierre shuddered and closed his eyes in fatigue. Nothing! He could do nothing!

The distant sound of hoof beats jerked his eyes open again. The troop of Dragoons had come clattering over the rise into view; but where was Andre?

Quickly checking on little Theodore's hiding spot, he turned his mule onto a slight path leading towards the nearby stream. He dismounted and led the animal down to the rushing waters where the bank hid him from view from the road. Pierre held his breath as he listened to the approaching hooves and the clatter of clanking swords ... and then they were past! I don't believe it, he whispered.

But he waited until the hoof beats vanished from earshot before he carefully forced the mule's mouth from the water and dragged it up the bank and through the bush. Here, he could view the whole roadway.

They were gone. And, turning he saw Theodore perched on his mule peering out from the bushes waiting for the wave to continue down the road. Suddenly, on the far rise, he saw the mounted figure of Andre waving the go-ahead. I don't understand, thought Pierre. What happened? Then he mounted and rode quickly, even passing Theodore in his haste, until he met up with his friend on the rise.

Andre was grinning a little skeptically and with a trace of guilt around his eyes.

"*Sacré bleu*, Pierre! That was close!" he shook his head in disbelief, "One moment we were fine! And then, suddenly, over the rise, I saw them cantering towards me! All I could do was ... keep going! I tried to ...   look normal ... like I was going on an errand!" He pushed his hat back on his head and wiped his damp brow. "They didn't even look at me! Just rode by on their business!"

"I did try to warn you, Andre!" Pierre chuckled hoarsely. "I could see over the ridge and saw them riding down the trail from the hills. You

]

wouldn't have seen them until you went over the rise!" Theodore had caught up with the two men and stopped in a cloud of dust. He was listening intently to the discussion – his face screwed up with concern and thought.

"Pierre, Andre, do you think perhaps that ... we are safer riding *back* to the Luberon ... than running to Switzerland?" his voice was much higher in tone.

Both the men looked at him with frowns. Then Pierre grinned and nodded.

"You may be right, Theodore!" He smiled at Andre; "Out of the mouths of babies ... comes truth?"

"Well, I would love to think we could relax our vigilance a little but maybe we should wait another day before we make any decisions ... Eh?" Pierre looked at the other two and received their nods. "All right then, back on the road!"

*   *   *   *   *

19th July 1687
Traveling south near Peyruis

Despite the overpowering sense of failure and bitterness that seemed to hang over his head like a heavy shroud, Pierre felt more relaxed than he had for some time. On a heavily grassed slope, he sat under the shade of an enormous red oak tree north of Peyruis. Late in the afternoon, they had left the road and taken a path to a high ridge overlooking the Durance River and, after a search, found a safe camping spot for the night.

His nose picked up the scent of a wild honeysuckle and as he rolled on his side, the pungent aromas of crushed thyme made him think of his mother's cooking. He watched the swallows in the late afternoon swooping and turning in their dives to capture food before sunset.

Despite the noises coming from the rear indicating that his friends had taken their turns in cleaning up and were soon to join him, Pierre still felt lonely. Suzanne's wistful smiling face floated into his mind. Although we were never ... that close, he thought, I had begun to think of Suzanne as a companion for life which is something close to being a ... wife. Hmm, he murmured aloud, with a touch of guilt, despite only two days, I am already beginning to think of her ... in the past!

In his reverie, he did not hear their steps until his friends both dropped down beside him and lay back after handing him a mug of tisane. Pierre breathed the refreshing scent before sipping.

"Now, this is really a peaceful scene!"

The sudden voice over their shoulders caused Pierre to choke on his hot drink and jump with pain as the spilled liquid burnt his chest. Theodore had covered his eyes in horror. But, Andre had nearly dropped his cup and rolled sideways to turn and dispel their fear with a cry.

"Renard – you damned mad fox!"

Still rubbing his sore chest, Pierre rolled his head around to see his cousin's image silhouetted against the deepening blue of the Provencal sky. His head was bare and his dark hair gleamed with the reddish tints that had given him his animal nickname.

"Cousin! Do you have to sneak up like that?" He climbed to his feet and extended his hand to grasp Renard's. "Just once I would like you to behave like a normal human being!" Renard grinned with his devilish air – obviously a little proud of his skills. He refused a drink and settled down next to them.

"Well, mes *Amis*," as he leaned back and rubbed his back gently on large warm slab of stone, "we have been shadowing you for some time, and," he brushed a fly from his face, "it looks like you are headed for Manosque and home?"

Both Pierre and Andre bobbed their heads in agreement.

"I thought I should caution you that you, Pierre," he nodded in his cousin's direction, "are still running around with a price on your head!"

Pierre's head jerked up in surprise. "Yes, I thought you may have forgotten that little matter! Our favourite *Capitaine* of the Dragoons is still eager to ... punish you for ruining his handsome features."

Pierre grimaced. Since leaving La Motte d'Aigues, he had pushed his "original sin" into the back of his mind – with survival his chief concern.

"Hmm! Right! Thanks for bringing it back again, Cousin!" Pierre was chagrined with himself for not having remembered the fact. "Well, we are still planning on returning to our villages," he glanced at Andre and received his nod, "so, we shall have to take a little more care from now on."

The three friends leaned back and sipped their cooling tisane but Pierre noted that Renard seemed to be buried in deep thought.

"And, Renard, do you have plans?" Renard broke out of his reverie and, leaning forward a little, peered around and grinned wryly at Andre.

"And, I thought my thoughts were private!" He stood up and looked into the distance. "That is a bad sign!" he hesitated and then turned to face Pierre. "It's probably a symptom of what I have been ... feeling lately. Do you," he pointed to Pierre, "remember when I first talked about the "Fox" idea?"

Pierre thought and nodded. "Well, I was upset and angry at the way the Dragoons – and the King – were handling us Believers. We are a folk who believe in our religious freedom - but we were being forced to accept their harassment. So, with a couple of friends – who felt the way I did – we adopted our disguises – and ... had some fun! That's what it was at first! But the Dragoons didn't like the nips the fox gave their behinds." He chuckled aloud. "They got revenge - but not in the way we expected! They killed people – in return."

Renard sighed with obvious frustration. "So we followed the Bible – and gave them an 'eye for an eye' – but that led to greater retaliation!" The friends were listening quietly without comment. "So, more disgruntled men began to join our little band. And, as they trained in our methods of survival, bands began to split off – firstly to carry out special missions; then they began to operate independently."

Both Pierre and Andre's eyes opened wide with surprise. " Yes, I

]

have been getting credit for exciting and spectacular forays as far north as the Loire valley and also, down south near Perpignan – in Catalan territory. Every day we hear of new antics somewhere I have never been!"

"That's unbelievable!" Andre blurted out.

"Yes, I think that the King himself must be plaguing his Generals to rid France of this despicable Renard!" All three grinning listeners yelled and punched the air in support.

"Well, Cousin, I must confess that ... I too have been giving the matter – of my notoriety – or fame – some deep thought! When I started out, it was a jest! It was fun! And, I was quick and alert – always a step ahead of those cursed Dragoons. And, when more followers came, I was eager to train others in the skills I had learned." He paused with some obvious discomfort showing on his slim face. "But, lately, I think I am wearing down a little too much! I am becoming careless! And, when you become careless, people die!" Pierre thought he saw a flash of tears in his cousin's eyes.

Pierre broke in. "I don't think you could have done more – or anything different – than you did!"

"Yes – I hear you, Pierre! But I still have to live with the thoughts – and the memories! The longer you stay at this business, the greater the backlash and the greater the risk of being caught. I know it – and so do all the men I have! Originally, if we were caught we would have been beaten and sent to the galleys in Marseilles. But now? We would be killed immediately – without hesitation." He nodded his head emphatically. "And, I, intend to live a long and exciting life!" He looked away as though to remind himself of the beauty of the river scene.

"So, I have reached a decision! I have handed over my command!" Theodore gasped aloud. "So the nickname of 'Renard', now belongs to the new leader and I have resumed my old identity of your wild cousin, Pierre Jaubert!"

He turned to look at the shocked faces of the listeners.

"But don't worry! I will not be joining your little band. I will be traveling with the shadowing group until we reach the Luberon Mountains. I will say goodbye to my parents and brothers and sisters and a small band of my group will head north to Lyon. And, then to Switzerland and safety – and a new life!"

"So the battle against the Dragoons – and the King ... will continue?" Pierre's face showed a mixture of both amazement and relief at the announcement.

"Yes! The groups have been well trained. And the more agony they cause the authorities, the greater is my pleasure – especially after Suzanne's death!"

Renard rose causing the rest to get to their feet.

"I must be off! You can sleep well knowing that a guardian angel is watching over you." He grinned. "Oh! A last thought! Don't forget that our friend, Alexander is somewhere out there!" and he waved his hand in a grand circle in the air.

"Hmm!" All three listeners grunted unanimously – indicating that they had, in fact, forgotten.

With a wave over his shoulder, Renard strode up the grassy slope and vanished over the rise. Slowly they settled down again and looked quietly over the panorama.

"Hmm!" grunted Andre, "it seems the only certain thing in our lives right now, is change itself!" and the others nodded.

*   *   *   *   *

... a few days earlier - 14th July 1687
Avignon – on the road to Lyon

The horses clattered into the courtyard of the inn at Avignon and snorted as though they were glad that the dusty ride was over for the day. Isabeau sighed with relief as she peered out of the carriage window at the deep shadows already playing tricks on the grimy walls of the two-story building.

"After all the worry and excitement of today, I think we should stop early," Uncle spoke thoughtfully. "Maybe ... spend the night at Avignon,"

Uncle Theodore had obviously made the decision as they approached the ancient city from the south but ruminated on it while they drove through the outskirts. "I think we could benefit from a good nights sleep!"

His decision was greeted by smiles from all the passengers. My good husband is probably already relishing the idea of some cool local wine, Isabeau thought with a small smile, while, I, would love to wash my face and hands and get cleaned up. Uncle was helping his wife, "Belle" down from the coach while Le Duc stood at his side ready to do the duties of a good husband.

It was noticeably cooler inside, as the burly proprietor of the Inn, welcomed his newly arrived customers. He took their orders for an evening meal – with a good local wine – and had the housemaid show the women to their rooms while the men excused themselves and enjoined to the pub.

The room assigned to the young couple smelled cold and stale and Isabeau's first action was to open the inner shutters and allow the breeze from outside to come flowing in. As she glanced down at the courtyard, she saw with a start, a mounted Dragoon quietly sitting in the shadows of the building opposite. When he looked up, startled by the movement of the shutters, he caught her glance and nudged his horse into motion turning away out of her sight.

Isabeau caught her breath momentarily as the incident brought back something curious from that morning. She furrowed her brow as she remembered exiting the last Inn at Cucuron on the Luberon hillside. As she had stepped into the bright sunshine she had noticed a mounted Dragoon standing in the shade of a tree near to the road out of town. As she had turned and glanced in that direction, he too had urged his horse out of sight into the trees.

She sighed aloud. Am I being over-anxious; or is fear driving me a little mad! When she leaned out, he was nowhere to be seen. That's silly, she thought, I must stop being so anxious. Cleaning up was a real

]

pleasure even though the water did not feel fresh and cool. It has probably been here for several days, she grunted to herself.

When she felt fresh enough, she decided that she would venture outside to enjoy the later afternoon sunshine. When she looked around the room for her shawl, she realized that she must have left it in the carriage. It had been her mother's and she desperately did not want to lose it. With a groan of frustration, she left the room and closing the doors, she slipped down the narrow steep stairs and quietly left the main door following it around to the right – where she had seen the groom leading the horses.

The livery stable was right behind - attached to the rear of the Inn. She picked her way across the cobblestones avoiding the piles of manure. As she hesitated in the gloom of the stable door and peered into the dim interior, the mixed stink of horse's manure coupled with the musty scene of hay made her twitch her nose.

She was startled by the crack of a whip followed by a sharp cry of pain. She stepped carefully inside enough to see. With horror, she observed a short stocky man, with his back to her, raising his riding whip and bringing it down again with a snap on the shoulders of a cowering young stable-boy who stood facing the side of one of the horses with a heavy brush in his hand.

"When I say work fast, I mean really fast, you useless rascal!"

Fury rose in Isabeau. As the man's arm rose again, she quickly stepped forward and when the whip reached its peak, she leaned out and jerked it backward from his grasp. The jerk threw him off balance and he tottered before he collapsed back onto the straw-covered floor with a sharp cry. She had had to jump back sharply to avoid him.

Although she felt a little scared, her anger was greater. He glared up at her in obvious confusion and fear. She swung the whip at him; with the whip point missing his nose. His eyes instinctively closed in fear.

"I don't know who you are but you have no right to treat a young boy like that!" His mouth fell open. "Now get up and out of the stable. I am going to report your behavior to the Innkeeper and if you try to punish the boy again, I shall ask my big husband to teach you a lesson!" The man rolled over awkwardly. Getting to his feet, he tore out of the stable door and vanished. The boy had frozen in his grooming duties and was staring wide-eyed at her. When she finally smiled, he grinned with relief as she handed him the whip.

"I was doing my job well – and quickly!" He gasped, "But, Batz beats us for no reason – no reason that I know!" He frowned and squinted his eyes. "I think he gets mad about something else – and then beats us boys ... for nothing!"

Isabeau smiled and nodded at his wisdom. "I shall tell the Innkeeper - as I said I would! Better get the horses finished!" She touched his shoulder and he smiled shyly at her as he brushed the horse's skin.

Isabeau turned and was relieved to see her shawl lying folded on the seat of the nearby carriage. Picking it up, she trod her way carefully out of the stable. Back at the Inn, she recounted her experience to the Innkeeper who listened with some obvious frustration.

"I am sorry *Madame*, for Batz's behavior – It's... no wonder that we have so many stable boys leave all the time. That is a nuisance for me too! Leave it to me, *Madame*!" He bowed slightly and left to visit the stable. Watching him, Isabeau decided not to tell her husband about her actions. He will get upset about my interfering in something that ... he feels is ... not my business!

The whole family really enjoyed supper that night. *Bœuf d'Avignon* with a rich herb gravy and roasted peppers, tomatoes and onions followed by a fresh herbed goat cheese and crusty baguettes coupled with a rich red wine from a nearby vineyard. Le Duc had a little too much wine and was asleep before Isabeau crawled in for the night.

They all rose early to get a quick start on the day. After a hearty breakfast of freshly baked bread with local conserves and fresh fruit they trooped out to their waiting carriage. Isabeau, eager for a breath of fresh air arrived before the rest and was greeted with a smile by the same stable boy that was holding the horses' heads.

She nodded to him and smiled back. But, glancing around to check to see who was watching, he gestured for her to approach.

"*Madame*, I want to thank you for your help. The Innkeeper came to assure me that ... I would be safe – from now on!" he shyly reported. When she turned to leave, he hissed at her, "Wait, *Madame*! There is something that you should know!"

She looked at him curiously, and he continued.

"*Madame* – I do not know what it means! But, the soldiers ... have been asking about you – and your party!" He peered furtively around as though trying to avoid any repercussions.

"Asking...?" Isabeau frowned and stared at him.

"Yes, *Madame*! The Dragoons were asking all about your behaviors, what you had done - while you were here. They asked us stable-boys too; and I saw them talking – and writing down – what was said – even to the Innkeeper himself!" He grinned wryly. "*Monsieur* Tremblay was unhappy about having to talk to them!"

"Hmm," she murmured, "That's curious! I don't know - but thank you for the information!" She touched his shoulder and he smiled. "I will see that my Uncle rewards you for your aid."

"Oh, no, *Madame*," he nodded his head, "You have been ... an angel in my life and it is I who should thank you. Thank you again, *Madame*!" And he made an awkward little bow. Isabeau grinned at him in response and turned to join the others as they emerged from the Inn door.

Once their luggage was tied onto the rear of the carriage, Isabeau found a moment to report to Uncle Antoine the warnings by the stable boy coupled with her observations of the previous day's sighting of Dragoons observing them.

Uncle listened attentively - but a little skeptically - to her story; and then, glancing over her shoulder, grunted: "That does sound a little funny, but, even as we stand talking, I can see a Dragoon - up ahead - waiting on the side of the road. Hmm!" He turned. "Let me go and have a

]

little talk with the landlord." Le Duc helped her into the carriage and then climbed in himself rocking the carriage when he settled his weight next to Isabeau. "Where has Uncle gone?"

"Oh, he had to ask for information from the Innkeeper. He'll be coming soon!" And then she turned to Aunt Belle to inquire about her night's sleeping and was assured that she had slept well.

Her Uncle finally emerged from the Inn's door and leaning out the window, she observed him go and talk to the stable boy and hand him some coins that resulted in much bowing and head nodding from the pleased youth. Once Uncle climbed aboard, the carriage started with a jerk and Isabeau was pleased to see the delighted stable boy running alongside their window and yelling his joyful thanks.

Le Duc frowned at his curious antics but as they rejoined the main road, Uncle told the party the story – to be received with gasps from the Aunt and worried frowns from Isabeau's husband.

"You went to the stable?" he grunted unhappily at her.

"And, Le Duc, just as well that she did!" Uncle Antoine reassured him. "You've got a very observant eye, young lady!" He grinned wryly at Isabeau; "If she hadn't noted those watching Dragoons and been warned by the stable lad, we might have found ourselves in a lot more trouble than we would like!"

He nodded back in the direction of the Inn, "The landlord confirms that he – and his staff - were questioned by a number of Dragoons – and warned not to tell us! And, he was upset about having to give information about his customers!"

He stared in obvious appreciation at Isabeau leaning in the corner of the carriage, "This is a bright young woman ... you have married, my young nephew!" He grinned and nodded in her direction. "Let us make sure that for the rest of the journey, all of us keep our eyes open for idle Dragoons. I would suggest that we do it carefully, so that we don't let them know that we are aware of them being there!"

He lounged back in his seat. "And," he added, "I have decided that we will not race up to Lyon! After all, if we were fleeing for our lives, we would race, right? So, we have to leave a distinct impression that – we are on a pleasant holiday! To prove the point, I took the liberty of arranging for the Landlord to pack a picnic lunch. With chicken, baguettes, fruit and wine."

All the party gasped in surprise and obvious pleasure. "So, near lunch time, all of you keep your eyes open for a shady pleasant spot by the Rhone River for a picnic – and let the watching Dragoons have their mouths drooling with envy!" And the burst of laughing eased the tension in the carriage.

*   *   *   *   *

20th July 1687
On the trail south – after Sisteron

For the first time in many days the three mules rode side by side up the dusty road along the winding Durance River - glinting in the late afternoon's sunshine. All three riders were quiet but felt safe riding close to farm carts returning home.   But Andre felt confused.   He leaned forward in his saddle to peer into Pierre's shadowed face.

"Are you alright, Pierre?"

Pierre glanced at his friend and nodded slowly without speaking.

"Well?" Andre urged him.

Pierre heaved a deep sigh and slowed his mule to a stop while the other animals, confused, circled round the silent rider.

"Well?" questioned Andre, "You should be overjoyed to almost be home again!"

Pierre looked at both of his companions and screwed his mouth up in concern.

"It's funny," he chose his words slowly and carefully, "I am really looking forward to seeing my parents – I had not expected ever to see them again! But, I also have to tell a father that his daughter - the one I promised to look after - is dead!"

He turned in the saddle and looked both ways up and down the road. "I only hope that all the Dragoons are gone from the Luberon!" He looked back at his friends. "Our village lost both Suzanne and our lookout, David – killed in the capture," He clenched his jaw and continued, "We do not bring much of a message ... of hope?"

Andre nodded as he added up: "Of the twenty-one people in our party, four died! Five went to the Convent in Aigues-Morte; but five crossed the border into the cantons of Switzerland; and the three rescued have joined the bandits. We three are free and going home to report to our village and, of course, our treacherous Alexander, has vanished?"

Pierre nodded in agreement. "When you total them up, it does not seem so bad! Four dead and five imprisoned - that's not bad - against twelve that are free!" He paused and frowned, "But, it doesn't mean much to the father who has lost his only daughter!"

All three looked at each other solemnly – the men with frowns on their brows and Theodore with glistening eyes. Without a word, they turned their mules south again and broke into a canter.

*   *   *   *   *

20th July 1687
On the trail south - Manosque France

Glancing over his shoulder to ensure that danger was not following them, he waved ahead to Andre on the next rise in the road to Manosque and urged his mule to canter down the dusty road.

Just a couple of farmers taking their vegetables to market and a large herd of sheep blocking a lot of the traffic, he mused. As the fresh morning air brushed his face, he found himself smiling. This pleased him

]

because it was such an improvement over the last couple of weeks of tragedy. And I am looking forward to seeing my parents again – something I had not thought I would ever do again.

As the wind blew the dust away, Pierre was startled to see that Andre, instead of moving down the road to the next rise as was their standard cautious strategy, was waiting for him and his little brother, Theodore to catch up. With further pressure, the reluctant mule broke into a gallop.

"What's wrong, Andre? Problems?" he grunted as he reined his mule in a cloud of dust. Andre simply pointed up into the tree instead and glancing up quickly, Pierre saw a piece of red ribbon hanging from the branch that leaned out into the road.

"Hmm! The Renard gang want to contact us ... what for?" He glanced around but Andre was already pointing to a treed glade south of the road along the Durance River below. Checking around for further dangers – and finding none – Andre led the way down a nearby path and through green brush into the shade of the overhanging trees. Here they all dismounted and watered their mules while they waited.

It was only minutes before a hooded figure slipped out of the foliage and waved to them.

"Pierre and Andre?" The two nodded while Theodore eagerly grinned at the newcomer. He motioned them to follow down a faint trail between the trees. Theodore took the reins of each mule and tethered them firmly while the two men followed down the path. Soon he caught up with them and tugged at his brother's arm.

"What now, Andre, what is going to happen?"

"Shh! Theodore, follow – and quietly!"

Suddenly the path rose up above a steep bank from which they could see the lazy river flowing placidly below. As they crested the rise, they saw several hooded men standing beside a tethered horse in a nearby hollow. The men turned and watched them approach. One's hood had a fox's features drafted on the front.

"Renard – your cousin, Pierre?" Andre grunted softly.

"No, I don't think so! He said he had handed over the local leadership."

The leader moved forward to meet then and extended his hand in welcome to Pierre.

"You are Pierre Jaubert? Your cousin suggested that I contact you before you return home to your village."

"And, you are...?" Pierre grasped the leader's hand firmly.

"You may call me Renard – the 'new' one!" The man chuckled and moved forward to greet the other two travelers.

"Let's sit in the shade!" and he gestured to a group of large rocks beneath the overhanging trees. The party settled themselves while the messenger moved some distance away from where he could keep an eye on the road traffic.

"We are putting together a party for a special task. We needed a couple of men who were familiar with the prisoners' role. Your cousin said you might be willing to help us out for a short period. Enough to disrupt the plans of the Dragoons!"

Pierre glanced at Andre with raised eyebrows. Andre nodded in agreement.

"Tell us more," Pierre looked back at the Leader.

"Your cousin met you recently near Peyruis?" Pierre nodded. "He forgot to mention to you the current situation with your own prisoner party." Pierre experienced a sharp pang of guilt. In the process of being freed and the search for Suzanne, he had not given the prisoners' party a further thought.

"Err ...Renard - I feel terrible! We have been so busy staying free, that I had not thought much more! What has happened?"

"We have been watching them carefully. But, after your successful escape, the Dragoons were much more careful and guarded! Alas, there has been no real opportunity to harass them again – without a danger of loss of men – or outright capture. Several times, we recognized that they were deliberately setting a trap for us! They are getting a lot more clever – or scared!" The leader shook his head in obvious frustration.

"So, what is your plan now? If we can help, we would like to!"

"Once they emerged from the mountain passes, they seemed to be more confident! Possibly because they were surrounded by much more traffic. Yesterday, they separated their party. They sent a light-guarded patrol of Dragoons to accompany a cart-load of women and children on a lengthy ride to the fortress of Aigues-Mortes where they will be kept as religious prisoners in the Tower of Constance. The mother from Bastide and her little boy; together with the twin girls accompanied by the young women from Grambois to look after them?"

Pierre nodded and turned to Andre: "Andre – that sounds like Laverne, wife of Theodore from Bastide – with Albert; and probably... Rochelle ... Daillon from Grambois – with the Gervaise twins, Nicole and Nadine?" Andre nodded sadly.

"We were reluctant to attack them – the children would have been at risk!" He stood up now and outlined his plan.

"They have changed their plan. They have moved to travel on the south side of the Durance. More villages to pass through. More witnesses and more impact on the village population – as a warning! But they also seem to have become a little more careless and confident – with a small party of ... three men. And, six Dragoons!"

"So what are your plans?" Andre spoke up.

"If you will join our group, we shall lay an ambush for them. We shall surround them when they sleep at night. We think we can free all the men without any loss of life! If, we act now! Once they return from the convent, they will be too many and too strong!"

Pierre looked at Andre and returned his nod of agreement.

"We are with you – and Theodore?" The boy jerked his head in excitement. "But, then we have to return to our village to ... tell them the sad – and glad – news!"

"Done!" The leader held out his hands and shook the hands of each of the party in turn." He gestured toward the roadway.

"Go back onto the road and before Manosque there is a bridge to the south. Take it and a messenger will meet you on the road and bring

]

you to the raiding party's camp. *Bonne chance!*" Both raiders slipped into the bush and vanished. Pierre and Andre grinned wryly at each other; shrugged and turned to walk up the path followed by Theodore skipping in excitement.

* * * * *

With the increased number of farm carts with produce and merchants traveling by mule and horse, the journey to the bridge on the Durance at Manosque was uneventful. The friends could ride together instead of in their safety patrol and sing folk songs as they rode. Several miles over the bridge they were contacted by a guide, called Louis, who led them onto the road south towards the village of Rians.

The late afternoon sun was setting giving the trees and shrubs a soft golden tinge. Louis pulled his mule to a halt and, as the party gathered around him, he pointed surreptitiously to a small piece of red ribbon tied to a branch on the left side of the road.

"We turn here, my friends!" And, checking up and down the road for safety, he led them down a slight path into the valley of a small stream surrounded by heavy woods. They were aware of a sequence of birdcalls alerting a camp among the trees to come alive with moving bodies. Pierre counted roughly at least ten men watching them from the shade of the overhanging trees.

"We camp here for the night," remarked Louis cheerfully, "I hope the supper is ready. You are hungry, aren't you?" The party all nodded with enthusiasm. "Water your mules at the stream; tether them; and we will get you fed. After that we will meet for a planning session. Come on!"

It was not surprising that Pierre found that most of the men wore neckerchiefs across their lower faces. They took their food and sat apart from each other while they ate their supper. Then before the gathering to discuss strategy, they all donned cloth bags with slashed eye-slits to cover their faces.

"They lead dangerous lives," explained Louis to Theodore who had questioned their unusual behavior. "The less chances they take, the better! If captured ... and tortured ... you would not be able to describe any of the bandits of Renard's gang!" Theodore nodded in excited agreement.

The leader, wearing his fox mask, explained the plan of attack. Their scouts reported that the small band of three prisoners had been increased to eight. There had been an addition of a small group of common thieves who were being transported to the galleys at Marseilles.

"The Dragoons have made ... recognition of our comrades easier for us! They have now given them red vests to wear ... to identify them ... as religious prisoners! Probably, for harsher treatment!" he continued. He explained that the number of Dragoons was still only six. They had stopped for the night a short ride south.

"They were camping on the banks of a stream in a wooded area like this," the leader waved his hand around, "A lone guard had been stationed on the roadway to both the north and south approaches.

According to their usual methods, two men would sleep after supper and be aroused at midnight to replace the road guards. So there would be two asleep around the fire; two on the road; and two ... supposedly, awake." He chuckled aloud as he said this and it was obvious that sometimes even the watchers within the camp also slept.

He indicated that since the riot in the mountains, they were now chaining the lines of prisoners between trees so that they were limited in their movement. He went on to explain the make-up of the raiding party and their tasks. "Timing is very important! Owl calls will alert us when to act!" He looked around. "No questions?" On receiving none, he nodded. "Get some sleep! We will be leaving early in the morning before the farmers get moving on the roads."

Louis brought each of the new party a hooded mask to ensure they were comfortable with its use. Then the party settled for the night.

Despite his obvious excitement, Pierre noted that Theodore was quickly snoring and smiled. Andre whispered hoarsely while he shared his plans for returning to his village of St. Martin. Pierre was relieved to hear that he and his brother were still committed to the escape route up the banks of the Rhone to Lyon; and then to a rush up the mountains to Geneva. Andre was still talking when Pierre lapsed into sleep.

*   *   *   *   *

21st July 1687
Ambush outside Manosque

Despite being in the middle of summer, the early morning air was almost cold near the banks of the little stream. A slight mist filled the hollow as men stirred and wrapped up their belongings. Louis delivered Andre and Pierre to two different groups. Pierre's group was identified with a piece of red ribbon hanging from the top of their hoods. Louis reported quietly that Andre's group had white ribbon to identify themselves. Theodore was to stay with Louis and would be in charge of the nearby tethered mules and horses when the attack took place.

Soon everyone mounted and followed a path down the stream for several miles until they turned sharply up the slope and dismounted in a heavy grove of trees. Renard led all members of the attack force to the edge of the grove.

Pierre stood with his 'red' party to the left of the leader as they stood in the shadows of the overhanging trees. Following the direction of 'Renard's' pointing finger, he could see the road winding down the slope to their right. The road crossed the small stream they had been following and to the left was another heavy clump of trees. Hidden from the road by the trees, was a smoldering fire on the stream bank. As their eyes became used to the limited light, he could make out the two road guards – one on the road below them leaning against a rock. In the distance, another guard sitting on the parapet of the bridge smoking a pipe – its faint plume of smoke traveling straight up in the morning air. Even at this distance, Pierre's nose twitched a little as thought he could almost smell the smoke. He could also make out four shapes lit by the glowing

]

embers of the campfire and some movement in the dark shadows of the trees. Are they the prisoners, he thought?

"You know your jobs! Listen to the owl calls! And, be careful! We don't want any mistakes – and definitely, no bodies!" he whispered hoarsely. Silently, the listeners nodded and turned to follow their leaders back into the trees.

Pierre knew his plans and had gone over them many times when he had wakened that night. Now, armed with a club and a sharp knife for protection, his band of four men was to follow the stream path down until they would be poised waiting for the owl call in the bush on this side of the fire. Andre's "white" group was to take the same deer path – but on the other side of the stream. Once they had passed the location of the fire, they would quietly cross the stream and position themselves on the far side of the fire. This would leave two groups of four men on each side of the encampment.

A couple of riders on mules would quietly trot down the road with the mules' hooves silenced by rags wrapped around them – followed by another pair later. They would be timed to have each pair arrive alongside each guard. The riders would wave a greeting to the guard and both would dismount. One would approach the guard for directions with a page of paper with a drawn map in his hand while the other held the mount's reins. At the signal, the first man would attempt to club the guard - with the second man to support him. The mules were well trained to simply wait even though their reins dragged on the roadway.

Just after the guards were attacked, the men from the red and white groups would slide out of the bush and attack the party at the fire.

Pierre grasped his club in his hand and with the other carefully loosened the knife in its scabbard. It was light enough for him to see that one Dragoon was obviously half dozing, seated against several large rocks around the glowing embers. Pierre's role was to subdue the sleeping man closest to him. The owl hoot sounded. Turning his head to the road, he saw the first pair of riders quietly ride by. Then the second. Then silence.

Then a hoot! The men around him galvanized into silent action. A tap on his shoulder sent him quietly running toward the prostrate figure. The crack of a twig behind him caused the prone figure to stir and a face turned upward with eyes still closed. A thump and grunt could be heard from the roadway followed by the stamping of mules' hooves.

Pierre lunged down with his club. Crack! The man groaned. Another, Crack! And the figure was silent. He spun round. Two men were forcing the dozing guard onto the ground and clubbing him. Then there was silence as each team looked at the other and raised their clubs in the air in salute. Pierre found himself breathing heavily. Then he remembered to finish his task. Unwrapping the unconscious man, he rolled him over and tied his wrists and ankles with pieces of leather thong.

From the depths of the darkness in the trees came cries of confusion from the manacled prisoners. Fresh twigs and branches had been added to the embers and, in the firelight, he joined his team members as they carried firebrands into the darkness.

The flickering firelight lit the confused faces of their comrades with joy and relief showing as they recognized the masks of their rescuers. He called Joseph's name and the young shepherd from Grambois grinned up and responded with recognition.

"Pierre! Am I glad to see you!"

"No names, Joseph! No names!"

"Oh! Sorry!" he grinned unable to hide his delight, "but, I am still glad!"

Chains separating the prisoners were uncoupled and each individual prisoner was led into the firelight for identification by the newcomers.

Still grinning Joseph and the mason, Isaac Gervaise, from Grambois were quickly released. The farm laborer from La Bastide-des-Jourdans, Theodore Claude asked hoarsely about the whereabouts of his wife, Laverne Coulan, and his baby, Albert.

The villagers were separated from the petty criminals to be mounted on some of the Dragoons' horses and mules and led up the pathway to their original camp. Pierre understood that the five thieves were mounted on Dragoons' horses and taken on to the village of Rians and released. Many so-called criminals were also considered "victims of the regime".

While Renard's group used some horses, most of the riders were mounted on mules to avoid being noticed.

One of the Dragoons had been left unconscious – but untied. He would release his companions when Renard's men were safely away. The leader felt that perhaps while they may suffer from embarrassment, they would be less likely to punish the local people for their loss. Broken into small groups the Renard's gang traveled like market goers and tradesmen leading their loaded mules to the nearest market.

All three rescued prisoners were anxious to do whatever was possible to rescue their womenfolk from their confinement at the Tower of Constance in the fortress of Aigues-Mortes near the marshes south of Marseilles. In the meantime, they had happily decided to join Renard's bandit group - to attempt a later rescue.

Within two days of roundabout travel, Pierre and his party finally rode across the Durance at Pertuis – towards home.

*   *   *   *   *

]

CHAPTER EIGHTEEN

Crouched in the bush in the stream-bed below La Motte, the three companions shook hands solemnly as though making a pledge. For safety, they had rested beside the tinkling brook until the evening shadows provided cover for their re-entry into the village.

Pierre watched as the grinning Theodore and Andre vanished upstream into the shadows. Then he heaved a sigh and crept silently up through the family vegetable garden below his home. Despite being mid-summer and the weather being ideal for celebrations, he was surprised that there were no auditory signs of the usual mid-week entertainment from the village square. At this time, the men would have been involved in their last hectic game of boules. The click of the metal balls and the yells of victory should have echoed through the narrow streets.

Hmm, he thought, maybe there are Dragoons still in the village after all?

For safety's sake, he decided to enter the house through the stable door. This way he could listen before entering the kitchen. As he opened the stable, the mule looked around anxiously, then snorted when it recognized him. He rubbed the ribs of his father's riding mule and then scratched its ears as it nuzzled him with pleasure.

A shaft of light lit the stable as the door opened at the top of the wooden stairs. His father stood on the landing holding a heavy wooden club and a lantern; peering down into the semi-darkness.

"Pierre?" His voice was low, shocked – and obviously, very surprised.

"What?" He heard his mother's voice from the end of the kitchen and heard her footsteps run over to her husband's shoulder. "Pierre, my son…"

Knowing it was safe, Pierre raced up the steps and hugged his father on the landing. But there was resistance in his parent's shoulders and he did not feel a return of the affection.

What is wrong, he thought? Are they aware – and ashamed – of my failure to keep Suzanne safe? His father turned away and stalked back towards the fireplace. He felt the affection in his mother's clasp but she cried quietly – and not with joy! He broke off and holding his arm around his mother, he walked into the center of the kitchen where his father waited stolidly.

"Is there something wrong?"

His mother choked a little sob and then looked at her husband. His father looked down at the stone floor and then shaking his head, he stared at Pierre – as though looking for ... hope!

"There are stories, my son! Tales of ... shame and disgrace ... all over the Luberon. We could not believe. We needed to hear it from you – our son!"

Pierre took a deep breath and let it out explosively. It was as he had dreaded it would be! He found his mouth twisting as he considered the words in his mind. Then he began slowly.

"You have heard then ... Suzanne, my future wife ... has been murdered!" From the change of appearance on his father's face and the gasp from his mother, he realized that this was a surprise they had not expected.

"Murdered, Pierre, *mon Dieu!*" his father raised his hand to the forehead and covered his eyes. His mother stood as though frozen, her eyes glazed over and a single tear began to trickle down her cheek.

Pierre leaned over and wiped up the tear on his finger and looked at it. His stomach churned inside. He did not know what to say or where to begin. Finally, he turned to his father.

"What have you heard, father?"

"When Alexander returned..."

"Alexander!" Pierre could not control the outburst, "He has returned?"

His father nodded slowly. "When he returned he was in great despair!" Pierre deliberately bit his lip and nodded to encourage his parent's story.

"He reported on the good progress the party had made up until... you took over the group – with Andre – and led them deliberately into the mountains - at Sisteron, was it not?" His father looked over to his wife for confirmation and she nodded. "He, Alexander, said that you were less cautious," his father squinted in the lamplight at his son, "that you took chances and," despite a snort of anger from Pierre, he continued grimly, "that the whole party had been captured. Except for Alexander and two other men escaping during the capture." He stood up erect for the first time and looked at Pierre for a response.

"Father," he hesitated and tried desperately to control his anger and frustration, "I never thought he would ever be able to show his ... treacherous face on the Luberon again!"

He held his arms out wide and gestured to the table. "Let us sit down and I will tell you the true story!" Both his parents nodded with some relief on their faces and sat quietly. Pierre pulled a stool up to the head of the table and as he sat down he smashed his closed fist down on the table. His mother jerked upright with fear on her face.

"This is not like you, my son! You have always been so quiet and so controlled in your manner. Please - don't scare me?" She spoke softly and he reached over the table and gently rubbed her hand.

"I'm sorry, my dear mother. But, we have all been through Hell! And," his voice dropped and a sob broke through, "I have been robbed of my future wife!" He took a deep breath and then slowly and carefully recounted the details of the escape journey.

He told of the disappointment at not being able to lead the group. Then of his acceptance of Alexander's reported expert knowledge. His father nodded in response. Then he spoke of the strategies they had developed for their safety and the roles that he and Andre had played in protecting their rearguard. He spoke of his growing awareness that all was not right with the world; of the cairns of pebbles at the signposts; and finally, of contact with the gang headed by the outlaw, Renard.

"Father, we were, both Andre and I, sure that something evil was taking place! And we became sure also that Alexander was behind it!" His father gasped with disbelief and shook his head slowly. Sadness grew in his chest and showed in his hoarse voice as he recounted the incident at the monastery hot pools – and Alexander's despicable behavior. Both his parents gasped aloud and mother covered her eyes with her apron.

"It was then that that swine, Alexander deserted the party – and Henri Deleman, from St. Martin - not me -took over the controls. And, it was his lack of caution that led to our capture." He shook his head in sorrow. "The poor man was killed when his daughter died!"

"And, it was not all a failure!" and Pierre then recounted the final result.

He told of the deaths of the father, Deleman and his daughter Francoise; and of their neighbor, David Blosset.

And of the six women and children who had been transported to the Convent near Marseilles.

"But five have reached safety in Switzerland in Geneva; and another three have joined the outlaws; and, we three, Andre, Theodore and I are planning on trying the Rhone route through Lyon –and we will make it to safety!"

His father rose from the table and looked out through the open shutters into the darkness of the early evening. He breathed loudly and rubbed his face in his hands. Then he turned and put his hands out across the table to Pierre; who grasped them tightly.

"I am glad that it is not a complete disaster! But, I knew, my son, I knew that the story could not be true! But the whole hillside of the Luberon has heard the tale and believes it! We," he gestured towards his wife, "We could not believe it – but we had nothing to work with..."

Pierre dropped his father's hands and stood up.

"Is the village safe – at this time – are the Dragoons here?"

"No, they have all gone. Everyone has abjured! Why should they stay? Why do you want to know?"

"We must call a village meeting, father ... to let them listen to the true story! Andre – and little Theodore – will back up the truth!" His father shook his head.

"I am not sure that it will be safe to try to tell your story! Perhaps, it would be wiser if I gather a group of reliable and wiser friends of mine - and let them listen to your story – without wanting to kill you!" He smiled at Pierre. "We don't want to rouse a lot of hotheads! After, all, It is your word against Alexander's – and he has put blame on your friend, Andre – as well!"

They spent some time talking about possibilities and making a mental list of supporters in both La Motte and St. Martin. Then Pierre gasped aloud.

"I forgot ... forgive me ... but I have to break the sad news to *Monsieur* Charpentier!" He nodded his head, "He gave me the ... responsibility of getting his daughter, Suzanne, to safety – and, I have failed! And, I need to tell him!" His mother gasped and looked at her husband.

"Pierre," his father's voice was grim, "I am afraid that that will not be possible. Our good neighbor, *Monsieur* Charpenter, died a week ago. They said that his heart gave up! The widow has left to live with relatives in Marseilles! The village is looking for a new baker now. The grief is all yours – and ours right now! We had both looked forward to knowing that we had a lovely daughter – and a wife – for our son! But if God has willed it - so be it!" And he put his arm around his son's shoulder and pulled him tightly towards him and hugged.

When he pulled away, there were tearstains on his father's face.

"I think, my son, that I will go and visit your friend, Andre, and his family. Your mother will pack you some food. I think the three of you would be safer in your hideout – the ancient borrie - until we can arrange a safe hearing in the community – probably for tomorrow evening!" He waved back as he opened the door cautiously and slipped out.

*   *   *   *   *

... just a few days earlier - 15th July 1687
Road to Lyon – Pont de Gard

As a Dragoon thundered by raising a great cloud of dust, Isabeau responded to Uncle Antoine's quick glance with a smile. Now that we know they are spying on us, our whole world becomes a much safer place, thought Isabeau. It makes you feel that you are one step ahead of the enemy!

The party now recognized the Dragoon's strategy. One soldier would ride up ahead enough to obtain a long distance look backward; and wait in the shade of a nearby tree – half-hidden. When the carriage passed his position, he would wait for the rear-guard major party and another Dragoon would ride past them to take a forward post.

"I wonder what they would do if we suddenly stopped?" she asked with a mischievous smile at her Uncle.

"Why not find out?" Uncle Antoine grinned back. "After all, I promised you a leisurely trip up to Lyon." He leaned out of the uncovered carriage window and peered up ahead. "The Dragoon has gone over the next rise! And there is a shady grove and a small stream coming up. Driver!" he called up as he twisted his head. "Pull off the road at the stream – we will take a break now!" He turned back in and chuckled. "Let's see how efficient their system is, shall we?"

]

The carriage swayed and slowed down before turning into the shade of the grove. Uncle Antoine jerked open the door and helped Aunt Belle and Isabeau down. Then he dusted himself off as he surreptitiously glanced down the dusty route. Isabeau led her Aunt down a safe path to a small pool nestled below the trees. But she also carefully watched back down the road. It only took a few minutes before the party of Dragoons appeared in a cloud of dust. They were chatting with each other and laughing and passed in a rush. Suddenly there were cries of consternation and the party broke from their canter and reined in a short distance down the road. Isabeau, her head peering through the green shrubs, began to giggle.

There was a flurry of cautious discussions with all the Dragoons avoiding looking back at the empty carriage. Then a decision was made. One Dragoon was delegated to turn and gallop back down towards Avignon. He rode past without casting a glance at the party. The others spurred their horses and cantered slowly onward. Isabeau looked back to the grove to see Uncle and son holding their stomachs as they chortled in glee.

After washing up in the pool, Isabeau and her Aunt climbed the bank to return to the carriage where the men were eagerly waiting.

"Well, my favorite niece, you got your wish, didn't you? Confusion to the enemy, eh?" Her Uncle put both of his hands firmly on her shoulders as he faced her and squeezed lightly.

"Yes, Uncle. Now what?"

"Well," he squinted his eyes into the morning sun, "I promised you a pleasant trip, so let's take our time. I had planned on spending tonight visiting friends at Orange. However, since we have a picnic lunch packed, I think we shall take the next road and have our lunch at the famous old Roman aqueduct at Pont du Gard!"

"Oh, Uncle, that's wonderful! I have heard so much about it – but never been there!"

"Neither has your Aunt, isn't that right, Belle?" Aunt Belle nodded her head with enthusiasm. They all climbed on board and Uncle joined them once he had given directions to the driver. Without looking directly, they spotted the patrol of Dragoons hidden in the next grove of trees and smiled at each other. This is becoming fun, thought Isabeau. And Uncle keeps his promises well!

*   *   *   *   *

24th July 1687
Village of St. Martin, Luberon hillside

The grapevine fire burnt fiercely with little smoke and provided enough light to throw golden flares up the sides of the nearby buildings and create grotesque designs on the doorways and shadowy trees and shrubs. The meeting had been arranged in the village square of St. Martin and a glance around the gathering highlighted tense faces of villagers from near and far.

Leaning carefully forward out of the shadows of an alley, Pierre could recognize faces from even as far away as Cucuron and Vaugines in the west and La Bastide des Jourdans in the east.

"It looks like a trial scene!" he grunted to Andre who crouched next to him shielding little Theodore protectively.

"I guess ... it would be important to the whole of the Luberon," whispered Andre. "Look who is going to speak!" and he pointed to the edge of the firelit area.

A large burly man with graying hair was coming into the center of the square. He paused at the spot where the light from the flickering fire lit up his features. He held up his hand and the buzz of conversations died out.

"*Mes amis!* I welcome all of you to this important meeting," he gazed around the firelit faces and nodded to various people as his gaze passed them, "I see that many of you have traveled long distances ... in a very short time ... to participate. I thank you!" He hesitated as though pondering his next move. "To those who do not know me, my name is Jacques Imbert from St. Martin. I have been chosen to ... adjudicate ... this gathering. Not to judge but to ensure that a fair hearing is given to this most serious of ... complaints. All our villages on the Luberon have been following the attempted escape of our loved ones. At first ... we were both anxious ... and excited ... about the reports of their progress. And, have now been horrified at the ... tragedy of the party's failure! And of the loss of freedom ... and the loss of hope."

An audible groan whispered around the square and Pierre felt a distinct wrench of his stomach at the sound. Andre grunted behind him in the dark. Someone appeared from the shadows and carried a wooden stool that was placed carefully at the edge of the firelight. He tapped Imbert on the shoulder; and pointed before vanishing in the shadows. Imbert nodded his thanks and sat down gracefully.

He continued, "As many of you know, to escape the disgrace of abjuring and the harassment of the Dragoons, a party of villagers were selected from the Luberon hillside," he paused and recited the villages involved, - from: La Motte d'Aigues, St. Martin, Grambois and La Bastide.

He looked around the deathly quiet shadowed square for confirmation and continued, "They left – what we thought was secretly - during the wedding festivities of the Richarde and Mallan families. They left in an attempt to escape – up the Durance valley – to the safety of Switzerland. As you all know, at the village of St. Martin's request, we were lucky to have the party led by a reliable young man from my village, Alexander Cramer, who reported that he was familiar with the Durance route." He waved his hand to his left and Pierre grunted in disgust. Alexander appeared from the shadows wearing a sad and abject face and stood in the firelight.

Looking around the faces, he nodded his head in recognition. Imbert continued, "The first note of the tragedy was when Alexander rode back into the Luberon to report the capture by the Dragoons before the party would have arrived at Grenoble?" He glanced at Alexander for confirmation and continued when he had received a tacit nod of agreement.

]

"Alexander reported being involved in a struggle with several Dragoons and managing to escape. He reported that at that moment, he had a choice! He could continue his escape to Geneva; or he could risk a dangerous journey back to the Luberon to report the disaster – which he chose!" Alexander nodded his head vehemently and a murmur of appreciation ran around the circle. Pierre grimaced and heard a grunt of disgust from behind him.

"He visited each of the villages in turn to report the disaster and then returned to hide from the Dragoons in St. Martin. Each village has grieved these losses. He fears that there may have been some loss of life! But he expects from past history that the men have been sent to the galleys in Marseilles and the women and children to a convent – but he has no details, yet!" A moan was heard around the square.

"He must have come directly home – without waiting to see what happened," whispered Andre behind him. Pierre nodded in the dark as Imbert continued.

"Now, I understand, several other members – from La Motte – have arrived back on the Luberon. Their story is different to that which Alexander reported." Pierre saw Alexander's face jerk around in shock as he stared at the speaker. Then, quickly, he turned and looked around the dark figures searchingly.

"You will remember," Imbert raised his finger and pointed around the circle of listeners, "that Alexander reported that he had run into growing opposition and interference to his leadership of the party from a small group of troublemakers. And, that this had finally broken into an outright mutiny," a murmur of anger crept around the firelight area, "before their capture. In fact, he reports that he was ousted from the party the day before." He looked again at Alexander for confirmation and Alexander spoke up finally.

"You're right! As I said, we were doing well." He gestured with both his hands flinging them into the air to accent his points. " No problems from Dragoons! And so close to safety!" He looked around the firelit faces, his face lit with excitement. "We all know that the people in that area of Savoy are accepting of our Belief! We would have been safe all the way to the border. Then, because of - the la Motte gang - I was thrown out!" Pierre could stand no more and, standing upright, he burst out of the shadows of the archway and walked into the firelight.

"Jaubert!"

"Jaubert, he's back!"

"The swine, he should be whipped!" Surprised voices called out from the shadowy figures. Imbert held up his hand and the uproar died down. He gestured to Pierre waving his finger to bring him around to his side - opposite to where Alexander was standing - his face in utter shock. Pierre glared at him. Then Alexander turned back to the crowd and pointed his finger at Pierre.

"That's him! It is that man who took your party into disaster!" He thrust his finger at Pierre again. "It is he that has to accept the blame – the tragedy of putting all your friends at serious risk!" Suddenly, he laughed aloud. "And, you can imagine the fine tale he will tell! He will lie! He will say anything to protect himself!"

"Enough! Alexander!" Imbert stood up and grasped Alexander with a strong hand and shook him. "I am running this meeting. We have all heard your story! But we must be fair!" Alexander threw his head back in a sardonic gesture and laughed aloud.

"Oh, certainly, M. Imbert! Let him tell his lies! Go ahead! It is my word against his, is it not?" Imbert shook his head.

"No, Alexander. He has two others with him!" Alexander jerked his head and peered around the circle. Andre holding Theodore's arm moved out of the shadows and walked around the fire to stand alongside Pierre.

"Oh sure, his best friend, Roux – and his little brother! It was them!" He thrust out his accusing finger. "It was those three who gave me all the trouble! It was they who took your party into disaster!" And he turned and looked at Imbert, "You expect the truth from them? Huh!" He laughed in disgust. "Go ahead, listen to their lies!"

Imbert nodded! "Yes, we will listen to them and ... judge for ourselves!" Then he turned to Pierre and addressed him politely. "The accusations against you and your friends have been made! We would like to hear your answers. Please..." and he seated himself again and waved to settle the hum of disquiet.

Pierre felt his breathing grow difficult and words churned through his mind. Settle down and breathe properly, he warned himself. This is not going to be easy! The fire lit the watching faces with anger and distrust. He caught a flicker of his father and mother's faces. His father nodded at him in encouragement. No, thought Pierre, I will not answer the accusations! I will tell a story – as it was, from the beginning.

"For those of you who don't know me, I am Pierre Jaubert of La Motte d'Aigues and I help my father manage his herd of sheep. Some of you I recognize! And, I think you know that I am honest and trustworthy." At the same time that he felt a solid pat on the back from Andre, he heard a groan from Alexander who theatrically held his hands palm up in a gesture of derision before rolled his eyes skyward. Pierre cleared his hoarse throat and continued.

"I will not answer accusations – for I don't know what they really are! But I will report on the journey of our party from the moment they left the Luberon!" Without looking he knew that Alexander had rolled his eyes upward again.

Pierre then described the journey explaining his actions with Andre in the rearguard protection. He described their relatively safe journey up to Manosque and on to Sisteron. Then his puzzlement when the route changed away from the safety of the Durance River. Alexander snorted in disgust and declared:

"You demanded that we take that route!"

Pierre turned briefly to look at him and continued. He reminded Alexander that he, Alexander, had made all the decisions – without consultation. He finished by reporting the party's safe journey to where they stayed at Monestier - where they had been fed and bathed in the hot springs by the monks. Here Alexander broke in again.

"It was he who accepted the hospitality of the Catholics! Can you imagine that? And, then, he took over the leadership of the whole party –

]

which led to their capture! Let him lie his way out of that!" Alexander's voice was becoming a little high and shrill.

Remain calm, Pierre, he told himself. Don't let your anger get out of control! Then, Theodore jumped forward and grabbed Pierre's arm.

"Tell them about the pebbles, Pierre! Tell them..."

"The pebbles, Pierre?" Imbert laid a hand on his arm, "What are these pebbles?"

Pierre hesitated. He felt that if the direction changed into side stories, he might lose control of the main theme. But Andre stepped forward.

"I am Andre Roux, also from La Motte. I worked mostly on the rearguard protection – with Pierre." He grinned at his friend, then continued, "We were puzzled about certain behaviors on the trip." And he continued to describe the peculiar actions of their leader, Alexander; of the mounds of pebbles at the signposts of villages; about how confused they were. And, of tests they made to verify if messages were being left for Dragoons. Pierre was horrified when this explanation by Andre suddenly led to the disclosure of how they were being trailed by a party of Dragoons.

"Dragoons?" Imbert's voice sounded incredulous; "You felt that Dragoons were shadowing you? Why?"

Pierre interrupted the process and outlined his surprise capture by an outlaw gang who warned him of the presence of the Dragoon squad following them.

"You say, it was Renard's group? They warned you...?"

Then Pierre told of his confusion about why the Dragoons – who were evidently aware of his presence, had not attempted to capture them. And he reported the further contacts with the friendly outlaws.

"But, why did you not report this to your leader, Alexander? Was that not very disloyal behavior on your part?" Imbert's voice was upset.

"Because, we had begun to question our leader's behaviors! We felt that he may have been betraying us to the Dragoons!" Andre spoke up hotly and pointed at Alexander.

"What a lying swine! And, what an incredible story! And they are all in this together!" Alexander broke out holding his face in his hands and laughing.

"Enough, Alexander! We recognize that it does sound a little ... far fetched! And, difficult to believe! That the Dragoons would follow the party all the way from the Luberon – nearly to Grenoble! Why would they do that?"

Imbert's voice and gestures made the whole tale questionable and the crowd's voices rose in anger. He waved his hands to quieten the outbursts and continued, "Carry on, Pierre, tell us about your leading the party and the capture!"

For the first time, Pierre sensed that the listening villagers were rejecting the description of the whole disaster. That they found the story too confusing; the alleged conspiracy too involved. He desperately juggled various directions in his confused mind. But he answered the question nevertheless.

"I did not lead the party when Alexander dropped out!" A buzz of confused murmurs greeted his words but he raised his voice and continued, "Henri Deleman – of St. Martin decided that - as the oldest member - he should lead the party. David Blosset continued to act as advance guard..."

"So where is Deleman? Where is your witness?" Alexander yelled at him.

"He is dead! He died in a riot with the Dragoons – after his daughter was assaulted ... and killed herself!" Andre stepped forward again. A groan of open pain burst from the listening group.

Imbert stood and raised his hands to try and restore order but Alexander seized the moment to raise his hands in the air and shout:

"How can you all stand there and listen to this contrived pack of lies! All lies! They," he jerked his arm around and pointed towards the friends, "They dragged the leadership away from me! I did not drop out! They collaborated with the Catholic monks at Monestier - before the party was captured! They led them into disaster! Can you imagine a whole patrol of Dragoons following us all the way to Switzerland? Why?" There was a confused silence around the square.

"And these mutineers have put all your people into prison – for life! And, for probable death!" He turned and called over his shoulder as he pushed his way through the angry upset crowd, "I will not listen to any more of these confused lies!"

And he vanished into the shadows. The incensed crowd moved forward growling and with arms and fists raised in the air in anger. Imbert was trying valiantly to try and regain control. He yelled for quiet. Reluctantly the villagers stood still and the yelling died away.

"What you have all heard is shocking - to all of us! Although there are three of you, you are all close friends!" He gestured with his hands open. "Do you have any witnesses? Have all the rest of the party been captured? You say my good friend, Henri Deleman, who you reported as having taken over control of the party – is also dead!"

Taking advantage of the silence of the listening crowd, Pierre, his voice growing hoarse outlined the end result of their journey. That after their capture, four had been murdered; five had reached safety in Switzerland; three had joined the outlaw band to try and free their loved ones; six had been sent to the Convent; and four had returned to the village – the three friends and Alexander.

"But – you have no witnesses to your ridiculous story!" A man waved his fist across the fire at Pierre.

Pierre took a deep breath and sighed. His face felt numb and cold despite the warm night air. A sense of hopelessness filled his stomach. He had failed to realize how confused and weak the whole explanation sounded to these angry villagers.

"No!" he said, "We have no witnesses - unless ... one of the three who joined the outlaws can be contacted!"

A dead silence hung over the village square. The agitated villagers glared helplessly at the three friends.

Suddenly a voice from the darkness of an alley:

"You want a witness? You've got a witness!"

All eyes jerked to the darkest corner of the square. Into the

]

firelight strode a tall slim wiry figure. Villagers gasped as they recognized the hood pulled over the head.

"*Le Renard!* *Le Renard!*" Imbert rose from his stool, amazement showing on his face.

"Am I an acceptable witness, M. Imbert?" Imbert's face now showed obvious relief.

"*Oui! Monsieur Renard!* We..." he waved at the crowd of villagers, "We are honoured by your unexpected visit. Can you help us deal with this mess?"

The hood nodded in assent. Renard raised his hand into the air and immediately silence returned to the square.

In a firm authoritative voice, he told of his decision to trail the escape party to ensure that they left the Luberon safely.

"Initially, we were worried that their safeguards were not strong enough – until we watched Pierre – here – suggest changes to their leader – which he accepted somewhat reluctantly."

A gasp went through the listeners.

"Then we became aware that a party of Dragoons was shadowing the refugees – and we could not understand the reasons. So we shadowed the Dragoons!" He laughed out loud and the villagers joined in. "After awhile, when it became obvious that the Dragoons had no intention of capturing the group, we decided to alert someone in the party – and we chose Pierre," he pointed at him, "because we knew he was honest and reliable." Another murmur of appreciation ran through the listeners. "Through Pierre, we set up a message system which worked reasonably well". Pierre noted that he did not outline the system.

Renard went on to explain that they became convinced that there was a traitor in the group - someone who was passing messages to the Dragoons. Shocked cries sounded around the square.

"Our party – of wanted men – outlaws - was never big enough to confront the militia! Our value was that they were not aware of our trailing them! I am sorry to say that because we were involved in other secret actions along the route, we missed the ambush and capture!"

" Renard, why do you think the Dragoons – after shadowing the party for so long – suddenly decided to capture them?" Imbert's voice was curious.

"I suspect, that once their informer was no longer safe within the party, the Dragoons would have to act! And they did – once Alexander had deserted the group!"

A surprised and angry rumble ran through the villagers. In response, he then shocked the listeners by detailing the circumstances of Alexander's leaving. With their firm moral standards, sneaking in to watch the women bathe, obviously shocked the group.

"We are sorry that people had to die! And that people had to be captured! But we are still hopeful that the women and children can be somehow freed!" Even in the dim firelight, Pierre could see tears run down the firelit faces. "Far from being criticized, I feel that Pierre, Andre and little Theodore behaved courageously!" Strong mutters of approval sounded in the group.

"Pierre even killed two Dragoons – by himself!" Theodore's voice piped up from behind his brother. A shocked gasp echoed around. "And, Andre also killed the big one!"

Pierre sighed at the shocked look on his father's face. He had hoped that the incident would not have to be exposed. To the silent audience, Theodore now recounted the whole attack. Pierre was shaken by the fact that the child, supposedly safe with the mules, had managed to watch the whole incident.

Following the dead quiet that followed the story, Renard raised his open hands in a questioning manner. "Well, you have the truth now – and a lot of the gory details! I must now leave you – and thank you all for your support – and your personal bravery!"

And then he turned and slipped into the darkness.

Imbert turned impulsively and shook the hands of all three in return. The excited crowd gathered around to renew their promises of support and affection.

Many wanted to know more details about the battle with the Dragoons and cornered Theodore who proudly related a more colorful story. Andre had to drag him away to bed. Pierre accepted many handshakes from local Luberon villagers as he peered around the darkness for his parents. Then he saw them standing in the shadows of a doorway watching him. He smilingly brushed the rest of the people away as he excused himself and joined his family.

"I am sorry ... that you had to hear that story from strangers, father!"

His father shook his head and, glancing for support from his wife, turned back to his son.

"We are not angry - just surprised! We did not know that you could do such courageous things! You have always been so - passive and careful!" He laughed softly. "In fact, we have always felt you needed to be more aggressive, more daring! No, Pierre, we were not disappointed – just a little shocked! But..." he looked around the square at the talking villagers, "Let's go home and talk about your plans – and have some wine!"

Pierre nodded with relief. He put his arms around his mother and father and the three slipped unnoticed out of the busy square and walked down the moonlit road out of town and back the short distance to their own village of La Motte d'Aigues nearby.

*   *   *   *   *

]

CHAPTER NINETEEN

25th July 1687
La Motte d'Aigues, Luberon hillside

He lay cuddled under his bed covers with his eyes fixed on the crack around the window's shutter. A heavy but clean smell of a light Provencal summer rain slipped into the dark room and tickled his nose.

A good day to travel, he thought. But Pierre recognized a distinct reluctance deep inside himself about even getting out of bed.

What is it? Then the full force of the "home" situation struck him. This will probably be the last time that I will ever leave this bed again! When I leave today ... it will be forever!

He felt his eyes water slightly and he brushed them with the back of his hand. He nodded his head slightly. Everyone has to leave home – but forever?

Down the stairs, he could hear his father moving around, blowing life into the embers in the fireplace and perhaps, packing food for his trip. Last night he had talked late with his parents. How he loved and respected them! How much he would miss them – both!

His father had urged a swift escape from the village. He was sure that Alexander would have alerted the wily Captain that his "attacker" was back on the Luberon. And he knew that the Captain would never give up his desire for revenge. I would like to have smashed his whole face in, thought Pierre in a moment of bitter anger.

And his thoughts flashed back to the memory of his lovely Suzanne - tossed aside like a piece of rubbish in the alpine meadow near Grenoble. Then his deep belief took over with a struggle. Alexander may be evil but we are not meant to harm people – but forgive? If I ever can!

With a deep sadness in his heart, Pierre shrugged off the covers and sat on the edge of his bed. He knew that Andre was anxious to start the trip up the Rhone River as early as possible. They would be sitting on their saddled mules at their meeting place by the small brook right now. But his father's late night thoughts had been wise!

Instead of racing north up on the banks of the Rhone, his father would escort them down to the nearby village of Pertuis - where he would have his son abjure his faith. The thought left a bad taste in Pierre's mouth; but he recognized the wisdom of "going through the legal ceremony" – even as a subterfuge!

Traveling with the Notary's certificate confirming that he had "changed faiths" - while it would make no difference if the Captain captured them – would provide some basic protection with any other authorities. Pierre nodded his head again emphatically and rose and dressed quickly. He re-made his bed – for the last time. As he felt a sharp pain of regret spear through his throat, he swallowed to choke his bitter tears.

*   *   *   *   *

25th July 1687
Leaving La Motte d'Aigues, Provence

The early morning mist was shrouding the distant Durance River in the valley as the four mules cantered over the rise and halted. Pierre signaled the party to stop and silently they drank in this beautiful pastoral scene. It was a sight - that for at least three of them - may never be seen again! An eagle screamed from a treetop above a thick grove of trees to their left.

Suddenly the elder Jaubert jerked! He pointed down the hillside to a break in foliage.

"Dragoons!" he whispered hoarsely. He yanked his mule's reins and swung the animal towards the grove of trees followed by the rest of the party. In the protection of the trees, they threw themselves from their mounts.

Each rider covered the nose of a mule and rubbed its ears to keep it calm and to prevent them snorting as the squadron of Dragoons clattered by leaving a heavy cloud of fine dust sifting through the morning air despite the early morning shower.

"There's your *Capitaine* Benoit – in the lead!" whispered Andre. "That was good timing! How did you spot them, sir?" and he glanced at the older man.

"I was lucky – or blessed!" he responded. "I saw a flash of light from a breast plate." He waved at Pierre who was busy readying himself to re-mount. "Wait awhile – you never know!" The party stood quietly rubbing their mules and watching the road through the gap in the foliage. Suddenly the hoof beats of further horses grew louder and the entire group sighed with relief as a rearguard of three riders clattered by.

The older Jaubert shook his head with obvious relief.

"Two lucky breaks in one morning is asking a little too much!" He nodded to his son: "I think we should travel swiftly to Pertuis and get the ceremony over with." It will take the Dragoons some time while they search the villages. You can use that extra time to get an early start on your final journey!"

They all mounted and this time, they copied the system they had learned on their road up the Durance – one rider in the front; two in the middle; and a rearguard rider behind.

*   *   *   *   *

... a little earlier - 15th July 1687
On the road to Lyon – Pont de Gard

"It's hard to believe that that magnificent structure has been standing there for ... a thousand years!" As she stood on a prominent rock with her Uncle, Isabeau was overwhelmed at the gigantic stone aqueduct that towered above her. "The Romans really knew something about building, didn't they?"

"It also used to be used as a roadway – on top ... up there!" Uncle Antoine pointed and Isabeau craned her head back to look at several youth who had climbed onto the top ledge. "But in the last couple of hundred years ... or so, the roadway has deteriorated. It's a pity that something is not done to repair it!"

"Isabeau, Antoine!" Aunt Belle's voice floated up the rough pathway. "The meal is ready – and smells lovely!"

"Come – it's well past my normal meal time!" Her Uncle grasped her arm for safety and led her back down the path. Isabeau stopped at the last turning and looked back at the aqueduct again. "I'm glad I saw it – at least once!" she announced and then ran to catch up with her Uncle.

*   *   *   *   *

The picnic lunch was succulent and worth waiting for. A baked rabbit pie with a wonderful pungent gravy flavored with the exciting taste of garlic and rosemary; with a mixed salad of the vegetables of Provence – including onions, olives, greens and chunks of rich cheese. The host had also included a rich apple tart and several bottles of local estate wine.

"I think we have been discovered!" Aunt Belle whispered softly and nodded her head in the direction of the river bottom. Several Dragoons had suddenly appeared on the broad stretch of golden sand across the river and, on sighting the picnic party, had withdrawn into the riverside brush.

"Poor devils – early afternoon and probably nothing to eat since morning!" Isabeau lay back and observed their hiding place from under the broad brim of her hat. She looked around the group – which included the driver – and nodded her head. "There is plenty left over to feed most of the patrol. Maybe we should leave the rest – and a bottle of wine – with the extra fruit?" Both Uncle and Aunt grinned and nodded. Her husband was less enthusiastic.

"Let the bastards starve!" he grunted.

"I do feel a little sorry for them. They are obeying orders, aren't they?"

After some discussion, it was agreed to leave the remainder prominently displayed on a nearby rock. The party packed up and with a last glance backward at the majestic stone structure, Isabeau and her family set out for Orange.

*   *   *   *   *

The two matched black horses were sweating slightly as they pulled the open carriage off the dusty road and into the open cobbled area before the riverside inn. As it jolted to a halt, the Captain cursed the driver.

"Can you not control your steeds, you useless oaf!"

"I am sorry, *mon Capitaine!* I will try harder!" The driver grimaced as he looked over his shoulder at the resplendent officer whose uniform was now covered with a light mist of Provencal dust.

"See if you can get me some ... fruit? Some local pears are supposed to be excellent! And some local wine – white!" The driver checked the brakes; nodding as he leapt to the cobblestones. The Captain drew his usual large white handkerchief from a pocket and attempted to flick the dust from the sleeves of his coat.

He stood up in the carriage and, raising his hand to shade his eyes from the strong noon sun, he peered over the heads of his escort of mounted Dragoons at the nearby languidly flowing waters of the Rhone.

He detested the Rhone – it was a poor example of a truly great river. He had not got over his longing for the spirit of the Seine and the soft still beauty of the Loire. He shrugged and his fingers touched the livid red scar on his cheek. Will it never heal up properly? Is this cursed wound simply a symptom of the festering sore of this Provence?

Every village is filled with these pesky Huguenots! You have to humiliate them, grind them into the filthy dust of Provence, before they finally abjure. And then they sign the papers. And we know they are perjuring themselves to escape the harassment. Yet, we let them lie to us – and escape!

"Damn these heretic Huguenots!" he raised his voice in frustration causing the escort's horses to jerk and prance. His carriage rocked and he grasped the rail to keep his balance.

The return of his driver accompanied by the laden Inn landlord brought the Captain back to the present.

"So, what have you got?" He peered over the rail at the Innkeeper. "Hmm, the pears look fresh – and cool. Good! And the wine, light and clear – and cool too! Hmm! You have done well!"

He nodded with obvious reluctance at the landlord whom he suspected was also of this cursed faith.

"Michel – move the carriage to the shade overlooking the river – and I will enjoy a light lunch. I will not be entering Avignon! But, I am expecting several messengers with reports on two different matters – and they will meet me here." He sank back into his seat with the bowl of pears on his lap. The wineglass and bottle were clutched in his hands. And soon the fresh pear juice dripped from his mouth and trickled glistening to his chin as he waited for his messages. Slowly the stark white handkerchief discolored as he placidly wiped his face – careful not to touch the scar.

*   *   *   *   *

Pierre approached the rise in the dusty road cautiously slowing the mule's approach until he could peer down the next slope. He breathed another short sigh of relief as his view extended all the way down the slope until an ancient stone bridge crossed a small stream at the bottom. His eye raced up the opposite slope to the next rise. Nothing – except a series of farmers' carts and wagons – some heading towards him destined for the markets at Pertuis and others heading away – probably for Cavillon, he mused.

He turned in his saddle and waved to Andre who was still waiting on the previous rise and received an enthusiastic approval as he cantered down the slope towards Pierre. He caught a flash of white teeth as Theodore grinned in excitement and urged his mule up the slope. Pierre waved and turned his mule towards the bridge. Sensing water, the mule broke into a canter.

Pierre tensed as a pair of riders came over the rise ahead galloping down the opposite slope towards the bridge. But a glance revealed that they were not Dragoons – just young – rather flashily dressed – ruffians. Before he reached the bridge, the pair galloped past carrying on a conversation of yells with each other.

Noticing a secluded stream bank alongside a heavy grove of trees, Pierre slowed down at the bridge and checked the site out. It seemed to provide an opportunity for the three friends to rest and water their mules and wash some of the dust from their faces. Pierre waited at the bridge for his friends to catch up.

Why do I feel so ... optimistic about this journey? My first escape to Marseilles ended up in disaster and failure. The second – up the Durance – ended in more disaster ... and death. Maybe, it's time! A slight grin came to his face as he remembered the meeting this morning with the Notary in Pertuis.

Since it was so early, they had met in his kitchen. His father sat opposite the old man who was gesturing with his quill as he drafted the document on the scarred wooden tabletop. He looked up and scanned over the faces of the young men.

"You do not have to look so anxious – abjuring is common these sad days!" He nodded in the direction of his father. "What he is doing ... is wise!" He tapped the documents on the table. "These will protect you as you travel and, I expect, that is what you are going to do?" They all looked at each other; then at the father ... for guidance. His father grinned slowly and nodded.

"And, you are going...?" Pierre nodded and said: "Lyon ... yes!"
The Notary nodded.

"I too, am a Believer!" The young men looked startled. "Yes, even I have abjured! It's common, " he said. "But ... it will only protect you from the ... ordinary militia. If, they are seeking you, then you need ... a reason ... for your travels. Hmm..." he stopped writing and stared at the glowing fire in the fireplace. Then he nodded.

"I will ask you to ... do me a favor!" he looked at the father who nodded slowly.

"Good, your reason for the travel will now be that you are carrying a letter from the Notary at Pertuis – me - to another Notary colleague in Lyon. Yes, an urgent message, I think! And, of course, at no extra charge!" He chuckled aloud and Pierre's father grinned back at him. Pierre felt himself relax at this point. The crafty old man!

Pierre now patted his chest and felt the abjuring document and the urgent letter in the inside pocket of his jacket and smiled with satisfaction. The beginning of this journey made him feel much more satisfied with his life. But the self-satisfaction did not last long.

"Hey, stop that!" A child's yell up the hill made Pierre spin his mule round. Theodore was struggling over the rise while his mule's reins were being grasped by one of the ruffians in a blue coat who had dismounted. His red-jacketed friend rode up alongside the child's mule and reached out in an attempt to grasp the boy's arm. Both the men's backs were towards him. Pierre slapped his mule and it sprang forward and raced back up behind them. As he rode, his hand burrowed under his bundle strapped behind him and he slid his short sword out into his right hand.

Hearing the hoof-beats, the man on the ground looked backward and yelled at his companion in warning. The red jacketed man urged his horse around behind Theodore and drew a knife from its sheath and waved it in Theodore's direction.

"Keep your distance! Or, I'll slice your little friend!" Pierre jerked his mule to a dusty stop and waved his sword under the blue-coated man's nose. The action was frozen for a second and then Andre's head appeared over the rise. At once, he understood; drew his sword and came up behind the red-coated rider whose face jerked around in dismay. Outnumbered and out-armed, he dropped the knife to the ground and held his arms up in the air.

Pierre gestured to Theodore to move away from the ruffians. Andre grinned grimly and nudged the rider with the point of his sword forcing him to dismount hurriedly. Then Pierre moved alongside the blue-jacket's horse and lowering his sword, he cut gently through the girth strap and with a kick of his boot, sent the saddle crashing to the dusty road.

"Hey!" the dismounted rider cried in protest.

"You prefer me ... to cut you instead?" The man slowly shook his head but glared at Pierre. Andre now urged his mule forward as well and leaning over sliced through the strap on the other horse and a second saddle hit the dust. Grinning, both Pierre and Andre slapped the men's horses with the flat of their swords on the rumps, and, startled, they reared and galloped off over the rise, their reins dragging alongside them.

"Let's go!" Pierre called and, as the three mules raced down the slope, Pierre turned round to see the two ruffians running carrying their useless saddles awkwardly on their shoulders into the dust thrown up by the departing horses.

At the bridge, Pierre gestured to his friends and they turned off the road and worked their way downstream until they found a safe spot to water their mules and wash the roads' dust from their faces.

*   *   *   *   *

It was mid-day when Andre suggested they stop for a meal. The town of Cavillon could be seen on the top of an approaching ridge. On the stream bank over the bridge the ground was well-packed and worn as though it had been used by farmers' carts when they took time to rest on their journey. A heavy grove of trees shaded the area from the strong Provencal sun. Pierre led the way through the trees until they were concealed from the road. Theodore eagerly slid down and asked for one of Pierre's mother's apples.

"Good thought, Theodore!" he called as he dismounted. Then he stopped and peered through the brush.

"Hmm – it looks like someone needs help." He slipped through the bush and into an open area away from the main road.

A heavily loaded traditional tumbrel was standing under a large tree hitched to a heavy farm horse. The farmer knelt in front of the wheel with arms extended as he tried to re-install the wheel on the axle. Heavy rounds of cut tree trunk had been placed beneath the axle to support it in order to remove the wheel for a temporary repair. But the weight of the load had forced the firewood into the soft ground. The farmer was obviously tired and frustrated.

"Can we help you?"

The farmer jerked his head around in surprise. A touch of fear creased his face. He said nothing - looked them over. Then leaning the wheel against the side of the tumbrel, he rose slowly to his feet. Ignoring his reluctance, Pierre went forward and surveyed the situation.

"Yes," he said to the watching farmer, "if we three lift the side of the cart between us – just a little – Theodore can slide the wheel back on the axle – right?"

While the farmer hesitated, Pierre gestured to his friends and they came forward with Theodore kneeling in front of the axle hub and holding the wheel ready. Pierre nodded to the side of the cart and the farmer moved over and took a stance next to Andre.

"Ready! Now!" All three grunted as they thrust upward. The cart lifted a fraction and Theodore yelled with delight as the wheel slipped on.

"There! It's done!" Pierre turned and gestured his friends to follow him. Still confused, the farmer grunted in delight.

"Wait!" he called out. "I thank you for your help." He raised his palms upward. "Can I pay you?"

Pierre stopped and looked back; then he grinned.

"Are those melons – in the cart?" The farmer nodded.

"Yes – for the afternoon market at la Roque d'Antheron – over the Durance."

"Well, I think a couple of those for our noon meal would be a just reward!"

Relieved, the grinning farmer climbed carefully up onto the cart and tossed two melons down to the waiting friends.

Theodore grinned and waved back to the farmer who then busied himself completing the repair as they vanished into the shade of the trees.

"The best melons in the whole of France!" chortled Andre as they cut them open. Theodore grinned as the delicious melon juice dripped from his chin.

*   *   *   *   *

17th July 1687
On the road to Lyon - Orange

Isabeau leant out of the window of the coach and waved with eager enthusiasm as it moved away from the warm and friendly home of friends of Uncle Antoine where they had spent a couple of nights. She had been thrilled at her first visit to the ancient city of Orange with its many historic buildings of Roman origin.

She sat back with a touch of sadness – remembering that she would never probably see them again.

"Oh what wonderful friends you have, Uncle! They were so ... welcoming to me; and their lovely home is gracious."

"Ah, my dear Isabeau, I think they found you easy to please!" Uncle Antoine smiled with pleasure, "I was ... proud of my new niece." He glanced at his wife, "And you too, Belle, is that not so?" Belle nodded with enthusiasm.

"And, I am curious, Isabeau, what was the highlight of your visit to Orange?"

"Oh there were so many!" She stopped and pondered silently while they waited.

"I think it was the small choir that sang on the ruined stage – in the Roman theatre – in the moonlight! Yes! That was it!" She flushed a little at her enthusiasm. She grinned around the coach. "I am seeing so many new sights; and learning so much that I get exhausted – and can't remember." While both the Uncle and Aunt joined in her enthusiastic memories, her husband had closed his eyes and had begun to snore.

Uncle Antoine nodded at Le Duc with recognition of his own youth. "I am afraid that your husband – and my nephew – had a little too much wine – too late last night! We shall let him sleep it off, shall we?"

Isabeau nodded. Then she looked at her new Uncle in a pensive manner.

"Is there something wrong, Isabeau...?"

"Well, yes, there is! Uncle, we have never really discussed ... the purpose of this trip."

"Purpose?"

"Yes, Uncle! My husband," she gestured slightly to the snoring spouse, "arranged this trip with you. I am not sure what he told you about our... difficulties in St. Martin?" She stopped and waited. She was relieved to see him nod his head.

"Yes! He told me things were getting a little bit … uncomfortable in the village. What with the harassment of the Dragoons; and the attentions of our over-lustful Captain?" He smiled as he obviously remembered the prone figure on the cobblestones. "Belle and I have agreed that if the right moment arrives in Lyon, we should attempt to cross the border into the Swiss cantons. We have made secret arrangements and are financially secure so that we can relocate and live anywhere!"

He reached out and took his wife's hand. "It will naturally be difficult – at our age – to start our lives again – without our friends and neighbors! But we will be free!" Aunt Belle reached her free hand over and grasped his and smiled with love.

"Oh I am so glad to hear you say that!" Isabeau felt relief running through her body. "My husband is … reluctant to leave France. He feels we should just try and live with the problem." She shook her head in a worried fashion. "I am not sure what we will do to live. Le Duc would probably have to start a new business of some kind. I am sure he will be able to trade anywhere."

"Well," said Uncle with some authority, "we do know that in the Swiss area we will be safe and free. But I suspect that Geneva will be flooded with the many refugees who are escaping. I am unsure whether it will be better to move to another Swiss city; or maybe move into one of the many Princedoms of Germany. I have even heard that some of the Princes are reported to be paying cash rewards to certain trained craftsmen to settle in their cities!"

"So, when, my dear husband, do we make this decision?" Belle questioned.

"I think that we take one step at a time – and enjoy each step separately!" Uncle released his wife's hands and clapped them enthusiastically.

The sudden noise jolted Le Duc awake.

"Huh! What's wrong?" he grunted and peered through half-open eyes as he rubbed them.

"No, my nephew, we have been discussing our future plans."

"And?"

"We have agreed that we shall take one step at a time – and enjoy each moment of the trip," Uncle looked around the carriage and accepted the smiles and nods from the womenfolk.

"Good," grunted Le Duc, "then, I'll go back to sleep for awhile, thank you!" And he did.

Uncle Antoine looked at his sleeping nephew with some affection, nodded and continued.

"We will stop for a mid-day meal at Bolene – on the banks of the Rhone. There is an excellent Inn overlooking the river. Then visit the picturesque old Chateau at St. Paul; and then stay the night with my cousin, Theo, in Montelimar."

"They make really wonderful sweetmeats there – I am sure you have never tasted anything so exotic before, Isabeau!" Aunt Belle nodded with enthusiasm and then brushed the gust of dusty air in front of her face as a Dragoon raced by on his horse.

"Oh Uncle, they're back keeping an eye on us again!" Isabeau leaned out and watched the soldier ride up ahead.

"Yes, Isabeau, we shall have to accept them as a condition of each day, won't we?" her Uncle nodded wisely. And Isabeau reluctantly found herself wondering where Captain Benoit was at this time.

*   *   *   *   *

... a day earlier - 16th July 1687
At Avignon, Provence

"What do you mean *'they are not behaving like they should'*?" the Captain's voice had chilled. It was immediately obvious to the trooper that he had taken unwarranted liberties in his report.

"Well, ... sir, they started out being ... scared! And, now they seem to be ... having fun!" The Dragoon was flustered – and showed it.

"Having fun?" The Captain sat up sharply waving his lace edged handkerchief frantically. "And, what are you doing that allows them to 'have fun'?"

"We are just watching them, *mon Capitaine!*"

The Captain turned his head and nodded at the observant Sergeant. He frowned and grunted aloud.

"Hmm! What do you think, *Sergent*?"

"I think, *mon Capitaine*, that they have ... sensed our strategy – and now, feel safe!"

"Well, then," he turned back and gazed over the Rhone River, "we had better change our strategy, hadn't we? Maybe give them a little shock!" He looked back at the Sergeant. "Maybe it's time for me to insert my nasty velvet glove into their plans, eh?"

The Sergeant nodded and smirked. He enjoyed when the Captain took firm action.

Dismissing the Dragoon with instructions to continue the current strategy, the Captain turned to observe another messenger approaching. The dusty Dragoon brought his tired horse alongside the Sergeant's and nodded his head in recognition. The two men exchanged hoarse whispers before the Sergeant returned to the carriage side.

"Interesting news, mon *Capitaine*! That bastard, Jaubert from La Motte has been located – on this road north."

The unhealed scar on the Captain's face noticeably flushed and his eyes narrowed.

"So? And..."

"Two men – evidently pederasts," and he snickered, "tried to abduct a young boy on the road north to Cavaillon. Another two men waylaid them! They sound like your attacker, Jaubert - and probably Roux - with his young brother from St. Martin. However, Jaubert

209

unhorsed them – and they were a little unhappy and were drinking and grumbling in a local inn."

"Damn that bastard!" the Captain swore. "How does he always avoid capture? Once on the road to Marseilles; then captured below Grenoble; chained and escaped again! Then missed him at the village when he returned. And is now hailed almost as a Saint! And he unmasked our 'rat', Alexander, in the process!"

During the tirade, the Sergeant nodded his head.

"Well, now on the road north! Damn that bastard!" He jerked around and looked at the dusty messenger. "Let him," he jerked his thumb in the Dragoon's direction, "take extra men back on the road – double the patrol! I cannot rest until he is either my prisoner – or dead!" He lowered his voice to a mumble. The Sergeant had to lean forward to catch his words. "Maybe this confounded wound would heal up then!"

The Sergeant spun his horse away from the carriage and arranged to feed the trooper at the inn before sending him back with the enlarged patrol. It was not a good time to be in close proximity to an upset Captain.

The Captain stood up in his carriage and studied the slow flowing river. His mind was back in Paris.

A lazy smile crept slowly onto his injured face. An image arose in his mind. That of Louise - that very young eighteen year-old maid of the lady-in-waiting to the Queen. Not very bright – who cared! Especially, when she was shy and so unsure - and kept her fabulous figure so well disguised beneath her gown. Catching her unawares and forcing her to submit. What a joy – for any man! Oh to be in Versailles again!

He looked around for his Sergeant. If I cannot be in Versailles, choosing between my pleasures, then I might as well have them right here, he thought with grim satisfaction. When we capture that bastard Jaubert – I'll enjoy giving him a few scars on the face – before I kill him!

His smirk brightened as the image arose of that bitch mocking him in St. Martin. Challenging my manhood, was she? For an instant, he saw her sprawled struggling on her back on the fresh straw of a stable as he ripped her clothes away. His smile grew as he felt the urge rise within him. Why not?

"*Sergent! Sergent*, where the Hell are you?"

*　　*　　*　　*　　*

26th July 1687
Up the banks of the Rhone - Avignon

"You know, Andre, I really feel different today!" Pierre turned in the saddle and looked back curiously at his friend as their mules followed each other through the narrow streets of Avignon. Pierre worried that both Andre and young Theodore had been restless in their sleep during the night they had spent at the home of one of his father's friends. Now, Theodore, on the lead mule, turned also to listen to this startling revelation as he kept his beast headed for the major northern gate in the ancient city's walls.

"Different?" Andre shrugged his shoulders and smiled wistfully.

"Yes! I feel ... like ...well, like we are really going to make it this time?" Pierre looked ahead again and nodded slowly.

"Yes! I understand! It's like ... we know where we are going. And, how to get there!" He hesitated. "Well, at least until we reach Lyon, we are on legitimate ... business? Then we have to be a lot more careful – wary?" Andre nodded and moved his mule out of the way of an incoming farmer's cart.

"The gate!" A quiet call from Theodore brought their alertness back. Pierre deliberately halted his mule and allowed the two brothers to ride past the guard together. As previously arranged, Andre stopped and asked the guard for directions to Orange and thanked him for his help. During this hesitation, Pierre trotted his mule past the two friends without a glance and rode down the dusty road in the direction of the out-pointed finger of the soldier.

The road was packed with two-wheeled tumbrels loaded high with freshly picked vegetables and fruit for the early morning market in Avignon. Theodore called out the contents he recognized as they rode along.

Carrots and onions mingled with baskets of apples and pears – often crowned with twig cages of chickens and ducks - allowed the party to stay fairly close together until mid-morning. Then they divided up into their separate stations until they began to join the more tardy farmers' carts heading into the ancient city of Orange.

Andre led the way into the busy square that was the center of the market area and located a quiet stream where the mules could slake their thirst. Pierre separated and wandered through the stalls until he found food for his group. He came back laden with bread, cheese, sausage and fruit. Andre had found a hidden cool spot where they sat on the banks of the shady stream and enjoyed their lunch.

After a snack, they remounted and followed the traffic heading for the north gate of Orange. Much to Andre's consternation, Pierre kept them together – much closer than in previous towns, without explanation.

"Just trust me, Andre! I'll explain later!" Andre grunted in frustration.

Pierre halted his mule at the busy inn just inside the gate. He motioned his friends to remain on their animals and he strode towards the innkeeper who was chatting to several patrons outside in the sunshine. He stood patiently waiting for a break in the chatter. Finally, the innkeeper turned his head and nodded in his direction.

"*Monsieur* – can you tell me what the quickest route to Lyon is? We have not traveled this way before." The keeper smiled slightly and pointed out the gate ahead.

"You are from...?"

"We are on a mission from Pertuis – in the south – to Lyon"

The Innkeeper nodded and waved his finger at the gate.

"Just follow the roadway through the villages of Bollène; then

Montélimar; Valence, Vienne and then reach Lyon. About … three days good journey." Pierre nodded in appreciation.

"Thank you, *Monsieur*. You are kind!" He doffed his hat and remounted his mule nodding his head again at the Innkeeper who beamed back.

Andre glanced over at Theodore and shook his head in consternation.

As they passed through the gates two guards scanned the passing traffic. Pierre deliberately nodded his head in greeting and directed his mule closer to the guard.

"*Pardon, Capitaine?*"

The guard grinned back wryly, "Hah! You recognize true quality in a solider, do you?"

"I have not traveled this way before – is this the route to Lyon?"

"Yes, it is!" The guard peered through the shade cast by Pierre's hat at his face.

"And, you have … papers?" Pierre looked concerned and frowned.

The guard stepped forward and grasped the reins near the mule's mouth.

"Too many of those damned Huguenots running from the law! Are you one of them?" Pierre grinned back ruefully.

"Used to be, *Capitaine*, used to be!" He dug into his jacket and produced the certificate of abjuration. He unfolded it and handed it to the guard. It was obvious to both Pierre and Andre that the guard could not read the document even though he opened it and peered at the writing.

"Good!" he said. "Good! And, your business?" Pierre dug again and produced the missive from the Notary at Pertuis. When the guard reached for it, he drew it back in safety.

"I am a courier for an important official in Pertuis. I carry a confidential message to a Notary in Lyon." He turned the message over displaying the heavy seal on the reverse. The guard raised his eyebrows and grinned somewhat in embarrassment.

"Sorry, *Monsieur*. We do not want to harass businessmen on their journey!" He pointed up the northern road, "Two days up that direction. Good journey!"

Pierre nodded his head in appreciation and urged the mule to move into the heavy traffic leaving the gate. He turned and waved at the guard as the dust rose to shield them.

"Pierre?" Andre challenged him from behind.

Pierre turned and grinned back at his friends.

"Sorry, my friends! But, I wanted to ensure that, if we are being followed, then they will be sure to take the road to Lyon through Montélimar!"

"But, why?" Andre's face was still frustrated. Pierre grinned as he nodded.

"Because, for safety sake, my father suggested that we turn across the Rhone at the big bridge at Pont-St.-Esprit – and travel up the less-used side of the river – while they search all the villages and towns on the other bank."

Andre's face broke into a grin as he nodded consent.
"Of course! I thought … you were going mad, Pierre!"

*　　　*　　　*　　　*　　　*

Within an hour, they reached the turnoff to the bridge. Pierre dismounted in the shade of a huge tree and they let the mules graze on the grass while they talked about strategies. Then the three re-mounted and waited for the right opportunity. Theodore waved excitedly as a four-wheeled wagon approached and turned down the road in the direction of Port-St.-Esprit.

This time Andre and Theodore led together while Pierre trailed behind in their dust. Andre rode up alongside the driver and opened a friendly conversation about market conditions and the weather. Luckily, the farmer was eager for some companionship and as agreed, Theodore urged his mule to travel alongside the lead horse – thus becoming part of the operation.

Quietly, Pierre urged his mule up close to the rear of the wagon. Eventually, the massive ancient bridge came into view and the two guards paid little attention to the farm wagon and its outriders. In the village on the other bank, Andre and Pierre bought the farmer a cool glass of local wine and chatted about the road north. They soon were ready to leave armed with many useful tips about possible safe sleeping locations up the bank to Lyon.

*　　　*　　　*　　　*　　　*

Captain Benoit was not a man who liked to be hurried. He had decided very early in his career to practice a relaxed degree of elegance and grace. He always made sure that he was carefully – and elegantly – dressed. That his grooming was perfect for the occasion – and even, a little beyond the occasion! He always ensured that he had a bounteous supply of perfectly laundered lace-edged white handkerchiefs to flourish with great dignity. That he spoke slowly - choosing his words with dignity, grace and elegance. That he amused – and injured - people around him with his caustic wit; with little touches of ironic humor; always keeping himself a little "above" his audience. He felt it left people – even important people – like King Louis himself – wondering whether … he knew something secret – and very important – that they themselves did not know!

Hmm – let them wonder! And, to succeed in this image, you had to believe in yourself – that you were an aristocrat; that you were elegant and dignified; that you were better!

But this moment – for the Captain – was different! For, at this moment, the Captain never felt less sure – and it was getting worse!

The dusty messenger had caught up with his carriage north of Orange.

The message was short. It was a request for an immediate meeting. Even in the hot sunshine, the Captain felt his insides chill. Despite the politeness of the message, the signature below made it an immediate demand.

I did not know he was even in the south of France, the Captain thought, as fear leaked into his system.

He had surprised his patrol of Dragoons by insisting that they turn around and race back to the city of Orange.

His anxiety showing, he had spent most of the trip automatically dusting off his clothes and licking his lips. There was no doubt that the King – in his world of Divine Right – ruled France with a steel fist in a velvet glove.

But the message was not from his Majesty - but from a man who lived in the shadowy corners of the salons of Versailles – and who was reputed to be the one courtier who put the steel in the glove! A promise from "The Man" was written in marble; a threat was sure death!

As he entered the small Inn, the Captain found himself struggling to retain his casual elegance. But his gestures seemed false and vaguely theatrical. The stupid valet made him wait outside the sitting room door while a whispered conversation took place inside. The Captain had to fight against the desire to eavesdrop through the door crack. He drew himself up to his full height. Elegant ... and confident! The door finally opened and the valet motioned him through the door and closed it behind.

The only light in the small room was from two candles on a desk facing the wall. The Man was signing documents with only the top of his silver head showing. The head moved upward silently and the black eyes glinted in the candlelight. The Man motioned with his quill in the direction of the waiting chair. Then, without a word, the quill motioned to the glass sitting on the edge of the desk. The Captain caught a whiff of brandy and noted that the Man also had a filled glass before him. Then the top of the head showed again as he continued signing the documents.

The Captain found himself sitting upright and stiff in the chair looking at the glass. He took a slight breath to relax and put him into control again. Then he leaned over and lifted the glass and breathed in the aroma. It was the very best of brandies! He felt that he was now looking better but knew it was nothing but a pose.

He thought back to his days of elegance at Versailles – it seemed so long ago – when he had first learned of the reputation of "This Man". Everybody whispered stories – but no one was really sure! And, now, this interview! Was this recognition ... or was this a quick trip to Hell? Just, wait and see *Capitaine*! The scratch of the pen was the only real sound in his world, right now!

Suddenly the head lifted and again the bleak glint from "The Man's" black eyes. The documents were pushed neatly to the side of the table and the quill laid on an ornate stand. The Man sat back in his chair and drew his cloak around him in an effort to keep warm – despite the stuffiness of the small room. He nodded in Benoit's direction and grunted.

"Thank you for coming, *Capitaine*!" The Captain leaned a little forward to respond but noticed immediately that The Man was wagging a finger in front of his mouth and shaking his head slightly. He got the message – he was here to listen and not to talk. He sat back and nodded.

"I have ... followed your career with interest, *mon Capitaine*! Yes, with interest! You are an ambitious ... rascal? But, you seem to know ... your limits ... reasonably well. Just ... how far to go!"

The Captain stirred slightly but the restrictive finger wagged again for silence. "Despite your ... flamboyant manner ... and your dalliance with many married women;" the Captain shifted uncomfortably on his chair, "including some of their very young maids;" the Captain's eyes widened without his recognition, "you have managed your campaign in the Luberon ... very well! Just the right touch of brutality ... with enough viciousness ... to get the attention ... and fear ...of those damned Huguenots!" The Man leaned back and nodded his head slightly. He picked up his glass of liquor and breathed in the fumes as he gazed up into the dark corners of the room. Then he placed the filled glass carefully on the edge of the table and leaned forward to emphasize his husky words.

"You must understand, *Capitaine* Benoit, that, ... while his Majesty is the ruler of France, he has been ... persuaded that he will gain ... recognition from above," and he waved his finger lazily skyward, "if he is able to stamp out this ... opposition to Catholicism. And, we ... must remain as the power behind the throne ... in this glorious crusade!"

He pointed now directly at the Captain's chest. "And, you are ... one ... of our tools; our weapons; and ... we ... are pleased with the way things are going!"

Although the fear was definitely still in his belly, the Captain smiled slightly at the compliment and nodded his head.

"I have not called you ... to report, *mon Capitaine*. There is no need for that! We are always fully aware of what is going on in the Luberon. We have ... our sources! We have arranged this little ... consultation ... so that you can listen!" As the Captain nodded again, the smile vanished from his lips.

"The New Believers had ... much strength in the whole of the Luberon! But you, and your Dragoons, have pressured them enough to abjure. That little old lady you burned to death ... a nice touch! Yes! Just the right shock to get their attention!" A hoarse chuckle trickled across the table. "But, you have some unfinished business! *Non*?"

The Captain had trouble meeting the firm glare in those dark black eyes. But he nodded slightly.

"Yes!" His finger waved as it pointed. "The wound on your face ... is seen as a scar on the face of his Majesty! And that young shepherd is still running free, isn't he?" The Captain nodded and grimaced. "And that ... impertinent young bride – the Mallan woman – she mocked you in front of her whole village!"

Shocked, the Captain felt himself cringe inwardly and smiled slightly to show he had a sense of humor.

"Yes, you did right to retreat ... in dignity! He who withdraws in dignity, avenges himself later, *non*?" The Captain nodded. "*Bien*! We see eye to eye! "And those bandits – led by ... a number of ... Foxes? We still need to make an example of them – and we shall!"

He picked up his brandy glass again and sniffed its contents while the Captain took time to drain the glass empty and looked down at it. A small bell tinkled and the valet entered immediately and refilled the Captain's glass. He left quietly.

"You," The Man leaned forward and growled in his soft voice, "must punish the woman – any way you like! The more disgusting, the better! And, the story of the disgrace must filter back to St. Martin! To make them realize ... they cannot win! And, it is vitally important that the man who scarred your face must be killed – and that story should return to his village to increase their level of fear ... and smash their sense of hope!" The Captain nodded in agreement. Right - smash their hopes!

"We will put more Dragoons into the search – and destroying – of that bandit, Renard. We will arrange that! But, you must keep your eyes open ... for clues." The Man pulled his cloak tightly around his body and shivered a little. He sat quietly pondering his thoughts. Then he leaned forward again.

"You have done ... a good job! But you must finish what you start. And, don't come back to Versailles until you do!"

Ooh! That doesn't feel good, thought the Captain.

"I will send you sufficient funds! Very generous funds! I suspect that both the bride and her family are actually going to escape across the border – and that shepherd as well. And, despite your best efforts, they may succeed! And, if they do, you must *go after them*. Not as a *Capitaine* of the Dragoons! But, as a ...spy?"

The Captain had been sipping the new brandy ... and almost choked. Out of France ... and as a spy? Although he had hoped to clean up the outstanding punishments before long, he had been quite willing to say "good riddance" if they escaped. But, now?

"But, how far?" The Captain finally spoke in a whisper as he nodded in reluctant agreement. The answer shocked him rigid!

"To the ends of the earth, *Capitaine*. Wherever it may lead. For I am sure, that your wound will not heal – will continue to fester and ache – until you have avenged the honour of the King! And, we will see you will have enough money to take your men with you!"

The Captain felt a chill run down his spine and found he was sweating heavily. The Man smiled a little crookedly.

"When the job is done, you can return to Versailles! Honour will be yours! I promise that! A lot of wealth – and perhaps - a title! *Non*?"

The warmth of the brandy finally reached his belly and warmed his soul a little. Now - that sounds good! Not only honour from the King; and money; perhaps even an estate – but a Title? For that, any Captain of the Dragoons would go - to the end of the world!

It was later, riding back in his escorted carriage, that the Captain realized that The Man had never taken a sip from the brandy glass. All business!

*   *   *   *   *

CHAPTER TWENTY

Pierre paused in the shadow cast by a huge church tower and watched as the local folk of Viviers vied with each other to sell their fresh bread, fruit and meat. They called to each other in cheerful voices as they haggled for prices. He grinned as a ribald old woman thrust a sliced pear into his hand. He bit into the fruit and fresh sweet juice ran down his chin.

"Well, young fellow – you will not get a better pear anywhere up – or down – the Rhone! And much better than those fly-bitten pears being sold by ... him!" and she gestured wildly in the direction of the stall across the cobbled roadway. Another old gray-bearded man, at the next stall, rolled his eyes in despair and held out a cut pear in an offer to taste.

"Don't believe that old woman! She steals my pears at night and passes them off as her own crop!"

Pierre grinned.

"I'll take some from each of you – you are both bandits of the first water!"

After paying for his purchases, he was slipping them into his bag when his arm was gripped frantically from behind and he swung around to find a desperate Theodore – his eyes wide with fear.

"Pierre," he whispered hoarsely, "they are here! In Viviers!"

"Who?"

"Those two men ... the ones who grabbed me on the highway!"

Pierre frowned and shook Theodore quietly.

"Don't panic, my little friend! Are you sure?"

"Yes, Pierre, I would never forget their faces! At least, there is one of them watering his horse at the fountain! He looked at me! And ... smiled in a horrible way! Please, Pierre! Andre was tying the mules up below the bridge after they were watered. So, I came to find you! Come quickly!" He turned to scamper back around the tower wall, turning to urge Pierre to follow. Placing the bag of food gently on his shoulder, Pierre followed around the wall and into the sunlit square.

Theodore crouched behind the edge of the fountain and pointed desperately towards the shaded area across the square where men were gathering outside the local Inn. Pierre quickly recognized the burly shape of one of the two men who had given them trouble on the road outside Pertuis. He grimaced and gestured to Theodore to quietly join his brother below the bridge while, pulling his hat down over his brow, he crossed the square. Pierre passed the table where the man was slurping wine. He did not appear to be taking much interest in the passing travelers.

Then Pierre slid down the bank to where Andre was listening to his anxious little brother. He raised his eyes to Pierre as he approached.

"It seems to be the same fellow, Andre – but he is more interested right now in enjoying his wine! I don't think it's a problem! But, maybe we should have our meal and keep moving!"

"But, Pierre, he looked at me! He remembered me!" Theodore was still agitated. "I didn't like that look at all!"

"It was good that you recognized the type, Theodore! But, I don't think we should be too disturbed! Come, let's have our lunch – and be on our way!" Mollified somewhat, Theodore settled down and they enjoyed their fresh fruit and bread together.

* * * * *

28th July 1687
Up the left bank of the Rhone

Traveling the left bank of the Rhone has been wonderful, thought Pierre. There is less traffic. We all seem less worried - less anxious. And, the fruit and vegetables had all been fresh. They had even stolen a few apples and pears from trees overhanging the stone walls as they rode by. The traffic was non-threatening – usually farmers cantering down the shaded road or wagons loaded for markets. Andre remarked that he had not seen a single Dragoon since they had crossed the river.

"It was a good idea, Pierre!" Andre reluctantly acknowledged. They were gathered under the shade of a huge oak that hung over the roadway beside the massive stone wall surrounding an ancient Bishop's palace. They had scaled the wall last night and slept peacefully in an abandoned tool shed. Now, in the early sunshine, they had finished their morning breakfast and were readying their mules for the day's journey.

"Pierre, Theodore wants to ask a favor." He turned to find the two brothers standing side by side and he raised his eyebrows quizzically as he looked down at the young lad.

"Pierre, I have ridden with you – and helped you – all the way along the roadways of the Durance – both there and back to our village – haven't I?" Pierre nodded seriously and waited.

"I think I know the plan – the strategy?" Pierre nodded. "Well ... Andre and you ... always take the most important jobs. Either watching out ahead or watching for trouble behind. And, whistling when there is trouble!" Pierre nodded and waited patiently with some idea of what the request would be.

"Well, I think I am ready to do something more important! More important than just riding along!" Andre breathed out heavily as though under stress. Pierre looked silently at him and pondered the decision.

"Andre feels that I am ready!" Theodore turned towards his brother for agreement and Andre nodded seriously. The boy looked back quickly at Pierre.

Pierre twisted his mouth in a thoughtful grimace and then

nodded in agreement.

"Yes!" Theodore pounded his little fist into the palm of his other hand and yelled in excitement.

"But, Theodore, I don't have to tell you to take no chances! We have a quieter route this side of the Rhone – but the Dragoons can be ... anywhere. Especially when there are so many of us Reformed church folk trying to reach safety."

The boy nodded - his face serious.

"I will ride in the middle and work with Theodore, Pierre." Andre reassured. Pierre nodded agreement and Theodore in his eagerness was saddled first.

As the farm carts passed on their way to the markets, the three friends waited for the right opening and Theodore grinned back at his two companions as he rode his mule into the dust first.

"He's growing up well, isn't he?" Pierre smiled wryly at his friend, who nodded and with a grin, rode his mule behind several loaded carts and crossed to the other side of the dusty road north where he could clearly see his little brother riding ahead.

*   *   *   *   *

17th July 1687
On the road to Lyon - Donzère

It was late afternoon when the damaged rear wheel of the carriage had been repaired well enough for the vehicle to limp into the next village of Donzère a short distance up the road beside the mighty Rhone River. All of them, Le Duc, Uncle Antoine and the driver were grubby and sweat stained.

Uncle Antoine wiped a dirty hand across his forehead leaving a trail of smeared dust behind and grinned at the two women sitting on a fallen tree with their backs to the river.

"I think we can make it as far as Donzère by nightfall. And I am surviving on a vision of a decent wash followed by a hot meal and a big glass of the local wine! Eh, Le Duc?"

Le Duc grunted. "You can skip the wash and the food. Wine would be my first choice!"

The two women rose and joined the men at the carriage door.

"Uncle, did you think it wise to have requested help from that passing Dragoon?" Isabeau's voice was quizzical.

"Well," Uncle smiled, "since they are keeping tags on us anyway, they might as well know where we are! Let's get aboard. I am going down to the riverbank to wash the worst from my hands and face. Come Le Duc!" And they vanished down the trail to the riverbank as the two women climbed into the carriage and opened the leather blinds to let the fresh afternoon air blow through.

*   *   *   *   *

220

17th July 1687
On the road to Lyon.

Close to the village Inn at Donzère, a small squad of Dragoons led by a burly Sergeant pulled their horses to a halt in the shade of the huge oak tree. One of the Dragoons took the reins of the horses and led them to the hitching rail away from the road while the Sergeant led his Dragoons to sit at a rough table under the tree.

The Sergeant glanced around at a number of the locals who were sitting enjoying the sun, drinking and smoking. One of his men asked about ordering wine and the Sergeant grunted.

"Not now – maybe later!" He pointed at a tall young Dragoon with a youthful face. "You know what to do?"

The soldier grinned and nodded. "I go in and wait for the young women to come downstairs - after cleaning up!" The Sergeant nodded and cautioned: "You must make sure she is alone – separated from the others in the party!" The young soldier nodded and continued.

"Then I tell her that a friend of hers ... a Pierre Jaubert ... has a message for her – alone! And ... that he is in the stable behind the inn?"

"Good! Keep it simple! And go directly around to the stable at the back!" The young soldier nodded again. "Good! Off you go! The rest of you come with me!" All the party rose and walked behind the Inn while the youthful Dragoon apprehensively entered the front door of the building.

Back at the outside tables, a man, who had been sitting apparently dozing before a bottle of wine at the table, pushed his hat back and peered under the brim towards the doorway of the Inn.

"Hmm! Now that is a curious situation, isn't it?" And, standing up, Renard finished off his wine and vanished around the other side of the Inn.

* * * * *

27th July 1687
Up the Rhone River - at Cruas

"You have done a really good job, Theodore!" Pierre's words of praise made the young boy turn a little red and he jerked around to grin up at his proud brother.

They had covered a lot more territory than usual - possibly due to the boy's infectious enthusiasm - thought Pierre.

They had passed through the ancient village of Le Teil where an old man had been pleased to explain the origins of the *chaine des coirons* – a long and rugged ridge with its castle-like pinnacles. "A wise old man told me it is caused by rivers of molten mud from a volcano," he had explained. And then Theodore wanted to know all about this new subject.

Now they were resting at mid-day for a meal. Above them, the ancient ruins of a massive old castle, shadowed the village of Meysse. And an immediate decision needed to be made about their route.

"Pierre, the road towards Privas – away from the river – is in much better condition – according to the local baker," recommended Andre. Pierre nodded frowning.

"I heard that too, Andre, but I think I would be more comfortable staying with the Rhone – and less traffic!" He nodded in the direction of Theodore who was rubbing down the sweaty mules. "It would be safer for him too!" Andre glanced at his young brother and nodded. "Yes, maybe you are right! Good enough!"

"Theodore!" called Pierre, "let us get moving! We are taking the road along the river to Cruas – where we shall spend the night!" Theodore waved back.

*   *   *   *   *

Looking over his shoulder, Pierre was shocked to see the glint of sunshine on armor as a cloud of dust came up the road well behind him. He whistled shrilly and as he drove his mule into the rough shrubs and trees alongside the road, he was relieved to see a wave of acknowledgment from Andre on the next crest.

Pierre hurriedly dismounted and crouched to rub the nose of his mule to ensure that it did not snort or bray.

A large squadron of Dragoons thundered by. Their handkerchiefs shielded their noses from the heavy dust and they had wrapped their cloaks around them to cover most of their uniforms as well. Only their officer seemed to be looking around him as he led them up the road.

All the men were leaning forward seemingly oblivious to any of the surroundings.

Phew, thought Pierre. Just as well we are watching our rearguard! Carefully checking the roadway to the south, he re-mounted his mule and drove it carefully out of the shrubs and foliage and was relieved to see Andre taking the same action on the next crest and waving to him. He cantered the mule to the next rise to join his friend. As the dust settled on the road ahead, both men grinned at each other as young Theodore also emerged from the brush alongside the road and waved to them.

"We will have to keep our eyes skinned as we travel to Cruas!" warned Andre as they rode down towards the boy. But they did not realize how careful they really had to be that day.

*   *   *   *   *

17th July 1687
On the road to Lyon - Donzère

Isabeau tugged the top of her chemise down a little lower than her husband would have liked. She grinned to herself as she remembered that he spent lots of time looking at the uncovered tops of breasts of other young women but demanded that his own wife keep her chemise line high – for safety sake, he said! It was good to get changed after a long hot dusty drive to Donzère and wash some of the dust from

222

your face and hands, she thought with pleasure. Her husband had kept to his pledge to make his first action on arrival to having a glass of wine downstairs and Uncle Antoine had reluctantly agreed to join him.

"I might as well go down and have a glass of local wine with them." She called through the closed door of her Aunt and Uncle's room and received an acknowledgment from her Aunt who liked to primp a lot before dinner.

Isabeau ran quickly down the steep stairs feeling light at heart. It felt wonderful when you know where you are going and why. At the bottom of the stairs she stopped and looked around. From the hum of conversation she recognized where the parlor was. Turning suddenly, she was confronted by a youthful Dragoon with a confused look on his face.

"*Mademoiselle?*"

"*Madame.*" She corrected him with a smile.

"I am seeking a *Madame Mallan* ... *Madame.* Can you help me?" He seemed flushed and stumbling in his request.

"*Madame Mallan* is ... still upstairs dressing."

"*Madame* ... Isabeau ... from St. Martin?" Isabeau looked surprised.

"Oh, that's me! Why did you want me?"

"Oh I am so glad!" He grinned a little and seemed relieved. "This is confusing." He pointed outside behind himself. "A traveling man ... promised me a glass of wine ... if I would give you a message! He said his name was ... I think ... Pierre Jaubert? But ... for some reason, he did not want to be seen in the Inn. He asked that you meet him at the stable behind the Inn – but to come alone – and quickly!"

"Pierre ... here? Are you sure he said that?" The Dragoon nodded and eagerly turned to leave. "But, was he tall with a reddish tinge to his hair – or stocky?"

"I do not remember, *Madame.* He was wearing a hat and riding a mule – so I don't know." He raised his hands and shrugged his head. Then turning, he pointed out the doorway in the direction of the stable and vanished out the door.

Isabeau stood confused. Which Pierre was outside? I suppose it does not matter anyway – I'll go and meet him. Looking over her shoulder at the busy Inn door, she hesitated. Come alone, he had said. Well a few minutes won't make a difference. She looked down at the gentle cleavage exposed; tugged it slightly and smiled. First impressions were important – even when you are married. She swirled and hurried out of the main door of the Inn and turned sharply to the right to follow the dirty tracks of carriages on the cobblestones towards the stables.

Isabeau's sudden surprise at finding the whole stable area deserted should have warned her. With the heavy road traffic, many stable hands should have been busy with their livery work. She frowned slightly, then shrugged and took a few cautious steps into the huge open stable doors. Inside, she ignored a flash of fear and peered into the dark shadowy interior.

"Pierre?" she called out tentatively. "Are you there?" The answering grunt allowed her to breathe a sigh of some relief. A dark figure appeared from behind one of the stall posts - hands gesturing her to enter.

"So, which one of the Pierre's are you?" She spoke in a teasing voice. She picked her way carefully through the straw covered cobbles toward the figure. She tentatively extended both hands in welcome. But a touch of apprehension grew quickly into a sense of panic. She hesitated. Why did Pierre not speak?

Suddenly, both the doors closed behind her with a thump. She gasped in surprise as she turned to discover two burly Dragoons fastening the inside drop-bar securely. In panic, she spun round again to see the figure emerge from the darkness and step into a patch of sunlight from a hole in the roof.

"*Le Capitaine*!" she gasped. She opened her mouth to scream but - from behind - a heavy gnarled hand clamped over her mouth. Another roughly circled her waist holding her tight. She kicked backward with her heel but with little effect. Fear rose as a further couple of Dragoons appeared behind their Captain. The patch of sunlight lit their yellowed teeth and wolfish grins.

The shaft of sunlight also lit up the red seeping scar as the Captain's face twisted into a leer.

"So ... you mocked me - in front of the whole village - you little bitch!" he sneered in a low voice. "I promised you I would get even! And, I shall! Your time has come, my dear little Isabeau!" Suspended tightly by the waist, she again lifted both feet from the dusty stable floor. She frantically kicked backward. At the same time she stretched both her free hands backward in an attempt to rake the face of the Dragoon behind. As her nails made contact, she heard him grunt with pain. But the arms about her tightened even more - until she had trouble breathing.

"Stop fighting, my dear! It will not save you from your promised reward!" His voice was filled with taut excitement. "If you are as clever as they say you are, you should be saving your strength instead! *N'est-ce pas?*"

Despite her panic, the reality of the situation struck her. To struggle would simply bring further grasping – and perhaps worse!

Dignity, where are you? She forced a deep breath into her body and relaxed her feet onto the straw and attempted to straighten her stance. Desperately she clung to her last iota of dignity!

"Gag the bitch's mouth!" The Captain drew his large handkerchief from his pocket and thrust it at the Dragoon standing next to him. In a couple of steps, the trooper had tied a knot in the middle. The soldier released his face hold long enough to force the knot into her mouth as she gasped for air. Then he tied it tight behind her head.

"Down!" the Captain whispered hoarsely. Isabeau felt herself lifted in the air; her feet grasped by two separate soldiers. She felt pain as her back hit the cobbles of the dusty straw floor. She lay stunned. Dust floated down to land on her pale perspiring cheeks. Sucking in a deep breath, she jerked her head up and stared at the Captain's face.

His mouth was opened wide in an enormous leer. In the shaft of sunlight his eyes flashed in sensual pleasure. "Spread her legs - and hold them!" The Dragoons grunted in obvious pleasure as they pinned her ankles wide apart.

He then gestured towards her exposed neckline. "Cut the ribbons!" Isabeau's eyes grew large and desperate. She jerked a frantic look down at her waist. The spot of sunlight flashed on the sharp knife slashing at her waist. She flinched instinctively. The ribbons popped, the jacket parted, exposing the top of her embroidered white chemise.

At a nod from the officer, a hand grasped the top of the fragile garment and ripped it downward to the waist. An audible gasp of pleasure echoed around the stable. The soldiers leaned forward eagerly. Her arms were stretched upward behind her head forcing the young perfectly shaped breasts to burst upward and gently sway back and forward as she frantically wriggled. She whimpered as a Dragoon's hand leaned over her shoulder and tweaked the erect nipple.

"Leave her!" the Captain grunted. "She is now mine – all mine – to do what I wish!" The Captain leaned forward gloating. "The little bitch is ... better than I had visualized! Hmm!" he grunted as he stood, legs apart relishing the view.

Then he gestured at her waist. "And let's have a good look at what she shows her husband - and her lovers!" He said hoarsely, gesturing with his one hand, "Lift the skirts! Let's see the rest of her!" A single Dragoon knelt and grasped the bottom of her skirt and petticoat. In a taunting fashion, he pulled them slowly upward as she struggled and grunted painfully. Gasps of glee from the soldiers echoed around the rafters as the garments moved up her slim shapely stocking-clad legs. The Dragoons grunted in unison when the ribbons appeared tied above her knees. A slight moan erupted as struggling thighs stretched above the stockings. Then, a groan of disappointment when they saw the rest of her slim torso covered by linen pantalets. Finally, with a flourish, the Dragoon folded the skirt and petticoats across her waist.

The Captain was having trouble breathing. "Expose her! Cut the ribbons at the waist!" The Dragoon leaned forward and fumbled at the waist searching for the elusive ribbons. Finally, in desperation, he simply grasped the bottoms of the pantalets and jerked them roughly until they tore aside, revealing the vee of dark brown pubic hair. Isabeau desperately forced her legs as close together as she could - with little success. Suddenly, despite her desperate fears, she forced her body to relax and lie still! Struggling was not going to save her. In fact, it seemed to be feeding the men's pleasure.

The Captain stood still and stared. His eyes finally lifted to meet hers and he grinned at her helplessness. Then his mouth twisted as he ran his gaze slowly down from her exposed breasts to her stocking-shod feet - ironically, the shoes still on. She sensed a change in his demeanor. He glared down at her, his face suddenly fierce and bitter.

"You spurned my advances, you little bitch! And then you mocked me in front of the whole village!" He paused. "I must admit – I lusted for the ... young bride ... in you! But, now I have you ... here – naked before me! You – and I - both know that I can ... do anything - to you!" He glanced around at the Dragoons. They were obviously feasting their eyes. All mouths were gaping open. Their labored breathing was highly audible in the silent stable.

And, what do I now see? Without your clothes – you are like all the rest of the women I have taken! Now it's my turn ... to spurn you, you little bitch! Instead of you enjoying the sexual pleasures I would have offered – that of an aristocratic gentleman – I'll give you - instead - into the crude hands of a bunch of ignorant Dragoons! Let them enjoy the body of a young *Provençal* bride!" He turned and nodded to the shocked array of surprised eager faces.

"Take your time, men! My gift to you! But ensure that she is able to walk away - back to her husband! I want her to spend the rest of her life remembering - our secret - that she has been used by a troop of Dragoons – men she would ... normally ... look down upon - in disgust!" He clapped his hands – almost in joy – and walked out of her vision without a backward glance.

She heard the doors open and close behind him. In desperate fear, she circled her head looking up into the eager eyes of the four Dragoons holding her. One with her arms twisted above her head; two holding her legs wide apart; and the fourth busy frantically struggling to undo the front of his drawers.

She was aghast!   In shock, tears began to stream down her cheeks leaving trails through the dust.

Her eyes widened in horror as they suddenly locked on the uncovering of his ... thing!

A sudden breath jerked into her mouth almost choking her. The only thing she had seen before was her husband's!

But ... this thing looked so ... huge!

What will it do to me?

Oh *Mon Dieu*, help me! Help me! Help me - now!

*   *   *   *   *

28th July 1687
Up the banks of the Rhone

With their mules loaded the next morning, Theo led the party's animals to the front of the shop where Andre personally thanked the owner for his kind hospitality. He smiled back at them with obvious pleasure.

"We all need to help each other ... these dangerous days, don't we?" They all nodded and mounted their mules.

Waving their hats, they rode to the outskirts of the town where they set up their protective strategy as usual. Theodore eagerly requested to lead the group again. Pierre hesitated – the thought of the Dragoon patrol fresh in his mind.

"Let him do it, Pierre! I will ride in the middle again and keep an eye on him!" Pierre shook his head in worry; then reluctantly nodded.

"But – be careful, Theodore!" The boy eagerly nodded his head.

"I'll be careful. I really will..." and looking up and down the road, ducked his mule through the dust of the incoming farm carts and set up northward towards Baix.

*   *   *   *   *

There it is again! Captain Benoit flinched as a sharp twinge of pain lanced through his face. He raised his hand sharply to touch the wound on his cheek carefully. Then he rubbed it gently until the ache slowly vanished. He stood and watched the brothers leave.

With the meeting over, the two men had run out to their tethered horses. In glee, they slapped each other on their backs and yelled in excitement.

Just like two overgrown children, the Captain mused. Definitely not my choice of companions – but in my business, you have to use whatever weapons are available – at any price!

They spun their horses in a dusty twirl and both doffed their plumed hats at him before turning to race off down the hot road south.

The Captain stood quietly watching their vanishing figures. He nodded his head several times as he reviewed the pact he had negotiated. It had not been a difficult negotiation. After all, they were the overfed and spoilt sons of an overpaid local government official. They did not have to work for a living! And, they had grown into dissolute raucous young men who spent most of their lives in drinking and partying.

He had quickly recognized that money was no reward to these fools. But tender young boys were! All he had to do was provide them with a chance at revenge against his own enemies! The man he detested most in the world – that shepherding peasant from la Motte, Jaubert. His cheek suddenly ached again as it reminded him of the man who had left him with his festering wound. And his best friend, Roux from St. Martin – two peas in a rotten pod!

He had given the brothers enough money to ensure that lack of funds would not prevent them from carrying out his task. He had written an authorization to use the services of any Dragoon they needed on the highway. And, all he had promised them was ... the young lad, Roux. He shrugged. What fools they were – but they would get the job done! And feed their dissolute appetites at the same time! He knew they were now heading to the last known contact with the trio of renegades. All he had to do was wait.

The Captain frowned. I should feel elated? I have taken steps to deal with *both* my immediate problems! The brothers will find Jaubert and his friends ... and I have dealt with the Mallan "bitch" – just recently! It was wonderful abusing her, tearing the clothes from her body – and I spurned her as well! A smile creased his face as he remembered the shocked mortified look on her face, as she lay half-naked on the straw of the stable. As the image returned a surge of power and lust uncontrollably swept through him.

Perhaps ... perhaps, I should have played a little? No, he shook his head again. Take my clothes off in front of a bunch of slobbering soldiers? No! Privacy is what I like! There will be another time! But, why am I not feeling ... in control of my destiny. The Man would be immensely pleased with my actions! He grunted again in disgust. But I am not pleased? Why?

Hmm! It's that bitch on the stable floor. Its unfinished business! Because I don't know what happened. Who went first – was it Gustav from Lyon - or that mustached oaf from Marseilles. Did she cry or lie there? Does the husband know? Hmm! I guess I should satisfy my curiosity; I don't really like unfinished things!

Turning, he strode towards his carriage as he called to his Dragoon escort lounging in the shade of the oak and gestured them to mount up.

*   *   *   *   *

28th July 1687
On the left bank of the Rhone - Cruas

The pleasure of these last happy days was still with him as Pierre took an interest in the surrounding countryside. Groves of olive and nut trees surrounded many of the stone farm buildings. Apple trees were ripe with early crops. Finally, what must have been the last of the farm carts, passed them and the road ahead was empty. The fields slowly vanished and were replaced by heavy groves of trees.

Ahead, a young man rode onto the dusty highway from a path going down to the right off the road and turned in his direction. He saluted with his hand and smiled as he rode by. Going into Cruas from the farm? Then another older farmer followed him out of the woods and galloped past doffing his hat as he passed. Pierre returned the salute and looking over his shoulder, saw them stop, shake hands and talk. Neighbors?

Then suddenly, he heard a yell and looking ahead saw Andre waving his hat before spurring over the crest. He urged his mule into a reluctant gallop and, breasting the crest, could not see Theodore anywhere. But Andre was turning his mule off the road ahead and then, drawing his short sword, he saw him gallop directly into the heavily wooded area to the left of the roadway. Pierre pulled his own sword loose - but left it sheathed and kept his mule galloping down the dusty road. What on earth was happening?

He jerked his horse into a sharp turn and faced the opening in the foliage. In an open glade, he recognized one of the two heavy brothers that Theodore had recognized in the village of Viviers – and he was alongside a struggling Theodore holding his reins and one arm. The other brother stood in his stirrups and menacingly waved a sword in the air. Andre rode straight at him. What should I do? Better wait until I see where I am best needed. Or should I race in and rescue Theodore?

As Andre closed in on the armed man, everything became very clear. From all around the glade, armed Dragoons appeared. It's a trap, silently yelled Pierre. Then he saw several Dragoons raise muskets. Shots rang out. He saw Andre stand in his stirrups and slowly sink backward to fall off his mule. As his body turned there was a bright red stain on his right shoulder.

Go Pierre! Go for your life!

He spun his mule and kneed it into a massive gallop down the road south. As he crested the hillside, he glanced back. So far, no Dragoons could be seen. Good!

Looking down the road ahead, he spotted the farmers he had seen moments ago, staring backward at the sound of the gunshot. As though realizing there was danger in the air, they began to canter quickly away.

Sudden inspiration struck Pierre. Jerking his mule hard to the right, he headed down a slightly worn trail into the woods on the same side of the road that the trap had been laid. Once concealed by the trees, he pulled his animal to halt; drew his sword and dismounted. He tethered the mule to a branch of a bush and crept forward to hide behind a tree where he was close enough to the pathway to observe the road.

Listening carefully, he heard several horses thunder by going south – following in the dust of the farmers! Then he was dismayed to hear another horse stop and circle on the roadway.

He crouched behind the tree trunk holding his breath. He heard the hooves coming slowly down the path towards him. Just one horse! It came closer and closer. As it drew alongside, Pierre quickly circled the tree and peered around the trunk to see the back of a thin young Dragoon. The soldier was standing up in his stirrups and leaning forward to peer down the path ahead listening carefully. Pierre glanced backward quickly. All clear! Then with a sharp jump he landed behind the stirrup and as the Dragoon desperately tried to turn his horse, he thrust the sword aiming for the vulnerable waist area between the breastplate and the belt. He heard a gasp of pain as the sword was thrust home. Then the horse reared and the body of the Dragoon came thudding to the ground jerking the sword free. As the Dragoon rolled over, Pierre gashed down at the exposed throat. Then – it was over!

Pierre, on his knees, took a deep breath to prevent the vomit from rising up his throat and flooding into his mouth. Feeling sick, he stared at the dying face of the solider.

I'm becoming a killing animal, he thought in desperation. Finally, he reached out and grasped the reins of the frightened horse and steadied him. Slowly he rose and tied the horse to the branch of a tree. Bending, he grasped the Dragoon's boots and tugged the body well into the surrounding brush. Then he fetched the horse and led it also into the bush.

Anxiety flooded his body and he felt his face going numb. What do I do now – how do I stay at least one step in front of the Dragoons. He listened frantically. There was no more clatter from the road. He carefully picked his way backwards through the bush in the rough direction of the spot where the Dragoons' trap was laid. I will be coming up behind their lines, so they should not expect me.

Soon, he could hear raised voices in argument. Bending and stepping carefully, he finally reached a point where he could listen to the talk and see the figures. Slowly sinking to his knees, he crawled forward. Parting some ferns slowly, he could see clearly.

Most of the Dragoons were still mounted in a circle listening to the heated discussion. Pierre was relieved to see Andre lying with his back against a tree trunk. There was a huge patch of blood on his right shoulder but he was obviously conscious. He was holding a padded cloth to the wound.

Thank God he is not dead! At his side was the trussed figure of Theodore – his face tearful but angry. The argument was between the two burly brothers and the officer.

"I don't really care what special arrangement you have with your Captain Benoit! I don't care a damn!" The senior brother tried to speak again but the officer brushed it aside.

"Shut up! These are my prisoners! And I will take them with me into Valance! When your Captain Benoit appears, I will listen to what he says! Until then, you can come along to safeguard your alleged reward! But you won't touch him until I say you can!"

He turned abruptly and stalked away to his horse. As he mounted, he called directions to his Dragoons to tie the captives to their mules and keep them under tight guard. "From everyone! Especially those child-lovers! I have no time for people like them!"

Disgusted, the two civilians mounted their horses and followed the party of Dragoons from the glade onto the road north to Valence. Peering over his shoulder, Pierre listened carefully.

Nothing! Pierre crawled back slowly until he felt safe to rise. Then with great care and silence, he worked his way back to the animals. He removed the Dragoon's valuables – every bit helps! He was pleased to discover that the soldier also had a small hand musket. He carefully wrapped the weapon and ammunition in a piece of cloth and concealed it in his pack. I'll take the horse and use my mule for a pack animal, he thought.

He surveyed the pathway. Then decided that going further down on the path might be the safest route.

The horse was temporarily unsettled with a strange rider but was soon under control. Then he stopped.

I don't have any plan! I can follow them or make my own way to Valence. But then, what do I do?

He ran through several possible alternatives and shook his head. I will have to play it by ear, he thought in disgust. Then he looked back over his shoulder to where the body was concealed.

Why not? At least I will have a plan! Nodding his head, he returned to the spot and soon emerged from the concealed area with another rolled bundle under his arm.

A short while later, he reloaded the mule and tethered it to the saddle of the horse. He set off down the path away from the ambush site. After a short trip he came across another path heading north and carefully cantered down it until he came to a small farm.

Circling the farmhouse and small field, he entered a rough orchard of olive trees and worked his way back to the road between Le Pouzin and Valence.

This road would also take him in the direction of Valence and would allow him to enter the city on a different route than that being used by the squadron of Dragoons. By traveling fast, he would probably arrive before the troops and search for a way of rescuing the two brothers.

Why is it ... that just when you feel you have things under control, disaster happens? He sat watching the traffic from a small grove of trees until he found the right opportunity.

A large group of well-dressed travelers galloped by on their horses. Pierre pulled into the dust behind them - looking like a valet with a mule-load of baggage.

*　　　*　　　*　　　*　　　*

17th July 1687
On the road to Lyon - Donzère

Isabeau squirmed hopelessly on the stable floor. Her mind was still racing with silent prayers to her God to ... do something! She was no longer aware or embarrassed at her nakedness. Her eyes were now locked on the new site of her inner terror – that thing! It was even bigger than before – it was standing out stiffly now – instead of hanging there!

Oh *Mon Dieu*! What will it do to me ... inside? There's not enough room, surely?

As if it were background noise, Isabeau was only dimly aware of the fact that the four Dragoons had begun - above her dusty body - to argue about "who would go first".

Vaguely, she saw a little flash of light behind the standing Dragoon - as he argued for the "first turn". Then - a thud! The Dragoon, looming above her feet, collapsed sideways to the floor - knocking another Dragoon over. Her left leg was free! She frantically gathered her tattered spirits - galvanized her muscles - and with a jerk, she twisted and kicked the face of the startled Dragoon holding the other leg. He yelped and rolled onto his back.

Both legs were free! Arching her back and twisting her lower body sideways, she threw the Dragoon behind her off-balance. Her inner rage burst outward. Gathering her knees beneath her she threw her half-naked body across his now sprawled figure. Grunting with fury, she raked her nails across the side of his face - tearing his cheeks. The man yelped in pain. She briefly turned her face as she heard a further thud.

Renard – of all people! He smashed another fallen Dragoon across the head with a heavy post. Then, with a quick grin in her direction, he swung his weapon striking the last Dragoon who was still struggling to crawl out from under the unconscious body of the soldier who was to have been her would-be rapist.

The Dragoon under her turned his bleeding face towards her in his efforts to roll clear of her body. Grimly clasping her two hands together for greater impact, she smashed her combined fists down striking him below his nose on the top of his upper lip. He grunted in intense pain and then lay there momentarily stunned - blood streaming from his mouth. In this little moment of victory, she raised her hands and ripped the gag from her mouth.

"Over here, Renard!" She rolled aside - leaving the stunned body of the Dragoon.

Isabeau suddenly became aware again of her nakedness. She jerked the remnants of her jacket off her shoulders and slipped her arms through the sleeves covering her breasts. Pierre took two steps past her and, wielding the pole struck the last Dragoon across the head. The soldier slumped down and lay still.

She stood up and shook her skirt down to her ankles again. Stunned, she stood and stared at her rescuer.

Renard bowed deeply grinning in his lazy fashion.

"The fox to the rescue, *Madame ... Mallan?*"

Isabeau stood as a sense of relief coursed through her body. A slight smile dawned painfully on her face where her mouth clearly showed the bruised lines made by the tight gag.

"Thank you, Renard, thank you!" She shook her head slowly. "That was ... a terrible, terrible moment! It seemed like a ... lifetime!" She breathed out sharply as though trying to exhaust the tension from her body. She looked around at the four unconscious Dragoons on the dusty straw floor of the stable. A groan came from the tall one who was lying on his back with his "thing" now wilted to a minute imitation of its previous glory. She made an almost hysterical little laugh as she gestured towards her rapist.

"It doesn't look nearly as threatening - now!" she whispered hoarsely.

Renard chuckled aloud. "I think it would be wise to escape before ... someone comes to ...get their share?" He glanced back over his shoulder. "Let's go out the way I came in, shall we?"

Isabeau nodded and was surprised to find that she needed to remind her legs about how to walk. She stumbled a little as she followed him through the back door of the stable and into the warm late afternoon sunlight.

Renard picked up a horse blanket lying on the rail and draped it over her shoulders to cover her naked back. He pointed to a set of wooden stairs that rose up the back of the Inn to the second floor.

"Up there, Isabeau!" She nodded and hesitated looking up at him in appreciation. He touched her arm and nodded.

"Go on, now! We were both lucky ... we got away too easily!" He turned and walked around the corner calling out to her as she left:

"I will go and have wine with your husband and Uncle. I will say ... you told me your dress was dirty and you were ... going to change?"

She nodded and as she ran up the steps, she called out:

"Thank you, again, Renard. I will not forget!"

*   *   *   *   *

CHAPTER TWENTYONE

28th July 1687
Up the bank of the Rhone River – Valence

As the group of travelers entered Valance, Pierre steered his horse and mule out of their dust and into the darkness of a narrow alley. He cantered into a small sunlit square and was relieved to see a fountain against the wall spewing a stream of fresh water into a large stone bowl. Looking around carefully, he allowed the animals to slake their thirst.

Now I need to find the Dragoon Headquarters, he thought. He turned the animals back toward the city gate. He located a livery stable and arranged to have the animals stabled. Then he stood in the darkness of a nearby ancient chapel and watched the travelers enter the gate.

Soon his quest was satisfied. A dust-covered Dragoon leading a pack-mule emerged and slowed his horse down as he confronted a walking soldier. They talked and gestured several minutes before the Dragoon turned and walked his tired horse in the pointed direction - with Pierre following in the shadows. Soon, the Dragoon stopped at a set of open heavy wooden doors surmounted by a flag-topped stone archway. He nudged his horse forward and was greeted by a sentry holding a musket.

Pierre used their discussion time to place himself against a wall opposite the gate where he sank down to rest in the shade. He pulled his heavy hat over his face but left enough space so that he could watch the doorway undetected. The Dragoon rode towards what was obviously the vicinity of the stables. The sentry's gaze passed over the resting peasant without really noticing him.

Pierre was amazed at the amount of traffic that entered the headquarters: food supplies, hay for the animals, wine carts, military couriers, off-duty soldiers and various craftsmen.

The arrival of another dusty Dragoon leading a pack animal caused a further conversation to take place. Pierre's ears pricked up at the short discussion. The Dragoon indicated that he wanted to eat and sleep the night as he was being transferred down south to Marseilles. The sentry pointed out the location of the stables, the kitchen and the barracks.

"I hear there are several others following me – also for Marseilles!" the Dragoon called as he rode away. Hmm, grunted Pierre, that's useful information!

Then, in a cloud of dust, the large squadron of Dragoons swept in, with a nod from the Captain, past the sentry. A lone Dragoon followed, holding the leather tethers to two mules carrying Theodore and the slumped form of Andre. Theodore had his hands trussed to the saddle.

The two burly brothers followed closely and spun their horses in the dust as they discussed their plans. They called out to the Dragoon that they would be bedding down at a nearby inn and would report to the Headquarters the next morning.

He nodded truculently and slowed his horse to a walk as he led the mules past the sentry and in a different direction than the stables. As the sentry peered at the prisoners, Pierre scuttled away from his present position and settled in a new location that allowed him to watch the prisoners.

The party stopped at a small white building with iron-barred window spaces. A single sentry leaned his musket against the wall as he helped his colleague lift Theodore to the dusty cobbles. He took a ring of keys from his belt and opened the door while the other Dragoon waited patiently outside with the still-mounted Andre.

The clanging inside told Pierre that the sentry had opened two steel cell doors. Soon he emerged and led Theodore into the dark doorway. After a further clang of a door closing, he emerged carrying the thongs used to bind the child.

Then the two soldiers slid the heavy form of Andre off the saddle and carrying him between them, they vanished inside. Finally, they returned and while the sentry stood on guard before an open door, the other Dragoon vanished.

He soon returned carrying two beakers of water that he took inside the cells. On leaving, he closed the door and the sentry locked up; and resumed his post while the Dragoon led the horse and two mules in the direction of the stables.

Pierre grunted again. A rough plan was forming in his mind as he gazed under his hat at the sun-bleached courtyard. It's dangerous – but it might work!

*   *   *   *   *

18th July 16878
On the road to Lyon - Montélimar

Uncle Antoine was disturbed. The beginning of the journey had been eventful – an exciting departure from St. Martin; followed by a daring game of hide-and-seek with the Dragoons. The first stroke of bad luck had been the broken wheel outside Donzère – but that had been fixed with a little sweat and swearing.

He had grown steadily thrilled with the surprising character of his new niece: lovely, charming, a great deal of courage – and style. But suddenly, she had emotionally changed. One minute lively and challenging - the next minute silent and far away. And from their evening with friends at Montélimar, she had continued to grow sharper

234

in tone, less patient and sensitive? He shook his head in consternation and his mouth winced in reluctant disappointment.

Bringing up the subject with his wife had provided little in the way of explanations. She shrugged her shoulders and suggested cautiously that perhaps the girl was having a monthly problem; or perhaps was now expecting...?

Uncle shook his head slowly. As they struggled up a short hill short of Valence – the end of a long day's drive – he thought that he should try and find a quiet moment and confront her himself. He felt a little anxious – perhaps scared – she was now so curt and short with all of them! Still, better to take the bull by the horns - than fear the thrust?

*   *   *   *   *

28th July 1687
On the banks of the Rhone - Valence

Pierre rode up the street towards the military enclave. Although the sun was close to setting making the shadows long and menacing, fear caused sweat to run down his face and dampen his collar still more.

Back at the stable he had opened his sleeping blanket to reveal the full blue uniform of the Dragoon he had killed in the woods. The dried red bloodstains matched the deep red lining of the jacket.

He had scrubbed the bloodstains at the collar and lapels until the cloth was worn but still stained. The jacket was dusty but this, Pierre felt, fitted the hot summer day. In an effort to conceal the damp stain, he had also patted dust heavily into the area.

Now he rode in a tired fashion trailing his pack mule carrying a bag stuffed full with hay from the stable supply. Some distance from the gate, he halted in the shadows and waited for a wagon filled with heavy wine casks to stop at the gate.

Then he urged his horse forward to follow directly behind the wagon. The guard's attention was busy on showing the carter the way to the stores when Pierre, with deep apprehension, followed him through with a tired wave to the soldier.

"On my way to Marseilles. I want to eat and sleep for the night." He said with a tired fixed grin.

The guard nodded, "More of your companions inside already." And he waved in the direction of the stables and then ran forward to wave the wagon in the correct direction. Pierre slumped pulling his hat down over his face in case of someone approaching.

Peals of laughter rang out from the barracks but the stable was deserted and quiet. A quick ride down the stables found Andre's mules. He dismounted and quickly shuffled the two mules in with his mule into the first three stalls by the doorway. He put his stolen horse further down the line. Then he climbed up into the loft above where he could keep an eye on the rear of the prison, the soldiers' barracks and the entry to the stable below; and waited.

Time dragged abominably before the sun finally sank and lanterns were lit outside the doorways to the buildings. Pierre wrinkled his nose as the smell of cooked food drifted up to tease him. He could recognize the sounds of men now drinking in the barracks and yelping as they played games of chance. Now – or never!

Carefully, he slid down from the loft. He checked the mules to ensure they could move quickly. Then, hefting two big bundles of straw onto his shoulder, he strode out to the side of the prison cell. There he dropped them and carefully peered around the edge of the building. The prison sentry was leaning against the wall half asleep. His heavy musket leaned against the wall beside him. A quick glance showed the main gates were closed and a sentry was seated on a stool and resting his back against the warm stone wall with a hat pulled down over his eyes.

Despite his anxiety, Pierre grinned. From his position it was clear that the Main Gate sentry was asleep. Pierre retreated carefully back to the side of the kitchen. Stacked outside was a supply of firewood. He carefully chose a sturdy piece of solid wood and crept back to the side of the prison.

Nothing had changed! Stepping silently, he rounded the corner with the log at his side and in two steps was directly in front of the sentry. The soldier grunted and raised his head exposing his throat. Pierre lunged forward and swung hard. There was a sharp cough as the soldier's throat collapsed and Pierre caught him and struggled to hold him up. A glance behind showed the guard at the gate still sleeping. With his arm around the sentry's neck he dragged him quickly into the shadows around the corner. He dropped the gasping sentry and hit him solidly behind the ear and he lay still.

Pierre pulled the body by the boots leaving a trail in the dust as he finally tucked him behind some barrels. He removed the heavy ring of keys from his belt. Then he loped back and took the sentry's position. Everything was still quiet except Pierre's heavy breathing.

Take bigger breaths, Pierre, he told himself and settle down. When he felt again in control, he carefully took the ring of keys and tried them in the prison door. The largest key squeaked as the door swung open. Looking over his shoulder, he was relieved to see the main gate sentry still dozing.

In the dim light of the doorway, he could make out four small iron barred cells. He was relieved to see that only two were in use.

"Theodore!" He whispered. There was a responding scuffle and a sudden gasp.

"Is that you? Is it really you, Pierre?" The voice rose higher with each word.

"Ssh, little one. Don't sound the alarm!" He peered into the next cell. "How is Andre?" He heard a grunt from inside and knew that his friend was at least awake.

"I am in pain from the gunshot wound. But, how did you get in here?" Andre's voice was low and tired.

Suddenly, footsteps outside made Pierre jerk around. He looked for a weapon of any sort. Other than the heavy keys, there was nothing! Even his sword was in the stable with the mules. A figure carrying a lantern stood in the doorway.

"Well, sentry, how is the patient? Eh?" The big obese figure peered at his face. "New man here, aren't you? Well, I am Louis Charlot – Doctor Charlot!" he pushed past Pierre as he stood there frozen in shock. Holding the lantern higher, he peered into the two cells and then concentrated on Andre's cell.

"Hmm. Gunshot wound in the right shoulder, they said. Can you talk?"

Andre nodded in the dim light. "Yes, Doctor! I am in pain but don't intend to die – not yet!"

"Cheeky young bastard, aren't you? Well, it looks like a good dose of boiling oil should clean and cauterize that wound. If you live through that, you should be ready for the gallows – so I hear! Haw- Haw!" he chuckled. "We'll do it first thing in the morning, sentry. Have him ready at sunrise!"

"Yes, Doctor. That will be all?" The Doctor nodded emphatically and stalked out the doorway. Pierre stood frozen, only just breathing. Then with two quick steps he looked out into the parade ground. Everything was still quiet. He gulped and took some heavy breaths again to recover. Then, inside again and fumbling he opened the cell doors. Theodore hugged him in joy and then helped Pierre lift Andre to his feet. Andre managed to stagger a little but they soon had him outside the prison and in the deep shadows against the high walls.

"Theodore and I will bring the mules! Lean against the wall and wait until we bring them! We will help you mount and then hang on!"

Grasping Theodore's hand he quietly ran in the cover of the shadows and into the stable. It was still deserted. Theodore led two of the animals quietly to the shadows beside Andre while Pierre brought up the last mule. With Andre mounted and hanging on, Pierre handed the reins to Theodore.

"Keep hidden in the shadows. I will have to cause a serious diversion – of some kind. Then I will join you."

"Pierre – be careful – and come back!" Theodore's voice whispered at his back as he ran back to the side of the prison.

Dragging the two bundles of straw inside the prison, he put a bundle in each cell. Taking the lantern from outside the door, he opened it and used it to start a fire in each cell. Then he closed the doors and locked the prison door. The main gate sentry was still sprawled sleeping. He loped quietly across the open area and joined the two brothers in the shadows. Flames were now showing and smoke was belching at the windows.

"Fire! Fire! Alarm! Fire!" Pierre turned away from the square so that his white military buttons did not show in the shadows. The gate guard had struggled to his feet and grabbed his musket. He shook his head and looked around for the danger. Then he dropped his weapon and staggered across the square and stood astounded in front of the blazing building.

He too, leaned his head back and yelled: "Fire, Fire, Help!" Then he rushed to the stables and returned with several pails of water. Men in various stages of dress were tumbling out from the barracks. Some ran back and returned with pails of water as well. An officer appeared and began to organize the fire fighting.

"Get something to break down the door!" He ordered and led a party back to the stable to search for tools. In the shadows, Pierre led the mules down closer to the gate. Then waving Theodore to wait with the animals, he picked up the sentry's musket and stood on guard himself.

When the attack on the fire was at a peak, he quietly opened one of the two main doors just enough to let a single mule leave. Then he motioned to Theodore who rode out of the shadows leading Pierre's mule. Pierre gasped with relief as he saw that Andre was guiding and riding his own mule. When they were both out of the gate, he led his mule out and glanced back inside. The soldiers were now smashing down the smoking door and no one was watching the main gate.

He mounted quickly and led his friends down the street and towards the gates of Valence. They slowed down as they approached the open gates. A guard stepped forward but then recognized the uniform Pierre was wearing and waved them through. Looking back through the open gates, Pierre could recognize a distinct golden glow above the shops and inns. He nudged his mule to catch up with the brothers as they galloped west across the bridge in the direction of St. Péray.

"We made it! Thank God! We made it!" he whispered and gratefully gulped the cool night air.

*　　　*　　　*　　　*　　　*

19th July 1687
On the road to Lyon - Valence

Uncle Antoine moved slightly in his chair so that the evening breeze from the open window could flush the smell of tobacco from his good friend's clay pipe away from his nose. It is becoming a popular habit in France – but still irritates my nose a lot, he mused!

He recognized that his mind was having trouble keeping up with the deep and fractious discussion his nephew was having with Antoine's old companion, Charles Blanc, who had run a very active trading business in Valence for many years.

Uncle's one eye was watching Isabeau as she helped her Aunt and Charles's wife, Marie tidy up the huge kitchen as the cook and maids did "the dirty work" of washing and cleaning. A fine meal – and really good wine, he thought.

There – Isabeau had turned and slid out of view. He leaned forward and glanced down the corridor. He saw her back disappearing into the darker sections. Then he saw a brief flash of light as she picked up a small lantern from a hallway table followed by a whiff of cool evening air. She has gone outside! Now is the time. He rose and the conversation stopped as the two men turned towards him.

"*Pardon, mes amis*, I will be gone for just a few minutes! I need to empty my pipe." He smiled as they nodded and turned to continue their discussion. Antoine slid quietly past the open kitchen arch and down the dark corridor. He found the door and opening it, stepped out into the darkened courtyard.

Isabeau was standing next to a large pillar. She started and spun round with a gasp. In the dim light of the small lantern resting on the stone ledge, he noticed what looked like a trail of tears on her cheeks. She quickly moved to rub her fingers across them in an attempt to wipe them dry and turned back hurriedly to face the dark garden.

Antoine quietly crossed the flagstones and came up behind her. As he laid his hands on her shoulders, she jerked and grunted. He pulled his hands back and moved carefully to her side, sitting on the balustrade and looked out into the dark shrubs – deliberately avoiding looking at her face.

"Isabeau," he said softly.

"Hmm!" she only acknowledged him.

"Isabeau!" He didn't know where to start! Oh well! "I have only known you a short while!" She said nothing. "But I have come to admire - greatly - your courage; your style; your grace." She stayed silent.

"I feel," and he gestured helplessly with his two hands – without looking at her, "that something has gone wrong – for you – and for us – in the last few days!" She remained still and quiet. "And, I feel helpless! I want you to trust me – and tell me. What we have done wrong!" He shook his head in frustration. She spoke at last – softly – her voice a little broken.

"You ... have done nothing wrong, Uncle!"

"My nephew, then?"

"None – of you!" Her voice broke as she spoke.

He turned now to face her slightly – to make eye contact. In his many years of trading, he had always found that looking at a person allowed them to trust him.

"Please," he whispered hoarsely, "How can I help?" Isabeau turned and looked around – somewhat in desperation. Then shrugged and turned and faced him.

She told him – with silent tears running down her cheeks. Slowly and in broken phrases, then faster like a rush of stream water breaks through a dam. Impulsively, he reached out and pulled her towards him. He felt an immediate tension strike her shoulders but as he pulled her face gently to him and rubbed her shoulders, he heard her sigh and felt the stress die. She now sobbed silently – without words.

"There ... there, little Isabeau. You were lucky that 'Renard' happened along!" He ran his hand gently over her hair smoothing out the waves. "Those swine – I'm glad he hit them – hard! I hope he broke their skulls!" He heard a gentle burble – like laughter – from his shoulder. She pulled back slowly.

"Must I tell ... my husband? I feel so ashamed!" She continued before he could advise her. "Not of what they did to me! But ashamed of not being able to look after myself!"

Uncle Antoine wanted to reassure her that she was "only one woman – against four or five men". But wisely he held his peace!

"I think, my little Isabeau, that it sounds like you – with a little help – were more than a match for four hulking Dragoons! Eh?" He saw a small grin flicker across her lips and a chuckle escaped her throat. "What would you have done differently – next time?" he asked. He saw her eyes narrow slightly.

"Perhaps," she whispered softly, "against my better nature, I should have asked you - or my husband, to come along with me – next time!" He nodded quietly.

"I think that would have been hard for you, Isabeau." And he saw her nod slightly. "You are a ... very independent young woman, aren't you?" She nodded emphatically. "But, it does seem – that in this world we both live in right now – we should both ... take a little more care?" She smiled up at him – openly and with the old Isabeau smile he was used to.

"Oh, I feel so much better now, Uncle. Thank you! It is so hard living with such ... terrible secrets!" He nodded and waited.

"Let us go in – smiling!" she grinned – a little. "With dignity!" And turning, she took his arm and holding the lantern in the other hand, she led him back inside.

*   *   *   *   *

28th July 1687
Up the banks of the Rhone - St. Peray

"Pierre, this looks like the right place!"

Pierre was riding alongside Andre and helping keep him upright in the saddle although he only grunted when spoken to. The party had ridden through St. Peray in the darkness and Pierre had urged the boy to ride ahead and look for an isolated barn or shed. They had been passing what looked like an affluent estate.

Now Theodore had stopped and was pointing to a roadside building. Pierre leaned around Andre to peer at the dark building. The barn had apparently once been part of the main farmyard but a newer set of buildings had been constructed closer to the chateau – leaving it isolated and now deteriorating. Theodore carefully steered his mule down a faint path until the old barn loomed overhead. He slid off his mount and led it toward the main door.

His face lit up in the moonlight as he glanced fearfully over his shoulder in the direction of the chateau where lights were very evident. Struggling, the boy managed to swing the massive door wide enough to lead his mule in. His eager voice whispered hoarsely.

"Pierre – it's dry and there is feed for the mules – and water!"

Andre slumped off into Pierre's arms and he dragged him moaning into the darkness. There was enough moonlight showing through the holes in the roof to allow him to tug his friend to a pile of scattered straw and lower him to the floor.

"Is my brother ... alright?" Pierre nodded.

"I think he has fainted." Pierre opened the jacket to peer at the wound that had now clotted. He touched it with his hand and winced at the heat.

240

"It does not look good! We must clean and bath the wound! Theodore, get some water - in your hat!" The boy grinned weakly and slipped outside into the dark.

With the water, Pierre carefully wiped the wound as his friend moaned with every stroke. Theodore had found an old candle and, shielding it carefully from the direction of the Chateau, he had lit it and was holding it above his brother so that he could watch.

When the door was jerked wide open, the surprise caused Theodore to drop the candle and it went out. However, a much brighter light from a lantern held by a young man clearly exposed the whole scene. Pierre spun round and grasped the hilt of his sword but another burly man stepped from behind and placed his boot firmly on the blade pinning the weapon to the straw.

A quick nudge from the man's other foot sent Pierre rolling onto his stomach. The shining blade of a dangerous looking scythe held by the lantern carrier made Pierre freeze. The burly older man, holding a sword in his hand, took the lantern from the younger man. Outnumbered, Pierre rolled on his side and watched the older man as he bent over Andre.

"Looks like a gunshot wound?" He looked in Pierre's direction, "Who shot him?"

"A Dragoon!" Theodore answered, "It's my brother!"

"You don't live around here! Where are you from?" Pierre looked at Theodore shaking his head slightly and answered.

"From the Luberon – La Motte d'Aigues." The man looked at him quizzically.

"And ... you are in trouble with the Dragoons?" Pierre nodded but said nothing.

"What is your name? I know many people from the Luberon range."

"Jaubert, Pierre."

For the first time the man lost his grim look and he smiled slightly.

"Hmm – you are not Jacque's son – the one that attacked the Dragoon Captain?"

Pierre nodded. "You know my father?"

The man nodded emphatically. "Yes – a good man! We all heard about the trouble with the villages on the Luberon. Are you escaping?" Pierre nodded again.

"We are also of the reformed faith! You don't have to worry! You are with friends! We must get your friend to my home. He looks like he needs immediate attention. We will fetch the cart and pull it between us to the main buildings." He turned and gestured to his companion. "Fetch the farm handcart, Abel!" Then he turned and extended a hand to Pierre and pulled him to his feet.

"You are welcome to our home!" he said and Pierre grasped his hand firmly in relief.

Between them they lifted Andre onto the cart and pushed and pulled it to the main building. The older man carefully avoided the lighted windows and urged them to carry Andre through a back doorway and down a long corridor and laid him down on a bed.

"I have sent for our friend in St. Peray – he is a retired Surgeon-Barber. Used to be with the army. Very used to treating gunshot wounds. He is a Catholic – but sympathetic towards our religious troubles!" he reassured Pierre and Theodore.

A young girl in her early twenties entered the room with a basin of warm water and clean white rags. "My daughter, Jeanne – she is used to dealing with injuries. Here, Jeanne, carefully wash the wound – front and back – and keep him as warm and comfortable – as you can. Nicholas Du Bois has been sent for!" The girl curtseyed slightly to the group and then set to work in a confident manner to wash the wound. She asked Theodore to aid her in holding Andre's arm away so that she could ensure the wound was clean. Theodore grinned weakly at her and held his brother's arm firmly.

"Come with me, Pierre – to get some food and drink from the kitchen. You must be hungry and tired." With a glance back at Andre and the young woman, Pierre nodded gratefully and followed the farmer down the corridor.

*   *   *   *   *

28th July 1687
Up the bank of the Rhone – St. Peray

A short time later, a couple of horses galloped into the yard and Pierre looked up from the kitchen table as a tall rangy man with a dark gray pointed beard burst into the room with a leather satchel swinging at his side. Pierre stood up with a piece of bread in his hand. The man's gray eyes bored into Pierre's. He spoke tersely.

"I am Nicholas Du Bois. I am a Surgeon - retired. Tell me about the wound."

Pierre explained briefly the circumstances of the gunshot wound.

"Hmm – so it was only this morning. Good! A Dragoon's musket. Right shoulder wound – in and out the back, you say! Bleeding but now sealed up – and hot to touch! Hmm!"

Pierre hesitated and then added:

"The Doctor at the Dragoons' barracks said that he would operate in the morning – fix the wound with a hot blade with a dose of boiling oil!"

"Hmm – like a typical Army doctor – most likely end up losing the arm as well! Well, I don't use that boiling oil solution – too much damage! I use Ambroise Pare's method – have much better results. However, may need your help? Come with me!" He turned and raced from the room and Pierre had to hurry to catch up with the Surgeon.

The daughter, Jeanne, looked up anxiously when Du Bois entered the room.

"Dr. Du Bois – I am glad you are here! I have cleaned and washed the wound but it has started to bleed again, I'm afraid!"

"No, that's good, Jeanne – my lovely girl! You have done the right thing! The wound needs to be bleeding to clean out all the dirt." As she stood up, he knelt down and studied the wound. "Looks good! I will use Pare's mixture. A hot blend of eggs with some of the turpentine and rose oil I have brought with me. It will cleanse the wound. Then I will close it up. Stop the bleeding but I will leave a couple of hollow straws in the wound. To allow any excess to seep out!"

Then he hurried out to help Jeanne fix the medication.

The owner, Samuel De Puy, nodded to Pierre.

"He is a good man – but always in a rush! But, he knows what he is doing – and is no butcher – like many doctors in the army!"

The whole party had gathered to watch the operation. The hot mixture had been applied to the bleeding wound with cries from Andre. Then the barber had placed several clean hollow straws into the wound before delicately stitching up the openings with fine threads soaked in turpentine. Then Du Bois slipped a small amount of liquid from a vial into the patient's mouth. Theodore watched anxiously as Andre lay moaning but the painful sounds died as Andre started to snore.

"Is he sleeping?" Theodore looked at the surgeon-barber who nodded and smiled.

"Your brother is now asleep. That little dose will keep him quiet for the rest of the night. Powerful stuff!" He looked at Jeanne. "He will be sore in the morning. Cold water cloths will ease the soreness. I have done the best I can – the body needs to heal itself." He looked at Pierre and grimaced. "He will not be able to move safely for at least three days – and then he must not overtire himself. Can you afford to take the time safely?"

Pierre looked over at De Puy who was leaning against the wall. The estate owner nodded.

"Your mules are in our stables and you should stay hidden – even from the servants and farm workers – while the hunt for you tapers off. You should be safe in this wing," he gestured out into the corridor. "My daughter will nurse him back to health. And, also provide you with meals. I am respected in this region. I don't expect anyone to be brazen enough to come asking questions."

The surgeon, Du Bois, spoke up again.

"Recovery from gunshot wounds is more than surgery and rest. It is also helped by the right foods. My wife is familiar with our local herbs and foods. I would recommend the yellow of the eggs, food from cows – cheese and butter, dark green vegetables and fruit – maybe, oranges. Dark meat – better use duck - with beans – and melons from the south." With a glance at her father, Jeanne nodded.

"That can be done. I didn't realize that the types of food you eat could effect your healing. I would like to learn more about that." She smiled at Pierre and then looked down with an anxious expression at her patient.

"When you have dealt with as many gun wounds as I have over the years, you learn a lot! I will send you a list of ideal foods by messenger in the morning." He stepped over and offered his hand to

Pierre who grasped it in appreciation. Du Bois turned and bowed slightly to De Puy.

"Thank you for allowing me to see this young man, Samuel!

The estate owner led the barber out thanking him gratefully for his discretion.

"I think we should let your friend sleep now," murmured Jeanne and urged Pierre and Theodore out into the corridor, "you will both sleep in the room next door." She showed them the doorway down the passage. "I have put warm water in your room to let you clean up for bed. I will be checking on ... Andre, several times in the night to see that he is doing well." She dipped her head shyly. "If you have to go ... outside, use that doorway." She pointed down the hallway in the opposite direction. "But, it will only be safe at night to go outside." She turned quickly and waved at them as she vanished down the corridor in the direction of the kitchen.

The two friends stood and watched her vanish.

"Sleep!" said Pierre wearily and Theodore nodded eagerly.

*   *   *   *   *

20th July 1687
On the road to Lyon – St-Rambert

Le Duc Mallan had been a little upset at the hard pace his Uncle demanded for the long journey from Valance to Lyon – in one day.

"What is different, Uncle? You said that we should take our time – enjoy the trip! Now suddenly, you want to race all the way to Lyon?"

Antoine grinned at his upset nephew. "A change of strategy, Le Duc. Always keep the enemy confused!"

Le Duc nodded but with frustration showing on his face. His Uncle continued:

"But I have ordered a ... large lunch ... to be served – country style – like a picnic! At about ... St-Rambert?" Food always mollified his nephew and he grunted happily and turned back to look at the passing scenery.

By the time they broke the journey for the picnic, Uncle Antoine had been pleasantly surprised at the speed that his nephew's wife recovered her previous good spirits. She was obviously delighted when the surprise showed on his face. She moved closer to him and whispered:

"Nothing has changed, Uncle! You have made it ... easier to bear!" He was surprised when she nudged him slightly with her hip. "I think I am ... a good actress – when I need to be. Just ... treat me the same ... as you used to!" He turned and looked steadily at her.

"I will! I promise!" And taking her hand, they ran back together to the waiting coach, watched in amazement by his wife and nephew.

*   *   *   *   *

"Wake up, Pierre! Wake up!" Pierre opened his eyes – with difficulty – and glared at Theodore leaning over him.

"What's wrong?" He glanced around the strange bedroom and shook his head to clear the cobwebs. Then he jolted himself upright.

"Andre? Is there something wrong?" Theodore grinned at him and shook his head emphatically.

"No! I saw my brother an hour ago – and he looks much, much better! But, half the morning has gone already!" He frowned at Pierre, "I have never seen you sleep so late before – I thought that there might be something wrong with you?"

Wearily, Pierre closed his eyes and grunted. Then he opened them again to meet the glance of the frustrated youth and grinned.

"Yes! I suppose so!" He stretched and peered at the rays of bright sunlight coming through the slats in the shutters. "Open up the shutters and we shall get moving." And he rolled the covers back and sat up.

*   *   *   *   *

An hour later – after a quick visit to the recovering patient and a delicious late breakfast of freshly baked bread, farm cheese, freshly cut melons and fruit and a hot tisane of herbs carefully selected and mixed by an enthusiastic Jeanne, Pierre and Theodore joined Andre in his sickroom.

Pierre noticed that while he looked pale and wan, his ready smile showed his vastly improved condition – although he winced when he changed position in his bed. Pierre also noticed how quickly Jeanne moved to the patient's side – and how she flushed when she noticed Pierre observing her behaviours.

As he was thinking of a way to tease Andre about the attention of his newly found nurse, the door opened quickly and her father, De Puy, entered the room and peered out the openings in the shutters while waving his hand asking for silence. They quieted and waited for him to speak. At last he turned and grimaced at them.

"That is third patrol to call on the farm this morning. All are looking for the wounded bandit and his companions. It really looks like you have kicked over a hornet's nest!"

"And...?" Pierre whispered hoarsely.

"I have managed to reassure them that you have not been seen! I acted a little angry and frustrated this time! I asked them why they were doing what the other patrols had already done – why were they not following up new leads. The *Sergent* admitted – a little ruefully – that all leads had led nowhere! So, they are having to retrace their earlier steps."

Andre turned and faced Samuel. "Are we safe then?"

De Puy shook his head slowly. "No – I don't think so! They had expected that they would find some report of your party racing for the safety of ... Avignon or Lyon. But, of course, they found nothing. Now they feel you may still be hiding in the district – which, of course, you are!"

Pierre pondered the problem. "We need to reach Lyon – it is big enough for us to get safely lost in for a while. Then we need to find a way of reaching the mountains – and the city of Geneva! If travel by road is dangerous – what about by the Rhone?" But Samuel shook his head grimly.

"No, the *Sergent* said that they have patrols watching – and searching – each vessel – and you would be more vulnerable on water."

"Father...?" Jeanne leaned forward from the chair at the head of the bed.

"Hush, daughter! I'm afraid this is work for adults!" and frowning, he turned his gaze again on Pierre. Jeanne frowned and shook her head in frustration.

"*Mon Pere!* I am not a child any more. So please listen to me!" Samuel had turned his head to glare at her. Then his gaze became gentler.

"Listen, my precocious daughter, we need to concentrate on a plan to escape..."

"But, father, I have a plan. You have told us many times about our Reformed ancestors escaping the tyranny of the King and his Dragoons a hundred years ago. Why not do the same ... why not dress them in ... a disguise!"

Her father frowned and shook his head. Then, he turned to Pierre and explained that his ancestors – women – had cut their hair and dressed as men to escape on board a boat to England in the mid-1500s.

"But, Jeanne, they were women. This is different!"

She simply smiled at him and then turning quickly, she spun with her long skirt rising up and flaring around her. "Why not ... dress as girls?"

"As girls?" He looked astounded and puzzled.

"Why, yes! You could escort ... your two daughters," she pointed at Andre – in bed, "your daughter, Jeanne ... and," she pointed at Theodore, "my little sister, Angelica".

Both Andre and Theodore burst into laughter that Andre soon controlled with a painful expression. But Samuel had narrowed his eyes as he looked at the two brothers and then he nodded slowly.

"It might just work!" He kept nodding his head as a slight smile crept onto this face. "Nice work, Jeanne – nice work!"

Both the brothers stared at each other with horror on their faces.

*   *   *   *   *

29th July 1687
On the banks of the Rhone – St. Peray

"Oh Theodore, you are delightful!" Jeanne's merry voice rang out as the youth spun and the skirt of the dress he was wearing rose up to show his heavy boots and stockings. "But you had better not show your boots – they are definitely not feminine!"

Theodore grinned at her. "This is going to be fun!" he announced, his shrill voice showing his excitement, "but we will have to do something ... with my brother!" and he pointed to his sibling who was standing awkwardly beside the bed dressed in a woman's skirt and blouse.

"I feel stupid, Pierre!" he grimaced as he ran his hands up from his waist. "I don't like the idea of wearing ... these oranges!" And he grasped the two round objects held tightly by a cloth wound around his chest under the blouse. Then he winced in pain.

"Be careful, Andre. You don't want to open up the wound!" Jeanne touched his shoulder gently. "Here, let me finish the dressing first." She draped a white shawl over his shoulders and crossed the ends across his chest tucking them into the top of the skirt. Then she grinned shyly at him as she fitted a white cap tightly over his head and pulled two hanks of hair from each side to peep out from the cap. She clapped her hands in delight. "You look lovely! But ... you have to practice walking and sitting so that you do not appear too ... man-like?" She turned to her father who had been watching the robing with a quizzical face. He nodded slowly.

"It's a big risk – but one which I think just might work!" He turned to Jeanne, "My daughter, I have arranged for you and your little sister to go over to the Manchette's estate – in secret - tonight. He will keep you for a couple of days – in hiding. Tomorrow – early - I will escort ... my two daughters to Lyon. Pierre will assist my coach driver, here. In livery, of course. And we will drive all through the day – and hope that we are not stopped." He looked around the room. "No one on my land knows of the plan – or of the presence of you three!" Then he smiled warmly. "It's a big gamble – but perhaps your only chance of escape. *Bonne chance!*"

Theodore grinned again in excitement but Andre looked anything but confident and sat down heavily on the bed. Jeanne bent over him and kissed him on the cheek; then Theodore and Pierre. Finally, she hugged her father and ran from the room with tears coursing down her cheeks.

*   *   *   *   *

29th July 1687
On the banks of the Rhone - St. Peray

The whole estate had been asleep when the "young women" entered the coach. The grizzled old driver, Marc, had offered his hand – with a grin – to Andre who had slapped it aside in disgust.

"No, Andre! You must remember your role! It is your life – and your young brother's life - that we are dealing with here!" De Puy sternly reminded him. "How is your shoulder this morning?" With a grunt, Andre settled back on the leather cushion with a glance of fleeting pain creasing his forehead.

"I am sorry, *Monsieur!* The pain is less this morning but ... it still cuts down on my alertness. I will take more care."

247

On the other hand, Theodore, with a devilish grin, extended his gloved hand to the driver. "I am ... honoured, *Monsieur!*" and was heaved into the open doorway. After the estate owner, De Puy entered, Pierre closed the door and climbed up beside the driver and settled with the heavy musket resting on its butt between his legs.

Inside, De Puy handed two folded lace covered fans to the two "girls".

"Try to avoid direct eye contact if we are stopped! Drop your face shyly and keep it covered with the fan. You will find it helpful in hiding any embarrassment, Andre! And, no fooling around, Theodore – this is serious business!" The two boys nodded and practiced with their fans. The estate owner nodded and rapped his silver-topped cane on the roof of the coach and it jerked into movement.

*　　*　　*　　*　　*

29th July 1687
On the banks of the Rhone - Tournan

"We are making good time so far! I hope our luck continues to hold up!" De Puy announced with some degree of pleasure as the coach crossed the Rhone River at the sleepy town of Tournon. "The busier traffic on the east bank of the Rhone will keep the Dragoons and Militia busy." He knocked on the roof with his cane. "We will stop at the next village, St. Vallier, to water the horses and have a little late breakfast – in the coach!" He called out to the driver and got a yelled response.

Andre woke up with a start and touched his shoulder gently. De Puy pulled a flask from the basket at his feet and handed it to the young man.

"Take a long swig of this concoction, Andre. Jeanne mixed it especially – it may not taste good but it contains a mixture of herbs – lemon balm, angelica and verwain – good for wounds, fevers and some pains." Andre took a sip; then a longer drink and nodded his head.

"The taste is not too bad ... and it reminds me of the ... sweetness of your daughter, *Monsieur.*" Then he closed his eyes and settled back with his cheeks and mouth tightened in a grimace.

Theodore peered around the edge of the flapping leather curtains to watch the passing traffic. Suddenly, he jerked his head back and looked at De Puy.

"Dragoons – a whole patrol of them – going south!" he whispered hoarsely.

De Puy leaned slightly forward and peeked through the opening. He nodded grimly and grunted.

"Some of them are looking backward – and the officer at the front is turning and giving an order!"

"Damn! A group of them have turned their horses. We can expect some ... undesirable attention, I think! Just stay quiet - and use your fans. Let me do all the talking!" The occupants of the coach could now hear the thunder of hoof-beats following their vehicle.

Theodore gently shook his older brother to alert him to the

248

danger. "Wake up, brother! We are in trouble!" His voice was low and tight with fright.

Andre stirred and opened his pain-filled eyes.

"Wake up – properly!" pleaded Theodore. "You have to be alert!" Andre struggled to straighten his posture groaning as he did. He finally propped himself up in the corner for support and grinned weakly at his younger brother.

"I'm as ready as I will ever be," he groaned. As the coach slowed, dust billowed in through the flapping leather curtains. Theodore coughed and wiped his face with his sleeve.

"What do we do, *Monsieur*?" He looked for guidance at the older man.

Well, don't do anything masculine – remember," De Puy whispered hoarsely, "you are ... young girls – and act like it! Try and avoid speaking. If you must, keep it limited – and feminine!"

De Puy dragged a handkerchief from his sleeve and wiped a bead of sweat running down his cheek. "I say again - let me do the talking!"

*   *   *   *   *

CHAPTER TWENTYTWO

29th July 1687
On the banks of the Rhone – near Vienne

Sergeant Scarron felt terrible. He rubbed his big belly harshly as he remembered a night of heavy drinking; and massaged the burning pain inside. That mad doctor's attempts to ease the pain had been useless! And, stupid advice like "cutting out drinking and fat foods – and losing weight" – were ridiculous solutions!

Scarron grunted and moved uncomfortably in his saddle. Why, his life revolved around lots of drink, lots of good food – and, of course, lots of women – and as much of each category as possible! A sly grin slowly grew on his porcine features as he recalled the riotous party last night at the inn.

"*Sergent! Sergent!*" Scarron shook himself away from the visions of Michelle's pendulous breasts as she had leaned over his body on the grubby bed. He raised his hand in acknowledgment of his officer's call. The voice drifted back through the clouds of dust.

"*Sergent* – wake up! That carriage we passed! Take a squad of men. Stop the coach and search it!" As he gestured to a group of men riding behind him, Scarron heard a late fading comment. "And don't get us into any trouble with the locals!"

He grinned wearily and nodded before slowing and jerking his horse around. A belch broke from his mouth leaving a nauseous taste of rotting fermented mutton. He spat into the air and the men following him cursed grimly. Damn that Doctor – maybe there is some truth in his prescription, Scarron grunted to himself.

Ahead the driver and guard of the coach appeared unaware of the squad's approach. As Scarron broke through the billowing cloud of dust alongside the carriage, he rose with some difficulty in his stirrups and bellowed.

"In the name of the King, stop the coach!" The two men on the driving seat peered over their shoulders; then at each other; and then jerked at the reins. Scarron noted that the stocky guard, alongside the driver, reached behind him and grasped a musket lying on a rack. Hmm, What's he got to fear?

The Dragoons' horses circled in the cloud of dust and Scarron saw a leather curtain jerked aside slightly and a man's startled face appeared briefly. Then the curtain dropped back.

As he swung heavily to the roadway, Scarron glanced backward quickly and noted with relief that his men had spaced themselves apart and two had their muskets out of the slings and covering the coach and driver. With harsh confidence, he shouted at the coach. "You inside! Everyone out – now!"

*   *   *   *   *

29th July 1687
On the road to Vienne – near St. Vallier

"In the name of the King - stop the coach!" A strident voice called out as the Dragoons drew alongside. A cloud of light dust swirled in through the flapping curtains. As the coach shuddered to a halt, De Puy opened the door and peered at the Dragoons. He noted with some alarm that they had dismounted. The heavy Sergeant was now standing before his men who were spread out behind him – two with muskets unlimbered and covering the coach. Putting a tight polite smile on his face he climbed to the ground and stamped his feet.

"Where is your officer?" He spoke with a degree of gentle frustration.

The portly Sergeant, frowning, raised his gloved hand in the air. His face hardened as he sought to re-gain control of the situation.

"*Monsieur! Bonjour!* You are traveling very early this morning?"

Pierre had swung down from the coach seat to drop the steps for the estate owner to alight. Now, he stood back with the musket held across the chest facing the soldiers, his hat pulled down to hide his face. De Puy wiped the dust from his coat but kept his eyes on the sergeant.

"*Sergent* – how far is it to the village of St. Vallier?"

Disconcerted, the officer frowned and then glanced at his men with raised eyebrows.

"Just a short drive, *Monsieur!*" A young Dragoon grunted.

"Good, we need to take a little break and rests the horses!"

"And, your destination! Your business, *Monsieur?*" the Sergeant got back to his task.

"Oh – up the road to Lyon! My business – I have an estate down south - on the Rhone. And, I am well known to the commandant of the Dragoons at Valence, *Sergent!* But if you must know, I am taking my two daughters to a special occasion with relatives – at Lyon! I will be engaged in negotiating the betrothal of my eldest daughter." He raised his eyebrows at the officer and waited.

"Well, *Monsieur*, could you ask ... your daughters to step out of the coach?"

De Puy shook his head fiercely and frowned. Then he stepped closer to the officer and lowered his voice.

"*Sergent*, that would be most disagreeable. My oldest is not only nervous – as you can imagine – but she is also a little ... uncomfortable ... right now! Female problems, you know!" The Sergeant's plump features winced a little and his frown increased – in obvious frustration.

"Perhaps, *Sergent*, you could peek inside – without causing any embarrassment?" Du Puy suggested softly.

Hmm, thought Scarron, another self-important estate owner! He stared through De Puy. Then reaching out, he gripped the man's arm and firmly jerked him forward so that he stood alongside and facing the Dragoons instead.

"Berette," he called on his drinking partner, "tell this gentleman why we are searching the coaches! Tell him how important our task is!"

Once he heard Berette begin his explanation, the Sergeant stepped silently forward and jerked the door open. He peered cautiously into the darkened interior. Just two women – but young women! Aha! .

The obviously younger – prettier - girl grinned rather nervously at the officer and covered the grin quickly with her fan. In the corner of the coach another older angular-faced young woman barely glanced at the soldier before turning her face away and raising her fan. Other than a couple of baskets on the coach floor, it was obvious that the coach was empty. Nevertheless, he climbed the steps and knelt in the doorway.

"*Pardon, Mesdemoiselles* – I must search every carriage – my duty!" He placed his hands on the floor of the carriage and leaning forward peered into the darkness under the seat. The older girl shrank into the corner and glared over the raised fan. Scarron smirked up at her. Then raising his hand, he pushed the skirt aside presumably to peer deeper into the dark recesses. As he leaned forward, he overbalanced slightly and clutched her knee to steady himself.

"*Pardon, Mademoiselle!* A slight mistake!" However, he made a point of running his hand up the leg and onto the hip before he levered himself upright again. The girl sat frozen in the corner.

Before he could swivel around to face the younger girl, she kicked him sharply in the crotch. He sucked his breath in pain and turned his head in shock to meet a fierce glare. Then she burst out in a high voice.

"You pig! You leave my sister alone. And - if you try to touch me at all – I will kick you right in your teeth and scream … and scream!"

Her ferocity shocked him. Someone so young – and so fierce. Just for stealing a little fondle! Then he remembered his Captain's warning.

"Oh, *non Mademoiselle!* Just a mistake – just a clumsy old Dragoon!" He saluted awkwardly and crawled carefully back and out of the carriage. As he slid to his feet, he found the barrel of the servant's musket firm against his large butt – and froze.

"Is there a problem – *Sergent?*" the guard grunted.

"None – No, none at all! I … am satisfied!" He turned and saluted De Puy who was peering at the carriage.

"I am sorry to disturb you, *Monsieur*. But we are looking for three young men who are escaping from … criminal acts!" He maneuvered around De Puy and struggled up onto his saddle. He turned his horse back down the road to the south. He gestured to his troopers and called back.

"*Bonne chance, Monsieur,* to you and your daughter … on your negotiations."

And the Dragoons galloped off in a cloud of dust as Pierre slapped De Puy on the back in congratulations.

"Well done, *Monsieur!* Climb aboard!" And the coach began its run into St. Vallier – en route to Lyon.

*   *   *   *   *

It was late in the morning before the Sergeant and his small squad caught up with the Captain as the larger force was crossing the Rhone to enter Valence. In the shade of a plane tree, the senior officer dismounted and pointed towards the cooler Headquarters building before settling down to a cool glass of wine while he called for a report.

Scarron stood stiffly at attention as he ripped through the report of his search of the coach – plus two other vehicles he had stopped while returning to the barracks. The Captain nodded.

"Good work, Sergent! But ... go back to that first coach. Where were they heading?"

Seeing the Captain in a relaxed and casual mood allowed Scarron to relax a little and embroider the story somewhat.

As an old veteran of the Dragoons, he mentioned the suspicious aggressive actions of the carriage guard and enjoyed the officer's nod of approval.

Then he expanded his familiarity as he leered a little while mentioning the two young women.

Obviously aware of Scarron's past record, the officer nudged him with a slight wink. The sergeant responded by letting slip his "accidental" fondling of the young woman.

"From my ... long experience, mon Capitaine," he simpered, "that estate owner will have a difficult time negotiating a marriage contract for that girl!"

"Hmm? Why is that, Sergent?"

"Well, the thighs I grabbed were strong and muscular – almost like those of a man. And with a strong, lean jaw behind the fan!" Scarron closed his eyes in recollection, "Even the little girl, although cuter, was no ... soft cuddly doll!"

The glass in the Captain's hand snapped splashing bright red wine onto the desktop – gleaming red against the white papers it stained.

The officer had jumped to his feet; his relaxed and friendly manner had vanished.

"Sergent Scarron – you stupid oaf! You have put your obnoxious interest in women before your duty today!" The sergeant stiffened again under the onslaught – a puzzled look playing over his furrowed brow.

"Mon Capitaine?"

"You fool, Sergent! I suspect you have allowed the two criminals, Roux and his younger brother, from La Motte – the ones who escaped from this very jail," he pointed out the doorway in the direction of the smoke-blackened jail, "to slip by disguised as two girls! And, I suspect, the frightened carriage guard, is none other than our notorious Pierre Jaubert - whom Capitaine Benoit – is desperately searching for ...Mon Dieu! What a fool you have made of all of us!"

Scarron stood stock still with a pained shocked face; eyes blinking in confusion; staring blankly past the officer.

"Don't stand there, you idiot! Get a messenger! We need to alert the Dragoons in Lyon! What fools we will be - before all of Provence! Go! Go!" and the sergeant swung round and staggered from the office.

*   *   *   *   *

20th July 1687
On the road to Lyon - Vienne

Le Duc Mallan's patience finally broke.   The long drive from Valance – even with the pleasant picnic luncheon on the banks of the picturesque Rhone River – was frustrating him to the point of anger.

"Really, Uncle, this rush is completely uncalled for!" He looked around the coach in disgust, "I really must protest! What has happened for us to suddenly race - as though the bloody Dragoons were right on our tail!" He bent his head and peered out the coach window backwards. His cheeks dusty, he pulled his head back in and glared at his relative. "There is nothing to rush from – nothing!"

Uncle Antoine grimaced; glanced briefly at Isabeau; shrugged and nodded slowly.

"Of course, Nephew! With your permission," he looked from his wife, Belle, to Isabeau, "we can stop for a glass of wine?" His wife nodded eagerly. Isabeau took a deep breath and exhaled. She appreciated her Uncle's empathy about the need for speed and safety but...

Then she nodded slowly. "Oh course, Uncle! That would be nice!"

Nodding, Uncle Antoine rapped on the ceiling of the coach and yelled out instructions.

"Driver – we are coming to Vienne soon. Let us stop there for a break. Choose a suitable Inn – somewhere peaceful – and we spend a few days looking at the countryside!"   An answering acknowledgment from above was heard above the rattle of the wheels and the coach slowed noticeably.

"It would be lovely to be able to wash my face and hands." Belle smiled, her face showing the fatigue of a really long day's travel.

*   *   *   *   *

21st July 1687
On the road to Lyon - Vienne

A strong breeze was blowing off the river as the coach clattered to a stop in the dusty cobblestone yard. Uncle had to hold the carriage door open as he helped the ladies down. As Isabeau stepped to the floor, a strong wind caught the shawl around her shoulders and whipped it wildly into the air. She gasped and grabbed at it but missed it. Away it went!

As it passed the Inn doorway, a hand appeared and skillfully grasped it like a victor's flag. Uncle cheered! A young Dragoon, his face grinning at his successful capture, wrapped it around his arm and trotted up to the owner.

"*Madame*," he proffered the shawl with a gleeful smile, "You lost

254

your shawl?"

Isabeau stood, her face frozen, her hands fixed at her side, staring at him. He leaned forward and thrust the garment closer towards her. She found she could not speak – her lips felt like they did not belong to her!

This is mad, she thought in panic. Belle, staring at her, leaned forward and grasped the shawl. She turned to face the confused soldier.

"Thank you, young man! That is kind of you." She smiled up at him: "You are quick with your hands!" The Dragoon turned to the older woman and bowed slightly.

You are welcome, *Madame!*" He glanced curiously at the silent Isabeau. Then he bowed as well and turned towards his horse tied to a nearby post.

"Isabeau," her husband whispered hoarsely, "that was almost ... rude! What has got into you?" Before she could answer, Uncle took her arm and announced:

"Let us get out of the wind – before we are blown into the river! Come..." and he led them into the sunlit doorway of the Inn.

Isabeau walked like she was in a trance. Whatever is happening to me? I felt like I was frozen – in time! She raised her hand to rub her lips and cheeks. They felt numb to the touch. All over a chance encounter with a young Dragoon? She shook her head in a queer mixture of anxiety and wonder. I felt I was doing so well – I had begun to feel normal again. In control! Le Duc must think I have gone mad – and maybe I have...

Inside the Inn, Isabeau was able to avoid her frustrated husband by joining Belle in a small side room to wash their faces and hands.

"Are you alright, my niece?" Her Aunt queried and Isabeau nodded dumbly.

Give me time, she thought and washed her hands for longer than usual. When left alone, she took extra large breaths and held them a long time before expelling them. She had found this method useful under pressure. Her lips and cheeks began to regain their normal feelings and settling herself down, she joined the rest of the family in the Inn.

"I am sorry," she quickly apologized to offset awkward questions, "I do not know what came over me. It was all so sudden!" Le Duc peered at her curiously before returning to his cup of wine. Uncle Antoine smiled meaningfully but said nothing.

Is that somehow connected to the horrible experience I went through? He looked like such a nice young man? Was it because he had a Dragoon's uniform on? Am I going to be like that every time I run into a soldier, she worried? I will have to think about what I can do to become myself again!

*   *   *   *   *

The sun was setting when the carriage entered the ancient Roman town of Vienne and De Puy leaned out the carriage window to direct the driver through the narrow streets until they turned through a dark archway to lurch to a stop before an ancient Manor.

"These are good friends of mine, Pierre," he called out as he swung the carriage door open. "They are reformed believers and will protect you until you are ready to move on!" Pierre's grin was tired as he dropped the steps for the two ""girls" to stagger down onto the worn cobblestones. Andre had to be supported as he descended. Servants carrying lanterns escorted the party through the huge opened doors and the hosts whisked them quickly down corridors and into hastily prepared rooms. Both the brothers removed their female attire - with much pleasure and relief.

"Food will be brought in soon," explained De Puy as he helped remove Andre's boots and aided him in lying down on the bed. "You'll need to swallow another dose of Jeanne's herbal mixture – it would help with the healing. After eating, my good friend's wife will change the dressing on the wound. Then you can finally get some good sleep!"

Andre grinned weakly and lay back exhausted.

"I suppose ... that you will be pleased to hear that Jeanne has been following us by a couple of hours?" Andre's closed eyes jerked open.

"*Monsieur* De Puy! You didn't tell us that ... before?" The father smiled grimly in return.

"I thought it wise to keep it a secret. She - and little sister - are following in an open cart - to prevent searches - under the care of a trusted older couple. Just a family traveling the road to Lyon! And, behind them, they trail your three riding mules and a pack animal. Ready to speed you on your journey - to Geneva - when you are well again. That is your plan, isn't it, Pierre?" And, he looked a little anxiously at him for confirmation.

Pierre nodded and heaved a heavy sigh of relief.

"Sometimes, *Monsieur*, things look black and dangerous ... and then, they are suddenly clear - thanks to you!"

De Puy's face was serious as he nodded back grimly. Then, he smiled again at the two brothers and left the room closing the door behind him carefully.

* * * * *

Andre stared at the concerned face of the older woman who had removed the dressing from the wound before cleaning the tender skin.

She smiled at him and rubbed his shoulder carefully.

"How is it? What do you think, *Madame*?" Despite his stoic bearing, his voice expressed a definite worry. She smiled.

"I think you know yourself! It's obviously getting better, isn't it?" He nodded.

"I can move my shoulder. And turn; without that sudden dart of pain?" She nodded her head slowly.

"I have looked after many wounds – and this one seems to be healing well."

Andre lay back with a smile and closed his eyes. She sat quietly looking at him. Then, turning she picked up the fresh poultice and laid it gently on the wound. His eyes opened and watched her as she wrapped his chest with torn strips of clean cloth and helped him shrug himself carefully into his shirt.

Hurrying footsteps outside in the hallway! Pierre rose quickly and crossed to the closed door and leaned heavily on the latch. The door bumped.

"Andre! Are you in there?" Jeanne's urgent voice reached them through the heavy door. Pierre stepped back and jerked it open. A flustered Jeanne fell in.

A sudden relieved smile broke across her face and she ran to the bedside and dropped down on her knees beside Andre grasping his hand.

"I am so glad to see that you are safe and looking so much more healthier than - was it just two days ago?" Andre grinned back at her.

"I am very glad to see you too," then he peered over her shoulder and smiled at ten-year-old little Josine who was staring wide-eyed at him. "Hello, Josine – it's good to see you too!" The little girl blushed red and, grinning shyly, hid her head behind her sister's back.

"Well, good news - and bad!" De Puy's voice echoed from the doorway. He entered and faced the three friends.

"As you can see, the two girls arrived safely in Vienne. But, I have arranged to take them on into Lyon tomorrow. They will be safer buried in a much larger city!"

A groan of unhappiness rose from the three friends. "The bad news is that somehow someone was smart enough to discover our secret. The word on the street is that the authorities are now looking for young men disguised as young women! Even these two," he pointed to the two sisters, "were subjected to being stopped three times in the last hour!" A horrified gasp went around the room and Andre grasped Jeanne's hand tightly.

"You," De Puy pointed to Andre, "need to rest as much as possible. You need to get ready to endure a long hard journey up the road to Geneva! I would suggest that, if you have to leave this house for any reason, that you go alone! Any two young men together will be dangerous!" The three friends nodded in unison.

"I ... we all are sorry to have caused you – and your family - so many problems, *Monsieur* De Puy!" Pierre stepped forward and confronted the estate owner.

The man shook his head firmly.

"No, Pierre! I think my family and I have been living in a dream world. Our estate is so peaceful – and quiet. Although, as you know, we are also reformed thinkers, in our little community of St. Peray, most of our neighbors respect our feelings – and the sad world just goes quietly by! But your arrival - shook us all up! We were jolted into the real world again. And, not a nice world!" Jeanne nodded in obvious agreement at her father's words.

"I'm afraid – in the light of what has happened in the last few days – we too – must make some serious – and painful - decisions!" The quiet in the room had become deafening. He stepped forward and took the hand of his little daughter and turned.

"*Bonsoir, Messieurs!* Jeanne – come quickly to the cart. Although I have promised to bring you back here to Vienne in a day - or so! When things settle down! Right now, we must get you and your sister to safety in Lyon!"

And, with a backward smile and wave from Josine, they vanished down the corridor.

Jeanne, in traditional Provencal style, kissed Andre three times on the cheek.

"I'll see you – both – in a few days from now!" and with a sad glance and a wave to the two other men, she slid into the darkness.

*   *   *   *   *

31st July 1687
On the banks of the Rhone - Vienne

Pierre hesitated at the door of their bedroom and listened. Ever since the return of the two De Puy girls, over a day ago, Pierre had to be more sensitive about barging into rooms.

He knocked lightly and, hearing nothing, he opened the door and peered inside. No Andre!

Then, through the opened shutters, he heard Jeanne's light teasing laugh. He grinned and went down the corridor and out into the small courtyard. Jeanne was standing leaning forward and waving a finger in Andre's face while she chided him.

"Jeanne!" he called out, "Your father is looking for you!" She turned and smiled and nodded. Then she pointed at the red-faced Andre.

"Pierre - you must talk to your friend! You must give him courage!"

"Courage?" Pierre stared at the frustrated maiden with curiosity. "Why - Andre is one of the bravest friends I know! How can you say such a thing?"

Jeanne threw out her hands in frustration. "He!" she pointed an accusing finger into Andre's face, "he tells me ... he loves me! But he is too scared to ask my father for my hand!"

Pierre burst into laughter and pushed Jeanne in the direction of the doorway. "Go and see your father - and I'll try and give Andre a push!" With a quick grin, she swirled and vanished into the house.

258

Pierre pulled up a stool to face his embarrassed friend. But, before he could speak, Andre clapped both hands on the top of his head and burst out:

"Pierre, my friend! I get ...so confused! Is this what love is like? Ever since ... ever since I woke up and found this beautiful girl tending my wounds, I have not been able to think of anything else! When she is with me, I am flustered and like a stumbling fool! And, when she is away, I feel ... hollow inside!" He heaved a heavy sigh and frowned. "Is this what love is like, Pierre? Did you feel this way ... about Suzanne?"

The sudden questions startled and shocked Pierre. Although he was looking at his friend, his eyes glazed over and his forehead furrowed. When he said nothing, Andre peered at his friend's face.

"Pierre? Are you alright?" When his friend remained silent, Andre shook his head. "Pierre, I ... am sorry I asked that question. I had not realized that you would be so ... so shocked by it!" Pierre shook his head in a confused fashion. His voice was a little choked when he spoke.

"Sorry, Andre ... but – until you spoke, I have never ... thought about the question." Pierre's frown came back and his eyes narrowed. "You know, I ... I never had that feeling with sweet Suzanne! When I think back ... getting her as my betrothed was ... a surprise and a shock!" Pierre shook his head a little ruefully and smiled slightly. "I admired her immensely – but I was never ... close enough to her ... emotionally – or physically – to develop that feeling you describe."

Andre's grin was a little weak. "Well ... good luck to you. It feels a little like a disease ... or a fever." He shook his head. "You know – uncomfortable but exciting at the same time." He chuckled a little. "Like you feel ... worked up enough to take on a whole army of Dragoons single-handedly – but are ravenously hungry as well!"

Although Pierre smiled at his friend's description, there was wariness in his gaze that made Andre look at him.

"Pierre! You have had that feeling too, haven't you?" Pierre's mouth winced a little and he said nothing. "Well, you have, haven't you? Well...?"

Pierre dropped his head and looked at the cobblestones. Then he raised it and looked intently at his friend. Then, he shook his head.

"Andre ... yes! I think I have had that feeling! Flustered when she speaks to you; stumbling with my words and thoughts; and, going away feeling empty inside. Yes! But," he hesitated, "I am not supposed to have them!"

"Why?"

Pierre stared at Andre and said nothing. The two sat and stared at each other.

"Because, Andre ... because, the lady is married to another man!"

"What! Pierre! You have never told me about her!" Andre leaned forward and grasped Pierre's arm. "What maiden ... affects you so!" He stared hard at his friend. "Oh no!" Andre leaned back and grinned suddenly. "Isabeau? Really?"

Pierre's eyes had glazed over again although he kept looking at his friend. He shook his head slightly.

"Andre – until you described the ... feeling, I never really knew what that was!" He stood up abruptly and shook his finger in his friend's face.

"Andre – what I told you is to be ... our secret!" He shook his head briskly again as though to vanquish the thoughts from his brain. "She told me once I had had a chance – and threw it away. So it's history, friend! Hmm! Until this moment, I never even recognized the possibility! Hmm!" he grunted and turning, he walked slowly away and out of the courtyard. Andre sat and looked at the blackened entryway. He pursed his mouth, half-closed his eyes and grinned slightly and shook his head.

"Poor Pierre!" he whispered softly.

*　　　*　　　*　　　*　　　*

24th July 1687
Arrival at Lyon

It was close to sunset when the carriage finally joined the heavy traffic that clogged the entries of the lovely old city of Lyon. Despite the rising dust, Belle was excitedly sticking her face out the window of the carriage to catch sights of familiar landmarks from her childhood spent visiting relatives in Lyon.

"Oh, look, Isabeau. I can see the spires of Cathédral St-Jean! Look, there!"

Isabeau smiled and nodded – sharing the excitement. She had never been to Lyon before. In fact, although her father had traveled extensively, she never remembered any mention of this great city.

Suddenly, weaving his horse between the carriages and carts, a burly Dragoon slowed down opposite the carriage window apparently waiting for a convenient opening in the heavy traffic. He glanced at the two women and smiled in a friendly manner.

Isabeau glanced over and saw Belle return a gentle smile. She felt her own cheeks and chin begin to numb out again. No, she thought, I have to master this terrible feeling of being lost! I have to get into control again – somehow. She rubbed her cheeks and forcibly made her mouth open slightly and then forced a slight smile.

The Dragoon pointed ahead at the heavy traffic and shrugged. Belle laughed slightly. Isabeau nodded with difficulty and forced a slight smile again. It seemed to come easier this time. Better! But I need to practice it more, she thought.

As the traffic slowed, the Dragoon waved slightly and lunged his horse ahead to vanish in the rising dust. Both the women pulled the blinds closed against the dust.

"What was happening? Out there?" Uncle Antoine gestured to the window.

Isabeau forced her cheeks to relax.

"Oh, just a Dragoon trying to pass – in the heavy traffic, Uncle." He stared at her thoughtfully; then responded:

"*Bon, Bon!* That's good, Isabeau." Belle looked at him – puzzled.

260

"I mean, it's good we have finally reached the lovely city of Lyon! *N'est-ce pas?*"

Isabeau smiled gently; rubbed her cheeks with her hands and settled back on her seat. Yes, it is good, she thought.

* * * * *

1st August 1687
On the banks of the Rhone - Vienne

"Pierre! Pierre!" The second call finally broke through Pierre's brown study. In the late afternoon sunlight, he had been slumped in the shade with his back to an ancient stone wall separating the barn from the pasture. The yells alerted a flock of sheep. Many raised their shaggy heads from their peaceful grazing to stare in frank curiosity at Pierre as he broke from his reverie and rose to his feet. "Here, Andre!"

"*Monsieur* De Puy would like to meet with us. Can you come?" Pierre thought Andre sounded concerned. Had he boosted his courage and approached Jeanne's father? Pierre waved an acknowledgment and heaved himself over the wall and trotted up to the door where his friend waited. One look at Andre's face told him that he had been correct in his assumption. Andre's normally relaxed face was reddened and he wore a silly grin.

"You did, you old scoundrel?" With affection, he punched Andre lightly on his arm. Andre's grin grew. "And...?" he chuckled.

"Jeanne's father listened to me – seriously!" Andre grunted hoarsely, "It went better than I thought – but," he hesitated and fixed a concerned gaze on Pierre as though he wanted some sort of reassurance, "he did not say either yes – or no!" he added hurriedly.

"So?" Pierre met his friend's gaze with some curiosity evident in his voice.

"He wants to talk about it – but with you along? Why – do you think?"

Pierre shrugged. "I guess ... we had better go and find out. *Non?*" He reached out and grasped Andre's shoulder and turned him towards the open doorway. Ahead of him in the darkened hallway, Andre's worried voice came over his shoulder.

"Now ... Pierre ... don't do anything to mess up my chances! This is not a joking matter, Pierre! This is my life!"" Pierre's chuckle caused Andre to stumble a little but before he could stop and turn, Pierre pushed him hurriedly with reassurance.

"Don't worry, *mon ami*, I won't let you down!" And he followed his friend into their bedroom.

The shutters were wide open letting the late afternoon sun flood the polished wooden floor highlighted by a colourful woven scatter rug embroidered with a collection of bright yellow sunflowers.

Jeanne's father, De Puy, had been standing looking out the window and turned as the young men entered. He smiled at them and waved his hand to two wooden chairs opposite the bed. Once seated, he himself sat on the edge of the bed. Self-consciously, he cleared his throat. Then he looked directly at Andre.

"This young friend of yours," he waved his forefinger in Andre's direction, "has approached me about becoming betrothed to my lovely young Jeanne." He hesitated and brushed the hair from the forehead. "Frankly, I never expected when I took pity on you two runaways that my gamble would end like this!" He waved his hand to quieten Andre's expected outburst. "Let me finish, Andre!" The young man sat back - his countenance serious now.

"On reflection, I realize that I had not really thought of Jeanne ... being ready for marriage. I have been made aware of the fact that she probably is; and that takes some getting used to!"

Andre made a movement again indicating that he wanted desperately to support his position – but De Puy waved him down again. "Andre – let me be open with you – right now!" Andre nodded reluctantly and sat still obviously having trouble keeping his patience in check. Pierre smiled at him in empathy and turned back to the father.

"Let me set your mind at rest, Andre," and he pointed at the anxious young man, "I am happy to know that my daughter is going to be betrothed to you – you are a fine young man – and worthy of her!" A glance back at Andre showed a pleased glow flushing his face.

"But – I have given it some serious thought." He rubbed his chin with his hand thoughtfully and continued: "If I gave her my blessing – and asked you to stay with me on my estate; you might be discovered, arrested and spend your days in prison – or rowing a galley in Marseilles! Or, if the two of you married and escaped to Switzerland – I would be left alone – without an heir – and I lose my daughter."

He turned to Pierre. "You see, Pierre," and he gestured with his hands, "I feel I have too much to lose by deserting my estate and taking my family away. I am too practical for that! I am going to abjure! And, at least act the part of a converted Catholic! But, I will still be a small family – me and my little ten year-old daughter, Josine."

Pierre and Andre were following him carefully and both nodding. Probably Andre is suspecting there is a catch somewhere along the line, mused Pierre. Finally, unable to contain himself, his friend burst out.

"*Monsieur* De Puy! I feel, if we are going to discuss your daughter's future, she should be here too." His future father-in-law leaned back and smiled ruefully at Andre. Then he shook his head.

"Andre – I would normally agree – but I need to negotiate a serious contract with you - first!" Andre looked astounded – and mystified. The father continued:

"It is difficult to give up a daughter – especially one as sweet and endearing as my Jeanne! But, I also, have my own future to look after. I need to suggest a trade to meet my – and my family's - needs." Andre stared at him.

"I will be very honest with you, Andre! I would like to trade my daughter," he hesitated and his face tightened under the strain, "for your young brother, Theodore!" Andre jumped to his feet astounded.

"What! My little brother! The light of my life! You must be mad!" Andre's eyes were wide open.

"Listen to me! Hear me out!" Andre sank down but kept shaking his head. Pierre leaned over and gripped his arm.

"Listen, Andre – listen to the man!" Andre returned Pierre's gaze but his eyes were glazed over in shock. He nodded slowly.

"I am going to grow old here – over the next twenty years. You and my daughter – and Pierre – will be gone – maybe settled in the duchies of the Germany Princes. All of you probably – will never be able to return. And – my future is gone!" De Puy stood slowly and walked over to the window and stared outside – while the two men waited. Then he turned back again and held his hands out palms up.

"I think Theodore has all the qualities to be a fine heir for me. He is intelligent, resourceful, kind – has a wonderful sense of adventure! I would adopt him! And within ten years, he will be the heir to a grand estate. He may," the man smiled slightly, "even marry my young daughter? But – he would definitely be the owner of my wonderful estate. And, I think, he will have no trouble acting - with me – the part of the converted Catholic. I think it may really appeal to his delightful sense of humour!" And De Puy grinned. Pierre nodded as well. Andre reluctantly agreed.

"I would have to leave my little brother behind – here in St. Péray? But, I get to take Jeanne - my betrothed - with me?" Andre looked askance at Pierre. Hmm, thought Pierre, he is considering the trade? He turned and looked back at the father.

"I am not sure that you can convince little Theodore to take that sort of deal!" Andre talked slowly and thoughtfully.

"That's where you - and Pierre - come into this plan. I think I understand the way your little brother thinks." De Puy responded, "Out of sheer loyalty to you, Andre, he would say absolutely not! So, you would have convince him that this is probably the most priceless – and most valuable – deal he could ever make in his life! And, it is! He would one day – not so long from now – be the owner of a huge and very valuable estate – a man with power and wealth. And, though I lose my daughter, I would have a new son to share my world with?"

"And I thought I was having trouble asking for Jeanne's hand! I had not bargained for this!" Andre turned to Pierre and stared at him.

"Pierre – what do you think? I cannot imagine life without my brother. But, if he was happy about trading a dangerous life on the road for a fabulous future - well? And, escaping without having to worry about a vulnerable little brother might be a lot easier than we planned." Andre – without waiting for a reply – turned back to De Puy.

"I should also tell you about the dangerous threats to Theodore's safety – from several 'boy-loving' pederasts!" And he recounted the villainous plot between the two despicable travelers and the Dragoon Captain.

"At least, he would be safe from their filthy hands. And, if we were captured while trying to escape, Heaven knows in whose hands, he would end up." From this line of thought, Pierre recognized that Andre was seriously considering the trade. Pierre nodded and spoke out.

"Andre, I agree that travel without little Theodore would be much easier. I feel that your little brother – even though I love him dearly – has become a recognition point for every Dragoon in this part of France – two men and a boy traveling together?"

"Yes, Pierre. Reluctantly, I feel you are probably right! Will you help me broach the subject with my sharp little brother?" Pierre nodded. All the men looked at each other and smiled a little sadly. Andre turned and faced De Puy.

"Does that mean, that the hand of Jeanne, depends on the acceptance by my little brother?" The older man looked at Andre without a word – then shook his head.

"No, Andre! I am asking for something in return." Andre nodded and stretched his hand out to De Puy. The man grasped the hand and they shook solemnly. Pierre leaned over and placed his hand on theirs.

"Well, *Messieurs*, it seems we have a difficult deal to negotiate?" and the three of them jointly smiled.

*   *   *   *   *

2nd August 1687
On the road to Lyon

The earliest rays of the sun were brushing the eddies in the mighty Rhône River as Pierre urged his mule into a canter. He joined the mass of farmers' carts heading north up the riverside road towards the markets in Lyon. As he rode, he checked each cart until he found his target - a lone older garrulous farmer with a shock of white hair hanging over his brow in a cart loaded with melons. Pierre slowed down to the pace of the cart and started a conversation. He finally persuaded the carter to stop briefly at a roadside inn to enjoy a quick glass of wine – at Pierre's cost. When they returned to their journey, the farmer invited Pierre to join him on the driver's bench to continue their discussion. Soon, Pierre was being regaled with stories of the "tried and true method" of protecting melons from a constant war by garden pests while his mule trotted behind hitched to the cart.

The effort paid off. Soon patrols of Dragoons were stopping closed carts for thorough searches. Carts containing groups of women were also being harassed. No Dragoon gave the lone melon wagon - driven by a father and son team - even a glance.

Finally, the spires of St-Jean Cathedral pictured against the Fourviere hillside heralded their arrival in Lyon. Soon the carts were crowded between the Saône and Rhône rivers and, in this slower traffic, Pierre took leave of his partner with grateful thanks. Waving to the carter, he turned off into the less traveled streets searching for someone who could read. Stopped at a busy street corner his constant review of the passing crowd drew the attention of a Dragoon officer. The pointed finger of the Sergeant sent three Dragoons to jostle him. Act quickly and cleanly, Pierre thought, as his breathing tightened.

"*Mon Capitaine*! I am pleased to see you!" The Sergeant frowned suspiciously.

Reaching inside his shirt, Pierre withdrew the now grimy letter from the Notary in the Luberon. He thrust it in the direction of the officer.

"I expect that you can read, *Monsieur*! I am trying to find someone to direct me to an address in Lyon!" The sergeant looked a little bit embarrassed; then shrugged and called over his shoulder to a skinny plainly dressed rider behind him.

"I don't bother to do clerk's work, *Monsieur*. Gustave, look at the paper!"

A thin trooper rode forward and grabbed the letter. Seeing the grime, he transferred it to two fingers, his face showing disgust. He glanced at the writing and then handed it back.

"It's addressed to the Notary down the next street." He called back to the officer.

"Hmm! Well, tell him how to get there – instead of blocking the traffic on market day!"

The directions were easy to follow. Down the street; turn on the right; and halfway down the road; turn right again into the arched alley.

Pierre doffed his hat. The sergeant turned his head in a frustrated manner and moved his squad of troopers back into the traffic.

The arched entrance turned out to be a long alley built under two buildings. In the dim light, a merchant, washing his windows, directed him to a doorway further down.

"Tie your mule to this post! It will be safe while I am cleaning up!" Pierre thanked him for the courtesy.

Inside the door, the Notary's clerk's nose wrinkled at the grimy condition of the letter. Despite this, he soon returned to guide Pierre into the large back office lit by heavy candles.

The Notary leaned back in his chair as he waved Pierre into a wood seat and stared quietly at him for some time before speaking.

"Thank you for the message from my colleague in the Luberon," he hesitated, then continued, "you people ... are suffering a lot!" He nodded with a slow smile flicking into his eyes, "I take it – from the date - that you have had ... trouble getting to Lyon?"

Pierre nodded without speaking – and waited.

"Well, you got here anyway! I will provide you with a receipt for the letter – which will act as an explanation to any authority who questions your journey. Will that be satisfactory?"

"That would be most useful, *Monsieur* Notary!" Pierre said, with appreciation.

"*Bien!* And, perhaps, you may soon be in need of another Courier duty, *n'est-ce pas*? Perhaps you could take a message from our office to a colleague ... say, in Geneva?"

Pierre's eyes sprang open wide with surprise. The Notary's slight smile now broadened into a grin.

"It worked before, *Monsieur* – why not again?" The Notary rose and extended his hand that Pierre grasped tightly in appreciation. Any help was priceless.

"*Merci, merci, Monsieur* Notary! It would be very ... useful!"

"*Bien*! I will instruct my clerk to provide the letter when you are ready to continue your journey."

As Pierre left the office, he noticed that his body felt much lighter and excitement had replaced fear about the next part of their journey.

Armed with the Notary's receipt, Pierre emerged from the dark alleyway and stood beside his mule surveying the passing traffic with interest. He felt confident enough to consider stopping for a meal and a drink at one of the street cafes.

Even on the Luberon in Provence, the city of Lyon is noted for its excellent cooking and food, he thought. He remembered his mother talking with a wistful smile about something she had relished many years before in Lyon. What was it?

An aroma wafting down the stone walls from a nearby café caught his nose. Onion soup! That was it! Leaving his mule tethered, he walked in the direction his nose was pointing and catching the eye of a passing waiter, he questioned the waiter about the soup.

"From your voice, I would say you are from Provence, *n'est-ce pas?*" The waiter grinned and nodded his head. "In my trade, we can pinpoint a person's home within three streets!" Pierre chuckled at the outrageous boast.

"Our soup is the best in the city, *Monsieur*. The best onions, the best garlic, the best wine, the best Gruyere cheese, the best of everything! With a healthy chunk of our rich bread! What more can any traveler ask?" Pierre seated himself down.

With his order placed, he stretched his shoulders in the morning sunshine and his nose twitched slightly as the scent of onions cooking wafted from the kitchen. He reached for the glass of red wine the waiter had left. Glancing around, Pierre carefully turned his chair so as to keep his back to the stone wall as he watched the approaching traffic.

The crowd was obviously enjoying the fine weather. As housewives strolled by carrying the days pick of vegetables; Pierre could smell a mixture of fresh carrots, wild thyme and parsley and see the silvery gleam of fish for the evening meal. Street vendors were selling their wares. A man went by with a huge load of fresh bread for some restaurant. Then Pierre was jolted upright.

Across the street, a woman had turned her back to him as she bent to study some fruit on a stand. His brow furrowed and his eyes narrowed. It could not be! Then she straightened and slightly tossed her dark brown hair. I don't believe it, he thought. What a coincidence! Standing, he waved to the waiter and then slid through the passing crowd until he reached her back.

"Isabeau?" he whispered hoarsely.

*   *   *   *   *

CHAPTER TWENTYTHREE

2nd August 1687
Lyon, France

Isabeau sat alone on the bed looking out the window at what she could see of the city of Lyon. She shrugged her shoulders in confusion. For the moment, I am safe – but feel a little disappointed – why?

Somehow, she mused, the promise of a "visit to Lyon to - meet the relatives" had been more exciting than the reality. Since their unsavory experiences with the Dragoons, Uncle Antoine had become cautious – frowning on any of her suggestions about visiting the wonderful shops of Lyon. Even the pleasure of tasting the gourmet foods, for which Lyon was already famous all over France, was withheld. She had become tired of his..."But, Isabeau, *ma Cherie*, it is too dangerous! You, Isabeau, of all people, should recognize that!" Even an appeal to her gallant husband, Le Duc, had been met with a shrug and a raised eyebrow.

After an early lunch, Uncle and Aunt Belle had "gone to rest for a couple of hours". Le Duc had left "for a couple of glasses of wine" with his robust male young cousins. She ran her hands over the smooth bedcovers and thought, No! I don't want to rest now! I guess ... I need to do something ... for myself! After all, we have been in Lyon for over a week! Since the 25th of July! And, now we are in August already!

Be daring, Isabeau – think for yourself! She looked down at her clothing. She wriggled her shoes on her feet. Good enough for a stroll down the busy street! If I need to hide myself, I'll pull this light scarf over my hair! Grabbing it off the bed end, she ran quietly down the steps and out onto the front steps. She stood in the mid-day sunshine and swished her hair. Its felt good to be free again!

She shrugged the scarf over her shoulders and slipped into the moving crowd. She gasped aloud at the jewelry in a shop window. Wrinkled her nose with pleasure at the café scents of cooked stews and herbs. Paused to run her hands over the colorful fabrics displayed on an open stand. Everything was so much bigger – and more exciting - than lovely little old St. Martin basking in the sunshine of the Luberon hillside.

She hesitated as the crowd moved into another busier thoroughfare. Several people bumped into her and apologized. She smiled and nodded. Then she moved into the stream of traffic with a quick glance backward over her shoulder to recognize the name of an inn on the corner. Wouldn't it be terrible if I got lost? The "Three Coins" – I'll remember that!

The street was wider with room to stop and look at the displays without impeding the traffic. Isabeau looked at men's hats; then a display of decorative statues; then the mixed scents of dried herbs – it reminded her how much she missed the Luberon hills where she could easily find and pick her choice fresh herbs. A glance through the crowd showed a street-side café and people drinking and eating on the opposite side. Then she turned to look at a display of fresh fruit – some she did not even recognize! Hmm, she thought, I must ask Uncle about them!

"Isabeau?"

Her whole body froze in absolute shock! Oh mon *Dieu* – save me! How could anyone know me? She grasped her scarf and pulled it over her hair before turning slowly – desperately seeking an escape route.

"Oh mon *Dieu*! Pierre Jaubert! Of all people!" Her knees felt weak – and she stumbled on the cobblestones. His hand shot out and grasped her elbow.

"I am so sorry, Isabeau!" He looked horrified. "I did not mean to frighten you!"

"Oh, Pierre," breath flooded out as she breathed heavily, "I am sorry. I have had some unfortunate experiences lately and I did not know what to think." She touched him firmly on the shoulder to balance herself.

"Isabeau - you are alone?" She nodded. "Then, would you honour me with your company while I enjoy some of Lyon's finest soup – onion soup! Made from an old – even ancient – recipe – so the waiter assures me?" Isabeau frowned a little; looked back up the street in the direction of the "Three Coins" Inn, then nodded slowly.

"Yes, I think that would be delightful. Maybe I will even have a little bowl of the soup." Pierre guided her by the elbow through the crush of people and, with a flourish of his serviette; the waiter seated her gallantly and rushed off for a *bol petit*.

Isabeau was momentarily uncomfortable. While she openly smiled in return to his open gaze, she wondered whether this was the right thing to do. She was sure her husband would certainly not be amused at her dallying openly on the street side with another man. But, after all, he had been a neighbour – and both of them were fleeing an enemy! She nodded in emphasis as he described a recent event but her mind was not really concentrating on his story. How would she explain to her new family that she had sat with a male friend and enjoyed a bowl of onion soup in the sunshine of Lyon? I won't, she decided. I'll slip back into the house and say nothing! For the moment, Isabeau, enjoy his company!

"So, Pierre, have you managed to elude your favorite ogre – *Capitaine* Benoit?" She dropped her head slightly and smiled impishly. *Sacre bleu*, Isabeau – you are letting yourself flirt with this man! Stop it, now! She lifted her head and looked openly into his brown eyes.

"I'm afraid not, Isabeau! *Le Monstre* – and his Dragoons – have been relentlessly pursuing us – Andre and his brother and I – up both banks of the Rhône!" He shook his head and frowned. "I have never seen anyone ... so obsessed ... as the *Capitaine*. Just for a little injury on the cheek. I think I would have given up a long time ago! But - tell me of your plans? I got two different stories from the village – one that you were visiting new relatives in Lyon; and another that you may be fleeing across the border to the Swiss cantons?"

She hesitated – deciding whether his experiences had been more dangerous than hers had. Then, she explained the actions of her "new" Uncle. How he had originally planned to visit the relatives to rescue her from the attentions of the amorous Captain. And, how this had later changed - to bolder plans – the more harassment they received. She felt so relaxed and trusting sitting talking in the sunshine to Pierre Jaubert that she had to catch herself before she blurted out the recent traumatic assault in the stable.

At the thought, she found herself saved from a decision by the arrival of the onion soup. The waiter, Philip, leaned on the back of a chair while he explained – in detail – what ingredients were in his famous soup.

"My chef would slaughter me if he knew I was giving his recipe to any of the citizens of Lyon – but to visitors – this is different!" he announced. "So I will tell you, *Madame*, the way!" Isabeau nodded smiling. "First slice the onions; then crush several cloves of garlic. Sauté in a little butter - with a large helping of the oil - of the olives."

"He adds a little flour to thicken it! Then a little dry white wine. You must reduce by cooking briskly. We add four times as much water - with some salt - and pepper – if you have it? Then a *bouquet garni* – some thyme, some marjoram, maybe some savory. And, more garlic – crushed. Then - oh, yes! Bring to a boil and simmer slowly for an hour. Soon, the soup will be almost ready."

Now," he gestured with his hands, "while it is cooking, I must have cut our lovely bread into slices - and dried them in the oven. While this is going on, my chef mixes the yellows of three eggs - with a little of the wine - of the Isle of Madeira. We remove the croutons from the hot oven. Now, you make it hotter and place a large bowl of water in the oven." He raised his hands and gestured again. "Now for the final movement! The soup is ready! You have removed the *bouquet garni*. You then add the egg-and-wine mixture and mix quickly. Pour the soup into bowls," he pointed to their bowls, "add the croutons; shake a little grated cheese on top; then, place the bowl of soup into the *bain-marie* - which is sitting in the oven; and cook for short time. Then *voilà!* These are surely *Chefs-d'œuvre*" he peered down at the two who had been spooning the soup while he talked. "Is it not a masterpiece? No?"

It was only after both had assured Philip that this was truly the best onion soup in the whole of France, that he smiled, waved his serviette in the air with a flourish; and rushed away to sell his *chefs-d'œuvre* to another customer.

They looked at each other and grinned conspiratorially.

"It really is absolutely ... wonderful! Isn't it, Pierre!" He nodded emphatically.

"I hate to say it, but it is better than my mother's!" And, he glanced around as if to see that no one was overhearing his blasphemy! Pierre glanced over quickly at Isabeau's down-turned face and felt warm inside. It had been a long time since he had felt so comfortable in a young woman's company - not since - Suzanne! He felt his stomach give a sharp jolt as bitter memories returned. No, Pierre, it is time to enjoy life again. And, I have always admired this lovely woman.

"Tell me about your relatives, Isabeau. How have you found them...?"

*   *   *   *   *

2nd August 1687
In Lyon, France

Captain Benoit climbed from the carriage and, moving to the shade, he lifted his gaze upward to view the magnificent facades of the ancient homes that graced this stately street in Lyon. Two squadrons of Dragoons were beginning to knock on each doorway as they made inquiries about visitors from the Luberon. He raised his hand to again massage the aching cheek. I need a drink, he thought, that's what I need right now!

The Dragoon holding the horses jerked around as the Captain called for his attention.

"I'll be at the Inn," and he pointed to the bottom of the street, "They tell me there is one down there! Tell my *Sergent* to bring me any reports!" He pulled his hat down over the side of his face to hide the embarrassing red scar and strutted with arrogance through the passing crowd.

He wrinkled his nose in disgust at the variety of smells that drifted up from the passing people. He whipped his lace-edged handkerchief from his wide sleeve and held its scented tip to his nose. I should have driven down in the carriage - avoided all this stench! He stopped outside the tavern but a blast of human sweat mixed with stale wine sent him reeling backward. Curse humanity, he swore!

He glanced over the crowded intersection and sighed with pleasure. Lyon is not only recognized for its excellent food but also for it's lovely women. Two elegantly dressed young women were ducking under their parasols to avoid the strong sun as they giggled and bobbed against the surge of the crowd.

Benoit's smile became a leer. I imagine they would both be wonderful in bed! Maybe, both of them together! He grunted in an odd mixture of both satisfaction and pain - as a wince ran through his cheek again. A quaint sidewalk café caught his eye. Even better – a glass of fine wine! A chance to sit in the shade and watch the Mesdemoiselles go by - yes!

Then a swirl of dark brown hair caught the sunlight and he grunted in further satisfaction. Maybe a quiet conversation with that lovely young woman, he smirked? The girl turned her head into the sunlight. Benoit grunted in amazement. No, it can't be! Of all things - that little bride bitch from St. Martin! I've found her - by myself!

Ducking his head and merging with the crowd, he strolled down the street until he was directly opposite her. Then he sidled to the far edge of the crowd where he could stand and peer across the street from under the lowered brim of his hat.

"*Mon Dieu!* The bitch is talking to none other than that other bastard from La Motte!" The Captain swiveled around slowly and peered up the street towards the door of the "Three Coins" tavern – not a Dragoon in sight! A backward glance threw him into a panic. Jaubert was standing and reaching for his purse. The bitch had pulled the shawl over her head again. She was probably leaving too! By the time I rush back to the street, they could both be gone! He grunted in dismay.   I'll have to do it myself, he growled!

Loosening up his sword in its scabbard, he rudely pushed through the crowd followed by blunt expletives as he forced his way to the edge of the café. Unaware of his presence, the couple were still laughing and talking. The hat still masking his face, he pushed between several occupied tables spilling wine as he bumped the diners. The yelled curses caught the couple's attention. Their faces froze. Jaubert's mouth fell open. A quick glance showed that Jaubert wore no sword – unarmed too!

"*Monsieur ... Madame* – I think it is ... the end of the journey ... for both of you!"

The couple stood speechless, the shared joy now vanished, their faces pale and drawn. A quick glance over his shoulder revealed still no Dragoons! Benoit turned back to face the couple again. A hush had settled over all the customers. The waiter's face peered curiously around the kitchen door – then vanished as quickly.

Pierre now looked around anxiously. Blank frightened faces stared at them. He looked back at the officer.

Recognizing the youth's desperate searching glance, Benoit smirked. Feeling more in control, he now withdrew his sword with a grating rasp that brought a gasp from the customers. He waved its point in a gentle circle and smiled slightly as he saw the couple following its sharp point with their desperate eyes. Benoit's eyes squinted like a pig locking his gaze on the young man's face.

"You, you bastard from the Luberon! I'm hoping - really hoping - that you make some dangerous moves! So I can," he pointed with his sword to Pierre's face, "thrust this little beauty right down your throat! So I can disfigure your face now! Just like you have ruined mine!" His voice lost its deepness – became harsh, sharp and shrill. The rage that lay rotting in his wounded cheek now shattered his famous self-control. He raised his elbow a little higher and felt his arm begin to tense for a thrust, when...

"*Monsieur*, would like some more of our wonderful hot soup?" Philip had appeared from nowhere. A large bowl of steaming hot soup held high in raised hands. His body thrust into the space between the two men. His head turned to face Pierre with a suggestive gleam in his brown eyes. "*Monsieur?*"

There was no hesitation in Pierre. Both his hands jerked out together. They hit the bowl thrusting it forward into the face of the startled Captain. He screamed as the hot pungent soup splashed his face and flooded burning down his chest. His backward movement, away from the bowl, overbalanced him. And he collapsed onto several tables and their occupants. With a sudden sway, Philip fell on top of the fallen officer. Benoit's gurgled scream echoed down the startled street. "Dragoons! Dragoons! *Attention! Attention!*"

Pierre grasped for Isabeau's hand and dragged her backward in the direction of the kitchens. Through the doorway, scattering the curious cooks who had gathered in the entry. Past the hot grills with several boiling pots spinning onto the tiled floors. Into the scullery where a little old aproned woman was rinsing plates.

"*Sortie? Sortie?*" he called. She toothlessly grinned and pointed past her down the passage. Without hesitating, the couple wound their way past her and, hitting the door, burst into the garbage littered alleyway.

A young couple were embracing – kissing against the outside wall. Probably a young prostitute, he thought. He reached out and shook them. They separated and stared at him in shock. Pierre grabbed Isabeau's shawl and draped it around the girl's neck. He pointed down the street away from the kitchen.

"Run! Run!" he grunted,. "The Militia – they are coming! Run for your life!"

He gave them a final nudge and the couple, wide eyed, raced off down the street, looking backward as they ran.

Pierre swung Isabeau round to jostle to a halt next to the passing crowd in the opposite direction. He turned to face the kitchen doorway. A Dragoon burst out with sword in hand and peered around. He tensed as he met Pierre's eyes. Pierre pointed down the alley at the running couple. The Dragoon looked away - saw the couple, yelled and, followed by three other Dragoons, raced off down the street.

"Now!" Pierre grunted and nudged an opening into the crowded street. He froze for a second as a group of Dragoons hurtled past the Three Coins tavern their swords raised in the air. They thrust their way to the edge of the café. Pierre and Isabeau rapidly filled into the wake the Dragoons had left and moved past the tavern and into the street where the Dragoons had already been searching.

More Dragoons were rushing down the street toward him. Pierre moved swiftly to an old woman that was struggling to move her pushcart of old clothes against the tide of the crowd.

"*Madame. Madame*, let me aid you!" He pulled her hand loose and placed it firmly on the side of the cart. Then he thrust forward with the cart, calling, "Good used clothes – just like new!"

With the arrival of this stocky man thrusting the cart forward, a space opened ahead and the startled old lady grinned as she hung on like a drowning dog in a flooded river. Isabeau, who had raced on ahead, gestured frantically to indicate her relative's home. Pierre grinned and nodded. With less traffic, the cart now moved forward easily. He stopped, bowed to the old woman and handed her several coins. She shook her head in wonder, grinned again and wandered off with her cart up the street. Pierre joined Isabeau at the doorway.

"Isabeau, we are all in trouble! Including your Uncle and his relatives!" He urged her to get her Uncle and Aunt into the carriage – without their trunks. "We can send for them later – when it is safe! I have to pick up a letter – down the street. Wait in the carriage on the river bank – down there!" and he pointed to the far end of the street. Isabeau nodded feverishly.

"Sorry about this mess!" she smiled apologetically. Then, with a quick glance up the street and with a wave of her hand, she was inside.

*   *   *   *   *

2nd August 1687
In Lyon, France

The clerk sitting at his desk in the Notary's office did not appear surprised when Pierre burst through the door.

"*Bonjour, Monsieur!* You are wanting the letter in a hurry *n'est-ce pas?*" A knowing little smile grew on his face. Pierre nodded frantically. The clerk continued: "My master and I discussed the matter when you left and he wisely ... made arrangements." The clerk frowned and nodded his head. "*Monsieur*, you need to get your horse from its lodgings; is it far?" Pierre shook his head.

"*Oui, Monsieur*, you go for your horse and I shall be waiting outside that door with your letter." Pierre attempted to express his gratitude but the clerk waved them away and indicated with a toss of his hand that Pierre should go about the important business of escape. The door slammed behind him as Pierre hurried down the street to where he had hitched his mule.

In minutes, Pierre, mounted on his mule, spun the animal outside the Notary's office. The clerk handed him the folded sealed parchment and had time to cry out "*Bonne chance, Monsieur, bon voyage!*" as Pierre turned and raced in the direction of the river.

*   *   *   *   *

"Do you think that we are safe here?" Uncle Antoine was obviously disturbed at their hasty departure as he and Isabeau stood beside the carriage on the banks of the Rhone making a small island at the side of the road in the heavy mid-day traffic. "Do you think your ... Pierre ... can find us ... in this?" Aunt Belle peeked out at the couple, her face still anxious about the luggage they had been forced to leave behind.

"Yes, Uncle, Pierre has always been reliable!" She peered with some surprise at her uncle, "Of course, you have never met Pierre Jaubert!" She knew she was making polite conversation to keep her own anxiety in check.

"Well, " said Uncle Antoine, "I think when you were married, he was in that escape party from the Luberon. Heading up the Durance River for Switzerland, *non?*"

Isabeau nodded but her eyes were scanning the heavy passing mixture of carts loaded with produce; carriages like theirs; and walking merchants of Lyon.

"There he is!" And she whipped a shawl off her shoulders and waved it in the dusty air.

Mingling in the crowded traffic, he recognized her signal and waved in response. With a quick look over his shoulder, he urged his mule through gaps in the crowded street and pulled to a halt in the vacuum behind the waiting carriage.

He leaned down and grasped the older man's outstretched hand and greeted him. Uncle Antoine looked decidedly relieved at his arrival.

"Sorry about having to leave your luggage, *Monsieur* Mallan. But we can safely make arrangements to have it spirited away in the next couple of days. Is that satisfactory, *Monsieur?*" The Uncle nodded emphatically.

"But, *Monsieur* Jaubert ... what about my nephew – Isabeau's husband?" Pierre nodded.

"Call me Pierre, *Monsieur!* And, by the time your Le Duc arrives home, we shall have a message to your relative's home giving him safe instructions on how to join up with our party!" On receiving the Uncle's relieved nod, he smiled slightly and nodded to Isabeau who was standing expectantly behind her Uncle.

"I will give directions to the carriage driver and ride alongside you as we go, Isabeau." She smiled back as she just stared at him.

He finally broke the gaze and instructed the driver. The carriage moved into the stream of traffic heading south in the direction of Vienne with Pierre trotting his mule at the riverside of the carriage to avoid the dust.

*   *   *   *   *

3rd August 1687
At Vienne, outside of Lyon, France

Uncle Antoine was leaning with his back against the gnarled trunk of an old apple tree, a half-filled cup of wine in his hand, looking at Pierre Jaubert with a slight tinge of amusement on his face. He shrugged his shoulders to remove tension and nodded his head.

"Well, Pierre, that's quite a story you have to tell!" He sipped a little more, then continued. "You have really been through some battles! I think if I had been about 20 years younger, I would have loved to have been through them with you – but I am an old man – and just want to be safe now!"

"*Monsieur* Mallan – I hope that perhaps we can ... work out a plan – a strategy – that would allow all of us to finish the journey – to safety and freedom!" Pierre felt a tinge of inner excitement that perhaps he could share his constant responsibilities with a wiser head.

"Hmm! *Oui*, Pierre!" The older man nodded emphatically. "Let me see. You have yourself and your friend, Andre – and his little brother. And, I am led to believe that we will have Andre's betrothed, Jeanne, as well. Now, I have my wife, Belle and I; and my nephew, Le Duc - another Pierre - and, of course, Isabeau, his wife – that you already know! That is eight all together!" Pierre nodded.

"I have some business acquaintances in both Savoy and in Geneva – so our coach - with my driver, a guard and the youth - and myself and the three ladies – with two outriders – riding ahead and behind – as you recommend," he pointed at Pierre, "could travel for a business and holiday visit."

Pierre nodded. "That is about as safe as we can get! I am not sure what the Dragoon traffic is going to be like on the road to Savoy – but we'll have to check with local sources – maybe the local Inns or markets?" Uncle Antoine nodded.

A door had shut loudly behind the men and they turned to find Isabeau leading her somewhat frustrated husband, Le Duc, by the hand.

"Your nephew has arrived, Uncle," she grinned a little mischievously, "He did not like being deserted in Lyon!" The younger Mallan did not appear to be a happy man.

" It was most ... inconvenient, Uncle – I got a message to 'stay with friends'; and then had to wait – without knowing what was happening – until your messenger arrived. Now," he waved his hands in the air with obvious disgust, "I am brought to this backwater of a town - while my companions are in Lyon!"

"Oh, come my husband!" Isabeau interrupted, "I am sure we can look after your entertainment needs – even in Vienne!" and she hugged his arm until he broke into a reluctant grin.

Then he nodded to Pierre: still lying on the grass. "So – what have you been discussing?" he grunted. His Uncle explained the basic plans and he nodded at each step of the way. Finally, he agreed. "That seems to be reasonable!" and sat on a stone wall with Isabeau perched next to him.

Pierre Jaubert rose and nodded to the older man.

"My friend, Andre and I have to do some further planning – with his little brother. So I will leave you and will keep you informed of any changes." They nodded and he smiled slightly at Isabeau; and went – with some apprehension – into the building in search of his friends.

*　　*　　*　　*　　*

3rd August 16887
At Vienne – near Lyon

"Did I not do well – on the road with you?"

"Are you throwing me aside – for a girl - for yourself?"

"Have I done something wrong?"

"Why? Why? Why?"

Both Andre and Pierre had been thoroughly punished by the tough and resilient little Theodore with a maturity way beyond his twelve years. There had been fierce tantrums – throwing himself on the bed in tears; yelling; sobbing – and finally, listening quietly and carefully to both sides of the negotiations. Finally it all was settled when he realized that the final decision was "his to make!"

"Be frank, be truthful with me, my brother! Has *Monsieur* De Puy said that it is either Jeanne or me – Theodore?" the boy was grim faced as he stared at both his older brother and Pierre. Andre shook his head forcefully.

"No, Theodore! He has asked for you – to be his heir! But, he has stated emphatically that – if you decide to not accept his offer – Jeanne can go with me to Geneva!"

"Really?" Theodore looked askance.

"Really! He admires you – and wants you – but he is not trading his daughter – for you!" Andre winced and added. "I feel really sorry for the man – he has been one of the most honourable and helpful men I have ever met – but he is also losing his daughter; and has only the little Josine to grow old with."

"Oh," the boy said thoughtfully, "does he have any … expectations … of me in that area?" His face reddened from the neck up as he spoke. Both Andre and Pierre exchanged smiles and raised both their eyebrows and their shoulders.

"Well," Pierre grinned slightly, "he did hope that … maybe one day you might even be married into the family?"

"Hmm," Theodore grunted thoughtfully, his eyes slightly glazed over as though pondering the possibility. "You know, she is very cute - and pretty – but would that be an … expectation?" Then he added, quickly, "but, don't get me wrong – I really like her – but … well … I am a little young to be thinking about things like that!"

"No, Theodore, I think all that is a long way down the road!" Andre reassured his little brother. "So, what do you think? Do you want more time?" The boy slowly nodded his head. It had been a long two hours of discussion and argument.

"No – I think we have talked about it enough!" He looked at the two older men seriously, "I will miss you – both – very much." His eyes shone a little with unshed tears.   "And I think *Monsieur* De Puy is one of the nicest older men I have ever met!" He frowned. "And, I really trust him!" Andre came forward and the two brothers embraced. Then when they parted, Pierre shook his hand and told him how much they would miss him on their next journeys. Theodore nodded his head and added:

"I would like to tell *Monsieur* De Puy, my decision. But," he added hurriedly, "I would like you both there – in case I have trouble saying what I have to say?"

Andre clapped his brother on the shoulder and assured him they would support him without taking control.   Theodore grinned in embarrassment.

Although the two older men were there to support him in his statement, there was no need for any action.   Both Andre and Pierre stood proudly by as a very solemn Theodore made his statement of intent to a very serious-faced De Puy. Hands were shaken all around. Jeanne hugged and "welcomed the boy to her family". Josine was in raptures about having a "big brother" – which she always wanted. Theodore gave her an excited hug but both Andre and Pierre felt that he looked more thoughtfully at the little girl than he had ever done before.

*   *   *   *   *

The mist was still filling the dips in the road as the convoy for Geneva set out from Vienne. They were on their way to the first "resting stop" halfway to the farming town of Port-de-Chéruy. Acting according to the strategy worked our by Andre and Pierre, a sentinel rider on a quick horse, Le Duc Mallan, would set off well in advance. He would ride to the top of the first ridge; look over; and if the road ahead was clear; he would wave, and the driver would drive the coach to that point while Mallan would ride on ahead to the next rise.

Andre, feeling that he had recovered enough to play a major role, was seated next to the driver and watching both forwards and backwards for signals. Inside the coach, Uncle Antoine rode with his wife, Belle, Isabeau and Jeanne – who was to act as "the young bride to be married in a weeks time" in Geneva. It had been decided that she too, would be a "niece" of her Uncle Antoine. Pierre Jaubert had been selected to ride the rearguard duty – watching for troops of Dragoons patrolling the road behind.

The action of the coach - at a negative signal - was to turn into the first farm road - which occurred often – and then look for a safe turning-round point. Once it was safe, the coach would return to the highway and continue.

Initially, many warning signals were received as single Dragoon messengers and small troops of militia were encountered. Sometimes an appropriate turning point was not found and the carriage would have to enter the farmyard and to the curiosity of the farming family would circle in their courtyard with Jeanne waving to them gaily.

After several tension-filled – but successful - hours of travel, young Mallan called a halt to the system.

"This system works well," he reported with some frustration, "but, despite all the precautions, I think we are being too fearful." He looked up and down the dusty road and shook his head. "They," he pointed to a vanishing pair of Dragoons, "Don't, seem to be in the least interested in either us riders – or the coach!" Pierre nodded grimly and reluctantly agreed with Mallan.

"The Dragoons don't seem to be vigilant – as they were last week. I am confused myself. Do you think something has changed?" he appealed to Uncle Antoine. The older man nodded - his brow furrowing.

"Maybe, Pierre, we should continue the system – but ignore the single riders. It will help us move along quicker. And," Uncle hesitated momentarily as he pondered, "When we arrive at Port-de-Chéruy, you will arrange to change horses, while I will go into the Inn and see what I can find out - in the way of gossip. Maybe something has changed!" The convoy moved out but began to make much better time as they began their new strategy.

*　　*　　*　　*　　*

The group sat on benches in the shade of an enormous oak tree next to the village Inn. Handing out a cool drink to all the ladies as they shook their long skirts to rid them of the dust, Pierre turned to see Uncle Antoine as he emerged from the village Inn door obviously struggling to keep his excitement contained.

"Our timing could not have been better for this trip, mon amis! But I bring mixed blessings! First, the good news!" He raised up his palms, "The word is out that his Majesty and his Ministers have decided that all those soldiers running about the countryside trying to seize 'us' heretics is too consuming and wasteful – of both money and manpower. So attention is to be concentrated on the borders – both with bordering countries – and at seaports." He frowned as he looked around the group, "So, we should be able to travel quickly and easily from here to Savoy – or maybe to the Swiss border?" His enthusiasm died at this point.

He continued: "But the bad news is … terrible! They have now set up a bounty system!" A gasp went around the group. "They will pay a rich cash prize to Dragoons - and the Militia - for heretics seized. And, even to ordinary people – like Inn owners – even farmers who turn in refugees! The word is that a wave of people have suddenly decided to join the Militia – with pictures of golden coin in their eyes - and dreams!"

"Hmm – terrible news!" commented Andre, "We used to worry about being reported by fervent Catholics – is it possible that we will not be able to trust even ordinary people now?" No one replied – all looked downcast.

"Well," said the young Mallan in an effort to cheer people up, "let's worry one day at a time. Let's speed on – doing what we have done so far - but move quickly towards the border into Savoy – how does everyone feel?" There were nods around the group.

"Ladies – let us get you into the carriage. My nephew, Le Duc – let us head up the riverbank for Sault-Brénaz; and then south to Groslée – maybe get there tonight?" Uncle Anthonie hurried them all along. Within minutes, the convoy was moving again. Le Duc Mallan rode again at the front and Pierre in the rearguard.

*   *   *   *   *

Jeanne, in her role as the future young bride, had completely charmed the innkeeper at the quaint old Inn at Groslée.

"I don't think he even noticed what the rest of us looked like!" grunted young Mallan as they helped the women into the carriage as the sun's rays crept into the valley and reflected off the nearby Rhone River.

Pierre grinned cheerfully. "Let us count it as a blessing!" And, reluctantly, the young husband grunted in assent.

Uncle Antoine was the final passenger to enter the coach. He smiled around at the waiting males. "The innkeeper suggests that we stay the night at the Abbey on Lac Bourget – Hautecombe Abbey. What do you think?"

"Who controls the Abbey? Is it Catholics?" Aunt Belle leaned out of the carriage window - a scared tone in her voice. Uncle Antoine nodded but smiled reassuringly. "Yes, my dear wife, but – there is a big difference. The Abbey is the chief burial place for the Dukes of Savoy!"

"Does that mean it is safe...?"

"I think so," he mused aloud, "The Kings of France are always trying to capture parts of Savoy ... but generally, the people of the Duchy, put their allegiance with the Dukes. That is, they may not agree with our views on religion – but they also like the peace they enjoy in Savoy!"

"*Monsieur* Mallan, you sound like you feel ... we can take a chance?" Pierre questioned, his face frowning as he tried to follow the older man's logic. Uncle Antoine did not reply immediately but looked serious. Then he nodded.

"I think it is as safe as we are going to find – the closer we get to the border with Switzerland. Yes," he added emphatically, "yes, I do!" Pierre nodded and looking around the group saw general nods in agreement.

"Everyone ready?" called out Pierre. A quick discussion led to a change in position. The young Mallan felt he was tired on constantly riding in the lead.

"You can worry today, Pierre!"

Pierre grinned and rode into the lead position. The convoy moved on down the dusty road towards Abbey Hautecombe on the largest lake in France – Lac Bourget.

In their enthusiasm for the next leg of the journey to safety, no one noticed a man standing in the morning shadows at the side of the stable partially concealed by his riding mule. He had pulled his hat well down over his eyes and as he looked up from the task of packing his saddlebags, he started in surprised recognition. But his eyes showed both surprise and fear.

*   *   *   *   *

5th August 1687
On the road to Geneva

The passengers had set a more leisurely pace as they left the Rhone River and rode through the green and rolling countryside with scattered farms and rutted roads. They wound their way up steep hillsides and raced down into the valleys. At times, they pulled the carriage off the road into a concealed glade at a high spot and enjoyed a picnic overlooking a vast valley while the horses recovered.

"I'll miss this lushness – this ... rough beauty," Pierre murmured to Andre as they chewed on a crusty chunk of bread. Andre nodded without speaking. They were close enough to see the sharp yellow eyes of a proud and vigilant eagle as it lazily floated over their heads and dived into the valley below. Pierre's nose twitched as the scent of crushed thyme rose up as he leaned forward.

"Pierre Jaubert – I did not know that you could ... think like a poet!" He jerked his head back as Isabeau's soft voice crept over his shoulder. She had quietly crossed the soft trodden foliage and now stood behind them. She met his startled gaze with a teasing smile. "I will miss it too," she said quietly in reassurance. He nodded and leaned forward to watch the progress of the lovely graceful bird.

Uncle Antoine joined them and pointed out the road ahead as it wove its way down the steep slope.

"There – we cross the Rhone River again. Then we follow it for some time before we have to go through a high pass and hug the cliff on the other side until we come to the Abbey. I hear it is quite an overpowering structure. It has a high tower and is built on the cliff face beside Lac Bourget."

"I hope they provide good food tonight at the Abbey. Not just ... bread and water!" The younger Mallan had joined them and put his arm around his wife's shoulders.

"Pierre, my husband! You are always thinking of food – lots of food!" Isabeau nudged him with her elbow. He squeezed her arm.

"You know, Isabeau, its not just food I'm always thinking of is it?"

"Le Duc!" She looked at him with a severe shocked stare. He shrugged and chuckled aloud. She heaved a sigh and turned and made her way back to the waiting carriage. He turned and watched her go. Then he turned to face the other men.

"Women! You never know how they are made! Tsk! Tsk!" He grinned at them and collapsed to look at the view. Andre met Pierre's glance and grimaced. Pierre nodded.

*   *   *   *   *

5th August 1687
On the road to Geneva – Abbey Hautecombe

Despite the magnificence of the scenery, the whole group was tired as the carriage paused at a vantagepoint and Pierre stood in his stirrups and pointed down the steep face. The carriage rocked to a stop and excited - but weary - faces appeared at the windows. The spectacular ancient Abbey was nestled on a long finger of rock as it stretched out into the azure blue of Lac Bourget. Its tall tower reared up like a middle finger surrounded by many ancient buildings.

"It's beautiful, isn't it?" As she poked her head around the leather curtains, Jeanne's voice was excited. "Is that where we spend the night?" Uncle Antoine nodded in the next window and added: "Although most people feel anyone living in Abbeys should lead Spartan lives, they certainly have a reputation for eating well!"

"Good! Good!" The young Mallan had ridden up behind the coach, "I am saddle weary – but nothing will interfere with my stomach!" And he rubbed his belly. Isabeau could be heard to snort inside the darkened coach.

"Well, down the hill to the Abbey!" Pierre called and spurred his horse down the steep slope.

*   *   *   *   *

5th August 1687
Lyon, France

Captain Benoit had deliberately had several of the lanterns removed and the table in front of him contained only a single glass of red wine and two flickering candles. He glanced over his shoulder at his Sergeant who – with another burly Dragoon – flanked him behind his chair.

"I want no smiles ... of welcome! I want him a little apprehensive! Perhaps ... a little scared!" The Sergeant nodded and then walked around the table and opened the door of the room. He said nothing but gestured to the man waiting in the dark outside to enter and closed the door behind him before returning to his supportive position in the shadows behind the Captain.

The Captain was drinking slowly from the wineglass and deliberately avoided eye contact with the visitor who stood, hat held before him, obviously ill at ease. The officer put the half-filled glass carefully on the table. Then he lifted his head and without any expression on his stern face, he stared at the man.

"*Mon Capitaine?*" His voice was hoarse and anxious. The officer nodded slowly and said nothing. Somewhere in the corridor behind him a board suddenly creaked and the man turned in fright and stared at the door. Then he jerked his head forward again. The stillness was frightening.

"You have ... information?" The officer's mouth hardly could be seen to move. The man jerked again and nodded eagerly. Even in the dim glow of the candle, beads of sweat could be seen gathered on his brow.

"*Oui, mon Capitaine!*" The man cleared his throat and coughed quickly behind his fist. "You..." he gestured with his hand towards the table, "Eh ... I know you are interested in the whereabouts of both Pierre Jaubert and the Mallan woman - Isabeau! *Non?*"

The Captain said nothing. But, as he reached for his glass and raised it slowly, his hand shook a little. With his free hand, he gently touched the inflamed scar on his cheek. Then he nodded slightly and raised his eyebrows.

"I know where they are!" The man's eyes had widened slightly with excitement. Then his brow furrowed with a worried frown as he corrected his words. "Well - I know where they were headed yesterday!" In the silence that followed, he looked less confident.

"And?" The man looked shocked and a little disconcerted. Then he stammered: *"mon Capitaine* – this man has wrecked my life! In my own village, I get no respect any more! On my hillside, I am treated like a traitor!"

"And?"

" I was able to help you before, *mon Capitaine!"* He gestured wildly with his free hand. "I would like to help the authorities ... the King ... in capturing these people!"

The Captain nodded his head slowly.

"But - for money? For the bounty? That ... is what you really want, isn't it?" The Captain's tone was soft – but cutting. The man looked stunned. His eyes seemed to glaze over. Then he shook his head fiercely.

"Non! mon Capitaine! You can keep the bounty! I just want revenge! Just pay my expenses – so that I can live a little better!"

The Captain smiled a little. "So, *Monsieur* Alexander Cramer of St. Martin – we meet again! You let us down once before, didn't you, Alexander – the little rat from the Luberon." Alexander's face had taken on an ashen hue – even in the poor lighting. He tried to speak in his defense but the officer waved him to silence.

"I remember well, *Monsieur* Cramer, you started your last task well. And, then you ran for cover! Not from a battle – but from," he leaned forward and looked up into the man's down-turned face, "from peeping at some little virgin!" Silence filled the room. Then the Captain grimaced a little and continued:

"Let me tell you, *Monsieur* Cramer, I don't allow myself to be betrayed twice! I will let you work with us - once more!" The officer waved a finger in front of Cramer, "But, let this be your final warning! If you fail me again – you will simply vanish, mon *ami!* Poof! You're gone – like magic! Not a threat, my dirty little rat – but a very solid promise!" Cramer stood silent staring at the floor.

"Well," Captain Benoit whispered softly, "nod your head, *Monsieur;* or leave with your life in your hands ... still!" Cramer nodded slowly and the Captain leant back satisfied.

"Well, tell me what you saw; and what you propose?"

And they talked for an hour – and the die was cast!

*   *   *   *   *

CHAPTER TWENTYFOUR

5th August 1687
Abbey Hautecombe, France

Uncle Antoine led his party of hungry travelers down the stone corridor following the garrulous guide – a young monk – who chattered along the way. A ravenous scent of lamb stew caught all their noses and smiles appeared on every face. Flickering firelight appeared in a doorway approaching on the left and the aroma increased. Pierre felt his mouth beginning to water and he grinned over Jeanne at his side to Andre who was holding her hand as they advanced.

"Hmm, smells good – my stomach grumbles at the scent!" Both Jeanne and Andre nodded eagerly.

But the monk led them past the doorway. As they hesitated, all the party peered inside. At many tables well-dressed groups of men and women – with some children – were eating and drinking wine with obvious enthusiasm. As they continued down the darkened corridor, Antoine tapped the monk on the shoulder.

"*Pardon*, Father ... but why do we not join them for dinner?" The monk's face creased in surprise. Then he smiled and nodded.

"*Pardon, Monsieur*, but they are all - of the Catholic faith!" He stopped and the group crowded around him in confusion. He peered around the faces.

"Did I make a mistake, *Monsieur Mallan*? I am so sorry – I thought you were of the Reformed faith?" He looked terribly concerned at his mistake. "Am I wrong, *Monsieur*?"

Uncle Antoine shook his head and reassured the father.

"No Father, you are correct. We are of the new faith! But are we not entitled to the ... same good food?" The monk looked up as though appealing to his God and smiled with relief.

"*Sacre Bleu!* I am so glad I have not erred! I do this duty so often that I sometimes forget to explain the differences, *Monsieur*." He pointed back at the firelit doorway. "We feel it would be safer if you were allowed to eat with your own kind, *Monsieur* – and the same food and wine!" He reassured the group; then turning, he waved his hand down the corridor and led them to the next arched doorway where similar smells of a lamb ragout issued.

"*Entrez mes amis!*" He waved his hand towards the doorway. "You will find many of your belief enjoying the good cooking and vintage wines of Hautecombe Abbey! Bless you all on your journey!"

Still somewhat shocked, Uncle Antoine followed a server who took them to several large uninhabited tables in the corner.

* * * * *

Following a bowl of wonderful vegetable soup with crusty rolls; they had a heaping plate of rich succulent lamb stew with potatoes done as *Gratin Savoyard* – thinly sliced and cooked in a beef broth with salt, pepper and local herbs between layers of alpine *Comté* cheese. This had been augmented by full-bodied local wines and followed by fresh apple tart from the local Abbey orchard and a variety of local cheeses.

Uncle Antoine had nodded recognition to several tables where he saw people he knew. Between the shoulders of the young Mallan and his Uncle, Pierre found himself watching the face of Isabeau sitting at the next table. Very contented, she was staring into space with a slight smile on her face.

She really is beautiful – in her own way, he thought, a strong face, determined to control her own life, the flickering firelight burnishing her dark brown smooth hair. Andre was so right, he mused guiltily, and I must stop this! She is a married woman!

He jerked with guilt as a heavy hand grasped each of his shoulders from behind holding him in his seat. Isabeau broke her meditation and a delighted smile filled her face. A low voice grunted in his ear.

"It seems they allow a high class of person into this establishment, don't they?" Pierre broke loose and spun round.

"Renard! My good cousin! What a surprise!" And, he sprang up to hug his relative with excitement. They broke apart finally to be greeted by applause not only from their tables but also from many of the other tables in the area. Renard raised his hand to acknowledge the recognition. Isabeau was at their sides. She grabbed Renard's arm and leaning forward hugged and kissed his cheek in the style of Provence.

"I am so pleased to see you ... again!" Then, in the firelit room, her face seemed suddenly flushed.

Renard bowed low and kissed her hand.

"*Madame Mallan*, it is always a pleasure to meet you again!" Then he went round the table greeting her husband - who was frowning with obvious confusion - and the Uncle and Aunt.

Hmm, thought Pierre, is there something I don't know about my cousin and ... Isabeau? Hmm!

After many glasses of wine and toasts all round, it was decided – with unanimous consent of the whole party – that Renard would join them in their – hopefully – final attempt to reach the safety of Switzerland.

After a hurried low-voiced discussion between Renard and Uncle Antoine, it was decided to leave early in the morning. As the crowd left the banqueting hall, Pierre managed to get alongside his cousin.

"Is there something I should know, cousin?" he whispered hoarsely. Renard grinned grimly and nodded. With a hand he restrained Pierre until the others were some distance down the darkened hallway.

"Pierre, I heard you had arrived late this afternoon – before me! But I also picked up some rumours that ... your party is being followed!"

"Again, Renard? Is it the Dragoons again?" Pierre was astounded. He had shepherded the party all the way from Vienne without trouble! He grunted in disgust.

"No – not Dragoons this time. But someone is being careful to watch without being seen by your party. However, he is careless to overlook the other travelers - who told me!"

"Like ... a spy?" Renard nodded slowly.

"Tomorrow, Uncle Mallan was going to suggest the trip up the lake north towards Switzerland. But, I warned him! And - suggested that we take the ... very first lake ferry over to the other side. That way we can watch to see who travels with us – or, at least leave the spy behind on the shore – for the next ferry! What do you think?" Pierre thought it over and then nodded emphatically.

"Good thinking, my wise old cousin!" He smacked Renard hard on the arm. "So, let's get to bed for an early start!" And the two cousins with arms round each other's shoulders strode down the corridor to catch the others on the stairs.

*   *   *   *   *

7th August 1687
Crossing Lac Bourget to Rumilly, France

Before the sun had made its way into the valley to bring light to Lac Bourget, the party – some with half-open eyes – helped move the carriage safely onto the little lake ferry on its first voyage that morning. Steam rose from the shining backs of the black horses to join the cloud of mist that covered the water. Especially shaped logs were jammed behind each wheel.

"This is a dangerous lake, *Monsieur!*" The operator of the ferry warned Uncle Antoine as he questioned the precautions, "It is notorious for its sudden squalls; and they say that hot water comes into the bottom of the lake from springs – making the currents volatile!" He turned and pointed to several locations on the lake. "Many boats have turned over – there, there and there!" Uncle nodded – now mollified somewhat.

Once the carriage was safely on board, Pierre was about to check the faces of the passengers waiting behind, when Renard nudged him in the back. He turned to see his cousin extending a colourful scarlet scarf to him.

"A gift, cousin?"

"No, Pierre, I am afraid not! Since you have been riding vanguard on the trip, it is expected – by anyone – that you will do the same this morning. Wrap this openly around your neck – with the end trailing in the breeze! That way you can be recognized – and remembered – by strangers on the road! Once we land on the other bank, most carriages will head north towards Annecy. I have suggested to Uncle Antoine that we avoid the main roads to Geneva. We can travel more safely – and hidden - through the countryside – through the village of Rumilly; then Frangy; along the old Chateau route until we get close to the border. I have heard that it is a safer place to cross – less traffic – therefore less Dragoons and militia!" Pierre nodded slowly memorizing the names of the villages.

"But why the scarf, cousin?"

"When we get to the other side we will take the winding road to the main highway. You and I will ride behind – as you have done before. Then on the highway north, I will lead the carriage off onto the Rumilly route. And you," he touched Pierre on the chest, "you will follow – not too close – another similar carriage heading north. If there is a spy – he will be galloping around the top of the lake. By the time he catches up, he will have to ask questions of people coming south. I would think the question would be 'Did you see a man riding a mule – with a red scarf around his neck'; and he will be following you – and the wrong carriage!"

"And I?" Renard grinned at him ruefully.

"Aha! So, when you reach Annecy, you find some way of losing the scarf – and the spy! Sneak out of Annecy and take the direct route from there to Rumilly. We will be waiting for you outside an Inn – it is said to be at the place where the two rivers meet – the Chéran and the Néphaz. All the local people will know the point!" He paused, "Can you remember the names of the torrents." Pierre nodded and repeated the names of the two streams.

"Maybe, I will find someone riding north – about my build – and give him a gift of a red scarf!"

"So – that's how you treat my gift, cousin!" Renard grinned and pushed Pierre towards the rear of the ferry.

Pierre, Andre and Renard had made a point of staying at the back of the ferry and carefully inspected the other passengers waiting to board. They recognized no one suspicious.

"If there is a spy, I don't think he would take the chance of boarding the ferry – not with us watching so carefully!" commented Renard under his breath and the other two nodded. They stood on guard until the boat left the shore.

Suddenly Andre pointed north.

"Look, you two! It looks like someone is in a hurry to ride around the end of the lake!" In the distance, a lone rider could be seen racing his horse up the road north leaving a dusty trail behind him. Grimly the two companions nodded.

*   *   *   *   *

7th August 1687
On Lac Bourget, France

Although the lake was reported to be volatile and dangerous, the journey that morning was calm and uneventful. The whole party enjoyed the trip looking back at Hautecombe Abbey nestling beneath the sharp peaks and azure sky as the mist cleared. While Andre stood with his arms around Jeanne holding her against the rail, Isabeau placed herself between the two cousins to watch the Abbey drift slowly away with her watchful husband balancing behind her resting a protective hand on her shoulder.

Once the carriage was safely delivered to the new shoreline, everyone climbed aboard or mounted their steeds - with the two cousins taking the vanguard position. The trip up the winding road to the main highway was a relief.

But here, Pierre waved adieu to his party with his cousin, Renard, riding in his place. As they vanished in a cloud of dust, he settled down on a rocky ledge while his mule grazed on nearby grass and checked the sun's position in the sky. He judged it would take about two to three hours for the suspected spy to round the end of the lake and return to the same highway. So, in an hour's time, he would seek out a similar carriage going north and begin to shadow it from a safe distance – making sure that his red scarf was clearly on display.

* * * * *

Pierre squinted into the late afternoon sun as he tried surreptitiously to check his rear for the person he felt was still tailing him. He then looked forward to the carriage ahead and waved to the driver in his usual manner signifying safe travel. For some time he recognized he was approaching the famous old town of Annecy - first spotting the old turreted Chateau high on the hill above the town overlooking Lac d'Annecy; and then the formidable Palais de l'Isle in the middle of what looked like a stream.

Suddenly he realized that the carriage ahead was slowing down as it crossed the canal and he slackened his pace as well. He gently nudged the mule to turn slowly in a circle in the road and under his hat brim he gazed down the road south. There he was! Moving rapidly through the cart traffic to slide his chestnut horse into the shadow of a livery stable. The stable boy ran out to hold the animal and backed away as the man shouted something at him. Hmm, thought Pierre with some pleasure. "That gave you away, you lousy rat!"

While the follower turned his back to cover his actions, Pierre took the opportunity to whip the scarf from this neck and move his mule quickly into the canal traffic. Once hidden from his nemesis, he surprised the mule by urging her into a canter and using the middle of the road, moved swiftly through the center of Annecy. When he judged - from the traffic - that he was safely on the road - heading north; he searched passing travelers until he found a man roughly his age and build with a similar hat. He rode up alongside and grinned in a friendly manner.

"Heading north, are you?" The man returned the smile with some curiosity and nodded.

"I'm heading home to a suspicious wife, myself," he said with another guilty grin, "I got this from my ... lover." And he jerked off the scarlet scarf and proffered it to the rider. "Here, you take it! I can't go home with it anyway!"

Surprised, the rider took it and grinned back in understanding.

"That's the wages for sinning, I suppose! Certainly – and thank you, *Monsieur.* I shall bless you as I ride home!" Turning his mule quickly and waving to the still surprised rider, Pierre urged his mule into a side alley. From his darkened cover, he watched the red-scarfed rider canter up the road north. He chuckled several minutes later as he saw a rider on a chestnut horse race by with his face covered – to protect him from the dust – and settle into a steady trot a safe distance from his quarry.

Quickly, Pierre nudged his mule onto the roadway again heading south and looking for a crossroads – and the route that would take him back to Rumilly.

*   *   *   *   *

7th August 1687
Rumilly, France

It was late in the evening when Pierre rode wearily into the quaint village of Rumilly. A couple of questions to a local farmer took him to the site where the two fierce streams broiled together as they met. There leaning against the bridge was his cousin, chewing a fresh apple.

"It's my third apple while I waited! Welcome, cousin, did it go as planned?"

Pierre dismounted before he replied.

"*Oui*, my wise cousin! Exactly as we discussed. Right now, our rat will have confronted some poor peasant on his way home and found that he is following another fake fox!" He looked around. "And, do you think we can still get some late dinner for a tired traveler?" Renard's white teeth glinted in the moonlight as he grinned.

"We have asked the Innkeeper next to the old Church to keep your dinner hot! They make a wonderful white wine here! Come; let's lead that poor animal to the stable.

*   *   *   *   *

7th August 1687
Annecy, Duchy of Savoy

The invitation for an update of events had been terse and formal. As Captain Benoit read the unexpected missive, he felt his stomach plunge followed by a sharp pain in his chest. Sudden sweating warned the officer of an approaching disaster. *Mon Dieu*, will I never be left in peace? He half crumpled the parchment as a second spasm hit his guts.

When "The Man" beckoned, you went! Benoit's mind raced over the past couple of months – what did he have to report that ... was positive – in any way? Was there something The Man knew that he did not? Is there someone in his troop of Dragoons that is leaking vital material to The Man? Pictures of his victims flashed through his racing mind – the sheep farmer, Jaubert? His reddened cheek felt more sensitive. That teasing little bitch of a bride from St. Martin on the Luberon? Her wealthy Uncle? Or, was it the elusive Renard – who is still popping up in a variety of villages? *Sacre bleu*, there is little positive to say on any of them – except perhaps embellishing the antics of his informer – that Huguenot Rat?

Enough! You must appear to be confident – not boastful – just secretive – but sure. Brush off any doubts! You have a mission – you are confident that your results will be satisfactory – even though they may still take a while to become certain!

The Captain wiped the ring of sweat from his brow with his lace-edged handkerchief and then looked at the damp rag with disgust. It would never do to flourish a disgustingly wet cloth in front of The Man!

"Sergent! I need another fresh handkerchief – maybe two? And ... we are going up the hill to the Chateau – for a consultation! Get my carriage ready!" The Sergeant ducked around the corner in response.

"Chateau?" He held a flagon of wine and looked confused. He peered at his Captain with the crumpled message in his hand. "Is it ... 'TheMan', mon Capitaine?"

"None of your damn business, Sergent! In Annecy, there is only one Chateau worth the title! Get moving!"

The Sergeant nodded briskly and vanished from sight. What I don't need is further questions, winced Benoit and he rubbed his infected cheek carefully; I have enough unanswered questions myself!

*   *   *   *   *

The appointment room was vast and with little in the way of furniture – mainly the huge carved desk cleared of all material except a single open notebook – looking like a diary – and a quill and ink holder. The illumination provided by only two candles cast an eerie dim light adding to the bitter tensions within the Captain.

Because there were no other chairs, he now stood, plumed hat in hand as the dark figure before him studied the details in the book. Benoit felt that somehow entry into the presence of The Man had reduced his size! It's the old waiting game, isn't it, he thought grimly. Be patient; keep control; no fluster; well thought-out responses. Let The Man play the cards!

The silence continued and despite his patience, the Captain felt his breathing quickening and sweat running down his spine. To maintain control, he carefully tugged the fresh lace-edged handkerchief from his right sleeve and gently brushed the tip of his nose.

"Well, mon Capitaine?" The voice was soft, ominous and paper-thin – and stopped abruptly.

"Monsieur?" The Captain kept his voice soft, terse and controlled – especially polite!

"Hmm! Don't play games with me, Capitaine!" The voice was low, harsh and as sharp as a sword blade. "Don't forget, you stupid swine, that ... I am the Master of game-playing! To live with ... his Majesty, requires a ... legion of games – every day – every hour!" The Captain stood speechless – anything he said would be disastrous!

"Bon! In ... moments like this ... it is better to be silent – than mumbling trivial nothings!" A short silence. Then:

"Report – on them all!"

Benoit reported. He kept it short and concise. No elaboration. Reports that the sheep farmer, Jaubert, had joined up with the rich trader, Mallan - and his nephew. And his "bitch" of a wife. They were traveling together. They had entered Annecy sometime today. And, a special agent was seeking their location. A man, suspected of being the outlaw, "the Fox" was now also with them. Here he stopped! Don't say too much or be too sure! Perhaps The Man knew something he did not!

"All that deadly ability ... in one basket, *Capitaine*? Is that wise?" The Captain mused - deliberately keeping a lid on the panic he felt was around the corner. Keep it positive – no negatives – but no reassurances!

"You are correct, *Monsieur*! A lot of deadly abilities gathered in one basket – but also - an opportunity to sweep them up in one blow – if it is handled right." Then he went on to try to extend his options. "You did promise - did you not – that I may have to follow them out of the country – if necessary?

"Hmm! I do not need a lecture to remind me of my promises, *Capitaine*! You know that! You and I have a deal! No need to remind me!" Quietness followed – and Benoit waited patiently – concentrating on his breathing. Then The Man continued.

"This special Agent? My reports tell me you have used him before – have you not?" Without waiting for a response, the voice continued. "And, he failed before – did he not?" The Captain simply nodded and waited. It was safer that way!

"If he ... fails again?" Silence. The Captain knew that he was expected to somehow promise something – anything!

"I have warned him, *Monsieur*! There is no doubt in his mind of the consequences of failure!" Silence. The Captain continued softly. "But...?"

"But?"

"I would be foolish if I said that I would destroy him immediately..."

"Why, *Capitaine*...?" The words crept along the floor like flaming brandy.

"Because, *Monsieur*, sometimes even - almost-dead rats - can be much more useful in tough situations!" An ominous chuckle broke out from the other side of the table. "Oh, *Capitaine*, you are learning ... so well!" The Captain waited – and was relieved at the change in tone and detail.

"I don't need to tell you, *mon Capitaine*, that your heavy use of the Dragoons on the villages of the Luberon – and in all of Provence – have had successful results. His Majesty is ... extremely pleased! And, I have given a lot of credit to you, Hugo!"

The officer unconsciously let out a sharp telltale breath – and immediately regretted it.

"Hmm! Don't get comfortable, *mon Capitaine*! Despite the 'Dragonades' success - despite the enormous wave of abjurations! It would still be useful and dramatic if a number of important victims were publicly humiliated in their villages, *non*?" The officer simply nodded – he understood the message!

"So – enough, *mon Capitaine*! You have a job to do! You have the tools to carry out the task! My aide – outside – will see that you have a large - generous - supply of freshly minted gold ducats – from Vienna! I don't have to remind you, *mon Capitaine*, that they are not traceable to Versailles! That - this is a ... personal crusade? Of your own!" The Man was now peering intensely at the officer.

The Captain nodded firmly. He understood. And, so did The Man. The officer bowed; stepped back and replaced his plumed hat; bowed again without making eye contact; turned and silently left the room. The Man's chuckle followed him out as the door closed.

* * * * *

8th August 1687
Annecy, Duchy of Savoy

Cramer stood – in pain – before the door of the Captain's carriage. He could not raise his head to meet the officer's steady accusing gaze.

For the first time in his life, he did not know what to say.

He could feel the presence of the Sergeant right behind him. Could hear him breathing – quicker! It was the end? Like this? Feeling stupid – instead of confident?

"Well, *Monsieur* Cramer?" The Captain's voice was soft – but deadly. A dozen excuses rose to his mind. Where – how – to begin? The Captain said nothing – sat there waiting. At last...

"*Mon Capitaine*, it was ... not my fault!"

"What was not ... your fault?"

"*Mon Capitaine*, I have followed the group – of scum – from Lyon ... to the Abbey. I never let them out of my sight!" His voice was desperate – it was his life!

"And?"

"I never let them see me – never! But they surprised me! They took the little Ferry across the lake. I was shocked! Why did they not just ride north?" But the Captain said nothing – he stared. Cramer stumbled onward.

"*Mon Capitaine* – I killed a horse in the ride around the lake!" The Captain nodded and commented:

"So – you were paid for the dead horse. Carry on!"

"I followed the sheep farmer, Jaubert, all the way into Annecy. I swear ... he never saw me! He was easy to follow – so stupid, I thought!"

"Easy?"

"*Oui, mon Capitaine*! He wore a red scarf around his neck. I saw him at the canal at the entrance to Annecy..." The voice of the Captain interrupted his flow.

"Very convenient of him, wasn't it - to wear a colourful scarf?" Cramer's eyes narrowed as the truth struck him.

"Hmm! That ... was stupid of me, *mon Capitaine*!" He struck the side of the carriage with his closed fist in frustration. "Stupid, Stupid!"

"Yes, *Monsieur* Cramer! Very stupid! And...". The informer was silent; his eyes screwed up in thought and frowning. Then he continued:

"It was ... definitely Jaubert! All the way to Annecy! But when he moved in the center of the town, I raced after him and the carriage."

"And, ... what went wrong, *Monsieur* Cramer?" Cramer disliked when the Captain talked softly – and politely! It hinted of danger – to come.

Cramer then disclosed with obvious frustration his trailing of the red scarf out onto the road north.

He reported how the rider had stopped to buy an apple from a wayside stall – and how he had suddenly realized that this was not his target! How he had approached the rider – in anger – about a "stolen scarf". How the mysterious rider had explained having the scarf; and how Cramer had rushed back and searched all the inns and stables in Annecy – without success. He now stood, his face flushed with shame and frustration.

Unseen by Cramer, the Captain smiled slightly. A half-dead rat was more use to him than a dead informer was!

"And, *Monsieur* Cramer – what are your thoughts! Where are they?" Cramer jerked his head up in surprise and he stared at the officer with wide eyes.

"Eh, they must be heading north – that is the only way they will escape! But, they must be using a different route!"

"And ... which route?" The "Rat" stood silent while options raced through his mind desperately seeking an alternative to his promised death.

"The only option is ... they could be headed up the route through Rumilly ... and Frangy! It is much less traveled and easier to check with local inns." He desperately looked up at the Captain. "I could be with them by tomorrow at noon!" The officer simply stared at him; then nodded quietly.

"Either you are right, is that not so, *Monsieur* Cramer – or you are wrong – and dead! Gone forever, is that not so, *Monsieur*?" Cramer took a deep breath and nodded. It was clear in his mind that there were no alternatives.

"Go, *Monsieur* Cramer!" The Captain gestured west with his index finger. "We will follow you with a large troop of Dragoons!"

Then he added quietly: "If you are right, there is something that they don't know – and you don't know either, *Monsieur* Cramer – but at the top of that route is a large encampment of Dragoons! They will be walking into Hell – instead of Heaven!" Suddenly, Cramer's face lightened and he broke into a surprising grin - of relief.

"What a lovely thought, *mon Capitaine* – what a lovely thought!" As he turned to run to his horse, the Captain added quickly:

"*Monsieur* Cramer! I think you should arrange to take a couple of Dragoons with you!" Cramer's smile vanished.

"You don't trust me ... any more, Captain?" The officer rolled his eyes skyward, apparently seeking understanding from some greater being.

"Maybe, *Monsieur* Cramer! But my main reason is that – if you find them – you can keep me informed at all times - without losing them again! Right?"

Cramer regained his smile and nodded emphatically.

Then he spun round; mounted and rode over to a group of Dragoons lounging on their horses. A few words and the three riders vanished in a cloud of dust.

*   *   *   *   *

8th August 1687
On the road to Geneva - Chaumont

Breakfast turned into a celebration when Renard told Pierre's story of misleading the spy and sending him off on a wild goose chase. Everyone applauded enthusiastically and Pierre found himself flushing with embarrassment. To re-gain some personal control, he suggested an early start that would make the traveling easier for both the horses and the carriages occupants.

"It's amazing how much less traffic – and soldiers – we are finding on this route!" Isabeau's husband waxed enthusiastically. "Maybe a courier every couple of hours. Even the people driving the carts are cheerful and helpful." Everyone nodded.

However, they still kept their security system in use – continually checking backwards and forwards by the outriders. However, the miles passed quickly and by noon they recognized Frangy when they passed the reported picturesque ruins of an old chateau. They stopped for a lunch break and enjoyed the famous white wine from this enclave.

It was early in the afternoon when they pulled into the village of Minzier to have a carriage wheel checked by the local blacksmith – who also ran the small livery stable. While the repair was being carried out, the group decided to sample the local wine at the small Inn.

Pierre was the last to enter the Inn when the Innkeeper touched him on the arm and nodded his head away from the door. Puzzled, Pierre turned and faced the grizzled and gray bearded portly man.

"*Monsieur* – I question whether ... you are ... of the reformed faith?" He looked a little uncomfortable.

"Why do you wish to know, *Monsieur*?" Pierre was cautious.

"Because we," the man gestured towards a small but spacious stone barn behind the building, "have a party of 'believers' resting in there – and the woman ... is ill! I think ... they could use some help!"

Pierre raised his eyebrows. Then he nodded.

"Thank you, *Monsieur!* I have a lady inside who is experienced in dealing with sickness!"

He turned and entered the inn; had a quiet talk with Isabeau; and the two of them left the Inn to check on the barn.

As Pierre reached for the door handle, Isabeau gasped behind him. Pierre stopped and turned in confusion. Her eyes were closed and she was breathing heavily – her face had whitened.

"Isabeau," he whispered, "is there something wrong? Are you alright?" As she slowly opened her eyes he sensed pain in them. She

293

exhaled and shook herself. Then she straightened up and waved him in the direction of the door.

However, now mystified and uncomfortable, he was more cautious. He nodded for her to stand well to the side of the door as he entered. He pushed the door open gingerly but backed up quickly as a man rose from the shadows and came quickly to the doorway.

Before his vision was clear, the man greeted him with both relief and amazement.

"Jaubert, Pierre Jaubert – is it not?" Pierre pushed the door wider to allow the sunlight to illuminate the greeter. Then he sighed with obvious relief.

"Jourdan, Paul ... from Cabrieries d'Aigues? - On the Luberon! " The young man nodded extending his hand, which Pierre grasped. "Pierre, you have others here too?" Jordan nodded. "Come in and greet them all!"

Pierre also met Paul's cousin, Pierre Jourdan, Pierre La Grange, Louis Corbon – all from Cabrieries d'Aigues on the Luberon. Also young Pelanchon from Sivergues in Provence.

Soon Pierre was surrounded and hands were shaken all around. Suddenly, he remembered that Isabeau was still waiting outside and leaned out to call her in.

"I expect you all know, Isabeau Richarde – now the wife of Pierre Mallan? All nodded and greetings were exchanged.

"I understand that you have a woman – who is ill?" Isabeau queried. They all nodded. An older man stepped forward and explained.

"I do not know whether you remember meeting me. I am Pierre Goiraud, son of Jacques from Cabrieries." His face saddened. "My wife, Francoise Roux, lost our child, Jacques, after he was born. She has had trouble recovering – from both the birth and the death! And, then we also had to leave our village and flee!" Isabeau's face lost some of her normal vitality. She nodded.

"Let me meet your sick wife, *Monsieur*."

Goiraud led the way into the rear of the darkened building. In the back of the building, a large trapdoor in the roof had been propped open allowing a huge amount of sunlight to pour in.

A slim young woman was resting on a large pile of hay huddled beneath a heavy cover. The weak smile on her face could not hide the extent of the sadness.

She raised her hand in greeting but did not speak. Isabeau took her hand and held it. Then she turned to the watching men.

"Pierre, could you leave us for a while. Perhaps ... you could send Jeanne out to stay with us – she can help me!" Everyone nodded and left the building. Inside, Pierre sent Jeanne out to help; and then bought a glass of wine for all their new friends.

Pierre cautiously questioned them on their plans for escape.

"We headed this way, Pierre, because we were told that there is a skilled guide in the Frangy area who has developed a successful escape route over the border." explained Goiraud in a hoarse whisper. "Because he is a heretic like us, we can surely trust him!"

"Do you know his name?" Pierre Mallan leaned forward to join the discussion.

"No. And, he keeps his face covered at all times – for his own protection, they say!" Goiraud assured them. "However, many groups are reported to have crossed the border."

"Have they received messages back about their successful arrival in Geneva?" Renard entered the conversation as well.

"Well, not that I know of. Why do you ask? Do you think there is something wrong?" Goiraud was puzzled and concerned.

"Hmm!" was all Renard said and he raised his eyebrows cynically. "There is a lot of bounty money being tossed around, you know!" He sounded cautious.

"Well, we have arrangements to meet with him tomorrow evening at a small Inn in Frangy. He collects a small fee per person – so he is not doing it for that money!" Goiraud reassured the group. Renard looked at Pierre and nodded.

"It certainly would not harm us to listen to the plan. We really haven't developed a strategy yet ourselves, have we?" Pierre pondered and then nodded.

"There was a slightly bigger inn back down the road a mile or two at ... was it Chaumont? We could stay there and look into the escape route."

Pierre agreed, "I will discuss it with our Uncle Antoine." And, he turned and joined the Uncle who was sitting with his wife in the sunlight.

*   *   *   *   *

8th August 1687
On the road to Geneva - Chaumont

A short while later, Isabeau and Jeanne returned to the rest of the party enjoying the warmth of the alpine sunshine outside the Inn.

"I have brewed a strong tisane from my own supply of herbs and added some of the local herbs growing outside the barn. I have told her she must rest as much as possible. Also, take a cup of the mixture every hour for the next couple of days – and longer if she needs it. Her husband will ensure that she has a lot of soup as well. Otherwise," she shrugged a little sadly, "just time will have to cure her! What a sad situation!" and they all nodded solemnly.

Uncle updated her on the plans to return to the last village and the plans to review the new escape plan. Then everyone joined the convoy again and the repaired carriage turned before the Inn to move down the road.

*   *   *   *   *

Cramer urged his horse back into the darkness of the woods and dismounted hurriedly while calling hoarsely to the two Dragoons.

"Dismount, quickly! And, hold your horse's noses. For some unknown reason, they are returning down the road from Minzier. We must keep our horses from neighing or snorting until they are safely past!"

Though the horses shuffled a little in consternation, the watching party was quiet as the carriage and riders passed safely. Then, from a safe distance behind, they shadowed the convoy until it reached Chaumont where they apparently settled for the evening.

"*Bien!*" Cramer whispered softly to one of the Dragoons: "Ride back down the road until you can contact *Capitaine* Benoit. Inform him that we have successfully located both the carriage and its riders – the Mallans, the Jauberts – both the cousins; and especially, the bride!" The Dragoon looked confused. "Don't worry, the *Capitaine* will understand!" The Dragoon shrugged; repeated the instructions successfully; and mounting, rode out in a cloud of dust.

Turning to the second Dragoon, Cramer handed him some money with instructions to arrange accommodation for himself - only - at the inn: "keep his eyes open and his mouth shut!"

"I have other plans for this evening!" he tersely reported "But, I will make contact with you early tomorrow – in the stable!" The Dragoon looked relieved and rode out of the trees and down the road.

*　　*　　*　　*　　*

CHAPTER TWENTYFIVE

"Look, *Monsieur* Goiraud, it sounds, because of your wife's illness, you need to use this Guide to get you and your party over the border quickly?" Renard waved a finger at Pierre Goiraud as they stood outside the village livery stable at the Chaumont. "We," he gestured to the two Pierres – Jaubert and Le Duc Mallan - standing beside him, "feel a little more wary – at this moment! So, we think you should negotiate on behalf of your group of five persons! But, without using names, you could also check out, with the Guide, about an additional eight persons in the escape party? How does that sound?" Goiraud nodded slowly as he mentally added up the figures.

"If you need to be more specific, you could say – from other villages of the Luberon?" The man from Cabrieries was more satisfied with this and nodded eagerly.

"Are you going to be there as well?" Renard looked at his cousin with raised eyebrows and, receiving no response, shook his head.

"No, well ... we are not sure yet! Probably not!" Goiraud looked disappointed but nodded.

Renard shook Goiraud's hand and wished him good luck and they watched as he and his partner, Pierre Jourdan, rode off under the starry sky.

"Well?" Renard grinned at his companions. They both grinned back and raced each other to saddle their animals in the stable.

*   *   *   *   *

"There are two entrances to the inn, Renard." After shadowing the two men from Cabrieries at a safe distance, the companions had waited until they entered the Inn at Frangy. After briefly separating to check the building out, they had regrouped in the darkness of the livery stable.

"I thought there might be! They said he meets his customers wearing a mask of some kind - for safety sake. But I'll bet he does not ride that way! So we need to watch from a close enough spot – without being seen ourselves." After a brief discussion, Renard crossed the road to be opposite the main entry – standing in ornamental shrubs outside an ancient home. The two Pierres took the side entrance – one each in the deep shadows on either side of the livery stable.

They did not have long to wait. Regular customers were arriving every few minutes – often in pairs – laughing and gossiping as they went. Then, Pierre was taken by surprise as two figures rode up together stopping in the shadows at the entry to the stable. A flash of moonlight on a shiny scabbard of a sword caught his eye. A Dragoon! He found himself holding his breath.

The brief conversation was low and muffled. Then the civilian swung to the ground. He handed the reins to the soldier and stood watching where the horse would be held. The Dragoon trotted both horses down the alley to stop at the rear of the next building. But, Pierre was surprised when the Dragoon remained mounted. Ready for a quick retreat?

Then the man moved briefly out into the moonlight before pulling his scarf up over his face. Pierre's quick intake of breath made the man turn sharply and peer around the darkened area. Pierre froze and held his breath. The masked man loosened his sword in its scabbard as he pulled his hat down over his forehead. His hand resting on the sword's hilt, he kept staring and moving his gaze slowly to cover the whole area.

Pierre never moved a muscle! And he was pleased that he had leaned close to an old dark pillar that concealed most of his body. Eventually, the man walked from shadow to shadow until he stood beside the side door. Then with a final glance backward, he entered quickly.

Mon Dieu, Pierre breathed out finally. He felt his heart racing and struggled to regain control. Then, as he was about to leave his hiding spot, the side door opened and the man peered out into the darkness. Pierre closed his eyes and waited. Be careful, Pierre – this scoundrel is very careful – freeze and wait!

Eventually, the door closed and Pierre made his way cautiously to the opposite end of the stable. Mallan sniffed quietly and moved to his side.

"Did you see him, Mallan?"

"I saw him – but not clearly! He is ... cautious, isn't he?" Pierre nodded.

"Did you recognize him?" Mallan shook his head. Pierre gripped his arm.

"Let's join Renard!" He whispered hoarsely and Mallan followed him in the shadows until they had reached the front of the Inn. Waiting for several customers to start a conversation, they crossed behind them and stood outside the old house. They never saw his cousin approach, until he was right behind them.

"*Mon Dieu,* Renard – you scare the hell out of me!" complained Mallan with a chuckle.

"*Bon!* I like that!" Renard gripped their arms, "What did you see?" Pierre expelled a snort of breath he had not been aware that he was holding.

"You are not going to like this, Renard. The masked man is our old friend, Cramer, the traitor from St. Martin!" Both Renard and Mallan swore aloud.

"Well, thank God we didn't go in! Forewarned is fore-armed!" grunted Renard.

Mallan shook his head in disgust. "What do we do now? Run for it?"

All the men were silent for a short while. Then Renard made a decision.

"Let's ride home – right now - and think along the way. Despite all Goiraud's enthusiasm, it probably is nothing but a damn trap! Let's ride!" They all mounted up and found themselves riding hard for Chaumont. Soon, Pierre yelled to them to slow down and they stopped to allow the horses to recover before riding the rest of the way in a gentle canter.

*   *   *   *   *

9th August 1687
Near the Swiss border - Chaumont

"There are few lights showing! It looks like all are abed." The three travelers sat in their saddles observing the inn at Chaumont.

"I think we should wait for the return of Goiraud and Jourdan in the dining area. We need to listen to his story – and without giving our information until he has thoroughly laid out the plan. What do you think?" Renard grimaced at his companions.

Pierre nodded but Le Duc looked up at his bedroom shutters before he reluctantly nodded. Lucky man thought Pierre; and for the first time in a long while, he recognized a deep need for a close partner. After they had prepared their horses for the night, they sat and discussed their dilemma.

*   *   *   *   *

After midnight, 10th August 1687
Near the Swiss border - Chaumont

About another hour passed slowly until they heard the sound of hoof beats. They all moved out to the open doorway to alert the men to their presence.

Jourdan was the first to dismount - his face already alive with enthusiasm.

"I'm sorry you were not there to meet with the Guide. He seems to really know his way around!" Pierre nodded and clapped him on his shoulder.

"Come on in and sit. Tell us all about it!" Both men hitched their horses to posts and followed the group into the inn.

Jourdan was the most verbose as he ran through the plan with Goiraud adding additional pieces.

The escape party would travel by horse and mule to the crossroads to the village of Vers – on the right. However, they would take the turn to the left. About a mile down the road, the Guide would meet them at the roadside. He had located a ravine that ran parallel to the main road all the way to the border. It was a safe trail – not large enough for a cart but well concealed by trees and foliage.

The Guide had insisted that the last mile be traveled most carefully so as not to alert any border guards. Scouts would go on ahead and signal when the border crossing was clear. Very early in the morning, long portions of the border were covered by only single guards. Once the guard had safely moved away from the pathway, a large number of riders could storm across. Sometimes the guide was able to bribe a guard to look the other way. But with the larger bounties now being paid, this was less possible.

"We told the Guide that we may have a larger party – including women – from the villages of La Motte and St. Martin," reported Goiraud with a smile. "He seemed to be pleased at that point." He paused and frowned. "Actually, I was surprised that he charged so little! With the amount of risk involved, I would have been willing to pay much more!"

The three friends listened intently to the whole announcement nodding their heads as they concentrated.

"Well, Pierre, Renard, what do you think?" Pierre winced at the degree of excitement in Jourdan's voice. It's a pity we have to disappoint him, he thought. He turned to look at his companions and Renard gestured with his finger to encourage him to speak. Pierre nodded and spoke with some regret obvious in voice.

"Paul Jourdan – I'm afraid we need ... to confess a little!"

"Confess! I don't understand! What have you done?" The young man was confused.

"Steady, Jourdan! I must admit," he turned and gestured at his companions, "we were a little more skeptical about the ambitions of someone like your Guide! So, after you rode out tonight to the meeting..." and he went on to outline their actions - and their frightening discoveries.

Both of the listeners' faces went through changes of emotions – confusion to shock; to frustration; to anger; and to horror. Jourdan's face was white with fear at the end of the disclosure.

"*Mon Dieu*, what have we done! Are we all at risk – right now!" He clenched and unclenched his hands in dismay and anger.

"No, Jourdan!" Renard spoke up. "As long as Cramer feels he has you – and us – on his fishing line, he will be patient! If we are correct in our assumption that he is the traitor – then he will want as many fish on his hook as possible. We must not scare him off."

"In fact," Pierre spoke up, "as long as we keep him feeling secure, we can make our own plans!" He put his hand on top of Jourdan's fists and squeezed them tight. "We are sorry to disappoint you – in this manner – really! But, at least we now know!" Jourdan reluctantly nodded and grimaced. Goiraud nodded his head as well and sighed.

"Right now, I think we all should get some sleep. But – at daybreak, we should divide up into two parties – and get an understanding of the countryside and what lies ahead – carefully!" Renard suggested, "Two of you go and inspect the trail – but not too far! You don't want to frighten Cramer – who probably will be watching you! Then come back and meet with your party to discuss and relax. We," he gestured to his friends, "will tell the landlord that we will be staying for another couple of days. But we will take the carriage and drive up the same road to survey the route. We will plan for a picnic for our group – look like we are celebrating and having fun! That should keep Cramer satisfied!"

"Yes, I agree too," Mallan added, "We need time to develop a better plan – and I need to get to bed!" He grinned and quietly loped up the stairs to his bedroom. The men solemnly shook hands and retired for the night.

*   *   *   *   *

10th August 1687
Near the Swiss border - Chaumont

It was obvious, despite their plans for a picnic, that the carriage group was in a somber mood. The discovery of the traitor, Cramer, in their territory had dampened most spirits.

As she rode in the carriage, Isabeau had also been mulling over her shameful "freezing" at the barn door and was upset she had confused Pierre with her peculiar behaviours – without being able to explain to him. She shook her head and twisted her mouth in disgust.

"Something wrong, Isabeau?" Belle's concern frightened her. She shook her head and blamed it on Cramer's arrival. Jeanne was being educated on the complicated background and plans, as the carriage approached the crossroads and slowed down. Isabeau stopped her explanation and peered out of the window.

In the midst of the crossroads a large open cart was leaning at a crazy angle. It was evident that a wheel had been damaged. Standing with her back to the carriage was a large woman wearing a feather-plumed mauve hat. Her face, as she turned, was tearstained and frustrated. Up the road ahead, Isabeau's Le Duc had ridden past without stopping. Why doesn't he care about the problems of other people, worried Isabeau in anger? He should be able to see that the lady needed help?

Uncle Antoine opened the door and was stepping down from the carriage as Pierre Jaubert rode up in a cloud of dust.

"Madame, bonjour! Can we be of assistance?" The lady, who introduced herself as Madame Roche, widow of Vers – the village down the road to the right – was appreciative of the offer but unsure of what they could do to help.

301

Pierre pointed out that the iron band holding the wheel together had broken – but could be fixed by any blacksmith.

"For shame!" she cried. "My husband, who has been taken by God two years ago, could have fixed it himself. He was good at blacksmith work, you know!" she told the watchers. But the nearest blacksmith is ... way down in Frangy! So..." And she held up her hands in confusion.

"Well, if you have the right equipment, I think I could fix the wheel. Do you live far from here?" Pierre offered. She was overjoyed and explained that she lived on her husband's farm several miles down the road to Vers.

"Pierre!" Andre, who had been riding on the top of the carriage, called out. When Pierre looked up, Andre pointed to an old evidently abandoned farm on the corner of the crossroads. There standing next to the disheveled barn was an old two-wheeled cart,

A quick discussion with the widow revealed that the owner, Shabbe, had had to abandon his small farm because of a relative's death in Lyon and had been gone for several years.

"He plans to come back, you know! He sent a message that he might return by the end of this year." *Madame Roche* explained that she was "keeping an eye on the farm for him".

"Pierre, maybe you can 'borrow' a wheel from his cart – to get the lady home." Renard added his ideas. Reassuring *Madame Roche* they would return the borrowed wheel, the three riders crossed the grass field and using cut firewood and brute force they left the cart balanced on a temporary platform. Then they returned with the borrowed wheel together with a long pole to raise the damaged vehicle and within minutes, the wagon was repaired temporarily – although the new wheel was slightly larger that the other three wheels.

"*Madame*, if you like, I will drive your lop-sided cart while you ride in the carriage?" Renard offered with a gallant smile.

"Oh, you are all so helpful! And, they tell me you were going on a picnic. What a shame to mess up your day!"

So, the convoy turned and rolled it's awkward way down the road towards Vers.

Madame Roche, from the window of the carriage, after several miles directed them to turn into an opening in a grove of large oak trees and the road wound down to the edge of a small fresh stream where her farm lay.

Aided by Renard – who claimed he was an "idea man" while his cousin, Pierre was the artisan – they soon had the fires going and using the antiquated equipment of the deceased Roche, Pierre soon had repaired and replaced the damaged wheel.

"I didn't know you could do things like that, Pierre!" burst out Isabeau who had been watching them work.

"Oh, that's my cousin, Pierre – he hides his talents very well!" Renard teased. "In La Motte, I always tell everyone how talented he is – that way they don't ask me to do anything laborious!" The ladies chuckled while Pierre flushed and shrugged. "Let's have that picnic now! While you people stood around and watched, I got hungry!"

They all gathered at the streamside and enjoyed their lunch.

*   *   *   *   *

Cramer was overjoyed at the reports given.

"So while the one group has picnicked; the other party took time to check out my escape route – that's good! And, they all met together after our Frangy meeting last night to discuss the plan! So far, so good! Listen carefully," Cramer pointed to the one Dragoon, "you will keep an eye on the Cabrieries' group in the barn at Minzier. You," he nodded to the second Dragoon, "will stay and watch the carriage. They will need it - to move the women when the time comes. I will report my success to Capitaine Benoit; and arrange for his involvement in the final ambush at the border. He will need to have his troop in place the night before!" Cramer was feeling a little lightheaded at the way his plan was unfolding. "And we will meet – here in Frangy – tomorrow night. Jourdan will come to the inn when they are ready to participate and name the day!"

*   *   *   *   *

10th August 1687
Near the Swiss border - Chaumont

The group had been surprised when their hostess asked them to stay for supper "because of all their wonderful kindness".

Madame Roche now bustled around the large black pot hanging from a heavy hook above the glowing fire. She stirred the contents and moaned a little with pleasure.

"'Tis good, mes *amis*! A hot and tasty lamb soup with lots of onions and some freshly-picked mushrooms – from outside the back door," and she gestured to the heavy wooden door set in the back wall of her tone farmhouse, "and, after helping me like you did today, you deserve a good warm - and healthy - supper!' She bent and dug into a worn old sack hanging from a hook on the cluttered wall. She drew out several loaves of crusty bread and dropped them on the well-worn and polished kitchen table.

"You ... Jeanne, isn't it?" In response to the nod, she ordered, "You cut the bread in nice thick slices and I'll ladle out this fine soup!'

Soon all the party was sipping the strong soup with little conversation to slow their eating. Their hostess encouraged them to enjoy a basket of fresh apples and several types of local cheese when they finished their meal.

"*Madame Roche* - did you and your husband farm this land?" Andre bit into a crisp apple with pleasure.

"*Oui, Monsieur,* " she chuckled a little grimly, "but, since my poor husband, Gustave went to heaven some years ago, I do what I can to sell the extra fruit and vegetables I grow. And the odd pig – and lamb – but, mostly, I ... do laundry," she grinned impishly at Andre, "and, I am now known as the widow Marie Roche - the laundry-woman!"

"For a nearby Chateau, *Madame*?" grunted young Le Duc Mallan, remembering passing a large estate on the dusty road into Chaumont.

"*Non, Monsieur!*" She gestured to another door in the opposite wall, "Come and see what type of washing I do!"

Pierre and the young Mallan together with Andre rose and followed her to the doorway. She swung it open and Pierre stepped cautiously into the darkened room. The old women followed him in bearing a lighted lamp. An uncontrollable gasp rose from Pierre as he found himself surrounded by a veritable sea of colourful uniforms – mostly Dragoons!

"*Madame!* You must be looking after ... a whole army!"

Madame Roche chuckled. "*Non, Monsieur,* but up the road – at Viry – there is a large encampment! These Dragoons trust me – mostly scoundrels, of course - but it provides me with a good living!'

"Hmm!" A loud grunt from Renard peering in at the doorway made Pierre look at him curiously. He simply winked and grinned mischievously back at his cousin, then shook his head and ducked from sight. Their hostess continued without paying attention to the interruption.

"That's why I need my cart so badly! I go in once a week to pick-up and deliver the laundry. Even the officers – they trust the work of the 'Laundry woman'! And then, every couple of days, I take a cart of fresh vegetables that I sell to the cook in the kitchen. Ah! They pay me well." Their admiring glances obviously gave her pleasure but she ushered them out of the room and back to finishing their meal. Pierre caught Renard's eye and raised his eyebrow but his cousin shook his head again and bit into an apple.

*   *   *   *   *

Unexpectedly, Renard rose and thanked *Madame Roche* for her excellent meal. Then he suggested some solutions.

"*Madame*, we need to repair *Monsieur Shabbe*'s cart before it is dark. I, together with the two Pierres, will take our mules and your cart. It should not take us long and we will soon be back to enjoy another glass of wine with you before we return to the inn at Chaumont. Thank you again for your wonderful meal!" *Madame Roche* blushed with pleasure and she nodded her head in consent. "Don't be too long now!" Pierre rose and left the warm kitchen with the other two men.

Renard hoarsely explained a possible plan to his friends as they loaded the wagon and drove back to the crossroad's farm. Pierre nodded silently as he considered the options presented while the Le Duc Mallan was highly skeptical.

"You could never get away with a plan like that!" he grunted. Renard grinned at Pierre without comment.

Once the cart was repaired Renard pulled in out of sight behind the barn.

"No sense in taking chances on having it stolen," he commented a little grimly.

*   *   *   *   *

When the men arrived back at the Roche farm, the group was ready to return home to Chaumont.

"We will be a few minutes," Renard told them, "Pierre and I need to talk to *Madame Roche*."

Inside, they interrupted the lady as she was preparing bags of fresh apples to be sent back with the party as a treat.

Madame Roche listened carefully and finally, after some initial reluctance, agreed to their offer.

Outside, she delivered the apples to the delighted company. Then she made her announcement.

"*Monsieur Jaubert* has ... very kindly ... offered to stay overnight so that he can accompany me when I deliver the clean uniforms to the Dragoon camp – in case there are more problems with my cart!" The group broke into spontaneous applause. They had really grown to like the courageous hardworking laundry lady.

Isabeau darted a curious look at Renard but he grinned at her and purposely looked away.

*   *   *   *   *

11th August 1687
On the road to the Swiss border - Viry

There was little doubt, Pierre thought with some sadness, that his hostess had sadly missed male company with whom to chat in her present life! Since the early wakening and throughout his plentiful breakfast she had been almost garrulous. Pierre had carefully provided short - but polite - answers to personal questions about himself and the party continually turning the conversation back to *Madame Roche* and her lifestyle.

It was soon obvious they were now approaching the village of Viry with more traffic on the road. *Madame Roche* pointed eagerly off to the right where the tents of the militia could now be seen in neat rows around what was once a good-sized farm.

As she turned off the road onto a worn track, she explained how they would have to pass the sentries.

"But, of course, they know me well. It will not be a problem!" She hesitated a little and coyly flushed. "I will ... explain ... that you are my nephew ... from Lyon!" She dropped her head and whispered hoarsely, "I don't want them to think I have ... found myself ... a younger man."

Pierre grinned at her as they approached the open gate where two sentries lounged on stools on either side of the entry.

"I would be ...very honoured, *Madame Roche!*" She grinned back at him and swung round to punch his arm softly. Both the guards chuckled as the cart stopped.

Madame made her announcement explaining his presence. "And, a saucy one he is too!" The guards laughed and waved her through.

Pierre let out his breath and relaxed as they drove up the road to the camp.

"That is the business office," she pointed to an extended shed behind the main farm house, "and the farm house is the headquarters of the General and his officers. I have never been in there – and, don't want to," she added hastily.

She pulled her laden cart up before the front door of the shed. Two clerks were seated at separate tables on the wide covered verandah. Both waved at her cheerfully.

"The one on the left is the clerk, Jules, who arranges the laundry; the other is the clerk who buys my vegetables and fruit, Alex. They are nice men – although I think they try to cheat me all the time!" she whispered hoarsely. "And, they expect me to do all the work! They are not gentlemen!"

"*Monsieur Jules*! I have your fresh laundered uniforms ready!" she called out; and he waved her to bring them in. Pierre sprang down and helped her alight. She leaned over and pulled the dust cover from the clean uniforms. Then she picked up a large batch of uniforms and Pierre followed with a further load, trailing her up the stairs on to the verandah and down the central poorly lit corridor.

She stopped at a doorway halfway down the corridor. She struggled with the handle; opened it; staggered in; and dropped her load on a large empty table. The huge room was obviously divided in the middle with dusty and soiled uniforms on the one side and rows of wooden empty racks with hooks on the other.

"The clerk writes the size with black ink in the waistband and neck of each uniform and gives a wooden ticket to the Dragoon," she explained, "When he brings in a dirty uniform, he hands in his ticket and gets the right size uniform. The officers they are very fussy, you know ... they have their uniforms especially made. They have their name written on each piece."

Turning, she added: "I bring in each load and they sort them out." When they had taken the last load, the clerk came in and counted each item ticking it off in a book he carried.

"Good work, *Madame Roche*! Let's go out and settle up your account while we enjoy a glass of free wine – compliments of the officers!" He chuckled aloud as he scurried from the room followed by his laundry lady.

Pierre moved quickly to the doorway in the side wall amongst the soiled uniforms. There was no lock – just a small wooden block with a nail in the center to close the door. Pierre breathed easier. Looking around quickly, he found that the block turned easily. He gently opened the door. It looked out onto the windowless farmhouse wall with a dusty roadway between the two buildings. He quickly closed the door and rapidly exited the room closing the door quietly behind him. No one seemed to have noticed his delay.

"Here, young man, have a glass of wine!" The clerk indicated a stool against the wall and passed a generous glass of red wine to Pierre. Then he turned back to his negotiations with *Madame Roche*. Pierre settled down and sipped the wine. It was good and was really probably part of the officers' stock. With a cautious check he noted that the other clerk worked seriously at his records without being disturbed or interested in the cheerful bickering between his counterpart and the *Madame*.

The less he notices me, the better, thought Pierre and he deliberately turned his back to the clerk and surveyed the actions of the camp.

As they climbed into their cart, the Supplies clerk glanced up from his work and called out to *Madame Roche*:

"Are you coming with more vegetables and fruit, *Madame* – today?" She shook her head.

"I'm afraid that I will be busy for another couple of days, *Monsieur Alex!* Maybe, three days from now?" He grimaced.

"I am running short now! I guess - I will have to look elsewhere. *Bonjour, Madame* – have a nice trip." And, he looked down at his books again. Good, thought Pierre, just what I needed to hear!

An hour later they were back at the farm. After enjoying a hearty country lunch, Pierre effusively thanked *Madame Roche* for her hospitality and, with gracious thanks from the lady herself, raced his mule down to the crossroads.

Here he stopped and checked that he was not being observed. Then dragging the cart from behind the ancient barn, he hitched his mule up to it.

Waving his willow switch, he set out on the road home south to Chaumont. The plan was taking shape.

*   *   *   *   **

11th August 1687
Near the border - Chaumont

Twilight had enveloped the village of Chaumont when Renard and Pierre carefully tucked the old cart, now fully loaded with freshly purchased local vegetables and bags of fresh fruit, into a barn on the outskirts of the village.

"Do you think I have a future as a vegetable trader, Renard?" His cousin grinned and covered the load with an old canvas.

"Well?"

"I think you have done a good job. The first step in our plan is now complete. Tomorrow – we either win or lose, right?"

Pierre nodded and washed his hands in the water from the horse trough outside the barn doors as Renard closed them.

*   *   *   *   **

12th August 1687
Near the border – Viry

It was well before sunrise when the two cousins rose and sneaked out the rear door of the inn at Chaumont – in case someone was watching them. They saddled their mules and led them out the back entrance to the property and did not mount until they were safely away from the area. At the old barn Pierre hitched his mule to the loaded cart. Renard led the way on his mule and the other mule followed without Pierre having to raise his switch. By daybreak they had safely reached the farm of the absent *Monsieur Sabbe*. Here Renard stabled and hobbled his mule and joined Pierre on the seat of the old cart. Both took a deep breath and expelled it together.

"This is the beginning of a hell of a day, but this is it, my friend!" Their joint smiles were weak and tense.

"Let's go!" And they rode towards Viry.

*   *   *   *   *

12 August 1687
Near the border - Viry

A mountain of cloud mantled the vivid blue sky as they approached the village of Viry. Wisps of mist still clung to the tops of trees and tips of the larger tents of the encampment. Renard put his hand on Pierre's in order to stop the cart. They had been traveling without speech for some time now.

"Let's run through the plan again, Pierre – for, from here, there is no turning back!" Pierre sighed and nodded as he stopped the mule. They looked at the layout of the camp and Pierre described the conditions he had encountered and reviewed the plan step by step. At the end, they looked at each other in silence.

"Well?" asked Renard. Pierre looked at the camp in the distance and pointed to the sheds.

"*Très bien!* See - the clerks are at their desks! Now is the time, my brave cousin!"

The mule moved forward and turned into the encampment.

Pierre handed Renard the reins as they drew near the sentries. He turned and delved under the cover and turned back in time to greet the soldier who had stood up.

"*Bonjour, Messieurs!* Vegetables and fruit for the troops!" He extended his hands and presented four fresh apples to each of the guards. "A gift from a poor peddler!"

The guards' eyes opened a little wider.

"Hmm! *Merci, Monsieur!* It looks like - a good start to our day!" He turned and tossed two of the apples to his partner.

"Do you happen to know what mood the supply clerk, Alex, *is* in today?" The guards looked disconcerted; then one replied:

"Alex is usually in a foul mood – any morning of the week, *Monsieur! Bonne chance* to you – anyway!" And they sat down on their stools again and began biting into the apples and nodding as the sharp clear juice broke into their mouths. Pierre automatically flicked the mule and it started up the roadway to the buildings.

"Good move, Pierre! That little gesture removed any suspicion. Better for us when we leave as well!" Pierre nodded and took another deep breath. Get yourself as relaxed and confident as possible, Pierre!

Pierre slowly drove the cart past the first clerk without meeting his gaze and stopped before the supply clerk who was still writing in his book. It was a relief to see the clothing clerk drop his stare and continue making notes in the records - without recognition.

"*Pardon, Monsieur Alex*? I understand that you need supplies of fruit and vegetables?" Pierre was certain from the speed at which Alex's eyes jerked up that the clerk had not been able to fill the quota. However, the eagerness vanished as the trading instincts of the clerk took over.

"I could use some extra – but not a great deal – right now!" Pierre simply nodded and swept back the covers. Alex rose and came over and looked at the contents.

"I am not sure I can use ... all that you have there!" His tone had become cautious. Pierre groaned a little and the clerk's sharp eyes lit up.

"Aha, *Monsieur* Alex, I am sorry about that! We have lost a sale in the village," he gestured in the direction of Viry, "and ... are reluctant to have to take these fresh goods all the way back to Chaumont!" He glanced at Renard as though seeking agreement from a partner – who nodded. "Maybe you can make a really special deal to help us out?"

The clerk's eyes lit up. And then extinguished quickly. He screwed up his eyes in thought.

"Well, that is a shame! Maybe..." He paused for a long time while the two men gazed at him appealingly. "Well, for the right price, I'll take all you have!" And, after some careful thought and much sighing from Pierre – they settled on a price that would have made any bandit happy for weeks. Alex first led the sack-laden Renard down the central corridor; opened the door on the right and showed him the bins and tables on which to leave the produce.

"Come and have a glass of good wine with us when you have finished unloading." he invited before he grabbed a bottle from the racks nearby and trotted back to his desk. Renard grunted his acceptance and then went out for another load. Unseen by the clerks, he also wrapped two bottles of wine in a sack and placed them in the back of the cart.

When the last batch of produce was being lugged in, Renard brushed past Pierre who was standing behind the two clerks. While Alex wrote details in his book, Pierre stood blocking the view of the corridor. Placing the items on the table, Renard gently closed the door and opened the door to the clothes storage and peered inside. There was no one there! He quickly crossed the floor and unlatched the opposite outside door. Then he gently closed that door and returned back to the verandah.

Alex nodded his thanks and proffered a cup of wine.

"My friend – poor soul – does not drink!" Pierre spoke up with a snicker. "Take the cart away and put the animal out of the sun!" Renard touched his forehead and lead the mule down the track and around the building stopping in the shade beside the side door of the clothing storage. He then hobbled the mule and gave it some carrots to chew on. He peered around the corner. Both clerks were now sipping wine with Pierre celebrating the purchase.

Quietly, Renard climbed the steps and gently pushed open the side door. He quickly collected an armful of the items he needed and loaded them into the back of the cart. Pulling the cover over his hoard, he checked the corner again. Both clerks were still busy laughing and drinking with Pierre. Good so far!

He returned for a final load. He also chuckled as he grasped his final prize – a Captain's plumed hat! Enough – go! He pushed a piece of straw to hold the block of wood in place as he gently closed the outside door. Then with his knife in the crack, he gently wriggled it until he heard the block drop to lock the door. Sweat was running down both his face and back as he slowly returned to the cart and covered its contents. Again, he peered around the corner. Pierre was standing on the step nodding thanks to Alex. Good timing!

Renard coughed slightly and Pierre turned and caught his eye. Nodding, Pierre saluted to the clerks and turned and loped up the road to where Renard was removing the hobbles from the mule's hooves.

They both climbed onto their seat and Pierre touched the mule to move forward toward the entryway. The short distance to the sentries seemed to last for ages! Renard leaned back and lifted the two bottles from the sack. As they slowed down at the guards, he extended a bottle to each guard.

"It was a good deal! Alex was in a buying mood! We share our good fortune with you – apples before, wine now!" The eyes of both guards widened with pleasure. They furtively took their prizes and hid them in their coat pockets and saluted the peddlers. A touch of Pierre's willow stick sent the mule cantering up the path to the open road. Both men expelled huge breaths of air. Pierre felt like his legs were made of soft mud!

"We did it, Renard, we did it!" Pierre whispered hoarsely! "The most important second step!" And they gripped hands silently as they turned the mule onto the roadway south.

*   *   *   *   *

13th August 1687
Near the Swiss border - Frangy

The two heretics, Goiraud and Jourdan, were obviously nervous. Beads of sweat rimmed both their foreheads as they waited for their mysterious Guide at the table. With hat pulled low and a scarf covering most of his face, he sat down quietly and looked steadily at the two refugees.

"Well?" When he finally spoke both men started and sat upright on their benches.

"Eh! ... *Oui, Monsieur!* We have managed to persuade our friends to join the escape party! Is the offer still open?" Cramer nodded silently and held out his hand.

Fumbling, the older man dug into his jacket pocket and a well-worn purse clinked dully on the table. Cramer hefted it in his hand and, without counting, slipped it into his pocket.

"We, the whole party, will meet you in the morning - long before daybreak – as discussed – on the road to Valleiry – after the crossroads. There will be ten men and four women. The men will all be mounted on horses or mules. The women will arrive in the coach. They will then be placed on mules and led down the path – by four of us." Although Cramer was thrilled by his success at involving both the Mallans and Jauberts, he sat silently. Goiraud stopped talking and asked: "Is that alright, *Monsieur*?" Cramer nodded and rose. Within seconds he had vanished. Jourdan wiped his forehead with his sleeve and grimaced.

"This is really frightening. I hope those Jauberts know what they are doing!"

"I think so! As you know, Renard is successful at taking chances – and winning; and Pierre is really solid – works hard and accomplishes what he sets out to do!" Goiraud grinned weakly. "In this world of uncertainty, what more can you ask? Let's go back to Minzier!" And they rose and went out into the night.

*   *   *   *   *

14th August 1687
Near the border – at the Viry crossroads

The rider could not have been seen by even the most alert of passing travelers. Heavy low-hanging branches shielded him from view but spaces between the leaves allowed him to clearly observe any action on the darkened road. But, Cramer was dead tired! He had been up most of the night escorting Captain Benoit and his enlarged troop of Dragoons to their hiding places at the top end of the path.

The Captain had been excited by the idea of the ambush - of *all* his enemies! Seeing him touch the unhealed scar on his cheek is a give-away, thought Alexander – that always-painful wound seems to ache more when he becomes nervous. Knowing this little weakness of his would be useful if we ever play cards together! He smiled in the dark – but the humour was short-lived. The Captain had made it clear that this trap had better succeed – or else!

Cramer tensed! Without hearing anything yet, he knew there was action down the dark road. He leaned forward slightly and cupped his ear in that direction. Hoof beats? How many? Hmm! Sounds like a single rider! He leaned over slightly and withdrew a heavy loaded musket and nudged his horse slightly sideways so that he would have a clear shot without panicking the animal. The rider appeared through the mist.

From the manner in which the Dragoon's cap was worn, he recognized it as Bion, his trooper – with news of the party at Minzier. As the figure slowed, Cramer coughed.

The Dragoon jerked his horse to a spinning stop. He peered into the dark shrubbery with a cautious "*Monsieur*?"

"Here, Bion! What have you to report?" The trooper urged his horse off the roadway and he drew alongside Cramer.

"Everything goes well, *Monsieur*." Although hoarsely whispered, the Dragoon was obviously excited. "The carriage arrived at the inn at

311

Minzier. The sick lady joined the other women inside and the old man climbed on top."

"How did they appear?" Cramer's voice was cautious compared with the Dragoon's enthusiasm.

"They were dressed warmly – in their peasant clothes."

"Not their clothes, you fool! How did they act? Scared? Happy? What could you tell?" Cramer's patience had worn thin during this long night.

"*Pardon, Monsieur!* I misunderstood! They ... shook hands and slapped each other on the back. They ... were happy and excited?" Cramer grunted and nodded.

"And, your partner, Coulan?"

"He signaled to me that I should report. And that, he would wait and follow the carriage – those were your orders, were they not, *Monsieur?*" Cramer nodded.

"*Bon! Bon!* – We wait patiently! But, Bion, I need you to find a safe place where you can observe. And keep count of the numbers as they head off behind me down the path. You can count, can't you?

"*Oui, Monsieur!*" Bion acted embarrassed. "I learned to count in the church school."

"*Bon!* How many are we expecting?" He peered at the soldier watching to see if he used his fingers.

"Eh! Four women and eleven men – fifteen all together!" Cramer nodded satisfied.

"You will count to ensure that we have no stragglers – no one spying on us. After they have gone, you will join up with Coulan and follow – but keep well back and do not get seen. If any escape the ambush and race back down the path, don't take prisoners. Use your sword and kill them!" He saw Bion's head jerk toward him sharply. "You will get your bounty – even for a dead body – without any tales being told by survivors!" He reassured the soldier who nodded and then searched around for a suitable hiding place.

Cramer nodded as the Dragoon located himself in heavy foliage across the road – his horse hobbled well back in the thicket. Then he shifted in his saddle and allowed his body to relax a little. The plan was going smoothly! He touched the scarf at his throat for reassurance and waited. It should be soon!

*   *   *   *   *

Cramer peered down through the light mist that swirled on the dusty road and closed his eyes to intensify his hearing. He thought he had heard a carriage approaching and had pulled his scarf upward. But the sound had quickly vanished. Anxiety was growing at the same rate as the slight pale pink and golden blush that was touching the distant hilltops – dawn was signaling her approach. They should have been here by now! We should already be moving down the ravine! Cramer's breath was shortened and he had trouble breathing. Where were those stupid heretics!

312

Ah! Hoof beats – at last! But – only one rider? The mist swirled and a rider thundered out of the darkness. A Dragoon – Courlan? *Mon Dieu*, what has happened now? Cramer's stomach dropped and he choked slightly. God, give me strength!

He called out and the rider turned and came directly to him.

"Coulan? What in the hell has happened?" The rider shook his head in confusion.

"*Pardon, Monsieur*, but I do not understand!" The Dragoon's face was twisted in fear. "I did what you told me to do! I stayed with the carriage – while I sent Bion to report that the groups had gathered together!" Cramer nodded impatiently and waited – with difficulty.

"After the carriage left – with the women, the driver and the old man, Mallan - the others simply stood around and talked."

"Then?"

"Finally, I found a way around the Inn without being seen. I chased after the carriage until I had it in my sight. Then I followed carefully."

"And?"

"Well, *Monsieur* ... when the carriage arrived at the crossroads, instead of turning to the left – to join you here – they went straight on – on the road past the encampment at Viry?" The Dragoon hesitated seeking words to explain his consternation. "I did not know what to do, *Monsieur*! But, you said, stay with the carriage – so I followed – all the way to Viry. But they went straight past the camp! And, through the village!"

"What – they went through the village?" Cramer was both dumfounded and suddenly dreadfully afraid.

"But, *Monsieur*, maybe it is not so bad after all." The Dragoon smiled slightly.

"No so bad? Why do you say that, you fool?"

"Well, *Monsieur*, as I rode back – in a hurry – a troop of Dragoons – I did not recognize any of them – led by a Captain - was racing up the road in their direction." The soldier tossed his hands in the air. "I yelled out for them to stop – but they ignored me – so I shouted out to them to check the carriage up ahead. And, *Monsieur*, the Captain looked back and raised his hat – in acknowledgment, *Monsieur*?"

The Dragoon waited in vain for any recognition that he had acted correctly – but none was forthcoming.

Cramer felt numb all over. He touched his face in desperation but it too felt cold and without any feeling. The last time he had had this feeling was in the village of La Motte d'Aigues when his world had crumbled overnight. I think Cramer, that you had better get the hell out of here – and vanish. Now!

Spinning his horse, he flashed past the waiting Dragoon and rode hell for leather into the early morning light. The two Dragoons joined each other in the middle of the road and stood mystified - staring into the cloud of dust that was settling slowly.

"I don't understand, Bion? What got into him?" His partner shook his head.

"I think we had better ... go and find *Capitaine* Benoit! Eh?" Coulan nodded and they turned their horses down into the ravine and cantered slowly out of sight.

* * * * *

CHAPTER TWENTYSIX

14th August 1687
On the border – near Geneva, Switzerland

The first rays of the crimson sun crept over the mountain crags staining all the tips of the other peaks a bright vivid pink. As neglected as he felt, the lone guard, Marcel Benezet, rubbing the slight gray beard that matched in colour his shaggy wispy hair, blessed the arrival of the sun. It looked like a good day ahead – and he felt he deserved a good day! His toothless mouth twisted in frustration as he thought of being stuck alone on the early morning vigil while the twenty other younger members of the militia slept in the nearby barn alongside the key road from Lyon to Geneva. Despite the firm orders from the General that a line of guards should be standing within sight of each other all along the border with Geneva, his stupid officer - in charge of this most important guard post - really was a lazy slovenly swine! Marcel spat on the dusty roadway in disgust.

Armed only with a pike, in frustration, he kicked the poles of the border barrier he was defending in this chilly dawn. Then he peered up the road where the sun lightly kissed the distant massive walls of Geneva. Two Swiss guards were swinging open the heavy ironbound doors of the city and one waved to him. He grinned and waved back. It pleased him that some other poor soldiers were up as early as he was.

The snap of a broken branch in the nearby woods caused him to spin around and level his weapon in the direction of the noise. He peered and cursed. A fawn, stepped carefully from the shadows and seeing the glint of his pike's point, spun and vanished into the dark woods.

"Hmm!" he grunted. How he would have liked to be the one who captured an escaping heretic! All the newly arrived militia volunteers had come mainly for the money – the new bounty offered by the King.

Catch one of the "new Believers" and you could be rewarded with "as much money as you earned in a month". Catch a whole party – and he could buy a share of a village inn – and then "He too could live like a King!"

Again, he thrust his pike forward savagely and grunted in pain. An old wound still sent a flash of agony through his tired body. Then he looked back over his shoulder at the barn door. He would bet if he caught a heretic, those sleeping youngsters – especially the officer - would take all the credit – and the money!

A sudden creak and a thump of a wagon wheel, as it hit a pothole, echoed up the winding road from the valley below. The arrival of the first of the morning traffic to Geneva – and the rest of the guards were still sleeping!

"*Bon,*" he whispered. The Dragoons had warned them that the escaping heretics were becoming tricky – sly like foxes! So, he grunted, I will be tough and trust no one! I will be suspicious! Traveling this early in the morning requires a very strong explanation! He moved into the middle of the rough road and peered through the fragments of drifting mist as the hot breath of the lead horses made tiny wreaths around the animals' nostrils. He raised his ancient shoulders in what he imagined was a dignified stand and held up his hand. The driver raised his hand in acknowledgment and pulled the reins to stop the team. He turned and nudged the sleeping older man beside him and gestured toward the guard.

The man pushed back the wide brimmed hat that had covered his waking face. He rose up cautiously on the wooden seat. As he rose, Marcel noted with some awe, the good quality of the material of the coat. Maybe a rich bribe would be in the offing? Turning, the man climbed wearily down the side of the coach and stamped his shining boots in the dust. He stood and looked at the guard without moving and automatically Marcel nodded his head in a slight salute and moved forward.

"*Monsieur, bonjour!*" The man nodded and smiled slightly.

"What is your business today – and so early, *Monsieur?*" The man kept silent but beckoned to Marcel with his finger to come forward. The guard checked over his shoulder quickly. He could hear no movement from the barn. Marcel felt a little uncomfortable about using this immense authority he bore on his old shoulders.

"Come..." the man whispered in a hoarse voice. Marcel moved forward, his pike held upright between himself and the man. Closer he leaned forward a little to listen.

"*Bonjour,* guard," the man pointed with his finger over his shoulder in the direction of the coach, "We do not wish to wake the ladies! *Non?*"

"Ladies...?"

"*Oui,* guard! I am transporting my lovely niece to be married in Geneva – today! She and her companions are sleeping. They do not wish to be disturbed." The man turned and gently opened the carriage door. "See!"

Marcel carefully walked a wide circle around the waiting Uncle still keeping his pike between them. These heretics could be very tricky! He carefully peered into the darkened interior of the coach.

An immense gathering of skirts and petticoats hampered his vision. A variety of gently flowered scents filled his nostrils. He wriggled his nose with some slight pleasure. He leaned a little further forward.

His eyes opened wide as he noted what was the very obvious bride – a young girl decked out in a wonderful white gown, her face tilted back in quiet repose. She leant against another attractive young woman with thick brown hair cascading on her shoulders – also sleeping. Marcel swiveled his head to the other side of the carriage. Two sleeping matrons shouldered against each other in peace. A quick glance showed

316

no hiding places for heretics. His suspicious eyes softened – obviously a wedding party – no reason for suspicion. But, wait, Marcel! Do what you are told to do! He turned and moved away from the coach and as the man softly closed the carriage door, he spoke.

"Papers, *Monsieur*? You have papers?"

"Of course, guard!" The man dug into his side pocket and produced a sheaf of notarized documents. The man eyed Marcel quizzically; then proffered them. Marcel hesitated before he took them and peered at each in turn with an air of authority. The man had suspected that the guard could not read. Marcel bobbed his head and handed them back with a flourish.

"You can pass, *Monsieur*! And, ... my best wishes to the bride!" The man looked relieved. Marcel turned and began to push the pole barricade slowly open when he saw the man's patient gaze shift over Marcel's shoulder – and the guard halted his actions.

"Marcel – what have we here?"

The truculent question rang out through the dawn's chilly air like a bolt of winter lightening. Marcel turned to face the officer who stood at the barn door shrugging into an elegantly braid-covered topcoat. With a flourish, he clapped his plumed hat on the back of his head and stepped onto the dusty road.

The man spoke first.

"If you please, *mon Capitaine*, do not raise your voice. The ladies," he gestured towards the carriage, "are sleeping. My niece is getting married today in Geneva," the man explained softly.

The Captain eyed the speaker with hostile suspicion. He reached his hand out for the notarized papers still held in the man's hand.

"I will see your papers, *s'il vous plait, Monsieur*!" The man glanced in the direction of Marcel. The Captain interpreted the glance.

"That old idiot," he gestured at Marcel, "cannot read! I will make the decision!" He took the papers and glanced through them hurriedly.

"Abjured heretics! I suppose you feel that," he waved the papers in the air, "these papers give you liberty to flit around the country ... and into Geneva? Huh!"

Marcel's head jerked up and his eyes opened at the descriptive terms. Heretics?" The Captain glared at the man who now had a distressed look on his features.

"But, the wedding is today, *mon Capitaine*..."

"You do plan to return to France after the wedding ... don't you?"

""*Oui, mon Capitaine, certainement*," the man assured the officer. The Captain hesitated, looked through the documents again and reluctantly nodded his head.

"But ... first I should inspect your cargo, *non, Monsieur*?" Handing back the documents, he called over his shoulder. "*Sergent!*" Then he walked arrogantly to the coach door. The second officer burst from the barn and rushed to join his superior who was waiting at the carriage door. The Captain gestured his soldier to the opposite door and then, grasping the handle, opened the door. It was obvious that the discussions had awakened the females in the carriage as they were now sitting up and tidying their hair.

"*Bonjour, Mesdames et Mesdemoiselles* ... sorry for the disturbance but ... a little inspection is ... necessary!" He caught the eye of the Sergeant and pointed at the youngest girl, "*Sergent* – I think, the future bride?" The Sergeant leered at his superior. After glancing at the two older women, he then pointed to the dark-haired girl next to the bride. "The bridesmaid, I think – and a lovely piece of work too!"

He turned to his sergeant and grinned. "Remember, *Sergent*, warnings from Headquarters – escaping heretics are ... sometimes disguised as women! Remember?" The Sergeant leered and nodded enthusiastically. Both men climbed the carriage steps and leaned into the interior. The Captain placed his hand on the window ledge and leaned towards the dark-haired girl. With a sudden movement, he grasped her nearest breast and squeezed firmly. The Sergeant had mirrored his superior's actions grasping the young girl's breasts as well – but using both hands. Both women shrieked.

"Hmm," grunted the Captain, "they seem real enough, don't they, *Sergent*?"

Suddenly the Captain's body froze and he grunted in pain. The dark-haired girl, fixing him with a fierce glare, spoke softly but firmly.

"*Oui, mon Capitaine*! That is ... a very sharp knife digging into your throat. If I were to move it quickly ... downward, you might never see tomorrow come!"

While his superior froze in silence, the Sergeant had released the young bride and stepped back on the ground. His forehead creased in sudden anxiety as he peered anxiously at his Captain for guidance.

"*Mon Capitaine*?"

But, the girl answered instead.

"I am sure your *Capitaine* is anxious that we leave immediately for the wedding! Is that not so, *Capitaine*?" He grunted but did not move. "*Sergent*, tell your guard to open the barricade! Now!"

A glance at the Captain's face made the Sergeant spin round and call out:

"Guard, open the barricade! Now!" Marcel with a curious smile on his face, leaned on the poles and the barricade opened. He propped them open with his body and waited. The rest happened quickly.

The older man had climbed up beside the driver. The driver flicked his whip and the horses moved suddenly forward past the barricade. As they passed the poles, a sudden shove from the dark-haired girl sent the Captain flying backward to sprawl in the dust – his blood covered hand clasped to the throat. Fresh bloodstains showed on his white cravat.

He climbed slowly to his feet helped by his sergeant and the two stared as the carriage raced up the dusty road to the distant gates of Geneva.

All the sleeping guards had now emerged half-clothed from the barn and were gathered behind their officers at the barricade when the thunder of fresh galloping hooves spun the soldiers around.

A troop of dust-covered Dragoons was racing up the road from Lyon with a splendidly garbed Captain at their head. The border guards gaped as the troop of riders thundered to a halt throwing a cloud of road dust into the morning air.

"*Capitaine*, are you in change of this checkpoint?" The border Captain was still startled and simply stared at the Dragoons' leader.

"Well, speak up, man! That blood?" And, he pointed to the officer's stained chest, "Are you injured?" The Captain started; looked with shock at his blood-covered hands and grunted; "Just an ... accident! ... Shaving!"

"Well, quickly then! We are looking for a carriage – of women! Has it passed through here?" The officer stared and turned towards the road to Geneva speechless. The Sergeant replied instead:

"*Oui, mon Capitaine*, it went through here just a short time ago. Women ... on their way to a wedding in the city," and he pointed up the road. "You can still see the carriage being inspected at the gates!"

"Oh *Mon Dieu, Capitaine*, I think you and your men are in real trouble. All those women are criminals – wanted criminals!" The young Captain spun his horse around towards the barricade. "I am a special aide – to the General himself! We," he gestured to his troop, "must bring them back – even if it means entering Geneva to do that! Open the barricade, Guard! Now! We can catch them – if we hurry".

Drawing his sword, he spurred towards the barricade. The guard pushed it open and stood back. The rest of the troop followed their leader through the barricades and up the long dusty road to the gates in the far distance.

Seeing the troop coming, the Geneva gate guards, armed only with pikes, allowed the carriage to pass through the gates.

Then they stood back and allowed the troop, led by their French Dragoon Captain, to flow through and yelled for reinforcements as they closed ranks behind them to prevent the troop from leaving.

The border officers stood, surrounded by their guards, and watched the gate and listened to the uproar from over the walls.

"Is he mad?" grunted the Captain gingerly wiping his bleeding throat. "He cannot ride – with impunity – into a Swiss city?" The Sergeant shrugged his shoulders and said nothing.

Some of the older guards voiced their concerns.

"They were awfully young for Dragoons, weren't they?"

"Some of them didn't even have boots on - or caps?"

"Didn't it seem that most of the group were riding ... mules?"

Marcel shook his head slowly. "They say that the heretics are very sly – like a fox?" He looked at the Sergeant. "And, they do disguise themselves, don't they?"

The Captain stared grimly at his men and then nodded to the Sergeant.

"I think – for everyone's benefit – we will all just forget this day! It never happened?" The Sergeant and all the men – except Marcel – nodded and closing the barrier, trooped in for a late breakfast. Marcel shook his head and smiled grimly, "*Oui* - very like ... a very sly fox!"

*   *   *   *   *

As the pikemen at the city gate flashed by, Pierre kept his horse close to his cousin, "Captain" Renard- who was still waving his sword wildly. Frightened faces of women peered from doorways. Businessmen scurried into the entrance of alleys and yelled in dismay. Ahead, he could make out the rear of the carriage.

Doors were open now and the ladies had spilled out onto the cobbled street and were hugging each other. Uncle Antoine Mallan was standing on the roof of the vehicle dancing a little jig of joy.

"*Halte! Halte!*" "Captain" Renard yelled out; and the horses and mules reared and circled. Young Andre Pelachon, wearing a uniform much too big for him, ran awkwardly up leading his mule and grasped as many of the reins as he could.

The women rushed to meet the dismounting riders. Jeanne, flushed and excited, threw her arms around Pierre's neck and hugged hard. Then she broke off grinning and grabbed her fiancé, Andre, and kissed him solidly. Pierre drew a deep breath and deliriously yelled out "We are free! Free!"

He turned again and found Isabeau standing panting from the run. Her hair swirled and gleamed in the flashes of early sunlight breaking over the rooftops. She smiled broadly, grasped his shoulders firmly and kissed him three times on the cheeks in the traditional Provencal manner. "It worked! It worked!" He grinned back.

Her husband, Le Duc, pushed through the riders and spun her around grinning wildly. "What an exciting adventure," he yelled. "This is living!"

Suddenly the jubilant spirits shattered as the excited group realized a large body of heavily armed and grim-faced guards surrounded them.

Renard, dressed in his ornate Captain of Dragoons uniform; his sword still in-hand, felt the naked blade of a sword pushed unceremoniously into his chest. A guard commander holding the hilt was glaring in a dangerous fashion.

"What right do you have, *Capitaine*, to ride your troop of ... unsavory ... Dragoons through the gates of our city ... in such a dangerous fashion?"

Renard stared at the officer; looked around in a brief moment of confusion; and then grinned openly at the startled soldier.

"I apologize, *Monsieur!* Most heartily! Could I ... surrender my sword?" The Commander looks nonplused; frowns in confusion.

"Surrender? I ... don't understand, *Monsieur!*"

Renard slowly reversed his sword, offering the hilt to the Commander.

"*Monsieur Capitaine* ... let me explain! We," and he waved his empty hand around the large group, "are escaping from France! We are what you would call refugees now! These uniforms - all of them - are stolen – a charade to allow us to get the carriage of ladies ... across the border! We beg for asylum, *Capitaine* – all of us!"

The officer dropped his sword tip and frowned in puzzled confusion. He screwed up his eyes slightly in thought. Then he suddenly grinned.

"That's clever, *Monsieur Capitaine*! I salute you! And, welcome to the city of Geneva – all of you!" Relieved, the whole group broke into a roar of applause. Four attractive ladies suddenly hugged the Gate Commander, to his obvious pleasure.

*   *   *   *   *

It is obvious, mused Pierre, that the successful escape had given rise to an unexpected wide range of feelings. Exaltation and joy that they had escaped and were finally free! And also a definite level of deep sadness - that they may all never see close friends and relatives again.

After the men had emptied their saddle bags to change into their own clothes, the Commander of the city Guard had asked to be allowed to keep the Dragoons' uniforms.

"I have a few ... ideas, where I think ... I might find the need for a troop of disguised Dragoons ... you never know!" He smiled mysteriously as he arranged for the uniforms to be carefully folded and taken into storage.

Through his kind efforts, the whole group had been housed in an unused double-story livery barn with their carriage, mules and horses in a nearby shed.

*   *   *   *   *

Late afternoon 14th August 1687
City of Geneva, Switzerland

Exhausted – but still exhilarated – the group all sat on bales of hay in the wide-open doorway on the second floor loft overlooking the busy Geneva street. The landlord had provided them with a gift of various local cheeses and fresh crusty bread to celebrate their liberty.

Andre Roux called out from the bottom of the ladder.

"If you want wine, I need some help down here!" There was a rush to help him carry up the large collection of mushroom-shaped wine bottles. Pierre's cousin, Renard, had generously offered to spend some of his ill-gained loot on the celebration.

Andre finally settled himself down with a glass of wine. Pierre noted his slight frown and under the cover of the lively conversation of the group, quietly put the question.

"Something wrong, or just tired?" The frown increased as Andre pondered his words. Then he shook his head and replied.

"It's probably my imagination, friend – but ... when I was in the inn – getting the wine - I actually thought I saw ... our two favourite villains."

"Villains?" Pierre smiled slightly.

"Well, it was a sideways glance into the darkened back of the inn, but, I thought I saw your Nemesis – *Capitaine* Benoit! And his *Sergent!*" Andre shook his head again. "But, since they were in ordinary clothes – I have never seen them out of uniform – No - I must have been mistaken." And, he laughed ruefully.

" Andre, I think that the shock of finally being free – and safe – may be playing tricks on your mind. Relax and enjoy yourself!"

They grinned at each other and turned to listen to the conversation. Uncle Antoine had enjoyed a long conversation with the landlord and was anxious to share his information.

"I think we should enjoy this freedom – as quickly as possible," he explained as he gestured with the full glass of wine, "for we should make plans to move on!"

"But we only just got here, Uncle!" Isabeau peered around the shoulder of his nephew, "Why so soon?"

"Just a case of too many refugees – like us!" and he went on to explain that the flood of New Believers escaping over the border had severely overloaded both the facilities and supplies of food for not only the City but also for other smaller nearby towns in the vicinity.

"Wagons of refugees are being sent daily up the road to Lausanne and even Basel and Zurich!" He also told them the story of how angered the King of France had been at the acceptance of so many of his heretic peasants by Geneva. He had sent a message to the Geneva authorities with an ultimatum, "Either empty your City of all heretics – or I will send in my General with an army of soldiers to capture and return them myself!"

All turned and stared with wide eyes – and waited. Uncle Antoine grinned wryly and nodded.

"And, of course, Geneva has a very limited army of guards! What else could they do but obey! The guards went through the city streets and herded all the refugees out the main city gate – the gate we came through! And closed the gates firmly – watched at the border by the French soldiers."

"Were they all captured?" voiced young Andre Pelachon?

"Well, no! You see the vast group of refugees was in this 'no-mans land' between the gates and the border. The large crowd simply wandered around the walls. But," he paused for obvious effect, "at the end of the day, the good citizens of Geneva – with the full knowledge of the Authorities - went out one of the other gates – away from the view of the French troops – and invited all the refugees to return!"

The group laughed and enjoyed the story. It was Renard who brought them all back to reality.

"So, now we have freedom – but have to keep moving – until when?"

Pierre nodded. "You are right! But, I remember my father had a wise old saying that goes like this: 'If you have no particular place to go, any road will take you there.' – so," he suggested, "we need to discuss what options we have – and develop a plan!"

"That sounds like a good idea," Andre nodded, "At least, we have the coach and our horses and mules! Thanks to the Dragoons!"

"That's just about it!" Isabeau spoke softly, "We are free; but we need to move; and we need to have a direction! But," she paused and held her glass for re-filling, "let us enjoy the present freedom – we have earned – for the next few days – and then, move on!"

"Agreed!" the band chorused, "Pass the wine around!"

THE END

(or - is it?)

Several streets away, in the back of a darkened wine room in an inn, a large group of nondescript men crowded around a table. Wine cups were filled but no one drank. All listened to their leader – somehow different when he was out of uniform.

"Listen and listen carefully! The Man from Versailles gave me a mission! And the funds to - not only do the job – but, if necessary, to travel out of the country to complete the task! The capture or destruction of three people!"

He paused. "The bastard that did this to my face!" and he pointed to the discoloured and seeping scar on his cheek with bitterness. "The man we suspect has plagued the Dragoons all over southern Provence – the bandit, Le Renard – whom I think is a cousin to my chief enemy. And, lastly, but not least, that little bitch of a "bride" from St. Martin – who not only made me lose face – but also has become a symbol of courage to the Luberon villagers."

He looked around the table. He knew each man personally.

He continued: "This is important to me – and to you! I will see that you are rewarded – by the King – through The Man – so that you will each be rich for the rest of your life."

The men glanced around the table and smirked. "At present they are celebrating their freedom – they feel safe now! And, as the old General said once to me, "There is no General more vulnerable than one who thinks that he is safe and secure! That is the time to strike! Drink up and celebrate our new mission - and our later fortune!"

And a cheer rang out from the men that made other patrons in the inn look over at the table with interest and concern.

*   *   *   *   *

NOW

THE END

RECOGNITION

In writing a novel of historic fiction, a "thank you" needs to be given in many quarters. Help with in-depth research; opportunities for promotion, requested criticism and finally, encouragement - long term!

Especially blessed is the wonderful **Internet** - sometimes just tapping in a few words resulted in major leaps in research retrieval. Let nothing in the future hamper this exciting resource.

Firstly, let tremendous gratitude go to a wonderful English teacher in Pietermaritzburg, South Africa, Miss Joyce Terblanche (now Mrs. Joyce Dowse - retired) for her fresh enthusiasm and skillful encouragement in my teenage days. Because of her I published my first "paid" short story at age 16 years! And the love of both reading and writing stayed with me for my whole life!

To my (deceased) mother, Kathleen Joubert for encouraging me - despite my Dad's criticism of my interest in "scribbling". And gratitude to my dear sister, Lynette Maurer, (sadly deceased) for her lifelong support and encouragement.

In my research: a gift of a 1600s Huguenot wedding ritual from the Huguenot Society Library at New Platz in New York; a thanks to the Mayor of St. Martin de la Brasque in Provence, France, M. Imbert, and his staff at the town hall for help in earth-shaking discoveries; and to the wonderful descriptive Dorling-Kindersley guide books for their extremely useful historic details.

To the courageous families who helped immensely by providing "Home-Exchanges". In Southern France in 1998 for my wife, Fern and I to visit the historic sites for the book: In Perpignan - Nicole Constanzo; and in Avignon - Alexander and Solange Ranelli and their lovely family. And, later in the Cape, South Africa, Nick and Elsa Lombard of Welgemoed - which allowed us to attend the International Huguenot Conference to present a paper on the difficult research for this novel.

A special mention of my South African friends and relatives who hosted us: Lennard and Joan Kloppenborg; Diana and Ron Curling; Thelma Trail, Stafanie Roos, Bernard and Vi Bradley, David and Sandra DuPlooy. And to my nieces - Corinne Nichols; and Gail (and Danie) Ankiewicz and for their support and patience.

A special thank you to Neels Britz of the University of Stellenbosch who was so supportive in helping me attend the 3rd International Huguenot Conference in South Africa. Also thanks to Dr. Christo Viljoen of the Huguenot Society for his enthusiastic support and guidance of my efforts.

Special gratitude goes to the people who "painfully" went through the manuscript to point out errors and offer welcome criticism: Lionel and Julie Benoit (Deceased); Doreen and Stan (deceased) Clapp; Sandy Zahara (Deceased) and Bonnie Barros. Also remembered are Dr. Glen Campbell and Cheryl in Calgary who spent endless hours helping translate early French documents.

Sometimes a detailed written description of a character is not enough to colour the author's imagination. In a search for inspiration in the early stages of this book, I found a young professional (Doctor of Chinese Medicine), Carolina Johansson. She caught my eye as the "portrait" of the "Isabeau" of this novel and she kindly posed for a snapshot. An enlarged copy - with her wistful smile - helped me capture a vision in many difficult chapters. Later, I added pictures of other possible characters that still hang in a row above my computer. Thank you, Carolina, it worked! Also to my Aussie nephew, Mark, whose portrait became the guide for the lively "Fox" in the novel.

My lifelong appreciation goes to my dear wife, Fern Beverley, whose patience has been never-ending! So much time was spent - down below in the basement - grimly grinding away! And, when I read her little pieces - usually over coffee breaks - she was always enthusiastic.

Kenn Joubert
Cedar-by-the-Sea, Nanaimo, BC Canada.

Kenn Joubert was born in South Africa and began his career as a writer with his first short story published (and paid for) at age 16. His early career was as a Banker and he eventually "banked" with three different Banks on three different continents. But, his hobby was writing - working for a while as a "District Correspondent" for the Natal Witness.

Determined to see more of the world before he "settled down", he quit his job and traveled to London to hitch-hike around most of Europe. At 23 he decided to add North America to his list of "spots visited"- with plans to return "home" to Africa in one year.

However, fell in love on the winter prairies of Western Canada with a pony-tailed girl; got married, had a family; and is now a Canadian citizen of over 50 years! Over this period, he has published commercial articles in national media in South Africa and Canada.

However, Canada was kind to Kenn! In 1967 at age 34 - as a "High School Drop-Out" - he returned to upgrade his education at the University of Calgary and obtained a Degree in Education (History). He later returned to Graduate School to complete a Masters in Clinical Psychology. After having now "changed work horses in mid-stream", he worked in a variety of positions as a "Community Psychologist" in Western Canada before settling on Vancouver Island BC. Although retired, he is still registered with the College of Psychologists in Alberta, Canada.

After retiring - on a part-time basis - he has provided "Trauma" support for groups involved in work-site disasters - and spent the rest of his spare time carrying out in-depth historic research and writing fiction.

Kenn has always sought challenges! In the early 1950s, he noticed a national career advertisement and sent his resume in the mail. Several months later, he was thrilled to receive a "letter of acceptance" from the Canadian Space Agency as a "Candidate" for Astronaut! He underwent many physical examinations. He was even asked to - research and review - the various Space experiments planned.

The original selection had over 3,700 applicants. Finally, when the numbers were cut from about 600 to the final 60 candidates, Kenn received his letter of rejection. However, he is still proud of the fact that he "at least applied"!

Kenn is a long-time member of the BC Federation of Writers in Canada and the SAWC (South African Writers Circle). He has participated in many writing courses and Writer's Conferences. He is a "Life Member" of the Huguenot Society of South Africa as well as a well-recognized Genealogist and historic researcher.

Kenn is living a retired life with his wife, Fern, in a lovely cottage overlooking the Straits of Georgia south of Nanaimo BC on the inner coast of Vancouver Island in the Pacific Ocean off the west coast of Canada. In front of his home in a fir-tree is a huge nest for a pair of Bald Eagles. Their annual antics are followed each of the last 20 years with great interest.

ISBN 141207180-1